Constance Heaven

★   ★   ★

THE WIND
FROM THE SEA

Mandarin

A Mandarin Paperback
THE WIND FROM THE SEA

First published in Great Britain 1991
by William Heinemann Ltd
This edition published 1992
by Mandarin Paperbacks
Michelin House, 81 Fulham Road, London SW3 6RB

Mandarin is an imprint of the Octopus Publishing Group,
a division of Reed International Books Limited

Copyright © Constance Heaven 1991

A CIP catalogue record for this title
is available from the British Library
ISBN 0 7493 1122 3

Printed and bound in Great Britain
by Cox & Wyman Ltd, Reading, Berkshire

THE WIND FROM THE SEA

He opened the door, a cloud of icy cold mist poured in and he jumped to the ground. Isabelle peered after him, seeing him appear and disappear as the fog eddied in thick clouds. She thought she could see some kind of a barrier and was almost sure there was another carriage beyond it with people moving around it. Suddenly she thought she knew what had happened. Robert would have been worried about her driving down through such a night and had come to meet her. She saw a tall figure detach himself from the group of people and move towards her. She climbed down from the carriage so filled with joy she did not stop to think.

'Robert,' she cried, 'Oh Robert, at last,' and ran towards him.

But it was not Robert's arms that closed around her. It was not Robert who looked down at her with that odd mocking smile. It was Lucien. Too late she realised her mistake.

BOOKS BY
CONSTANCE HEAVEN

The House of Kuragin
The Astrov Inheritance
Castle of Eagles
The Place of Stones
The Fires of Glenlochy
The Queen and the Gypsy
Lord of Ravensley
Heir to Kuragin
The Wildcliffe Bird
The Ravensley Touch
Daughter of Marignac
Castle of Doves
Larksghyll
The Raging Fire
*The Fire Still Burns

*available from
Mandarin Paperbacks

For LUCIA *with my love*

But O, self traitor, I do bring
The spider love, which transubstantiates all,
And can convert Manna to gall,
And that this place may thoroughly be thought
True Paradise, I have the serpent brought.

John Donne

Prologue

A gust of wind drove a shower of icy sleet across the deck of the ship as it ploughed through the Channel towards the English coast. Isabelle drew closer into the small shelter provided by the hatchway, pulling the thick woollen shawl closer around the small boy who was huddled against her.

'It's so cold,' he muttered fretfully, 'and I still feel sick.'

'It won't be long now. It can't be and once we're there, it will be all over.'

Guy looked up at his sister, his face pinched and white in the faint light of the lantern that swayed dizzily above their heads. He was the man of the family now, it was he who ought to be brave, it was the last thing his father had said to him on that dreadful day but it was not easy when he was not quite eleven; he had never in his short life felt so utterly wretched and behind him lay a nightmare he did not dare to remember.

'What is going to happen to us, Belle? Supposing there is no one there to meet us?'

'There will be,' she said reassuringly, trying to still her own grave doubts. 'And even if there isn't, we know where to go and in England we'll be safe. No harm can come to us there.'

'Are you sure?'

'Quite sure.'

She pulled him closer against her, two lost and friendless children in a world suddenly grown frighteningly hostile.

There was only one other passenger on deck. He had been standing in the shadows, leaning back against the pillar of the mast, staring across the grey choppy sea. The murmur of voices woke him from his abstraction. It seemed that others had fled from the tiny saloon below, where the few passengers were crowded together in a thick haze of rum and tobacco smoke.

3

The sour stench of bilge water and other more disgusting odours had driven him up on to the deck, where the wind was biting but filled with the clean salt tang of the sea. This was not the usual packet service plying between Calais and Dover, but a small vessel carrying a dubious cargo, almost certainly contraband, and a few ill-assorted passengers who for various reasons were anxious to avoid the customs officials and the law officers and had paid heavily for it just as he had done himself.

The swaying lantern steadied for a moment. He saw the girl's face clearly and was instantly struck by her beauty, so pale it might have been carved in alabaster, the eyes dark mysterious pools, the shawl pushed back from the damp clustering hair, one arm around the child who clung to her, his face buried against her shoulder.

Refugees undoubtedly, *émigrés* from a Paris whose gutters were awash with blood. Ever since the King had gone to his death in January, the massacres had grown steadily: forty, fifty, sixty, every day, rattling along the streets in those hideous tumbrils, old and young, rich and poor, innocent and guilty, and now these two – my God, were they sending children to the guillotine now! An angry compassion drove him towards them.

'Wouldn't you be better off in the saloon with your friends?' he said gently. 'At least it is warmer there.'

'We have no friends,' said the girl, chin uplifted, rejecting his compassion with dignity and pride, 'and my brother is not well. He is better up here in the air.'

Seasick, of course, poor little devil! He unwound the plaid he had wrapped around his own shoulders and held it out.

'Take this. It will at least keep off some of the sleet.'

'Thank you, Monsieur, but you must not concern yourself.'

She had the air of a great lady towards an importunate servant, yet she could not have been more than twelve, if that. It both amused and irritated him.

'Take it,' he said brusquely. 'Your brother is in need of it even if you're not.'

He shook out the heavy folds, tucking the rug around them both and noticing how she bit her lip, how the delicate colour

4

raced up into the pale cheeks as he pushed the small frozen hands firmly under the warm blanket.

'Thank you. You are very kind,' she murmured in a thread of a voice.

'It shouldn't be too long now,' he said, pointing towards the east where the faintest streak of light appeared in a rift of dark clouds. 'It will be dawn soon and we shall be coming into harbour.'

He stood still for a moment, looking down at the forlorn pair and fighting an almost irresistible desire to touch with a caressing hand the damp curls clustering around the white forehead, the tragic scenes he had witnessed during the last few months moving him to an almost unbearable feeling of pity. A few years ago when the revolution broke, the great surge forward, the cutting away from the shackles of the past, had seemed to him, as to many other young Englishmen, a most wonderful thing; a moment in history when it was good to be alive – Liberty, Equality, Fraternity, marvellous watchwords for the future. But now the glory had dimmed, vanished into a welter of blood and tyranny and into a useless and devasting war for which Britain was hopelessly unprepared.

He leaned on the rail, impatient for the voyage to end so that he could be on his way and the vital information he carried safely delivered.

The girl leaned her head wearily back against the hatchway and studied him in the shifting light of the lantern, a tall man wearing a long heavily caped coat, the hat pulled down to his brows so that all she could see was the stern profile, the straight nose, uncompromising mouth and firm chin. Quite young, she thought, but with something dark and secretive about him. His French had been impeccable yet not quite native, and it would not have surprised her to know that the name and occupation on the papers in his breast pocket were not his own. Then he had walked away from them and back into the shadows.

It was two hours later when the first dark streak of the shore appeared, seeming at first to be no more than a deepening of the heavy clouds on the horizon and then gradually taking shape through the mist. It was seven o'clock but barely light.

5

The rain had stopped though it was icily cold and everything dripped with water. She roused Guy and stood up, folding the heavy rug and looking to return it, but its owner had disappeared below so she hung it over her arm and crossed to the rail.

'Look, Guy,' she said, 'come and look. There is England at last.'

It was not an inviting prospect. A bare shingle beach stretched as far as she could see, while a sharp wind blew the mist into thin shreds. There seemed to be little habitation, no more than a few scattered black huts where here and there points of light bobbed and glimmered.

The ship had put down a dinghy and passengers were being rowed ashore. The light strengthened as she waited for it to return. She clutched the big carpet bag tied roughly with rope, fingering nervously the little leather pouch which was tied around her waist and hidden beneath her cloak. The few coins it contained and a name hastily scrawled on a scrap of paper were all that stood between them and destitution in this unknown foreign country.

The last time the boat returned, she scrambled awkwardly down the swaying ladder, aware of watching eyes as she tried to hold down her billowing skirts. A kind-hearted sailor swung the boy to his shoulder, carried him down and dumped him beside her. The man in the caped coat was already standing in the bows, his neat elegant portmanteau at his feet.

When they reached the beach he leaped out and strode across the shingle towards the cottages and she followed him, splashing through the surf and stumbling over the pebbles in her thin shoes, carrying the heavy bag and pulling Guy along with her.

As she drew closer, she saw that one of the huts boasted a faded sign flapping creakily in the wind, and depicting a white-wigged, red-faced King George, 'Farmer' George, who had sat on the English throne for nearly fifty years and was now said to be raving mad.

Some of the passengers had already gone inside, trying to combat the chill of the morning with piping hot grog but the man in the caped coat was obviously well known, for after a

6

moment the innkeeper himself came out to him and stood in deferential conversation. A rough-haired boy appeared and went around to the back of the building, returning a few minutes later with a horse ready saddled. The traveller stood impatiently tapping his boot with his riding crop while the portmanteau was strapped on, and Isabelle took a deep breath and walked towards him.

'Your rug, Monsieur,' she said, and held the plaid out to him.

He turned to look at her, his mind obviously so concerned with other matters that it was a few minutes before he spoke.

'Good God, are you still here? Is there no one to meet you?'

'No.'

She still held out the rug and he pushed it back awkwardly.

'Keep it. You may find it useful. Do you know where it is you have to go?'

'I have an address.'

'Better let me see it.'

Time passed and he was anxious to be gone. He had no wish to involve himself but he couldn't leave these two young creatures alone at this desolate place without offering some kind of assistance.

She fumbled under her cloak for the leather pouch and brought it out. Her icy fingers were clumsy and one of the coins fell to the ground. He saw the gleam of gold and picked it up quickly.

'Put that money well away and take care to show it to no one or you'll not keep it long. This is rough company.'

Then he took the folded paper she held out and opened it, leaning towards the light streaming from the open door.

'Sir Joshua Brydges, High Willows,' he read.

'Who is he?' he asked.

'My uncle.'

'And he has sent no one?'

'No, but there may not have been time and . . .' she looked around her, 'and he might not know where we were to land.'

'I see. Well, we are close to Rye Harbour here. Have you any idea where High Willows is?'

7

She shook her head. 'I thought I might hire a carriage,' she said tentatively.

'Not in this place, Mademoiselle, not any kind of conveyance, you can be quite sure of that.'

They had been talking in French. Now he beckoned to the innkeeper, who had been listening intently and looking from one to the other.

'Do you know this gentleman, Isaac?'

The man squinted down at the paper. 'Aye, sir, I do that. There's not many in these parts as don't know Sir Joshua. He's one of them as sits up in London and makes the laws as keep the likes of us beggars.'

There was spite in the voice and the traveller raised his eyebrows.

'Member of Parliament, is he, and not popular I take it,' he commented drily. 'Well, never mind about that. Where is High Willows and how can this young lady and her brother reach there?'

The innkeeper scratched his head doubtfully but his sharp eyes had seen the gleam of gold and if there was profit to be made out of it, then he was the man for the job.

'Ah, that's just the trouble, sir. High Willows is out on the Marsh and there's nowt that can be hired hereabouts as I know of save only Tod. He'll be goin' that way through to Camber and Lydd with his market cart. He might perhaps drop 'em off for a consideration.'

It sounded like rough going but there was little choice. It was unthinkable that a girl like that should stay in this place for a day or possibly two while Sir Joshua was contacted.

'Where is this Tod?'

'Inside this very minute, sir, takin' somethin' to keep out the damp.'

'I see.' He glanced at the girl watching him anxiously and then turned back to the innkeeper. 'Now you listen to me. You tell this Tod to carry these two children to Sir Joshua's High Willows as soon as he can and in the meantime you find them some decent food. What have you got?'

'Nowt much, sir, leastways not for the likes of them.'

8

'For God's sake, man, you've got milk, I suppose, and bread. You make sure that wife of yours gives them a bowl of bread and milk with plenty of sugar and a mug of hot chocolate and don't tell me you've none of it because I know well enough what the luggers bring in.'

'And who's goin' to pay for it, you tell me that,' grumbled the man, 'couple of beggarly Frenchies. I've had a bellyfull of them all this past year.'

'Maybe you have, but this time I'll be paying and you make sure they're treated properly because if I hear to the contrary, and I will, you'll lose your licence and I'll make damned sure you'll get nothing more from me or from anyone else. Understand?'

The man cringed. 'Aye, sir, aye, I'll see to it, don't you fear.'

'Take care you do.' He watched the innkeeper move reluctantly to the door before he turned back to Isabelle and began to explain in French, but she interrupted him.

'You need not translate, Monsieur. I have understood well enough what you have been saying and I'm grateful.'

'You speak English?' he said in some surprise.

'Oh yes, from a child. My mother was Sir Joshua's sister.'

He wondered briefly what had taken the sister of this unpopular Kentish squire to France and marriage with a French aristocrat, because it was obvious that the girl and her brother were gently bred.

She was looking at him with those large and haunting eyes that he was to find so extraordinarily difficult to forget.

'May I know to whom Guy and I are indebted for so much kindness?'

He hesitated and then shook his head. 'I think not, Mademoiselle, at least not for the time being.' He grinned almost boyishly. 'I have put the fear of the Lord into friend Isaac. He will see you and your brother safely to your uncle.' He paused, then on impulse took the girl's small hand and kissed it lightly.

'Good luck, my dear, and to you, *mon brave*,' and for an instant the boy's hand was held in the firm warm clasp. Then he had taken the reins from the lad who was still holding the horse, swung himself into the saddle and trotted up the shingle beach.

9

'Why do you think that man was so kind to us, Belle?' said the boy, watching the upright figure disappear into the thin layers of mist that still drifted across the low-lying fields. 'Do you think he guessed who we were?'

'How could he? It was just pity, the kind of pity a man like that feels for a starving dog. We've got to grow used to being treated like that now.'

Her voice was filled with an angry pride but was it quite true? She was not sure. In a queer way she had sensed a warmth beneath that cool exterior but maybe that was just imagination, something she longed to believe at this wretchedly lonely moment. Then she braced herself.

'Come along,' she said, resolutely taking Guy by the hand. 'Let's go in.'

Men's eyes turned to stare as she entered the miserable hut but she walked past them with so much dignity and self-possession that a couple seated on a bench close to the fire hastily moved up to make room for them.

They had been promised breakfast and, with the practical good sense that was so much part of her character, she was going to make quite sure they got it before the long day that no doubt still lay in front of them.

Tod's wagon was piled with lumpy sacks of root vegetables, potatoes, turnips, swedes, carrots. Warned by Isaac, he grumblingly made a kind of nest with sacks and an old torn blanket, and there they were forced to sit, jostled, bumped, bruised and shivering in the icy wind despite the traveller's thick plaid rug. It was not a great distance as the crow flies but Tod had deliveries to make and goods to be picked up which necessitated diversions down heavily rutted lanes thick with mud and ploughed up by the feet of cattle and horses, so that as the afternoon drew on every bone in Isabelle's slender body seemed to have its own separate ache.

Once a farmer's wife gave them a look of pity and a slice of stale pie, another time a serving girl brought them a cup of goat's milk over which Guy wrinkled a disdainful nose. Worn out by the night on the ship, he slept for most of the day, his head on Isabelle's lap, and she was left to her own thoughts.

'I will not remember,' she said to herself. 'I must not remember. I must think of the future and not of the past.' So she tried to concentrate on the country they were passing through, the bustling little town of Rye with its cobbled streets and fine church set high on a ridge, the long stretches of sandy beach blown into enormous dunes and in the far distance the sea lapping gently as milk. Then they were out on the marshes, heavily dyked fields that seemed to extend to the horizon with scarcely a tree, only waving reeds and tall whispering grasses and hundreds, thousands of sheep, heavily fleeced sturdy sheep, bred especially for the rich pasture of these water-sodden meadows. But hard as she tried, the memories came crowding back, horribly vivid pictures against which she was powerless to shut her mind.

Was it only a year since they had been so happy in the gracious family château with its splendid gardens, the green turf and shaded walks where they played hide-and-seek and chased their dogs, sunlit days filled with small pleasures, the turmoil in Paris still only a distant anxiety about which Father and Grandfather often spoke in low voices, but which scarcely touched as yet the children's peaceful lives? It was true that Isabelle had been sometimes aware of a dark shadow hovering above them as it had done long ago in the months after Guy was born and their mother had sickened and died.

Then suddenly it seemed everything had changed. There were strangers, men in red caps and tricolour sashes, shouting in the village market place, their arms flung up towards the skies as if they called down the wrath of God on all around them. She saw one of them when she drove through with her governess, and Mademoiselle Julie said in a horrified whisper, 'Don't listen. Shut your ears against such wickedness.' But she couldn't, no one could, it was like trying to hold back an angry sea.

The château was invaded. She saw them from an upper window marching up the drive, hundreds of them, the peasants who worked in their fields, the women who had called a greeting

11

and curtsied respectfully when she and Guy rode by. Now they were armed with anything they could lay hands on: scythes, billhooks, cudgels, axes, guns, old and rusty but with the power to kill; and her grandfather outfacing them bravely, uselessly. A day of terror with her father bundling them out of the house through the servants' quarters, Mademoiselle Julie distractedly putting together cloaks and dresses and underwear, pushing them into the carriage and Jean Pierre, her father's old coachman, saying, 'Hurry, hurry, Monsieur! Hurry, *mes enfants!*' And at the last, worst of all, a hideous sickening glimpse of her beloved grandfather dragged into the midst of them, the white hair all dabbled with blood . . .

The cart had jolted to a halt, Guy had woken up and was shaking her, the memories were abruptly cut off and she was staring at the stone pillars, a pair of handsome gates and a long neatly sanded drive curving away, bordered by thick hedges.

'High Willows,' said Tod laconically, and climbed down from his high perch.

Guy was rubbing his eyes and looking dazedly around him. Tod swung him to the ground and held out a dirty hand to Isabelle.

'There you are, Miss,' he went on not unkindly, 'and good luck to the pair of ye. You're goin' to need it. He's a hard man is Sir Joshua and as mean an old skinflint as you're like to meet in a mort o' Sundays. You'd better mind how you go.'

He grinned, showing half a dozen blackened teeth, and with that word of warning he climbed back into the cart and whipped up his patient horse.

They watched him trundle away and then hand in hand trudged up the long drive till the house came into view, large, imposing, its shuttered windows unfriendly, no lights showing, no sound of barking dogs, no cheerful bustle. It stood four-square, solid and unwelcoming in the fading light of the winter afternoon.

They climbed the steps and Isabelle had already raised the brass knocker when a shrill young voice interrupted her.

'Mamma doesn't care for beggars to be received at the front

12

door. If you've come about the position of kitchen maid, you should go to the servants' entrance.'

Isabelle looked round. A young girl in a blue velvet mantle trimmed with grey fur stood below them on the drive, holding a small dog on a leash, and surprisingly it was Guy who stepped forward to answer her, small and angrily defiant.

'Don't you dare to speak to my sister like that. She is Isabelle de Sauvigny and I am the Comte de Sauvigny.'

Coming from a dishevelled boy in a dirty peasant smock, stained breeches and muddy boots, it sounded so absurd that the girl giggled.

'La, what a mouthful! If you're the Comte whatever it is, then I'm the Queen of Sheba. You look more like two of the play-actors from the summer fair.'

Before Isabelle could reply, the door was opened and a young man in a handsome green livery stood there, frowning across them at the young girl on the path.

'Oh there you are, Miss Venetia. Your lady mother has been looking for you this past hour. You know she doesn't like you to be out in the park after dusk.'

The girl tossed her head. 'I was only walking Fluff. I'm coming in now.' She ran up the steps, pushing past Isabelle. 'You'd better send these beggars packing, Franklin, or Mamma will be very displeased.'

The footman looked them over superciliously. 'As for you two, if it's food you're after, you'd best go round to the kitchen quarters and be quick about it. They'll know how to deal with people of your sort.'

'We're not beggars and I'm not applying for the position of kitchen maid,' said Isabelle in her precise English. 'I wish to see Sir Joshua Brydges at once.'

'Oh you do, do you? Well, you're unlucky, Sir Joshua is away from home and what makes you think he'll want to see the likes of you?'

'Oh he will see me, you can be quite sure of that. I am his niece and this is my brother.'

'What!' The young man was taken aback, somewhat impressed by her manner in spite of himself.

13

'You'd better come in,' he said doubtfully. 'I'll have to speak to the mistress.'

He ushered them into a large hall and shut the door.

'Wait here and mind you don't touch anything,' he said threateningly and disappeared up an imposing staircase at the far end.

The floor was of black and white marble, the dark red walls hung with large gilt-framed portraits, one or two pieces of heavy oak furniture stood against the walls and it was icy cold. Isabelle shivered and gripped Guy's hand more tightly.

'What does he think we are – thieves?' he whispered. 'I don't like it here, Belle. Do we have to stay?'

She could have echoed his wish but there was no alternative. They had no place else to go.

'Ssh,' she said warningly, 'someone is coming.'

Augusta Brydges was a fine figure of a woman in a gown of corded silk, priceless lace at her bosom and falling in cascades from elbow length sleeves. She had never liked her husband's half sister, had in fact heartily detested her for reasons which she could never reveal to anyone. Clarissa had been more than twelve years younger than her brother and a flighty beauty from all accounts. Their father had married for the second time and both he and his wife had died in one of the cholera epidemics that periodically devastated the country districts, leaving Joshua as sole guardian of the little girl barely six years old. In Augusta's opinion Joshua had become far too fond of the lovely wayward Clarissa, which explained his cold icy rage when, at nineteen and in flat defiance of all his own plans for her, she had run off with a handsome Frenchman. Augusta was betrothed to him by then and vividly remembered the look of baffled fury at the very mention of her name. He had never forgiven her.

Had Clarissa married her lover or hadn't she? She was thinking about it as she came down the stairs. All communication had been abruptly cut off, her letters burned unopened, so there had been no news of her from that day to this. The very substantial inheritance that should have been hers when she came of age had come to Joshua. She did not think he would

14

have any wish to see it jeopardised, not now when he was steadily rising in the world of politics and needed every penny to keep abreast of the rich and the fashionable. Could these two be her children? Was it possible? Driven out of France where such shocking things seemed to be happening every day? Were they genuine or were they imposters with a likely tale cooked up by some unscrupulous liar?

She frowned at the two children in their travel-stained peasant clothes.

'It seems you claim to be my husband's niece?' she said coldly to Isabelle.

'I am his niece. My mother was Sir Joshua's sister.'

'So you say. Well, that remains to be seen, doesn't it? Sir Joshua has been in London but I am expecting him to return this evening. Till then . . .' she paused and then abruptly made up her mind. She turned to the hovering footman. 'Franklin, take these persons to the kitchens and ask Mrs Bedford to see that they are given food. When Sir Joshua returns, he will decide what is to be done with them.'

'Very well, Madam.' He smiled triumphantly. He had been right after all. 'Come along you two. This way.'

Guy had gone red in the face. He was bursting with righteous indignation at their treatment but Isabelle shook her head at him. In the absence of written proof, she supposed her uncle's wife had a certain right to be doubtful.

The news had already spread among the servants but whether she believed it or not, Mrs Bedford, the housekeeper, had a kinder heart than her mistress.

She found a warm corner for them in the huge kitchen. She ordered the servants to bring them bowls of hot soup with new baked crusty bread followed by generous slices of game pie. Isabelle thought she was starving but, when it came to it, found it difficult to choke down more than a few mouthfuls, but Guy, with the healthy appetite of a small boy, ate everything that was put in front of him and the maids giggled as they piled the plate. The kitchen was filled with the rich aroma of roasting ducks, of broiling beef and fruit pies with creamy custards in preparation for the master's supper. After the long cold day the children

15

dozed in the heat and it was after nine when they were roused by the sound of carriage wheels outside, loud voices, dogs barking excitedly, and realized that their uncle had returned at last. They sat up waiting tensely for their fate to be decided. The servants had begun to dish up the food under the watchful eye of the stout red-faced cook when Mrs Bedford herself came to fetch them.

'This way, my dears,' she said kindly enough. 'Sir Joshua wishes to see you before he sups.'

The dining room was richly panelled in oak, two giant candelabra lighting up the long table set with silver and glass.

Sir Joshua was standing warming his hands at the blazing fire as they came in. He turned as they stopped short, hand in hand, staring at the tall imposing figure still in breeches and boots, his handsome riding coat open revealing the elaborately embroidered waistcoat, the dark curled hair tied back with a black ribbon, piercing eyes under tufted eyebrows. He frowned down at them and Guy's small hand clutched nervously at his sister's fingers.

'Come here to me, girl,' he boomed. 'Here, under the light.'

She hesitated, frightened of him though she hardly knew why. Then one large hand seized her chin and jerked her face near the candles so that she was staring up at him, so close she could smell the wine on his breath. There was a breathless moment. She trembled in his grip, then suddenly he uttered a barking laugh, released her chin and slapped her on the shoulder.

'By God, she is Clarissa's daughter right enough, the spitting image, no doubt about that. What do they call you, niece?'

'Isabelle, Uncle,' she answered feeling a little giddy now that the first ordeal was over.

'And this is your brother, I presume.'

'Yes, this is Guy.'

'I see, and where the devil is your father? Did he not bring you himself? It's all here in the letter he wrote and which came during my absence in London.'

'Papa is dead,' said Isabelle quietly.

'And your mother?'

16

She raised her eyes to his and it was as if a shadow crossed his face and then was gone.

'Mamma died some years ago.'

'They took Papa away from us,' burst out Guy stepping boldly forward, 'they cut off his head and they would have cut our heads off too if Mademoiselle Julie had not hidden us in the attic . . .'

'She had been our governess,' went on Isabelle, putting a hand on her brother's shoulder. 'It was she who saved us when the soldiers came. She made us dress in these peasant clothes and pretend to be Jean Pierre's grandchildren – he was Papa's coachman – and he drove us all the way to Calais and bribed a Captain to take us on his ship because, you see, we had no real papers of identity . . .

'Did he, by God? One of those damned smugglers I'll be bound, and where was it that he landed you?'

'They said it was close to Rye Harbour.'

Isabelle was about to tell him of the traveller's kindness and then stopped. For some inexplicable reason she did not want to share it with her uncle and aunt. It was something secret that belonged to her and Guy and to no one else.

'And how did you find your way here?'

'There was a man called Tod with a vegetable wagon.'

Sir Joshua looked at his wife and she said quickly, 'He is one of the carriers, my dear, he works all the farms around here.'

'So you had a pretty rough time of it, eh?' He ran his eye over the pair, his gaze dwelling on Isabelle for so long a moment that it made her feel uneasy. 'Well, we shall have to see what can be done with you, won't we, now you're here. Have you been given food?'

'Oh yes, your housekeeper has been very kind.'

'Good.' He glanced across to where Mrs Bedford still stood just in front of the door. 'Perhaps you will be good enough to see that suitable rooms are prepared for them and let them get to bed. Tomorrow will be time enough to talk about the future.'

Isabelle glanced from her uncle's harshly handsome face to her aunt's stony expression, acutely conscious of how very unwelcome they were and wishing passionately that she could

17

take her brother's hand and walk out into the dark. It was galling to be so helpless and so utterly dependent on those who so obviously did not want them, were perhaps in their secret hearts wishing they had followed their father to the guillotine.

She braced herself to acknowledge their grudging welcome with courtesy.

'Thank you, Uncle.'

She dropped a little curtsey to him and to her aunt, took Guy's hand and followed Mrs Bedford out of the room and up the stairs while a procession of servants started from the kitchen quarters carrying loaded trays.

At the first landing they met the young girl whom they had seen outside the house. She was elaborately dressed, her blue silk gown trimmed with flounces of lace and her fair ringlets tied up with pink satin ribbons.

'Oh look,' she exclaimed, 'the play-actors again. Where are you taking them, Mrs Bedford?'

'They are not actors, Miss Venetia, but your cousins come all the way from France.'

'I thought Papa said we were at war with the Frenchies.'

'So we are, but not with your cousins. Now hurry down, Miss, you know your father does not like you to be late for supper.'

'Papa won't mind tonight. He'll be too pleased to see me.' She waved an imperious hand. 'Out of my way, cousin.'

Isabelle did not move from the top step. 'In my country we were taught to say please, ' she said quietly.

The girl flushed scarlet, pushed rudely by and went on down the stairs.

'You mustn't mind Miss Venetia,' said Mrs Bedford uncomfortably. 'She will have her little ways.'

On the second floor she showed them into two small adjoining rooms. 'I'll send one of the maids with hot bricks for the beds, Miss. Do you want me to help unpack your bag?'

'We haven't very much. I think we can do it ourselves but thank you. You have been very kind.'

'Well, if we can't do a little to help others, I always say, then it's a poor old life,' went on the housekeeper. 'My room is at the far end of the corridor if you should want anything.'

There was little enough in the carpet bag but Isabelle pulled out a nightshirt for Guy, made him wash his face and hands in the ice-cold water and presently saw him safely into bed. He clutched at her as she bent to kiss him goodnight. She hugged him briefly, then blew out the candle and went to her own room.

The maid had come and put one hot brick in the middle of the bed but Isabelle didn't undress immediately. Instead she went to the window, pushed back the shutter and opened the casement. It was very cold outside; a thin sliver of a new moon had risen in the dark sky and a light frost spangled shrubs and skeleton trees. So much had happened since that last terrible day that it was almost impossible to realise that it was only a few days away, and yet it remained so horribly vivid in her memory.

It had taken them several days travelling mostly by night to reach the outskirts of Paris and they had gone at once to the house of their father's friend. Henri Rivage was a doctor. He and Gaston de Sauvigny had been at the Sorbonne together, one studying law and the other medicine. Isabelle had known him well. Many years earlier, before she was born, he had been responsible for some student riot against the government and had been packed off to the West Indies, returning later a fully fledged doctor who had established a successful practice in Paris. He had come often to the château but she could not like him, though she did not know why. Perhaps it was his coal black hair and small well-trimmed beard, perhaps it was his strident voice and the long arguments he used to have with her father. She only knew that she shrank from his boisterous kisses, his habit of teasing Guy till the child burst into tears, the contemptuous way he would sometimes look at her grandfather as if he despised the old man's creed of loyalty and honour.

He was unmarried and his housekeeper had received them with kindness. It was late in the evening when he had joined them, sporting a red cockade in his hat and a tricolour sash at his waist, laughing too loudly at their shocked faces.

19

'We must all be actors these days,' he had said, 'even an aristo like you, Gaston. We must all play a part if we wish to survive.'

'Don't be afraid,' her father had whispered to her afterwards. 'Henri has always been an ardent liberal but he is loyal, a good friend, he will see us safely out of the country.'

Even then she had thought her father was too trusting, unwilling to believe ill of a man whom he had called friend.

The last day came. They were to leave that morning, the baggage had been packed, the carriage already waiting, Mademoiselle Julie in tears as she kissed them goodbye when they had heard the tramp of feet, the ominous hammering on the door and froze in terror. The men had broken in, flaunting the red cap of liberty, arresting her father on a charge of treason, her gentle father who had never consciously harmed anyone, who had always been content with his books, the poetry he wrote, the music he played with friends, and standing at one side had been Dr Rivage, saying nothing, his hands in the sash at his waist, a smile lurking round his mouth and she had known at once that it was his doing, it was he who had betrayed them. Did he nurse a secret jealousy, an envy in his inmost heart for the young man who had enjoyed privileges that he had never known, whose gentle brilliance had so often overshadowed his braggart skills? She was not sure, only that it was scarred into her soul, something that she could never forget.

They had hardly even been allowed a last embrace. Their father had been torn from their arms and one of the men, a big hulking brute, had swung her round so that she could see him forced into the cart that would carry him to death.

'Look, little citizeness, look hard at what happens to the enemies of the Republic.'

He had made an obscene gesture so that she seemed to see the gaunt spectre of the guillotine, hear the blade rush down, see in horror the beloved head rolling – rolling – and shut her eyes against it.

When she had opened them Mademoiselle Julie was gripping her arm.

'Listen to me, you must go, both of you, leave Paris now, not a minute to lose,' she was whispering. 'There are some who would pursue hatred even to the last innocent child. Jean Pierre will take you. Change clothes quickly. You must look like his grandchildren. We have papers of a sort, a little money, he will drive you to the seashore, put you on a ship. I have here your uncle's name, your mother's brother. I know your father has written already but the Good God knows if in these terrible times the letter will have reached him.'

After that there had been only the terrifying journey, their hearts nearly stopping at every barrier, driving on and on, and one breathless moment when a guard dragged Isabelle out of the carriage.

'She's no child, no peasant's brat, but a woman grown.'

Coarse hands had fumbled at her budding breasts under the rough smock until Jean Pierre dragged her away.

'She is my granddaughter, I tell you. Didn't I see her taken from my daughter's womb with my own eyes? Take your filthy hands from her,' and he had hit out with such force that the man fell backwards in the mud among his jeering comrades as they galloped away.

It was time to shut the doors tight on those memories, to think only of the future which looked bleak enough. She was about to close the casement when she heard the singing, very faint but sweet. Listening, she began to distinguish the words –

'The wind from the sea
Blew my lover to me
He came with the moon
And was gone too soon –
Oh wind from the sea
Bring back my lover to me . . .'

The singing died away, there was a slight scuffle and a giggle – one of the maidservants perhaps running out into the night to meet her lover.

The silence flowed back and after a moment Isabelle closed the window and turned back into the room. The plaid rug, checkered dark green with grey and a thin red stripe, lay on the

21

bed. The traveller on the ship was certainly not a young girl's dream of a lover but all the same she stroked the rug gently. In that moment of loneliness and despair he had shown a kindness that had warmed her heart. When she was in bed, she drew it over her and lay with it pressed against her cheek.

Downstairs in the dining room Sir Joshua was sprawled in his high-backed chair, his booted feet stretched towards the heat of the fire, his eyes half closed, a glass of fine French brandy in his hand. He was not above buying a contraband keg or two even while he enforced the laws that hunted the smugglers down mercilessly. The French lace on his wife's gown had come via the same route and was the envy of her London acquaintances.

She was seated on the other side of the hearth, her hands idle in her lap, while she wondered how best to say what was in her mind now that Venetia had been sent to bed. Her husband could be unpredictable, and so far she had no clue as to how he viewed the unexpected and very unwelcome problem that had landed on their doorstep.

Augusta Brydges was the granddaughter of a Yorkshire tradesman who had risen from being the manager of a dozen looms in as many cottages to founding his own fine woollen mill and bringing up his only son a gentleman, a decision he regretted when the young man distanced himself from his father's country mode of life and infiltrated his inherited affluence into a famous banking house. The old man had not been averse to his granddaughter marrying into a family who had been landed gentry for generations, if not particularly distinguished. Since then Augusta had made very sure that she steadily climbed the social ladder. It was her dowry that had bought the house in an exclusive London square. Sir Joshua had few social graces but he was regarded as a coming man in political circles, and she had ruthlessly exploited both him and his colleagues with her small brilliant dinner parties where the food was good, the wine even better, and the conversation outstanding. She had every confidence that in a couple of years, when Venetia was ready to be launched into society, she could persuade her reluctant husband into the Carlton House set that circled around the Prince of Wales and his fashionable toadies. She intended to see her daughter a Countess yet and her ambition was not to be jeopardised by a pale-faced aristocratic French chit whose beauty and poise even in beggarly rags already had an indefinable quality sadly lacking in her own daughter.

She leaned across and tapped her husband on the knee.

'What are you going to do with them, Joshua?' she asked.

'Do with them? What should I do with them, for God's sake? Cast them adrift when from what I hear every fool between Rye and Dover will be talking about them in the next couple of days.'

She got to her feet, taking the glass from his hand and refilling it from the decanter at his elbow.

'We could drop one or two hints,' she said tentatively.

'Such as?' He held the glass to the firelight and then sipped it appreciatively. 'Good stuff this. Those artful rascals know how to ferret out the best.' His voice softened a little. 'You know, Gussie, that girl is uncommonly like Clarissa before she took off with that French jackanapes.'

His wife frowned. She knew that in his rough undemonstrative way her husband had been fond of his sister, far too fond in her opinion. His reaction to her flight had been a deep and savage anger. There had been a time when she had been bitterly jealous of the girl, had hated the beauty and charm that had made her acutely conscious of her own plain face, despite the advantages of her grandfather's money. It was still there burning within her.

She said quickly, 'She may have her looks but I fear this girl has a good deal of her wilful temperament too. She showed a boldness I don't think becoming in so young a girl. She is going to need watching.'

He glanced across at her. 'What the devil do you mean by that?'

'Don't you think we need to know a little more about them, Joshua? Are you quite certain Clarissa was ever married to that Vicomte of hers?'

'So far as we know. He possessed a devilish pride, I remember

23

that.' His eyes narrowed. 'Is that what you meant just now? Drop a hint or two that they are base-born, illegitimate?'

'Well, there's no proof is there? And if they really are what they pretend to be, what about the rest of the family? Why did they abandon them, leave them to come begging to us? Wouldn't the boy be the heir?'

'You don't know what a topsy turvy they are creating over there, my dear, where Jack is master and it's off with his head for the rest, God help them.'

He stared into the leaping flames. Augusta certainly had her wits about her. If these two were believed to be his sister's by-blows, he might be expected to provide for them but certainly not at the expense of his own wife and children. The idea had its appeal in these awkward circumstances and yet there was something about that girl. He thought of Clarissa, so lovely and so wilful. She had slid out of his grasp when he had believed he had all her love. He put the bitter uncomfortable memory behind him.

He said heavily, 'It's true enough that things are not going to be easy from now on. There's already talk of a war tax, as if enough isn't being filched from our pockets as it is, and the city is in a state of chaos. Pitt talks about it being all over in a matter of months but in my opinion that's wishful thinking. He's always been a man of peace. I've spoken to a few who've been over there and got away at the last moment. They tell me they have been recruiting every man who can walk and handle a gun so I'm not so hopeful.'

'It's you I'm thinking about, Josh,' his wife went on virtuously. 'We're going to be faced with heavy expense with Venetia coming out in a year or two, and then there's James to be thought of.'

'That young devil will be the death of me,' growled her husband. 'My father would have had the hide off my back if I'd done half the things that lad gets up to.'

Augusta's adored son was seventeen, leading a riotous life in his first year at Oxford and in consequence on very bad terms with his father.

'He's only a boy, Josh, you must make allowances, and after all he has made some very important friends.'

'Young rakes with money to burn and as dissolute as himself. That boy will end up by bleeding me dry, you mark my words.'

He sat up and put down his glass. 'Now look here, Gussie, the girl's your province, not mine. Can't she stay here? Set her to work in the house under Mrs Bedford. In a few years she'll have to earn her own living, y'know. I can't be expected to launch her into society without a penny piece to her name.'

'You'll be giving her a good home. She'll have to realise that and be grateful. And what about the boy?'

'Puny little creature, he looks. We'll send him to the local school for a year or two. This war is not going to be over next year or the one after. There'll be room for youngsters in the armed forces and if that doesn't materialise, then I'll set him to work under Nick Forrest. He's always belly-aching about needing an assistant with the book work. The boy can consider himself lucky if I don't send him out with the sheep except I don't think Nell here would understand French, would you, old girl,' and he stirred the big dog at his feet.

He guffawed and hauled himself out of the chair, pleased with the decision, admiring himself for his own benevolence and happy to have settled what had seemed for an hour or two to be an annoying and expensive problem when he had so much else to worry him. He yawned and stretched himself.

'Damned if I don't get to bed. It was a bone-cracking journey from London, the coach in and out of bogs and forced to lend a shoulder to shift it free.'

Augusta picked up the two candlesticks left ready for them on the hall table and preceded her husband up the stairs, well satisfied with the way Joshua had taken her suggestion and adopted it as his own. She had learned over the years how to persuade him into thinking as she did and once convinced he could be relied upon to carry it out.

Part One

LUCIEN
1801

1

Isabelle woke early as she always did and knew at once by the sun that slanted across her bed through the uncurtained window that it was going to be another glorious morning. Her spirits rose though God knows there was no particular reason for it. Nothing had changed, but all the same it *was* her birthday. Today she was nineteen and though in all the years she had been at High Willows no one had ever remarked on it or given her a greeting except Guy, and even he had forgotten it these last two years, to her it was still foolishly perhaps a special day.

She got out of bed and crossed to the window, shivering a little in her thin cotton nightgown and yet still filled with an unreasoning certainty that something was going to happen, something momentous that would change for ever the grey monotony of her day to day existence.

There was one good thing, she told herself, as she poured water into the basin and slipped off her nightdress, her uncle and aunt with Cousin Venetia and hateful Cousin James were still in London even though it was mid June. They usually fled from the heat and smells of the capital before this, but no word had come from them and that meant she still had a few hours of freedom.

It was strange how her life had seemed to split into two parts, the months when the family were in residence and she played the part of the quiet, docile, submissive young girl living on her benefactor's bounty, as her aunt's sharp tongue constantly reminded her, and the other times when they were away in London and, provided she performed the many duties assigned to her, the easy-going Mrs Bedford permitted her a freedom enjoyed by very few young girls, even the daughters of neighbouring farmers and tradesmen, and in that time she had made

29

friends, even if they were all people who Aunt Augusta called contemptuously the lower orders, friends whose loyalty had carried her through the wretchedness of those first years.

This was an ideal morning for taking Juno out and riding down to the sea and it could be her very last chance since Sir Joshua forbade her to ride any of his horses when he was at High Willows, having the poorest possible opinion of any young woman's ability to ride anything but an ambling hack. She put aside the faded cotton gown and dragged out the pair of Guy's breeches which she had adapted to her own use. Fortunately he had shot up these last few years from a rather puny little boy into a sturdy seventeen, nearly six feet tall, while she still remained small-boned and very slender. The breeches were badly worn but she had mended them. She belted them around her narrow waist and pulled on a frilled white shirt and an old leather waistcoat which she had stolen from a battered tin trunk when helping to clear the attics and altered to fit herself. A pair of soft leather boots from the same source were rather too large but, wearing them stuffed with paper to make them fit, she felt ready for anything.

She slid quietly down the back stairs taking care to avoid the kitchens. Mrs Bedford, thank goodness, didn't usually emerge from her room till after seven but Cook's temper could be unpredictable. Then she was through the garden door and running around to the stables. Jason, the under-groom, was one of her most valuable friends. He was in the tack room whistling to himself as he worked on the leather and brass of the carriage harness.

'Top o' the morning to you, Miss,' he said cheerfully, 'You're down bright and early.' He gave her a knowing wink. 'Is it Juno you're wantin'?'

'Please, Jason. It may be the last opportunity.'

'Aye,' he looked her up and down, 'it will be an' all especially if her ladyship were to see you dressed up like that.'

He grinned and her eyes sparkled back at him.

'But she won't and you won't tell her, will you?'

'Nay, 'tain't none of my business but I don't know as I'd like a sister o' mine to go about dressed up like a boy.'

'You haven't got a sister and anyway I couldn't manage Juno in a skirt, even you must see that.'

Once years ago at the beginning she had innocently asked her aunt if she could be given a suitable habit and be allowed to ride in the mornings, as she had always done at the château, and had been told crushingly that beggars couldn't expect to be given everything they fancied and she must grow accustomed to life being very different now. She had never mentioned it again, but had secretly made sure she got her own way even if it always held a strong spice of danger in case anyone should give her away.

Jason brought the mare out ready saddled. Isabelle rubbed the velvet nose and offered a piece of sugar she had saved from the kitchen. Juno sniffed it with caution before crunching it appreciatively. Jason gave Isabelle a leg up and put a warning hand on the bridle.

'Mind you're back by eight, Miss, before Mr Crane shows up. He could start asking questions.'

'I will,' she promised and then was away out of the stable block and riding down the bridle road that took her to Denge Marsh and to the sea.

During that first long, hard winter she had thought she would never grow accustomed to the naked bleakness of the marshes; the great stretches of dyked fields, so flat, so empty of trees; the winds that blasted bitingly across them lashing the freezing rain into the faces of those who ventured out; the snow that fell so thickly you couldn't see where the road ended and both men and sheep stumbled into the half frozen sluices and often drowned before they could be rescued.

The months had seemed interminable, lonely, desperately unhappy. They had been made to feel utterly dependent and aware from the covert glances, the whispering, that lies had been spread about them, that they were illegitimate, children of no consequence, thrown out of France with no roots anywhere, lucky not to be sent into the misery of an orphanage.

She had repudiated the slander with a bitter, angry pride but she might have been talking to the wind. It was far easier to believe, to say what could you expect from a nation that cut off the head of its king and had the impudence to declare war on Britain? Guy, sent to school in Rye, had come home covered with blood and bruises from the battles he fought with his rough schoolmates, most of them bigger than he was, and only too ready to make cruel fun of the pale-faced boy with his absurd pretensions of noble birth (who had ever heard of a Comte de Sauvigny?) and his funny way of speaking. She had tried hard to give him some of her own courage, her own certainty that a time would come when they would be able to prove who they really were and in the meantime they must make the best of it. But she had only partly succeeded. For the past two years, since he had been taken away from school, he had been set to work with Mr Forrest, her uncle's farm manager, a blunt, forthright man who was good at his job, knew every last thing about sheep, but had absolutely no sympathy or patience with a moody adolescent who felt life had cheated him. Guy loathed everything about him and about High Willows and constantly talked to Isabelle of running away and taking the King's shilling, enlisting in one of the regiments which were being recruited up and down the country.

'But you can't fight the French. They are our people,' she objected.

'Not any longer they aren't, not after what they did to Father and to us.'

She lived in fear that in a rebellious moment he might do what he threatened with no notion of the horrors he would have to face as a private soldier in the ranks.

But on this lovely summer morning she was not fretting over any of these problems. She let Juno go at her own pace down the grassy track, thinking of how amazing it was that the marshes had now become her greatest solace. She loved the feeling of freedom they gave her, the marvellous light that was like no place else, the stillness, the enormous drifting clouds, the sunsets that flamed in great arcs of colour, of green and gold and crimson stretching to the distant grey blue hills. She was humming as she trotted along, that haunting little tune she had heard on that first evening.

Oh wind from the sea, blow my lover to me . . .

Gwennie, the housemaid, used to sing it when she hung out the washing, watching it flutter in the strong breeze, but sadly the young man she had run out to meet had been unluckily trapped by the Press Gang marching up from Rye Harbour, and was now far away with the Fleet with no prospect of coming back to England for months, possibly years.

'Danged silly fule, I'll be tellin' him what I think of him,' she confided angrily to Isabelle, 'lettin' himself be caught instead of runnin' like a hare and I keep wonderin' how many other girls he's kissin' out in those foreign parts and me gettin' older every minute,' she went on, trying to still the dread that, far from kissing girls, he might by now be lying stark dead at the bottom of the sea.

At the Ship and Anchor where the fishermen gathered before going out with their boats, she pulled up for a moment and Mary Hope came out with a cup of milk and an appreciative pat on Juno's glossy neck.

'Your uncle's not back from London yet, Miss?'

'Not yet, and not like to be for some days.'

Jonty Daley had come out with her. Jonty worked at the inn, a Jack-of-all-trades, broad-shouldered, stocky with a mop of untidy brown hair and a coarsely handsome face. He gave her a sharp look and a nod before he picked up a spade and bucket and went round to the back of the building.

Isabelle guessed that there had been more in the artless question than appeared on the surface. The huge cavernous cellars, dating from medieval times, were probably stocked with the smugglers' loot ready to be packed on the backs of the stout little ponies during the next night or two, and distributed throughout the marshes before her uncle or the Revenue Officers got wind of it, and she gravely suspected Jonty of being one of the leaders of the gang. It was better to know nothing about such matters.

She drank the milk gratefully, handed back the cup and went on her way towards Dungeness, skirting the lighthouse and looking across the vast empty waste of shingle towards the sea.

33

The tide was on the ebb and there was a long narrow stretch of sand that ran all around the curve of the bay towards the beaches that lay about a mile back from New Romney.

Seagulls screamed and soared above her head. The marshes were alive with birds at all seasons and she had gradually learned how to distinguish some of them, widgeon, terns and redstarts, while in and out of the dykes fluttered peewits, lapwings and reed warblers. It never ceased to surprise her that across the great banks of shingle were green oases of flowers, clumps of dwarf broom brilliant in gold and lemon, campion and sea pink, thrift and creamy masses which they called sea cabbage.

She guided Juno carefully down the long line of planks put down by the fishermen to reach their boats, then she reached the firm sand and Juno began to trot and then to canter, the wind from the sea ruffling her mane and blowing Isabelle's hair into a wild tangle. She let the mare have her head and it was wonderfully exhilarating. The lighthouse was almost out of sight when she glimpsed something lying ahead, a bundle of rags perhaps, flotsam swept in by the tide from one of the ships in the Channel. As she grew nearer she thought she saw a tangle of dark hair, an arm flung out, and wondered if the bundle was a human being. Juno took the jump lightly but Isabelle couldn't go racing on, she had to go back and find out. She pulled up, slipped from the saddle and turned round, leading the mare. She had once seen a dead boy washed up on the beach and it had not been a pleasant sight; the face half eaten away had haunted her for days.

Reluctantly she dropped the bridle and knelt down. She could see now that it was a man, lying face down, his cheek half buried in the sandy shingle, the shirt and trousers torn and ragged, his feet bare. She touched the outstretched hand cautiously and it was still warm, not the icy cold, sea-sodden flesh she had imagined. This man was alive. She leaned forward and turned him over. He groaned and vomited a gush of sea water. There were bruises on his face and a deep cut high up at the hairline which had begun to ooze blood again. It ran down his cheek. She raised his head a little and with her handkerchief wiped the sand from his face and mouth. His eyes opened, large and very dark under curved brows. They stared blankly for a moment, then life crept back into them. He made an effort to sit up and she put an arm around his shoulders to raise him.

'Where am I?' he muttered in French.

Taken by surprise, she answered in the same language.

'This is Dungeness. It is England, the coast of Kent.'

'*Mon Dieu*, my head!'

He put a hand to his forehead, then stared at the sticky blood on his fingers. She wondered if he were a refugee. There had been one or two lately who had paid a high price to the smugglers for an escape across the Channel and had been robbed of their gold, their bodies thrown into the sea. If so, this victim had miraculously escaped.

'You're hurt,' she said. 'I'll go and fetch help.'

'No, no, no!' he muttered. His tone was so urgent that it stopped her as she was about to get to her feet. His hand gripped hers with surprising strength. 'No, no one, please.'

Was he perhaps a criminal escaping from justice? That might explain his torn and ragged clothing.

'If I could just rest somewhere,' he murmured.

She looked around her. This was a very deserted part of the shore. The few black huts clustered around the lighthouse were almost out of sight. Beyond the shingle stretched fields where tussocky grass struggled to grow on the stony ground and a thin pasture on which a few sheep seemed to have strayed. The only shelter was a wooden shack sometimes used by the shepherds when the winters were exceptionally hard and they were marooned by snow or by drifting storms.

With some difficulty she hoisted him to his feet. He stood wavering, one hand clutching Juno's mane, the other gripping her shoulder. Step by slow step she guided him to the hut. It was quite bare except that in one corner there was a pile of brushwood with an old sack spread across it. He sank down on it and closed his eyes as if all his strength was spent. She looked down at him wondering what she should do, all her sympathies captured by this forlorn outcast from the sea. She could not just leave him lying there, sick, in pain and soaking wet after the cruel buffeting of the waves. He could die without food and warmth.

She bent over him. 'Don't be afraid. I will go and bring something that will help you.'

'No one must know,' he said, the words dragging themselves out, his eyes wild with alarm.

'No one will know. I'll come alone.'

She would have to hurry or there would be awkward questions to be answered, but fortunately it was still very early. She galloped Juno back to the house, taking the shortest route across the fields, raced up to her bedroom and collected the checkered rug with a few simple remedies, a healing liniment and some old handkerchiefs to serve as bandage, and then went down to the kitchens. Luckily Gwennie was there.

'I think I'll take my breakfast to the beach,' she said gaily.

And the maid, accustomed to Isabelle's eccentric ways, brought her milk in a little closed can, some fresh bread and creamy cheese and an apple. Then she was out of the house. With any luck she could be there and back again before Mr Crane made his appearance and noticed Juno's empty stall. Beth, who had been lying stretched out in the yard enjoying the early morning sunshine, went with her.

Beth was a sheepdog who was afraid of sheep. Her mother was the shepherd's most trusted companion. In fact Barty used to say she could do the job as well as he could, if not better, even to shifting a thousand sheep from one dyked field to another or digging them out when the silly creatures got themselves lost and buried in the snows of winter. But Beth, who looked so beautiful with her black and white silky coat, never took to it. A sheep had only to turn on her with a loud bleat and she would tuck her tail between her legs and flee.

'Useless danged bitch!' Barty had growled to Mr Forrest. 'She en't worth the food she eats. She'll have to be put down.'

Beth's future hung in the balance until the two hard-faced men reluctantly yielded to Isabelle's impassioned pleading and Beth survived on sufferance, learning very soon to go to ground when Sir Joshua was there, but in his absence fed surreptitiously by Gwennie and not above creeping up the back stairs to her

36

saviour's bedroom and trying in her doggy way to prove her gratitude.

Isabelle called her to heel and approached the hut cautiously although the stretch of shingle was still mainly empty at this hour of the morning. Far away around the lighthouse half a dozen children were playing in and out of the waves that were slowly creeping up the beach to swallow the sand. She looped Juno's bridle over a decayed post that had once held a gate, commanded Beth to sit beside it and with a quick look around her went into the hut.

The stranger was stretched out on the bed of straw and bracken. He had stripped off the torn shirt and lay so still that for a heart-stopping moment she thought he was dead. Then she saw the rise and fall of the naked chest and knew he was asleep, profoundly asleep, worn out probably by the long battle with the sea. She knelt down beside him, gently wiping the blood from his face and examining the wound under the thick black hair. There was extensive bruising and blood still oozed. She put on some of the healing ointment she had brought with her and then raised his head a little to wind the bandage around it. He stirred and muttered but did not waken.

It was a handsome face, long and narrow, with arched black brows and a beautifully moulded mouth. She touched his lips gently with one finger. A long shudder ran through him and she drew back quickly. It struck her then that lying there in the soaked breeches could bring on chills and fever, yet she did not want to rouse him from what could be a healing sleep.

She hesitated and then abruptly made up her mind. With great daring, she unbuckled the belt at his waist and slowly drew down the ragged breeches. She noticed that one leg was heavily bruised and swollen and as she touched his ankle, he quivered, moving his head restlessly. She had never seen a naked man before and she gazed down at the long slender but muscular body, fascinated and at the same time a little ashamed, as if she were intruding into privacy. The hot colour raced up into her cheeks. She picked up the rug she had brought with her and threw it over him, tucking it around the chilled limbs. One thing was certain. The stranger was no sunburned

37

fisherman, no country rustic. The hand flung out was long and finely formed and had obviously not been employed in any manual work; and there was nothing in the pockets, nothing to show who he was or where he had come from or why he should have been thrown up on this barren shore.

Time was passing and she dared not stay too long. She placed the milk and the food close beside him, spread out the wet clothes to dry in the sun and wind that came through a broken window, and then went out. The door had no latch but she drew it close behind her. She would come back, find some excuse to walk from High Willows later in the day and bring more food. She scrambled back into the saddle and rode Juno hard across the fields to the house just in time for Jason to give the mare a quick rub down before Mr Crane's eagle eye fell on her.

Half an hour later, soberly dressed in her plain cotton gown, her hair nearly tied back with a ribbon, she went to join Mrs Bedford in the tiresome task of sorting through the extensive linen chests deciding what needed to be renewed and what must be repaired, a labour she hated. But Isabelle even by the age of twelve had been taught fine needlework and it had certainly proved useful, since Aunt Augusta saw no point in wasting good money on new clothes for a beggarly orphan when Venetia was so extravagant. Her cousin's cast-offs were far too large and in a style and colour Isabelle loathed but it was surprising sometimes what she made out of them.

At half past four she was released.

'You've worked very hard, my dear,' said Mrs Bedford kindly, 'and it's a lovely day. You need some fresh air. Take a turn in the garden.'

'I thought I could walk across the fields to see Mr Holland. I have a book I ought to return.'

'You do that and take a pot of my strawberry preserve to his sister. I know poor Harriet finds it hard to make ends meet on their miserable stipend, but make sure you're not late back. I don't like you to be out on the marshes when it grows dusk.'

'I won't forget, and thank you.'

38

The housekeeper sighed as she watched the girl go quickly from the room. She knew she should not have allowed her to become friendly with Gilbert Holland but the child had few enough pleasures, goodness knows. Not treated as one of the family and yet not one of the servants, she missed out on both counts. What was to become of her and her brother? From what she had heard lately, that young man was getting into bad company. Sooner or later a decision would have to be made about their future.

The Reverend Gilbert Holland was Vicar of Snargate, a tiny hamlet across Walland Marsh between the big house and Rye. Officially it was attached to the parish of Lydd with its magnificent church and its ancient history. Cardinal Wolsey was once rector there and had built its stately tower rising like a beacon from the flat land surrounding it, its pinnacles seen by every ship sailing down the Channel. Gilbert Holland was a scholar, far more absorbed in his books and his passionate interest in the flora and fauna surrounding him than in his few rustic parishioners, and for the last two years he had become one of Isabelle's dearest friends. It had come about by accident.

He was out on the marsh one afternoon hunting for the rare Pyramid Orchis and the stinking Goosefoot, both of which were said to bloom in these parts, when he saw the young girl leaning back against a tussock of marram grass absorbed in the book she had balanced on her drawn-up knees. He knew who she was. Everyone on the marshes knew about the refugee children who had landed on Sir Joshua's doorstep and whose past was so doubtful. When in residence, the family drove in state to Lydd church on Sunday mornings and due to an unfortunate estrangement on a matter of principle he had very little contact with them except through his sister who very occasionally took tea with Mrs Bedford.

Beth, who was a friendly dog, shook herself and gave a short bark when he approached. Isabelle looked up and then scrambled to her feet.

'Don't run away, child,' he said kindly. 'Tell me what you have been reading so assiduously.' He took the book from her reluctant hands. 'Good God, the Odes of Horace! Can you read Latin?'

'A little, not very well. In France I used to share my brother's tutor.'

'I see.'

'I found this in my uncle's library but it is very hard.'

'You could have scarcely chosen anything more difficult,' said Mr Holland drily.

'I didn't want to forget everything,' she said defensively.

'Would you like to learn more?'

He didn't know what prompted him to say such a thing when, like many true scholars, he hated teaching and had found the few coaching sessions he had been asked to undertake tedious beyond words, but something about the lovely shy grace of this French girl touched his heart.

She was gazing at him, her hands clasped, her face alight. 'Oh yes, yes, more than anything.'

He frowned, remembering the old quarrel. 'Would Sir Joshua permit you to take lessons with me?'

'I don't think my uncle cares what I do if it doesn't cost him anything,' she said frankly and then paused. 'But perhaps you . . .'

'No, no, no,' he said hurriedly. 'I want no fee. It would be a pleasure.'

'Then in that case I could ask Mrs Bedford.'

'You do that and let me know.'

And that's how it began. Nothing about it was mentioned at High Willows, though Mrs Bedford was sometimes uneasy, and it became a secret pleasure that they shared between them. Twice a week she ran across the fields and spent an hour, or more often two, in the company of a cultivated, well-stocked mind and they not only studied Latin but a great many other subjects. He lent her books and opened her mind to history, poetry and music while his sister, who privately thought her much too thin, fed her with rich meat pasties and buttered scones and other home-made delicacies.

The Hollands lived in an old timbered house beside the church. It lay in a hollow and was always damp. In the winter when the snow piled up outside they sat in the kitchen which was the warmest room in the house, their books spread around them and their feet close to the hob.

On this afternoon of her birthday, however, the sun flooded through the door and window mercilessly showing up the shabby furniture and the discoloured walls, and yet Isabelle loved it. She was reminded of her childhood, the smell of old leather in her father's study, the tangle of flowers in the garden, the sharp peppery smell of the herbs growing under the window. She felt at home there as she never did at High Willows.

This day she was not as attentive as usual. Once or twice Mr Holland had to bring her back to the poetry they were reading together.

'I'm sorry but my mind is straying all over the place this afternoon,' she said apologetically.

The old man wondered why. She led such an isolated life, meeting no one, not allowed to take part even in the country festivities. She had told him more than once very seriously that Sir Joshua had made it quite clear that very soon she must go out and earn her own living. 'I must learn and learn,' she went on, 'so that I can teach others and be able to keep my brother and myself.'

He was filled with pity. It could be a harsh loveless life for a girl who, in happier times, might have graced the cream of society.

He usually enjoyed a cup of tea in the afternoon and very often she shared it with him but today she wouldn't stay.

'I have to hurry. I'm wanted at the house.'

'What a pity,' said his sister coming in with a loaded tray. 'Just when I've been baking all your favourites.'

Isabelle hesitated. 'Could I – would it be dreadfully greedy if I asked if I could take one with me?'

'Take as many as you like, my dear,' exclaimed Harriet, her worst fears confirmed. That old miser, Sir Joshua, obviously kept them all on short commons when the family were in London. She wrapped two of the meat pasties and a batch of buttered scones in a white cloth. 'You take these and enjoy them.'

'Thank you, thank you a thousand times,' said Isabelle and leaned forward to give Harriet a quick kiss. 'You're so good to me.'

It would be food for her stranger till she had organized Gwennie and the kitchen at High Willows.

She went off, her step light, her face alive with some secret pleasure and Mr Holland despite his sixty years felt a pang of envy. Had she met someone, some youngster perhaps to laugh with her, to share innocent pleasures? He hoped to God it was not someone who might bring her to harm.

He turned back from the gate, looking for his cup of tea, and saw his sister struggling surreptitiously with what looked uncommonly like a keg of brandy. It could have only one source in this straitened household and he was deeply shocked.

'What have you got there, my dear?' he exclaimed.

She looked up guiltily and then bravely took it on the chin. In for a penny, in for a pound.

'What does it look like?' she retorted.

'Harriet, you know perfectly well how I feel about this. Haven't I said it a hundred times? I will not have any dealings with the smugglers. It is against the law.'

'Well, in that case you must stop them from using the ruined chapel in the church as a transit station for their contraband,' she said tartly.

'Harriet, you don't know what you are saying. It's not true. I won't believe it.'

'Of course it's true. Ever since that side chapel had to be locked against the congregation because of the danger of the falling ceiling, they have used it as a dumping ground, and if you weren't as blind as a bat with your nose always in your books and had taken a walk around that part of the graveyard, you could have seen the hoofprints of their ponies and the fine new lock attached to the small side door.'

He looked at her aghast. 'How long have you know about this?' he asked sternly.

'Oh I don't know,' she said airily, 'it must be more than a year by now. My bedroom window looks out on that side. I was wakeful one night and heard a rustling noise, stealthy footsteps.

I was anxious fearing robbers so I got up and looked out and there they all were.'

'Good God, did they see you?'

'I don't think so. They were far too busy, but soon after that I found the keg hidden in the woodshed.'

'And how many times since have we been accepting their bounty?' he asked sarcastically.

'I don't know exactly, it's not regular,' she said evasively. 'I didn't see why we shouldn't take it and you do so much enjoy your toddy on cold winter nights and a good nip when you have one of your poorly spells. How else do you think I could manage it?'

'Well, if we can't afford such things, then we must do without them. It's disgraceful. I ought to report it to the Revenue Officers at Hythe immediately.'

'And send a dozen or more men to prison or to be transported or hanged leaving wives and children starving and thrown on the parish. And for what? A few miserable taxes lost by the government. Is that what you call Christian? I warn you, Gilbert, that if you do, I shall be arrested too because I shall say it was all my doing and you knew nothing about it.'

He dropped down at the table and his eyes fell on the tea caddy and the pot waiting to be filled from the steaming kettle.

'I suppose this is part of it too,' he said bitterly.

She nodded. 'Sometimes.'

'It's infamous, it's abominable. I preach against it and this is what happens. We ought to refuse to accept any of their ill-gotten goods at once.'

But she knew he was wavering and sat down beside him putting her hand on his.

'I've always hated to see you do without a few little luxuries,' she said coaxingly. 'You're paid so little and I'm such a burden on you. It's unfair to be expected to make do on so small an income but if you really wish it, I will leave a note next time saying we want no more from them . . . except it doesn't pay to offend them . . . and after all, dearest, you know them all so well. You marry them and bury them and baptise their children.'

43

It was true. He weakened and she knew she had won. She had always to be practical for them both and if the government up in London imposed unfair taxes, then it was up to a sensible woman to circumvent them if she could.

She patted his arm. 'You have your cup of tea, dear. You'll feel all the better for it afterwards.'

She did not mention that sometimes lately, cautiously looking from her window, she thought she had recognised one of the young men busy with the unloading. Better to say nothing about it as yet, but all the same it worried her.

'The wind from the sea blew my lover to me,' sang Isabelle under her breath as she hurried down the path, Beth careering joyously ahead of her. She had known this was going to be a special day from the moment she woke and it was. This is what she and Guy used to call an adventure when they were at the château. It was so completely different from the humdrum life of everyday and she felt quite childishly happy.

She arrived at the hut flushed and excited, wondering if he would still be there or if he would have vanished like one of those dreams that seem so real and are gone so swiftly as soon as you wake. The heat of the day had abated and the vast stretch of the beach was filled with the golden light of early evening. She paused in the doorway, a little breathless, the big dog beside her, with no notion of the picture she made in her faded pink cotton gown falling from the high waist to her feet, the square neck edged with lace filched from one of those old gowns in the attic, the hair blown by the wind into little tendrils about the charming face.

The young man, propped up against the back wall of the hut, was staring in surprise and enchantment. She saw that he had pulled on his shirt, the dark hair flopped across the bandage she had fixed that morning and his eyes were not black as she had thought at first but a deep velvety brown. For the space of a few seconds they gazed at one another, then Beth gave a short sharp bark and abruptly the spell was broken.

The young man leaned forward. 'Who the devil are you?' he asked in remarkably good English.

She took a step inside. 'Don't you remember? It was I who brought you here this morning.'

'Oh no, that wasn't you. I might have been half dead but I remember distinctly that it was a boy, a fisher lad who spoke to me in French.'

She laughed, a delicious infectious gurgle. 'I *was* that boy and I *am* French.'

'Then it was you who left me milk and bread and bound up my head, stripped my wet clothes from me and brought me this blanket?'

'Yes,' she blushed a little at the memory of the slender naked body hidden under the rug.

'Mon Dieu! An angel of mercy and a most beautiful angel too!'

'Very far from an angel,' she said drily and came further into the hut. 'I see you have dressed again. Were the clothes dry?'

'Dry enough.' He frowned. 'What are you doing here if you are French?'

'That's a long story. How are you feeling now?' She knelt down beside him and put down her bundle, unfolding the white cloth. 'I've brought you some more food. It's the best I could find and it is fresh baked today,' she said anxiously.

'It looks delicious and smells even better. Did you steal it for me?'

'Not exactly. I have friends. Let me see your head wound first. I was worried about you this morning.'

'It's not too bad. Pains a little if I jerk my head.' He took a huge bite of the meat pasty. 'It's my leg that's the trouble. I tried to walk and could only manage a few steps. I'm going to be on your hands for a few more days I'm afraid. How safe am I here?'

She hesitated. She had not thought as far as that or what might happen if he were found there, though vagrants and tramps did sometimes shelter in these deserted huts.

'Not many people come up so far as here except the fishermen sometimes.' She sat back on her heels looking at him earnestly. 'What really happened? Were you trying to escape from France?'

'Looks like it, doesn't it?' he said ruefully, 'and making a grand hash of it. You see I had no wish to be forced into Bonaparte's conscript army but getting away is not so easy. I found a Captain in Calais who was willing to bring me over for a price but we ran into trouble in mid Channel . . .'

'One of the revenue cutters, I expect, on the prowl. So then they took your money and pushed you overboard.'

'You know?'

'I guessed. It has happened before. The law is very hard on anyone coming into the country illegally and on those who help.'

'And now when I'm caught, I have only to open my mouth to be taken up as a spy and clapped into prison.'

'It's possible. There are a great number now in Dover Castle.'

'Ugh!' he shuddereed. 'I'd rather be put up against a wall and shot.'

'Oh no. That would be terrible.'

'I have friends in London but how to reach them, that's the problem.'

'I'm sure we can find a way. You could stay here for a few days,' she went on eagerly. 'I could bring you food and when you are recovered . . .'

'I could be on my way.' He gave her a ravishing smile. 'I knew it the moment I set eyes on you. You are destined to be my guardian angel.'

He reached out for her hand, kissing it lightly, and Beth, who had sat patiently waiting in the doorway, started to her feet and growled.

'I don't think your dog approves of me,' he said smiling.

'Oh Beth is a very friendly dog but she is a little possessive sometimes.' She held out her hand. 'Come along, silly, come and be introduced.'

But Beth, normally prepared to love everyone, remained stubbornly aloof, refusing to come near the stranger and rejecting the piece of buttered scone he held out to her.

'She's telling you I'm not to be trusted,' he said. '*Je suis désolé.*'

'It's not that at all. She's telling me it's her supper time and she's right.' Isabelle got to her feet. 'I mustn't stay. If I'm late, questions will be asked but I will come again early in the morning, and I'll bring a herbal compress for your leg.'

'Physician too. How fortunate I am.' He caught at her hand as she moved away. 'What do I call my rescuer?'

'Isabelle,' she said shyly. 'And you?'

'My mother called me Lucien.'

For a moment she could not move, held in an enchantment staring into those deep brown eyes. Then she pulled away abruptly.

'I must run. Goodbye till tomorrow.'

'Till tomorrow, *ma belle* Isabelle.'

She had gone and he lay back with a sigh of relief. He had fretted all day at the disastrous failure of his plan, but now he had been granted a reprieve and in the most delightful way possible. She might betray him, of course, but he didn't think so. A difficult childhood beset with problems had taught him to judge people shrewdly and he had a fair conceit of his own power to charm. He had a few days' respite in which to think out his next move.

It was after seven by the time Isabelle arrived back at the house. She hurried up to her room to wash her hands and make herself tidy before going to supper with Mrs Bedford. While the family were in London, she and Guy usually ate their evening meal in the housekeeper's room.

'You're very late, my dear,' she said mildly. 'You've surely not been all this time with Mr Holland?'

'No, it was such a lovely evening, I walked down to the sea with Beth. It was delightfully cool down there after the heat of the day and I went further than I intended.'

'You shouldn't walk down there in the evening. You never know whom you might meet.'

'Usually there are only the fishermen and the children. I know most of them.'

Mrs Bedford frowned. 'Was your brother with you?'

'Not tonight. I expect Mr Forrest has kept him.'

'Well, we won't wait for him. Ring the bell, will you, my dear?'

Supper was served and Guy didn't come. Afterwards Isabelle escaped to her own room. It felt warm and stuffy so she opened the windows wide before she spread out her books. She had a piece of Latin verse to translate for Mr Holland before her next lesson but, try as she would, tonight her thoughts were not on the elegant poems of Horace.

> Quis multa gracilia te puer in rosa
> perfumis liquidis urget odoribus . . .

'What boy his hair scented with fragrant oils makes love to you, Pyrrha, in the rose-covered cave . . .'

No, that was clumsy, she threw down her pencil in disgust. It had none of the grace of the original. It was no good, tonight the words just wouldn't flow and her mind kept straying to the strange events of the day. Lucien, she mused. She'd never known anyone by that name. Was it his real one? Where had he come from and why? There was something intriguing, something exotic, about those dark velvet eyes and pale olive skin. He was different from anyone she had ever known, but then her experience was so limited.

She pushed aside her books and got up, going across to the window and leaning on the sill, breathing deep of the scented summer night. She was suddenly desperately weary of this narrow, confined life. There must be some way out of it, there had to be. She had a violent longing to run out of the house, go down to the sea, feel the wind in her hair, caressing her cheek, touching her lips with a salt laden kiss. The stranger had a beautiful mouth. She shivered and for a fleeting second saw again the slender naked body. The blood raced up into her cheeks and she pressed her palms against them, half ashamed and yet half delighting in the stir in her body, in feelings she had never known or even dreamed of before today. Then a door slammed below, the dogs barked and she came back to reality. What on earth was she doing, dreaming of a beggar, a vagrant, a criminal, he could so easily be any of these things. The cool,

48

practical side of her temperament told her she was behaving like a fool, a romantic idiot. Far better return to her books. Through them she might one day be able to escape into a wider world.

It was near to midnight when at last she undressed and got into bed. It was still very warm and she found it hard to sleep. When at last she did begin to drowse, she was abruptly wakened by the sound of running feet on the stairs and the slam of a door. That must be Guy and he was very late. Where on earth could he have been? He was seventeen now but he still seemed like the little brother she felt she had to protect. She slipped out of bed, pulled on her dressing gown, relit the candle and went out of the room. She tapped softly on his door. There was no answer so she went in. Guy was lying face downwards on the bed still in his working clothes. She shut the door and came further into the room.

'Guy, what is it? Why didn't you come to supper? Are you ill?'

'Go away. Leave me alone,' he said in a muffled voice.

But she had seen a dark streak of what looked like blood on his cheek, and the knuckles of the hand clenched on the pillow were bruised and bleeding.

She put down the candle and crossed to the bed. 'Guy, have you been fighting again?'

'What if I have? What concern is it of yours?'

She sighed. 'Let me see.'

He rolled over, staring up at her sullenly. 'It's nothing.'

She took a towel, dipped it in the water jug and came back to the bed. He sat up half resentfully and let her wash the dried blood from the long shallow cut on his face and gently bathe the damaged hand.

'Why must you do it? What good does it do? Who was it this time?'

His eyes glittered in the light of the candle.

'Do you know what he called me? A coward, too timid to tell my uncle what I thought of the way he treats me, a yellow belly like all Frenchmen, a bastard whose mother was no more than a whore . . . that was when I hit him. One comfort is he got the worst of it. I've spoiled his good looks for the next few days.'

'Oh Guy, was it Dick Forrest? Why do you listen to him? You know what will happen. His father will be running to complain to Sir Joshua when he comes down.'

'Let him. He can beat me for all I care.' He suddenly gripped Isabelle's hand so tightly that it hurt. 'I wouldn't stay here another minute, I'd be off like a shot, if it weren't for you. I couldn't leave you with *him*. We're all that's left, aren't we? We've got to stick together but sometimes something seems to explode inside me and I have to hit out. I could not come back tonight, sit and chat with Mrs Bedford like a tame pussy cat. I walked along the beaches, miles and miles, with only me and the sea . . .'

She had a sudden spasm of anxiety. 'Did you meet anyone?'

'Not a soul stirring.' He grinned suddenly. 'There is a moon tonight so there was no one out, not a boat, not a ripple on the sea.'

'Guy, you'd not go with them, would you? You'd not join with the smugglers?'

'I've thought of it. Jonty Daley's young brother was at school with me. He has hinted at it more than once. They'd be glad of someone who could speak French. It would be such a splendid smack in the eye for Sir Joshua, wouldn't it? He's so damned righteous and he drinks their brandy with one hand and strikes them down with the other.'

'No, Guy, you mustn't. Promise me that you won't go with them. It's dangerous.' She thought of the stranger who could so easily have drowned. 'There have been many who have died.'

He lay back against the pillows. 'Don't fret, Belle. It's a fool's game. It leads nowhere. Do you think I don't realise that?'

But he was not looking at her. He wouldn't meet her eyes and she was afraid that he had gone much deeper into it than he was willing to admit. Danger was the very spice to make it tempting to a boy bursting with frustration.

She got up. 'It's terribly late and I must be up early.'

'Are you going to take Juno out?'

'If I can. There won't be many more opportunities.'

'Shall I come with you?'

'You ought to get some sleep. I like riding alone.'

He grinned up at her teasingly. 'Whom do you meet down there? A lover?'

'Don't be silly. Whom could I meet in this place?'

'No, you're right. He likes to keep us chained. Why, Belle, why does he? It's not just that he's a tight-fisted bully, is it?'

'I don't know and this isn't the time to wonder about it.' She bent down and kissed him. 'Goodnight, dearest.'

Back in bed she lay staring sleeplessly into the darkness, waiting for the first streak of dawn and thought that Guy was right. There *was* something else. Now and again she believed that despite his bullying manner, Sir Joshua was afraid.

2

It turned into a summer idyll. Isabelle's good sense told her time and time again that it could have no future, it was all the purest folly, but for once her own cool judgment deserted her. Her drab life had suddenly blossomed, she seemed to race from one breathless moment to the next, and she gave herself up to it during those few precious days, living on a knife edge of discovery which only gave it an added intensity.

She would ride Juno down to the sea in the early morning, carrying the breakfast which they ate together. If Gwennie wondered, she did not question and loyally said nothing.

'Everyone's entitled to have a bit o' fun now and then, 'tis only right,' she whispered to Beth, putting down a generous plateful of scraps. 'You look after her, old girl, see she don't come to no harm.'

Sometimes Isabelle would escape for an hour in the afternoon, shamefully neglecting Mr Holland and her books. By some miracle the spell of fine weather continued and when his leg improved, Lucien would limp slowly beside her along the edge of the beach, the breeze from the sea tempering the heat in the golden light of early evening.

He talked and she listened enraptured. He told her that his name was Lucien de Vosges, that up to a few years ago he had lived all his life on the island of Martinique in the West Indies. He conjured up picture after picture for her, the long, low white house surrounded by its acres of exotic flower gardens, the blistering heat of midday and the cool nights, the sea glowing with a magical phosphorescence when they took out the boats, the fish darting like silver arrows through the water, the divers bathed in a blazing whirl of milky fire, till the moon rose drenching everything with its pearly light.

He told her of parties at the villa where the guests drank white rum laced with sliced limes and nutmeg, and ate delicious seafood and baby lamb cooked whole, succulent and golden. He described the carnivals with singing, fireworks and dancing in the streets when blacks and whites, dressed up as dragons or tigers or sea monsters or demon kings, mingled freely together for three riotous nights and days. He mentioned lightly that he had once visited La Pagerie where Josephine de Tascher had grown up, and legend whispered that she had been told by an old negro fortune-teller that one day she would be an Empress.

'She is not that yet even if she is now the wife of General Bonaparte,' objected Isabelle. 'He could still be defeated.'

'So he could, but not yet. He could still crown himself Emperor.'

'Have you ever seen him?' she asked curiously.

'Once only. He is a small man, smaller than I am and very plainly dressed, almost insignificant till you see his eyes and hear him speak.'

'And then?' she went on.

'Then you believe he could achieve anything, charm a nation to do his bidding, conquer the whole world.'

'But he did not impress you?'

His eyes blazed for an instant and then were immediately veiled by those absurdly long lashes.

'No, not me. I have no trust in such fiery eloquence. It flames and dies all too quickly.'

He was a magician with words and she was enchanted as much by the light and play on his handsome face as by what he said. But as they walked on the seashore or sat close together in the little hut, eating the food she had brought and sipping the wine from the bottle which, greatly daring, she had stolen from the cellar at High Willows, there were a great many things which he did not tell her. The pictures he drew so brilliantly had another and a darker side.

He did not say that his mother was only a servant in that great household, one white woman toiling from dawn till night among a horde of black slaves, that until he was fourteen he ran barefoot and in rags, employed in the sugar refinery for a

53

pittance by day and running errands at night for an eccentric Englishman, who lived alone half a mile away and, when he was not drunk, amused himself teaching the good looking boy to read and write and speak the King's English. He never once mentioned that, till the time came when he escaped to France, he never knew who his father was.

And in the meantime, while he recovered health and strength in the company of his charming companion, he thought of how he might use her to the best advantage. Those cursed smugglers on the ship had robbed him of everything, papers, credentials, money, but he did have a contact in London. Once there it would be plain sailing but how to get there, that was the problem. He needed money and clothes. Isabelle had confided a very little of her own circumstances. He knew she was not the peasant he had thought at first; but it was extremely unlikely that her unpleasant uncle, member of Parliament and local dignitary, would be willing to do anything for a penniless French refugee except clap him into prison as a possible spy till further enquiries had been made, and his contact in London would not care for that at all, would more than likely leave him to his fate. She spoke of a brother but he could not help feeling the fewer people involved the better. He would have to find some other solution and he was still turning it over in his mind when Isabelle found it for him.

It was almost a week after he had been washed up by the sea when he knew he had finally shaken off the worst effects of that very unpleasant experience. The wound on the forehead was beginning to heal, the headache had long gone, the slight fever that had bedevilled him all that first day and night had vanished and the damaged ankle had begun to knit together.

That evening, strolling beside Isabelle, he said gaily, 'See, I can walk easily again, even run a little if I must. It is time I went on my way.'

She felt as if the brilliance of the summer evening had suddenly dimmed, which was stupid because of course he would have to go. Hadn't she always known that?

'Maybe I could start walking,' he went on. 'How many miles is it to London?'

'I'm not sure. I have never been there but I think I've heard my uncle say it is more than sixty miles.'

'If I can keep up ten miles a day, it should not take me more than a week,' he went on thoughtfully.

'But you can't go, not like that. What would you do for food and lodging? You need decent clothes and money.'

'And where are they to come from?' he said with a humorous shrug of the shoulders. 'Alas, they do not grow on trees.'

She had already given some thought to this knotty problem. There was Guy, but then like her he mostly had to make do with James's cast-offs. But there were the old trunks in the attics. She might be able to search out something to fit him, a coat and breeches perhaps.

'I think I could find something,' she said doubtfully, 'but it would be second-hand and might not fit very well.'

'Anything, anything in the world to cover my nakedness,' he said dramatically. 'Can you do it? Are you sure? When? Soon?'

'Maybe not for a day or two. I will have to seize my opportunity.'

He wondered if she were going to make a raid on her uncle's wardrobe in his absence and that could lead to trouble. Oh what the hell! He would probably be gone long before it was discovered.

'I knew you were my guardian angel! How can I ever thank you?'

He fell on his knees and clasped her around the waist, burying his face against her cotton skirt.

She laughed, a trifle embarrassed. 'Don't be silly, Lucien. Get up. Suppose someone should see us.'

'Let them.'

He rose to his feet, slowly letting his arms run up around her body till they were facing one another. He held her close against him, one hand tilting up her chin so that she was looking into his eyes.

'You're so beautiful, Isabelle,' he whispered. 'Has no one ever told you how beautiful you are?'

She shook her head, mesmerised by his touch, by the warmth

55

of his body burning through the thin shirt, so close she could almost feel the beating of his heart.

He lowered his head and kissed her, lightly at first and then with increasing strength, teasing her lips open, feeling her tremble against him. She could not move. She had never been kissed like that before, never felt the hard strength of a man's body pressed against hers. She wanted it to go on for ever and it was he who released her so that she swayed, shaking a little.

'I'm sorry,' he murmured huskily, 'I shouldn't have done that. I wanted to say thank you and – and somehow I couldn't help myself.'

'It's all right. It doesn't matter.'

'But it does matter. I value your friendship too highly to risk losing it.'

'Does it mean so much to you?' she whispered.

'Do you need to ask?'

He had both her hands in his. He was drawing her towards him. She knew she should resist and couldn't. Then Beth, who still distrusted him, came bustling between them and Isabelle took refuge from her disturbing feelings in fondling the dog.

'She's telling me it's growing late and high time I went home.'

They walked back to the hut not saying very much and when they parted, he took one of her hands and kissed it.

'Am I forgiven?'

'There's nothing to forgive.'

He watched her as she went hurrying across the fields. He guessed that he could have seduced her easily and it would have been very enjoyable. If she had been the fisher girl he had thought at first, he would probably have had few scruples about indulging himself but there was something about Isabelle, something innocent and untouched, some indefinable quality, not like any of the other girls who had given him a night's pleasure. She was an aristocrat, she belonged amongst those delicately bred women he had once looked up to as living in another world than his and, much to his annoyance, despite what Céline had taught him when he was still little more than a boy, that feeling lingered.

Madame Céline de Ragny had been forty years old, rich,

bored and regretfully running to fat from too much extravagant living when she first caught sight of the handsome lad who sometimes worked in her gardens. Merely to gratify a whim, she had him washed and his wild dark hair brushed and curled. She had him dressed up in a flowing white silk shirt and breeches with a scarlet cummerbund and set him to serving the drinks at one of her elegant parties. Slim, with a pale gold skin and velvet brown eyes whose glance was a caress, he was an instant success and she was the envy of all the other women until the Revolution in Paris at last reached those distant shores and put an end to the pleasure-loving life of the wealthy French colonialists. Her elderly husband was recalled to France.

Lucien was barely seventeen when Céline first took him to her bed, teaching him all the arts of love, and he began to see her as his one hope of escape from the narrow, confined existence in the island.

She took him with her to a Paris only recently recovered from the shock of those first massacres, reeling under the dynamic leadership of a young Corsican called Napoleon Bonaparte and already at war not only with Britain but with half the countries of Europe. It was not really the place for a decadent aristocrat and Monsieur de Ragny swept his wife off to Italy leaving Lucien penniless and starving. But he still had one card to play and staked his all on it.

Once long ago in Martinique he had rescued Josephine's pampered little dog from the ragged children who were tormenting it. He hung about her pretty little house in the rue Chantereine on the slopes of Montmartre with his eye on the main chance, and luck played into his hands. One morning, down the pathway under the pleached limes, the little pug called Fortuné raced in pursuit of a cat and Lucien scooped him up from under the hooves of a horse and presented himself among the many petitioners with a bloody rag ostentatiously bound round his bitten thumb. Josephine had no memory of the earlier incident but received him graciously, not immune from the admiration in the fine dark eyes raised humbly to hers. Always carelessly generous, she gave him money and better still an introduction to her new and adoring husband on one of his

57

flying visits to the capital. From that had come other introductions, some not so pleasant, but he had swallowed his pride, had crawled and flattered, for the sake of the glowing future that could be his, that must be his. He would not let this temporary setback defeat him.

All the next day passed and Isabelle did not come. He had food. She had always taken the precaution of bringing more than they could eat; there was bread and cheese and the coffee he could boil up in a little panikin on a fire of twigs, so he didn't starve but he was tormented with anxiety. What had happened? Had they discovered what she had been doing? Had Sir Joshua returned unexpectedly? Had she been forced to confess, and would the soldiers be coming to arrest him? He kept a careful watch but no one crossed the stretch of tussocky grass except two children chasing a goat that had broken away from its tether and an old man trudging home with the day's catch in a fish basket slung across his shoulders. The hours passed so desperately slowly that he felt he would run mad.

He thought once of making a bolt for it but in his ragged state he was not likely to get very far. He could not sleep and felt so stifled in the little hut that midnight found him pacing along beside the sea. It was a black night, heavy clouds massing overhead. The heat wave would be breaking soon but as yet there was no breath of air. It was like wading through thick humid water. At the first streak of dawn he flung himself on the blanket covered bracken and a couple of hours later woke from a heavy sleep to see her standing in the doorway, breathless, excited, weighed down with a heavy carpet bag.

He was up in an instant and seized her by the shoulders shaking her.

'Where the devil have you been? Why didn't you come? I've been near out of my mind wondering what could have happened to you.'

'I'm sorry, Lucien, I'm sorry. I couldn't help it, really I couldn't.' She dropped the bag and came inside the hut. 'When I returned home the night before last, Mrs Bedford told me a message had come from London. My uncle will be returning within the next three days and the whole house was in a turmoil over it, so much had to be done. I couldn't find any opportunity to come away.'

'But you *have* brought me some clothes,' he said, impatiently brushing aside her excuses.

'Yes, they are the best I could find,' she said anxiously. 'I had so little time.'

From when she had got up at six o'clock till late at night, High Willows had been turned upside down. Mrs Bedford had insisted on everything being freshly cleaned and dusted, ornaments washed and replaced on tables and in cabinets. Guests were expected, so the linen must be sorted through, extra bedrooms aired, carpets sprinkled with tea leaves and brushed. Cook was consulted and the larder meticulously gone through and restocked. All day Isabelle had run hither and thither carrying messages to Mr Forrest and from him to Barty, the shepherd, about killing a sheep, then to Jason about the fowls that must be slaughtered and hung. In the afternoon he had driven her and Mrs Bedford into Rye Market and then to Hastings. High Willows was largely self supporting but there were always extra delicacies to be selected and purchased.

It had been past eleven before the housekeeper retired exhausted to her bed, and Isabelle was free to take her candle and creep up the back stairs to the attics. The servants' bedrooms were on the floor below and she met Gwennie on the landing.

'Wherever be you goin' at this time o' night, Miss?'

'I lost something when I fetched that little ebony table that Mrs Bedford wanted for the drawing room,' she improvised. 'It's a locket, the clasp was never very reliable.'

'Wouldn't tomorrow mornin' do?'

'It was my mother's. I don't want to lose it.'

'Shall I come and help you look for it, Miss Isabelle?'

'No, Gwennie, no, it's kind of you but you've had a much harder day than I have. You go to bed. It won't take a minute. I think I know where it must have fallen.'

She had lit a second candle, but even then it had not been easy to find anything suitable in the flickering light, so now she watched Lucien pulling out a waisted blue coat with a black velvet collar and large silver buttons that would have been the height of fashion thirty years before.

'Will it do?'

'Why not?' he said, frowning at it.

There was a pair of velvet breeches with grey stockings and buckled shoes. One of them had a hole in the sole. She saw the look on his face as he tried them on.

'I'm sorry they are not better.'

'I can manage.'

'Lucien,' she went on, 'it was so difficult to get away. I daren't stay any longer now. They will be looking for me. There is still so much to be done.'

He dropped the coat to the floor and took hold of her by the shoulders.

'I know, believe me, I *do* know what you risk for me. But there *is* something else. Money, just a little money to help me on my way.'

'I'll try, Lucien, I will try.'

This was the stumbling block, and she didn't know how she was to get round it.

'I'm sure you will and I'm so tremendously grateful. You do not realise how very much all this means to me.'

He slid his arms around her and she could not resist yielding just for an instant to the pleasure of feeling him so close. He was lightly kissing her eyes, her cheeks and at last her lips, so that for a moment her senses swam and she gave herself up to the long, passionate embrace. Then abruptly she pulled herself away.

'Let me go, Lucien, please let me go. I mustn't stay, but I will come back this evening. Somehow I'll find the money, I promise. There is some food for you in the carpet bag but now I must go.'

He walked back with her to where she had tethered Juno. She was wearing the breeches and shirt she had worn when she first rescued him and, lifting her into the saddle, her breasts pressed against his chest, he almost regretted his restraint. He watched her ride away at a brisk trot – perhaps this evening when she came back to him. He let himself dwell for an instant on the heady delight of holding that slim naked body in his arms, feeling it tremble with pleasure and surrender for the first time. Then he put the thought away from him. There were other and more important matters to concern him and he returned to a closer examination of the garments she had brought him.

They had all worked so hard on the previous day that they could afford to take things a little more easily. Isabelle spent most of the afternoon helping Mrs Bedford clean and polish the finest of the silver, the giant candelabra, the coffee pot and jugs, the enormous silver serving dishes, the baskets for serving cakes and fruit which were only used when the family were there and dinner parties were being planned. When the last piece had been carefully put away in its wash leather bag, she asked if she could take Beth for a short walk across the marshes.

It had been a day of heavy cloud and very little sun, but the storm had not broken and it was so humid that Isabelle felt her muslin gown stick to her at the slighest exertion.

'Take care it doesn't rain,' said the housekeeper doubtfully. 'Carry a cloak with you. There's no shelter in those fields.'

'I'd be glad if it did rain. It's so stuffily warm, I feel as if I can't breathe.'

'Off you go then, but don't be late back.'

Up in her bedroom Isabelle had a decision to make. All day it had been in her mind, and now she took from the drawer where she had hidden it the little leather pouch which still contained the coins she had brought with her from Paris. She spilled them into her hand, four golden guineas. Where Mademoiselle Julie had obtained English coins on that last frantic day, she still didn't know. She had had very little to do with money. Her uncle and aunt had never so much as given her a penny for herself, and she was not at all sure how far a guinea would take Lucien but she guessed that two would be sufficient to carry him to London and perhaps buy a modest meal and lodging at an inn on the journey. The money belonged to her and Guy. She had kept it for an emergency so she scrupulously put two guineas back in the bag. That must still be saved for her brother. She had thought of sharing the secret with him, but guessed that she would have to tell him all and that he would strongly disapprove. The other two coins were hers to dispose of as she chose and this was her emergency.

She wrapped then in a handkerchief, picked up the little basket that contained two large wedges of game pie, two wings of chicken and the cakes she had carefully saved from her own meal. It was no more than a children's picnic but it was all she had and must serve for a farewell supper. Then she picked up her light cloak and went downstairs and out by the back door. Beth, who had just licked her own plate clean, went galloping with her.

She ran most of the way so as to have as long with him as possible and stopped a few yards from the hut as the incongruous figure came to meet her. The coat fitted reasonably well, considering she had been forced to choose it by guess and candlelight. The breeches were a little too large but he had belted them into his narrow waist, and had pulled out the collar of one of Guy's old linen shirts which she had stuffed into the bag as an afterthought. With his long black hair tied back with a string and the dark stubble now showing faintly on his chin, he needed only gold rings in his ears to look every inch the handsome pirate of a child's storybook.

She ran towards him smiling in spite of herself, and he frowned.

'Don't dare to laugh,' he said reproachfully. 'Behold the nonpareil of fashion!' and he spun round before giving her a courtly bow.

She exploded into laughter and he joined her, pulling her arm through his.

'I feel like a scarecrow. At any moment birds will be nesting in my hair.'

Their humble supper turned into a hilarious picnic with Lucien at his most amusing, full of jokes and laughter, telling tales of other suppers as if he had been part of them instead of a bitterly envious youngster carrying trays of food he was forbidden to taste and pouring iced wine that was never for him.

The time went by all too quickly. Soon now he would be gone and it would be all over. It had been so brief and her heart sank

62

at its finality. How was she to go on living through the long, dragging days?

She got to her feet. 'I must leave soon or they'll be sending someone to look for me, but first I've brought you these.' She took the handkerchief from her pocket and held out the two gold coins. 'It's all I have. Will it be enough?'

He was not laughing now. He stood up facing her, looking down at her outstretched hand.

'Where did you get them? Did you steal them for me?'

'No, they are mine to spend as I wish.'

He hesitated for a moment, half ashamed of the use he was making of her. Then he took the coins and buried them deep in one of the coat's pockets.

'Isabelle,' he said huskily, 'I don't know what to say . . .'

She turned away her head, unwilling to let him see that there were tears in her eyes, and he took hold of her, yielding to the crazy impulse that swept through him. He was kissing her roughly, one hand on her back pressing her against him, the other pushing aside the neck of her gown so that he could kiss her throat and the swell of her breasts. For a few moments she gave herself up to the almost delirious joy that seemed to pulse through her whole body until suddenly it became too much for her, too frightening, and she thrust him away.

'No, Lucien, no . . . no . . .'

'Come with me,' he was whispering, 'come with me. Why not? We'll run off together.'

For a moment the crazy folly of it tempted her, then she shook her head.

'They would only come after me and it would be you who would suffer.'

He swung her back into his arms. 'Shall I come back, Isabelle?' he said in a muffled voice. 'Shall I come back some day . . . shall I?' and even while he spoke the words knew that it would be impossible.

'I don't know . . . I don't know . . .'

She was trembling violently, and the realisation of the rashness of what he was saying overcame him and he dropped his hands.

63

'You're right. This is madness, isn't it? But I'll not forget, Isabelle, I swear I'll never forget. One day, my love, one day . . .'

She guessed they might be empty promises even while she longed to believe in them.

'Will you go tonight?' she asked in a stifled voice.

'Either that or at dawn tomorrow.'

'So we must say goodbye.'

'Yes.'

She had picked up her cloak and was putting it around her shoulders with a shaking hand.

Outside the hut he made an attempt to return to their former gaiety. He took one of the coins from his pocket and tossed it lightly in the air.

'With this you have given me my ticket of leave.'

Both of them were far too absorbed in one another to notice the solitary horseman who was riding slowly down the path across the field and could see quite clearly the two figures outlined against the evening sky. He observed them with idle curiosity, which sparked into interest as he recognised the girl, saw how close they were standing, saw her slip into her lover's arms.

'By God,' said James Brydges to himself, 'what the devil does that French cousin of mine think she's doing hugging and kissing some damned rogue like a slut from the stews?'

James was in an exceedingly bad temper and more than ready to pick a quarrel with anyone. He had recently come from a blistering argument with his father over his very considerable debts. As if any young man of fashion wasn't entitled to gamble every now and then, he told himself indignantly, and if his friends happened to be of the first rank and accustomed to play for high stakes, was he expected to withdraw like some cursed ninny of a pauper? But Sir Joshua saw the situation differently. James had been ordered peremptorily to spend the rest of the summer at High Willows on very short commons. He would dearly have loved to rebel, but his father still held the purse strings and could be very tight-fisted, and this time not even his mother could help. It was Venetia who was her father's pet and could get away with murder, he thought resentfully. He had never had much affection for his sister, who paraded her beaux in front of him, the latest a sober strait-laced fellow whose wealthy father lived in some God-forsaken castle in Scotland and who had been held up to him as an example, God rot him! He was spoiling for a fight and here was one being handed to him on a plate. He leaped from his horse and charged towards the couple who stood so close together.

'What the hell do you think you're doing, fellow?'

He thrust them apart so violently that Lucien went reeling back and Isabelle stumbled and fell to her knees.

Beth, who had never liked James, rushed to her defence, leaping up and seizing hold of his coat while Lucien, lithe and agile, had learned to defend himself in a rough school and came back quick and deadly as a serpent. His fist caught James on the point of his chin so that he fell backwards, crashing into the wall of the hut and, hampered by the dog, went helplessly sliding down it. While Isabelle tugged at Beth's collar, Lucien saw his chance. Quick as lightning he seized the bridle of the horse and was in the saddle and galloping across the fields before James had struggled to his feet, bruised, bewildered and furiously angry at being worsted by some common vagabond while his damned cousin stood by holding the panting growling dog and trying not to laugh at the ridiculous spectacle he presented.

'Keep that cursed bitch away from me or I swear I'll have her shot,' he muttered. Then indignant rage got the better of him. 'That wretch has had the impudence to steal my horse.'

'I daresay it's only a jest,' said Isabelle, 'he will probably make sure it is returned.'

'More likely sell it and pocket the cash,' he growled. 'Who is he? And what the devil were you doing carrying on publicly with a ragamuffin like that?'

'If you'd only waited instead of charging in like an angry bull, you would have known,' she said, still cool and calm despite an inward quaking. This was the very last thing she had expected to happen and she greatly feared what James might do or say. In the little time he had spent at High Willows over the years they had never been on good terms, and there had been a time when she was barely fifteen and he had believed her easy game like the girls he fondled at Oxford. She had repulsed him furiously in an unpleasant incident she hated to remember.

'Well,' he said, his eyes narrowing as he looked at her, taking in the thin cotton gown, the dishevelled hair, the basket which she had picked up, 'who is he? You'd better tell me before Father gets wind of it.'

'He is just someone I met casually, a young Frenchman, a refugee like us, on his way to London.'

'And is it because he's French that you hand over cash for his trip and invite him to fondle and kiss you?' he said sarcastically.

He must have seen more than she thought. She took refuge in a haughty indignation.

'How dare you speak to me like that! I have done nothing wrong. It was just a gesture of friendship and goodwill.'

'Was it indeed? Let's hope Sir Joshua sees it like that and now what the devil am I to do with no damned horse?'

'Walk back to High Willows just as I am going to do,' said Isabelle unsympathetically, 'and you'd better start now because very soon it's going to rain.'

And indeed while they had been talking, the sky had darkened and the first heavy drops of the coming storm began to fall. She pulled the hood of the cloak over her head, called Beth and began to walk quickly across the fields, outwardly calm and self possessed, but filled with an inner anxiety. If he should relate the story to her uncle, she didn't know what might come of it. It had all been so innocent but many would see it otherwise. The only hopeful part was that Sir Joshua hadn't arrived yet and by the time he did, Lucien would be well away and out of his reach.

She was still a long way from the house when the rain came down in torrents. She and Beth were soaked through by the time they arrived and an hour or so later when she had changed and was rubbing her hair dry, she saw James come trudging up the drive, bedraggled, covered in mud and in an even worse temper. He yelled at his servant, whom he had sent on in advance with his portmanteau, sent the maids flying to bring him cans of hot water and fresh clothes, and bit Guy's head off when the boy saw him arriving outside and asked innocently if he'd had a fall and if so what had he done with his horse?

Later they all three of them ate supper in a gloomy silence, Mrs Bedford having taken one look at James's scowling face and wisely excused herself. They were just finishing when Franklin came in.

'There's a fellow outside asking for you, sir,' he said a little tentatively to James.

'What kind of a fellow? Who the devil is he?'

He reached for the wine and refilled his glass.

'He's a stableman from the White Hart in Hythe, sir. He says he has a message for you.'

'Can't he hand it over to you?'

'He says he's been ordered to deliver it personally.'

'Damn his impudence!' James swallowed his wine at a gulp and got up.

Isabella exchanged a look with Guy and then went out after him.

Outside on the front drive the stablehand was holding the bridles of the horses. The rain had stopped, the clouds were thinning and there was a welcome freshness in the air.

'Well, my man, what's all this about a message?'

'It were a foreign gentleman, sir. He ordered me to rub down the nag, give him a feed and then bring him back to High Willows, and I was to say to you most particular, that he was deeply grateful for the loan and hoped it didn't cause you too much inconvenience.'

'Cursed kind of him, I must say,' said James sarcastically, 'and where did this foreign gentleman go?'

'Couldn't say, sir. He went in to speak to the master while I did what he asked, rubbed down the horse, gave him a feed of oats and brought him back.'

He stood there, waiting expectantly, until at last, grudgingly, James tossed him a coin.

'Thank 'ee, sir, much obliged. I'll be on my way then.' The boy climbed back into the saddle and went trotting down the drive on his old hack while James caught Isabelle's eye, swore to himself and yelled for Jason to take his horse to the stables.

'What was all that about?' asked Guy. 'What have you been up to, Isabelle? James looked as if he could murder you.'

'It was nothing.'

'Have you been meeting someone down there on the beach?'

'What makes you say that?'

'Something I heard. I told the fellow to go and boil his head, but was there someone?'

'Yes, in a way. It was a young Frenchman, a refugee like us. I met him by chance as he was passing through,' she said reluctantly.

'Better take care. I don't trust James. He could invent any lying tale if he thought it might do him a bit of good.'

That was what she feared, but nothing more was said that night. During the next couple of days James went drinking with his friends or lounged about the house making himself obnoxious, until Sir Joshua arrived with Aunt Augusta and Venetia, and by pure chance the whole situation blew up in Isabelle's face.

It was after dinner on the first evening. The two girls had meekly followed Augusta to the drawing room, leaving the men to their wine. Guy, who didn't like Sir Joshua or James, hurriedly excused himself and disappeared.

Sir Joshua refilled his glass and pushed the decanter towards his son.

'Have you been dipping your sticky fingers into my strong box again, James?' he said unpleasantly.

'No, I have not,' he replied in righteous indignation. 'I'd have you know, Father, I'm not a schoolboy pilfering pockets. What money is it?'

'Mr Forrest brought me some last payments of rents and says he left them in the drawer of my desk. The bag is there but part of the money is missing.'

'And so you immediately think of me,' said James. 'I take that very badly if I may say so. There are the servants or what about Guy or Isabelle come to that?'

'Isabelle? Nonsense! What need has she of money?'

'To give away to her fancy man perhaps.' It came out before he could stop himself and for a moment Sir Joshua stared at him.

'What the devil do you mean by that?'

'It was the day I came down here.' James hesitated, then it all poured out; what he had seen that evening, and what had followed and somehow in the telling he put a very unpleasant light on it. His father listened in silence.

'You've never cared for the girl, have you?' he said at last. 'Is this true, James, or are you inventing the whole sorry tale?'

'It's as true as I sit here, Father. I kept quiet about it, but if you're going to start accusing me of what I haven't done – well then, I thought you ought to know.'

'Yes, yes, yes.' He felt anger rise up inside him, a stifling rage coupled with a queer feeling of disappointment. He said heavily, 'When you go to the drawing room, tell Isabelle I'd like to speak to her. I'll be in my study.'

'Now, Father, this evening?'

'Yes, now. Go on, do as I say.'

'You won't . . .' James hesitated, feeling a momentary pang of shame. It could after all have meant nothing, and he knew only too well his father's difficult temper.

'Go on with you,' said Sir Joshua roughly. 'What are you waiting for?'

'Very well. I'll tell her,' he said and went out quickly.

In the drawing room his sister was at the piano, trying over one of the short pieces she had brought down with her. Isabelle was bent over a book on the window seat trying to get the best of the light. He came up behind her and looked over her shoulder.

'Good lord, verses. How can you read that stuff?'

'I like it.' She closed the book and stood up. 'I'd better tell the servants that we are ready for the tea tray.'

'Leave that. Father wants to see you in his study.'

'Now? What for? Do you know?'

'Ask me another, and you needn't look so accusingly at me – I've said nothing but I advise you to take care. He's in one of his moods.'

69

She gave him a quick suspicious glance before she went out, uncertain what to expect.

He looked after her. It was a little like sending a lamb to the slaughter. Then he shook off his misgivings impatiently. She would get round him, women usually did. Look at Venetia. She always ended up by getting her own way.

Her uncle was standing at the window when Isabelle knocked and went in.

'James said you wanted to speak to me.'

'Yes. Come in, come in,' he said testily, 'and shut the door.'

He came to behind the desk and stood looking at her standing quietly before him. Her simple dress of flowered cambric had looked dowdy on Venetia, but she had contrived to give it one or two touches of distinction. These new fashions the women were wearing nowadays were all too damned revealing, he thought irritably, and wished she did not look so much like her mother. Clarissa had once faced him with just that look of innocence that he knew to his cost had hid a steely determination and a resilience that he had never been able to break down.

He said abruptly, 'If you needed money, why didn't you come to me or to your aunt rather than helping yourself from my drawer?'

'Are you accusing me of stealing? I never enter this room, not even to dust. Mrs Bedford does it herself. Why should I need money?'

'Perhaps to give to your lover.'

'Lover? What lover? I don't understand you, Uncle,' she said calmly enough, though inwardly quaking.

'Don't play the innocent with me,' he said roughly. 'James has told me what he saw and heard and how this French rogue of yours had the impudence to steal his horse.'

'That was a jest,' she flashed back at him. 'He did not steal it, he borrowed it, and sent it back that same evening with his thanks.'

'And what else did he borrow, this Frenchman of yours with his glib tongue, what else did he steal, eh? Answer me that.' Anger was rising in him. 'How often did you lie with him down

70

there on the beach disgracing my name, making yourself a byword, behaving like some common trull?'

'I don't know what tale James has told you,' she said passionately, 'but it is all lies. I have done nothing wrong. It's true that I did meet him once or twice and I spoke with him because he was a refugee like me, like Guy, and it felt good to speak my native tongue once again and to hear him talk of the country that is still mine. What was there wrong in that?'

'If that was the case, then why not ask him here? Why speak to him in secret telling no one? What was this vagabond of yours hiding?'

'He was hiding nothing, and when has any friend of mine been made welcome in your house?'

'Have you forgotten that we are at war with France? Where did this man come from? What was his name? What was his purpose in coming here?'

The questions thundered at her one after the other and she gathered her strength to reply firmly and proudly.

'He did not choose to tell me and I didn't ask. We spoke of other things.'

'Don't lie to me, Isabelle.' He had come round from behind the desk and had seized her by the shoulders. 'By God, I'll have the truth if I have to beat it out of you.'

She was frightened of the look on his face but still stood her ground.

'He was not my lover,' she said steadily, 'and his name and his purpose in coming to England belong to him and to him alone. I am saying nothing.'

'We'll see about that.'

Anger flooded up in him in a hot red tide. It was not Isabelle he saw, but his sister Clarissa standing there, flushed and triumphant, defying the brother who had been so close to her all her life, who loved her with a possessive passion that often frightened her. She had escaped him, she had run to her French lover and he had cut her out of his life as one cuts out a cancer, but this time her daughter should not escape. His riding whip lay across one of the chairs. He picked it up and gripped her painfully by the shoulder.

'His name? Tell me his name. Tell me what you did together.'

'I have told you. There was nothing, nothing.'

'Damn you! Damn you for a liar!'

The frustration, the anger surged up and would not be denied. He thrust her against the edge of the desk. One powerful hand tore at her dress and the thin cotton chemise beneath, and brought the whip down bitingly on the naked flesh.

She quivered, biting her lip till the blood came, but said nothing.

Her defiance woke in him a frenzy of baffled rage. He brought down the whip again and again, but still she did not cry out or beg for mercy and he let the rage carry him away till one of the red wheals showed a thin streak of blood and he seemed to wake to what he was doing. He stopped abruptly, aghast at himself. Then he flung the whip from him and turned his back on her.

'Get out,' he said thickly, 'get out of my sight! Go!'

For a few moments she could not move; the shock and the pain made her head swim so dizzily she thought she would faint. She clung to the back of a chair, her eyes closed, fighting for the strength to walk. Then slowly she pulled the remnant of her dress around her and walked stiffly from the room.

She could hear Venetia singing, the melancholy little melody followed her as she crept up the stairs, every movement sending waves of fresh agony through her. Fortunately she met no one till she reached her bedroom and fell face downwards on the bed. He had wanted to humiliate her, make her cry out for mercy, confess to something she had not done, but he had not succeeded. She had told him nothing and Lucien was still safe. At least she could console herself with that. Now what would he do? She could not think so far, the pain and the misery were too intense and, despite herself, it brought unwilling tears into her eyes.

It was past ten o'clock when Gwennie, on her way to bed, heard the stifled sound as she passed the room and paused uncertainly. She knocked and, when there was no answer, opened the door and went in. The room was dark but she could see the figure lying on the bed and moved across with her

72

lighted candle. She exclaimed with horror when she saw the lacerated back.

'Oh Miss Isabelle, whatever has happened to you? Who has done such a dreadful thing to you?'

'Never mind who it was, Gwennie,' Isabelle dragged herself up a little. 'Can you help me?'

'Shall I fetch Mrs Bedford? We ought to send Jason for the doctor.'

'No, no, it's not as bad as that. You help me with it, please Gwennie. There are salves and ointments in one of the drawers of my chest. They are what Miss Holland gave me for Guy when he was in so many fights at school. Can you find them and put them on for me? They will help to heal the cuts.'

'I'll do my best,' murmured Gwennie, still doubtful, but she came from a family of eight children who could never afford the expensive treatment of a physician except in the rarest of cases. She knew a great deal about treating cuts and bruises and lacerated flesh. She fetched the ointments and put them on the wheals with gentle fingers, afterwards laying a piece of soft linen across them and then helping Isabelle into her nightgown.

'Who did it, Miss?' she whispered. 'Was it the Master?'

It was useless to deny it. Isabelle nodded.

'My uncle was very angry with me and he lost his temper.'

'He ought to be ashamed,' said Gwennie fiercely. 'He'd never lift a finger to Master James nor to Miss Venetia neither whatever they did.'

'Probably not,' sighed Isabelle. 'Don't tell anyone about it, Gwennie, please. I . . . I don't want it to be known. It's so . . . so humiliating. I'll keep to my room for a few days. Tell them I'm ill – a summer cold and fever – and they'd best keep away from me in case it's contagious. Will you do that for me, Gwennie?'

'Trust me, Miss,' she said sturdily, 'but I still think it's a wicked thing and if I had my way I'd give the Master a piece of my mind, that I would.'

The thought of little Gwennie tackling the formidable Sir Joshua made Isabelle smile faintly but, strangely enough, what she most dreaded did not happen. No one guessed at what had

73

taken place that night. Sir Joshua said nothing to anyone and bit James's head off when he made a tentative enquiry.

'I don't want to hear anything more about it,' he said, 'and I'd thank you not to encourage servants' tittle-tattle in future.'

The missing money turned out to be a miscalculation on Mr Forrest's part and he came up with it the next morning full of apologies.

Isabelle was left in peace. Aunt Augusta after one enquiry left her severely alone. Mrs Bedford looked in to ask kindly if there was anything she wanted and Guy put his head round the door to ask how she was.

'Gwennie says you're not feeling quite the thing. Anything I can do, Belle?'

'It's only a chill. The weather changed so suddenly and I did get soaked through on the day of the storm.'

'You take care of yourself and stay in bed. The house is being turned upside down. It seems we're to have a party.'

That meant Aunt Augusta would be angry because she was not there to run hither and thither at her beck and call.

Venetia confirmed it, bouncing in one afternoon a day or so later.

'Gwennie told Mamma you had a feverish cold.'

'Yes, I have. You'd better keep away.'

'Pooh, I'm not frightened. You don't look very ill.'

'I'm feeling a lot better.' Isabelle was sitting up in the bed. Gwennie had put the softest of down pillows at her back. The worst of the agony had eased but every movement still caused her spasms of pain. 'I expect I shall get up tomorrow.'

'You'd better,' said Venetia flatly. 'Mamma is planning one of her dinner parties.' She plumped herself down on the bed and gave a little squeal when Beth poked her head out. 'You shouldn't have that dog up here. There'll be an awful row if Mamma catches you.'

'She won't unless you tell her,' said Isabelle quickly.

'Oh I won't say a word, don't worry.'

She was vain, spoiled and selfish but not really ill-natured, and it was a pity that the girls had so little in common and had never really got on together. Sometimes Isabelle regretted it.

She said with an effort to be friendly, 'Who are the guests? Is there anyone special?'

'There could be.' Venetia leaned forward confidentially, longing to tell someone about it. 'His name is Robert Armitage, Viscount Kilgour. He's not really handsome but very distinguished. You know what I mean. He has the kind of looks that make other young men seem callow and silly. His father is the Earl of Glenmuir and he has a castle up in Scotland.'

So Venetia was looking to be a Countess one day.

'Has he offered for you yet?'

'Not yet, but Mamma thinks he might,' she said ingenuously. 'He came to one of our musical parties and was very attentive. He stood by the piano when I played and said lovely things about my singing. Then we met him at the opera. He came to our box in the interval with his sister Marian. She is older than he is and unmarried so she lives with him in London. He is about thirty, I suppose, but older men are so much more exciting than boys, aren't they?' went on Venetia a little wistfully, as if she were trying to convince herself.

'I can't wait to meet this paragon of yours,' said Isabelle a little drily.

Venetia got up and crossed to the mirror, examining her face critically. She was a very pretty girl with her pale gold hair and English rose complexion.

'You know, Isabelle, isn't it dreadful? I shall be twenty-one next month and I'm not even engaged yet. I could have been, you know, several times. I've had two offers this past year but they were only younger sons and Papa didn't think they were good enough.'

'Did you care for either of them?'

'There was one,' confessed Venetia, twisting one of her curls between her fingers. 'He is a Lieutenant in the Navy and he was home on sick leave. He was charming and so very attentive. He couldn't dance because of his damaged leg so we used to sit and talk and . . . Oh what's the use of thinking about that now? You're so lucky, Isabelle, you could marry anyone, even the ploughboy, and no one would mind or create a fuss or keep reminding you of what you owe to the family.'

75

'I suppose I could,' said Isabelle ruefully, 'I might try it one day,' and she thought of Lucien, so handsome and so charming. How many of Venetia's admirers could stand comparison with him? He had promised to come back one day but would he? Would he ever know what she had suffered for his sake? Would those few days that had changed her from an innocent young girl into a woman who could feel passionately mean as much to him as they had done to her? Common sense told her it was very unlikely, but she could still dream.

Venetia was looking at her curiously. 'Is there anyone, Isabelle?' she asked. 'James mumbled something at dinner one night but Papa shut him up.'

'No, of course there isn't. Who could I meet down here except for fishermen . . . or ploughboys?'

'No, I suppose not. Do you hate it – living down here I mean?' she went on with a rare touch of sympathy.

'Sometimes. You'd better go, Venetia, your Mamma won't like you to spend so much time up here with me.'

'No, she won't,' sighed Venetia. She turned back on her way to the door. 'I have a new dress in pale blue that makes me look washed out. Would you like to borrow it for the party?'

It was kindly meant but the thought revolted her.

'No, thank you, Venetia. It is generous of you to offer but I still have the white one you gave me a year or so ago. I can make do with it. No one is likely to be interested in me.'

'Please yourself.' Slightly huffed at the rejection of her offer, Venetia went out slamming the door.

After a moment Isabelle struggled off the bed and examined her own face in the mirror. Beside Venetia's blonde prettiness she thought she looked pale and uninteresting. There were shadows under the large eyes and her hair hung loose and untidy around her thin cheeks. Who on earth would dream of glancing at her twice?

She went back to bed feeling so depressed she could have burst into tears, but Isabelle possessed a good deal of inner resilience. The next morning, waking to a new day, she felt differently about it. She was not going to let her uncle believe he had defeated her or daunted her spirit. The sun had roused her very early so she determinedly got out of bed and dressed, trying to ignore the pain and the stiffness. She threw a thick shawl around her shoulders, called Beth and went down the stairs and out into the freshness of the morning.

She had done nothing and yet her uncle had made her feel guilty, humiliated, unclean. She badly needed the keen salt wind of the sea to blow away the miasma of the last few days. The dog, free of her long vigil in the sickroom, was bounding ahead barking joyously and Isabelle followed. She would make her way to the hut so full of memories, and then find refuge and solace in walking at the sea's edge as she had done so often in her years at High Willows.

3

The sun had begun to break through the early morning haze by the time Robert Armitage left his horse at the Ship and Anchor and strolled past the lighthouse and along the stretch of shingle beach. He had put up at the Salutation Inn in Rye, a quiet hostelry which he preferred to the busy George and where Mr Lambe, the discreet landlord, was an old acquaintance of his. He had been invited to stay at High Willows but had gracefully excused himself, preferring to avoid a guest's obligation and be free to pursue quietly the real purpose which had brought him down to Kent.

For the past few years the war with revolutionary France had gone badly for Britain. Since 1795 a certain Corsican Lieutenant of Artillery, small, thin, half starved and twenty-six years old, had rapidly risen to become a formidable opponent and a strategist of genius. In the spring the country had been shaken by a political crisis that had ended in the resignation of William Pitt and the brilliant men surrounding him had followed their chief into exile. Henry Addington, well-meaning and mediocre, was the stop-gap Prime Minister leading a cabinet that did not inspire confidence.

An embargo on ships in foreign ports coupled with two years of disastrous harvests had brought starvation throughout the country. There had been mutiny in the Navy and in towns and villages children were reported to be begging from door to door for a few halfpence. The country, worn down by taxes, high prices and bloodshed, was weary of it. If it had not been for two outstanding victories, Nelson in Copenhagen and Abercrombie in Egypt, there might well have been revolution in England's green and pleasant land, thought Robert grimly.

Perhaps now was the moment to put out peace feelers and

hope for a respite but all the same, in the innermost heart of the Foreign Office, anxiety at a possible invasion still occupied the minds of those responsible for the country's defence. Reports of the barges massing on the shores of France struck terror into the bravest. The local militia drilling on the cliffs with inadequate weapons was not going to be enough. There must be investigation into the creation of coastal defence, and a preliminary survey of the conditions and cautious discussion with some of the leading dignitaries was part of Robert's mission.

He had taken on undercover work for the Foreign Office ever since he had been almost accidentally recruited when he was only twenty-two. He kept this secret from everyone, even his sister, so that when she asked him why he was going down to Kent, when she would have greatly preferred him to accompany her to Glenmuir on a short visit to their father, he simply shrugged his shoulders.

'Sir Joshua gave me an invitation and I decided to accept.'

'But why, for heaven's sake? He is not at all your type of person. I must admit I don't care for him or his wife; they are pushing people, always looking to their own advantage and toadying up to anyone, including you, whom they think may advance them socially.'

'You exaggerate, my dear,' he said mildly.

'No, I don't, and what's more, I'm quite certain that Lady Brydges has her eye fixed on you as a possible husband for that daughter of hers.'

'Well, you are always urging me to marry and provide an heir for Glenmuir,' he replied teasingly.

'But not Venetia Brydges! Oh Robert, you wouldn't!'

'You must admit she is very pretty.'

'Maybe, but she's also an empty-headed little ninny. She'd drive you out of your mind in a week.'

'Do you think so? She plays the piano nicely and sings very sweetly.'

'Robert, you can't be serious!'

She stared at him aghast and he smiled.

'No, not entirely, but it suits me for the time being to let them think so.'

79

'You don't tell me half of what you're really up to, do you?' she said ruefully.

'Perhaps not, but I do tell you anything that's important and I promise that when I do choose a bride, you will be the first to know.'

With that she had to be content. She was five years older than her brother and loved him dearly, but during the years she had lived with him in London she had learned not to enquire too closely into what he did when he went away, sometimes for weeks at a time, aware that the reasons he gave were very often far from the truth.

However he was not thinking of Venetia Brydges on that lovely morning which had succeeded days of storm and rain. Although he had passed through Rye time and time again, he was not familiar with this part of the marshes. He took deep breaths of the salt laden air, one part of his mind registering what an ideal spot this long stretch of empty coast presented for an invading force, and another part delighting in the feeling of space and light, the clumps of flowers, gold, pink and white, the birds that soared above his head or flew up startled at his approach.

The sea was coming up to high tide so he was walking on the grassy verge when he heard the barking of an excited dog and a ripple of girl's laughter. He peered across the bank of shingle thrown up by the incoming sea and saw a girl standing knee deep in the water, the waves breaking against her and he watched for an instant charmed by the picture she made, the slender naked back, the hair blown by the wind into a dark cloud around her head – Aphrodite, he thought, who rose from the foam of the sea to enchant the world of men. Then she turned and raised her arm to throw a stick for the dog. The sun came from behind a cloud and he saw quite clearly the cruel marks on her back. Good God, who would want to thrash such perfection was his first thought, followed quickly by the realisation that she must not know he had seen her. Very quietly he turned his back, retracing his steps. At a little distance he paused, looking away from the sea across the dyked fields, and began to whistle a lively tune. He gave her a few minutes and

80

then turned to walk back and was met by a furiously barking dog, soaking wet and shaking a spray of sea water over his buff breeches and green riding coat. His lovely goddess had by now hastily pulled on her cotton gown, draped a shawl around her shoulders and was running towards him barefooted, carrying her shoes in her hand.

'Don't be alarmed, sir,' she exclaimed breathlessly. 'Beth loves to bark but she won't hurt you.'

At Glenmuir his father had a dozen dogs, large and small. By the time she reached him he was already rubbing the ears of the excited dog who had instantly recognised a friend.

'I'm afraid she has made you very wet,' said Isabelle apologetically, tugging at Beth's collar.

'It's of no consequence.' He took out a handkerchief to wipe his wet hands. 'Isn't it a little early in the morning to be sea bathing?'

'Oh no, it's the best time because the beach is usually deserted.' The colour suddenly ran up into her cheeks. 'Oh heavens, did you . . .?'

'I thought I had a glimpse of a mermaid, that is all, believe me.'

In the moment she raised her eyes to his, those large eyes fringed with dark lashes in the pale oval of her face, memory had come rushing back. He recognised her now. The lovely child on the ship had grown into a beautiful woman, but what on earth was she doing dressed like a serving maid and bathing on a deserted beach with the marks of a savage whipping on her back? He had almost forgotten the incident over the years but now the memory was vivid. She obviously did not remember him and why should she from that chance meeting on that cold dark night? He and Sir Joshua had not mixed in the same social circles until recently, and though now and again he had wondered what had happened to those two forlorn refugees, he had not been anxious to disclose his own presence on the smuggler's boat.

She had bent down to pull on her sandals, then she straightened up.

'Were you looking for the right path, sir? Can I help you?'

'I left my horse at the inn and simply thought I would like a stroll, the morning being so fine. I must walk back and look for breakfast.'

'If you wait until I collect my rug, I will come with you. I can show you a shorter way.'

She darted back to the beach and came back a moment later with a plaid over her arm. It was so similar to the rug he had given her all those years ago it had to be his plaid, and she had kept it.

She showed him a path across the fields and in answer to his questions told him about the dykes, how skilfully the fields had been drained and how she had heard that there was talk of them being flooded against the French invasion.

'Only that would be disastrous,' she went on earnestly. 'What would happen to the hundreds of sheep and the country people who depend on them for their livelihood? There has been terrible poverty and starvation among the cottagers these last two years. I know because I sometimes go with Miss Holland to take them food and clothes.'

He listened with interest, watching the play of light on the lovely face, and was intrigued. That evening when he joined the family for dinner he would doubtless learn a great deal more, but for the moment he said nothing about their earlier meeting.

They parted a few yards from the inn.

'I must hurry,' she said, 'or I shall be scolded for being late. Mary Hope will look after you. They are good people at the inn.'

He watched her running up the bridle path, the dog racing beside her, before he turned back into the Ship and Anchor.

Mary Hope brought him a tray of coffee and asked if he could do with a thick slice of their home-cured ham and fresh eggs laid that very morning, talking all the time she went in and out.

'I saw you walkin' with Miss Isabelle, sir. She and her brother are kin to Sir Joshua Brydges up at High Willows though they do say as there was something not quite right about it. Their mother went runnin' off with some Frenchman. She were his half sister, you know, oh years back it were now. We weren't livin' here then but they do say he cut up very rough

82

about it. Then when their father had his head cut off by those savages over the water, the sister and brother arrived on Sir Joshua's doorstep, starving and penniless, and he none too pleased about it neither, not that it is any of our business and I must say Miss Isabelle does have a nice ladylike way with her, I don't care what anyone says.'

The information added to his interest. If Mary Hope was right, Sir Joshua had grudgingly given the boy and girl a home and then treated them like unpaid servants. He found himself looking forward to an evening that up to then he had expected to find tedious in the extreme.

Isabelle was not thinking about him at all. If she had been surprised to meet a well dressed stranger on the usually deserted beach at such an early hour, she did not connect him with the expected guests at High Willows. She was eager to examine more closely what she had found in the deserted hut very early that morning. She had not visited it since Lucien had gone and she had stood in the doorway looking about her, filled with memories and a most desolate feeling of loss. It had been bare and tidy, no sign left of occupation except for the plaid rug she had brought to cover him neatly folded in one corner. When she had picked it up, a scrap of paper had fallen out of the folds. He must have left it there for her knowing full well that he intended to leave that night. It had been wrapped around a tiny gold ring, a cheap ornament she remembered seeing on his little finger. Now in the privacy of her own room she looked at it again. It was engraved with the letter R and she wondered if it had belonged to his mother . . .

'*Ma belle Isabelle*,' he had written in French on the scrap of paper, 'you saved not only my life but my reason, since I would have sure run mad in a prison, so keep this as a token that I owe you a life. You know what they say – if you save a life it remains yours for ever.'

She sat on her bed and read and reread it. Had she meant something to him after all or was he simply playing with her in the charming way he had? The ring fitted her finger with some difficulty but she would not wear it. It would cause too much comment, too many questions could be asked. She wrapped it again in the paper and then in a handkerchief and buried it in the drawer of the chest where she kept her few possessions. One day, who knows, they would meet again and then . . . She stood by the window looking out towards the far distant sea, letting her dreams run on, remembering his arms around her, his searching kisses, the trembling, the longing that would never now be fulfilled. Then a loud knocking on the door brought her back to reality.

'It's the mistress,' whispered Gwennie breathlessly. 'She says if you're well enough to run out of the house, then you are well enough to make yourself useful.'

'Very well, I'll come.'

'Best hurry, Miss, she's not in the sweetest of tempers.'

There were several guests that evening, among them Reverend William Westcott from Lydd with his wife, the Mayor of New Romney with his daughter since he was a widower, and Captain Durrant of the Dragoons whose barracks were at Hythe.

Robert was the last to arrive and as he entered the drawing room in his elegantly cut dark blue coat, wearing his own hair cut short and curled in the new style, though by no means a dandy, he contrived to make everyone else in their breeches, silk stockings, lavishly embroidered waistcoats and old-fashioned white wigs look vastly overdressed. He bowed to his hostess, kissed Venetia's hand and went the round of introductions with a few well chosen words. They in their turn were inclined to eye him doubtfully, this fashionable young man from Whitehall who seemed so well informed, whose quiet grey eyes could on a sudden become astonishingly penetrating and whose few remarks had a disconcerting way of going at once to the heart of the matter.

He had to admit that the dinner was excellent, the turbot with an anchovy sauce quite delicious and the ducks spit-roasted to a turn. Robert was a sparing eater and so had time to notice that the boy and girl in whom he was interested slid into the dining room when the rest of the guests were already seated and took their places at the far end of the long table. He saw Lady Brydges frown but she made no comment, and he

84

surprised a look on his host's face that puzzled him, a look of anger mingled with a kind of discomfort.

Isabelle's plain white muslin dress with no ornament made her look like a schoolgirl, and indeed it had been made for Venetia two years before when she was still attending Mrs Smithson's Academy for Young Ladies and had been well washed since. The pale seasick little boy he remembered had grown to a lanky six feet, bony wrists emerging from the cuffs of a coat he had long grown out of, untidy dark hair, good-looking except for the sulky expression around the full mouth, and the impatient frown when he whispered a word to his sister.

All this Robert took in while he ate, paid Venetia, who was sitting next to him, a few graceful compliments and listened to the talk, mostly about the war and largely ill-informed. He took a great deal more interest when it turned to local matters, as it did when the ladies followed their hostess out of the room leaving the gentlemen to their wine. He saw James rise to open the door for his mother and couldn't help noticing how Isabelle flinched away from him when he contrived to run his hand along the back of her neck and down her bare arm. Ill-mannered puppy, he thought to himself, someone needs to teach him a lesson!

Pressed for the latest news about the possibility of peace, Robert was cautious.

'It is true enough that most of our European allies have fallen away from us, but their support was always doubtful and their alliance never more than half-hearted. With our backs to the wall, our army and navy have proved themselves in Denmark and in Egypt and we are of the opinion that Bonaparte is as anxious for a respite as we are, but while finding our way to a peaceful solution we must not forget the importance of our defences.'

Watching their dismayed faces he led the conversation to what had been largely his own suggestion, frowned on by Henry Addington, but heartily supported by William Pitt, who as Warden of the Cinque Ports had a more detailed knowledge of the area.

'I would like to put before you, gentlemen, the proposition

85

that we construct a canal stretching possibly from Appledore along the coast to Hythe. Exact locations will have to be considered but if Bonaparte's invasion barges were to land an army on these marshes, they would then be seriously hampered in bringing their guns and supply wagons through the fields and across a deep channel which would be strongly defended.'

It was news to them and certainly more advantageous than unblocking the sluices and flooding the land but it was likely to be very costly and no doubt a good deal of the expense would have to be borne locally. The proposal was discussed, pros and cons fiercely argued, each one concerned as to how it might affect his own land and his own pocket, but it was not rejected and opportunities to explore the plan further was all Robert required at this stage.

He looked around the company with his ironic smile. 'As Sir Joshua has just pointed out, we have at present no information that invasion is imminent but if we wait until we do and we have provided no barrier, we shall undoubtedly wake up one morning to find the enemy across the marshes and halfway to London before we have even assembled our defending forces.'

When they joined the ladies an hour or so later Isabelle was helping her aunt to serve the tea, carrying around the cups and the silver dishes of small sweet cakes.

Robert accepted a cup but shook his head at the sweetmeats and smiled down at her.

'I hope I was not responsible for any scolding this morning.'

'It was of no consequence,' she said lightly, though her cheek still burned from the stinging slap Aunt Augusta had thought to give her for neglecting her duties. 'I did not realise that you were one of my uncle's guests.'

'Are you disappointed?'

'No, of course not. Excuse me.' She moved away quickly in response to her aunt's impatient gesture.

She had only just realized that this was the Robert Armitage whom Venetia had described in such glowing terms. She glanced at him now and again as she obediently continued with her task. She saw his profile etched against the window as he bent his head to speak to Venetia, and it struck the chord of memory so suddenly that the cup she was holding slipped from her hand to the floor, missing the rug and smashing on the polished oak.

'Isabelle!' Aunt Augusta's voice had a distinct rasp. 'How can you be so clumsy! You'd better pick up the pieces and then ring for Franklin.'

Startled guests looked around and, mortified, Isabelle felt the colour rush up into her face.

'I'm sorry,' she muttered, but before she could go down on her knees she had been forestalled.

'Allow me,' said Robert, picking up the broken fragments and putting them on the small silver tray she was still holding. 'Fortunately the cup was empty. Take care you don't cut yourself.'

'Thank you,' she whispered and carried the smashed pieces of fine bone china back to the tea table to be met with a whispered rebuke.

'Please do not try to force yourself upon the attention of our guests in that vulgar manner,' said Aunt Augusta stingingly.

Isabelle bit back the angry retort. It was the very last thing she had wanted to do.

'Why don't you sing us something, Venetia?' interrupted Sir Joshua with the jollity that seemed to sit so uncomfortably on him. 'You know how much Lord Kilgour enjoys listening to you.'

'Oh Papa,' murmured Venetia blushing, 'I'm sure he doesn't want to hear me again.'

'Indeed I do, Miss Venetia. A delightful experience can only gain from a second hearing.'

She smiled coquettishly up at him. 'If you are sure . . .'

She was looking exceedingly pretty in a dress of rose-coloured silk with silver embroidery at the neck and on the puffed sleeves. She looked as delectable as the rarest kind of expensive confectionery, but then he had never cared for sweet things.

While he busied himself opening the piano for her and helping her sort through the pile of song sheets, he noticed that Isabelle had finished her duties at the tea table and had taken the opportunity to escape, slipping through the open windows and into the garden.

Later when Venetia had sung two ballads, had been greatly applauded, and the Mayor's daughter had been persuaded to play her party piece, Robert declined courteously the invitation to join the gentlemen in a hand of whist, and unobtrusively avoiding his hostess made his own escape.

It was not yet quite dark. There had been a light shower during the afternoon, and the garden had an evening freshness filled with the fragrance of flowers and new-cut grass very welcome after the stuffy warmth of the drawing room. He had no immediate intention of seeking Isabelle, but following the path that ran around a corner of the house he caught sight of the white dress on the stone seat against the ivy-covered wall and walked towards her. Absorbed in her book Isabelle did not hear him until he was almost beside her and she started up so suddenly the book fell to the ground. He stooped to pick it up with the paper that had fluttered from it.

'Don't go. I'll join you if I may. Surely you cannot see to read in this half light.'

'Not very well. May I have the book back please?'

'What were you studying so assiduously?' Then his voice changed. 'Good heavens, Virgil. Can you really read Latin?'

'Yes, I really can,' she said defensively, 'and I have a lesson to prepare for Mr Holland and I've been too busy all day to finish it.'

'And who is Mr Holland?'

The name had slipped out in spite of herself. 'He's just someone who reads Latin with me and Greek and history and even Mathematics,' she burst out.

'Does he indeed? You astonish me. Is Sir Joshua aware that he harbours a scholar under his roof?'

There was a teasing note in his voice and she reacted against it fiercely.

'Don't laugh at me. I suppose you're like my uncle and think young women are only fit for household duties, to wash and clean and sew and bear children and never be allowed to study or read or have minds of their own.'

'Did I say any such thing? Let me see what you have translated so far.'

She tried to snatch the sheet of paper from him but he held it high out of her reach.

'"Nowhere is it safe to be trustful. I found him, a castaway, A beggar and shared all I had with him. I must have been crazy . . ." If I remember rightly that is Dido upbraiding Aeneas for deserting her. It's not bad, not bad at all. Do I detect a personal experience?'

He had cut too near the bone. Angry at the condescension she thought she heard in his tone, she grabbed the book and paper from him and would have gone if he had not stretched out a hand and taken her firmly by the arm.

'Don't run away from me. I'm not laughing, believe me. I'm only surprised. I don't often meet young ladies who can not only read Latin but translate it a great deal better than I can.'

'Please let me go.'

'Not yet.' He still held her by the arm. 'Come now, sit beside me for a moment. I want to ask you something.'

Reluctantly she let him draw her down on the stone bench.

'Isabelle – may I call you that since we have not been formally introduced – do you remember me?'

'We met this morning by the sea.'

'No, not this morning. Six – or is it seven years ago, on board a ship sailing from France on a cold November night.'

'I didn't at first,' she confessed a little shyly. 'But this evening when you were talking to Venetia it suddenly all came back to me.'

So that was why she had dropped the cup. Had it pleased or frightened her?

'I never really wanted to remember that night,' she went on, looking away from him.

'Because of what had happened before?'

'Yes. The only way to go on was to blot it out of my mind.'

'But you kept my plaid.'

'It reminded me of your kindness when Guy and I needed it

most.' She paused and then raised her eyes to him. 'And you, Mr Armitage, when did you know?'

'This morning when you rescued me from your savage dog.'

'Beth is not savage,' she said quickly.

'Of course she isn't and I'm not at all afraid of dogs. My father breeds a great deal of them up in Scotland and in London my sister has two pet spaniels that plague me sorely.'

'But you don't mind?'

'Why should I?'

'My uncle would have had Beth put down because she doesn't earn her keep.'

'So now she is yours.'

'On sufferance only.' She smiled at him suddenly and bewitchingly. 'We play a game of hide and seek.'

What kind of hide and seek, he wondered, and was it her uncle's whip that had raised those cruel wheals on her back?

From somewhere came the silvery chime of a clock and she got up quickly.

'It's late. I must go. My aunt will be looking for me.'

But he caught hold of her hand, drawing her back to him.

'Tell me something, Isabelle. Are you happy here?'

'Of course I am,' she said far too quickly. 'They have been very good to Guy and me.'

'Are you sure?'

'I have to be sure, don't I?'

He was still holding her hand in his when Venetia appeared at the end of the path and came hurrying towards them.

'Oh there you are, Isabelle, wherever have you been hiding?' Her voice had just a suspicion of her mother's rasp. 'They've been looking for you everywhere. And Papa is asking for you, my lord. Some of the gentlemen are leaving and would like to make arrangements for meeting you tomorrow.'

Isabelle had already pulled her hand away and he watched her running through the dusk of the garden before he turned to Venetia.

'I will come at once. I'm sorry that you should have had the trouble of coming in search of me. I hadn't realised how late it had become.'

90

'Have you been talking all this while with my cousin?' asked Venetia, giving him a quick suspicious look.

'A few minutes only. She was more interested in the book she was reading than in me.'

'Oh Isabelle is quite a blue stocking, as they say. She was always at the books in Papa's library until he forbade it, but then of course she has nothing else, has she?'

'Isn't that a little unkind? She has her youth and her beauty.'

'Do you think she's beautiful, no one else does, and anyway that is not everything, is it? Mamma is already asking among her friends about a suitable post for her. Poor Isabelle, I'm afraid very soon now she will have to go out as a governess or a schoolteacher.'

To be bullied by parents demanding the best for their children at the least cost to themselves or growing old and withered in one of those educational establishments for the daughters of gentlemen, of which Marian had give him a horrifying description: what a cruel fate for any young woman. Venetia's complacent indifference to her cousin's fate revolted him.

'I doubt if any of her future pupils will be able to read Latin,' he remarked drily.

'Heavens, no!' Venetia put a hand on his arm, laughing up at him very prettily. 'We didn't learn anything like that at Mrs Smithson's Academy.' Then she frowned. 'I wonder where Isabelle is learning to read Latin.'

Obviously this was something she had hidden from the rest of the family and he had very nearly given the game away. He shrugged his shoulders.

'Possibly with her brother. They would appear to be very devoted to one another.'

'Guy works all day with Papa's agent, Mr Forrest,' said Venetia doubtfully. 'I wonder if I ought to tell Mamma about it.'

'Oh I shouldn't if I were you. Maybe I was mistaken in the book she was reading.'

'Or perhaps she was just boasting about it. Isabelle does that, you know. She used to show off how well she spoke French in front of everybody so as to put me to shame.'

91

'Well, after all, it is her native tongue,' he said mildly.

'That's what Mamma said. She was very angry about it.'

By this time they had reached the house and went into the drawing room together.

'Ah, my lord, there you are,' said Sir Joshua jovially, 'walking in the garden with my little girl, is that it? Well, never mind. The Mayor here is anxious to introduce you to Fred Howard who is the engineer in charge of the upkeep of the sluices and he would like to know if you are free at any time tomorrow.'

'Certainly I am and I would be very glad indeed to have the opportunity of meeting him.'

Arrangements were made, farewells were said and Ian Mackie brought round his master's horse. He had been born and bred at Glenmuir and had served Robert from the day he left his home to go to the university of St Andrew. He had a great contempt for anyone who was not Scottish, was utterly loyal and rarely uttered two words if one would do. One look at his master's face told him that he was not in the mood for gossip so he trotted silently at Robert's heels as they rode back to Rye.

They dismounted in the innyard and as he took the bridles of the horses to lead them into the stables, he glanced at Robert and said airily, 'Yon lassie for all she looks so meek and mild is a rare one for a lark.'

Robert paused on his way to the door. 'What the devil do you mean by that?'

'It seems that when Sir Joshua is off to London, she's down at daybreak and awa' with his best horse to the seashore dressed up in a pair of her brother's breeks.'

'And where did you hear all that?'

'Aye, well, after a few drinks, one of the stable lads was tellin' me, a fine joke he thought it. It seems the master is none too popular so they keep their mouths tight shut about it.'

Robert frowned. 'And you take care to keep yours tight shut too.'

'Oh you know me, close as an oyster. Never a word out o' season, but I thought as how you might be interested seein' as you met with the lady herself this very morn by the seashore.'

Damn the fellow! Was there anything Ian didn't know about him, thought Robert, torn between irritation and amusement.

'And I'd be grateful if you'd keep your big mouth shut about that too,' he said shortly.

'Aye, I will that, don't you fret now. Goodnight, sir.'

And Ian Mackie departed grinning slyly to himself. Caught Master Robert out that time and no mistake and that didn't happen often, not that he had the smallest intention of openng his mouth to anyone, not even to Lady Marian.

Up in his room Robert stripped off his evening coat, unwound the starched neckcloth, pulled his frilled shirt over his head, and then stood for a moment looking at himself in the mirror. The candlelight flickered over ruffled dark brown hair, frowning grey eyes, a lean tanned face with a strong jawline, not the kind of looks to make any young woman swoon with delight, yet, dash it all, here he was at close on thirty, attracted by a slip of a girl who possessed none of the qualities his father would look for in a bride for his only son. Not that Robert was likely to pay very much heed to the Earl's approval or disapproval, but wasn't it utterly absurd to be enchanted because he had seen her slim naked beauty rise from the sea in what had seemed like the very dawn of the world, because she had a rare simplicity and possessed none of the feminine allurements of the young women trying to capture his attention, because she read Latin and translated it prettily and he had won a first in Classics at St Andrews?

He had fallen in love only once before, or thought he had. He had been young then, barely twenty-one and newly come to London. Leila was older, rarely beautiful, and married to a man twice her age who was serving in the Royal Navy. He had believed himself in bliss for the few months it lasted. It was brought abruptly to an end when her husband returned unexpectedly on sick leave and he knew suddenly that he could not endure the lies, the deceit, the furtive secret meetings. She had been furiously angry with him, and he had found it hard to explain that while her husband was away it had been different but that now a kind of young idealism forbade him to cuckold a man he admired and whom he met frequently. For a few months he had gone through hell and then realized it was physical only, his body missed her unbearably, but his mind, his spirit, felt wonderfully liberated.

He finished undressing, pulled on his nightshirt, blew out the candle and got into the bed, resolutely turning his thoughts to what he had learned that day and to the enquiries he must pursue tomorrow if he was to make an intelligent report on the conditions and possibilities of the defences, and then found to his annoyance that his mind kept turning to what Ian had said.

'I found him a castaway, a beggar, and shared all I had with him ' When she rode her uncle's horse down to the sea in her brother's breeches, did she go to meet a lover?

Oh nonsense! He was out of his mind even to think of such a thing, no doubt it was all servants' gossip, and anyway what was it to do with him? Better by far to concentrate on a disturbing report that had reached him that one of the smugglers in these parts spoke excellent French and was said to have gone with them on one of their trips to France. Why? For what reason? It's true that this was an ideal place to bring in spies illegally along with all the other forbidden luxuries. It might be worth further investigation. Captain Durrant of the Dragoons had asked him to dine with him at Hythe and it appeared that his men sometimes worked along with the Revenue Officers who kept a careful watch on the gangs operating along this part of the coast. It might be to his advantage to accept the invitation and find out more about it.

4

'You wish to see me, Aunt Augusta?'

Isabelle was standing in the doorway of the morning room where Lady Brydges was in the habit of dealing with household affairs. It was a pleasant room, especially in summer when sunlight flooded in through the wide windows, though Mrs Bedford worried about the fading of the expensive carpet and the fine needlework of the chairs embroidered by Sir Joshua's grandmother.

Augusta glanced up from her small bureau.

'Come in, Isabelle, I will deal with you later.' She turned to the housekeeper who was standing uneasily beside her chair. 'I think that is all for this morning, Mrs Bedford. The cold chicken and game pie will be sufficient for our luncheon today as Sir Joshua is out. Perhaps you will speak to Cook about dinner as he may be bringing a guest back with him.'

'Very good, my lady.'

Mrs Bedford bustled out giving Isabelle a quick sympathetic glance as she passed her.

'Close the door and come here to me,' said her aunt with that abrasive rasp in her voice that always spelled trouble.

Isabelle did as she was told and stood meekly enough with downcast eyes and hands clasped in front of her, waiting to hear what she had done wrong this time.

Augusta studied her for a moment, the dark curls that clustered around her head and neck and needed no frizzing iron, the delicate pale oval of her face, the winged eyebrows, the large eyes with their fringed lashes. She had done everything in her power to reduce the wretched girl to a nonentity and now this had to happen.

'I gather that when Sir Joshua and I are away from the

house,' she began crisply, 'you are in the habit of running to the Reverend Gilbert Holland at Snargate and begging him to give you lessons.'

Isabelle looked up quickly. 'Who told you that?'

'Does it matter? It is true, is it not? Why have I been left in ignorance? Why do I have to question my housekeeper about what goes on in my absence? Venetia informed me that last night she caught you in the garden boasting to Viscount Kilgour of your ability to translate Latin!'

There was a wealth of sarcasm in the icy voice.

'I did nothing of the kind,' said Isabelle stung to anger. 'He asked me what book I was reading and I told him. That is all.'

'And is that why you were seen holding his hand and doing your best to force your attentions upon him, one of our most valued guests! It's quite unpardonable. I dread to think what he must have thought of you or of us.'

'It so happened that it seemed to amuse him and I don't see why Venetia should be so upset. He is not engaged to her yet.'

A rebellious resentment was rising up in her so strongly that she found it impossible to choke the words back.

'Don't be insolent, girl,' snapped her aunt irritably. 'You must surely know by now that your uncle is not on good terms with Mr Holland. Some years ago he saw fit to support our tenants publicly in their unjust claims against Sir Joshua. It was most unpleasant and it caused a deep rift between them. Neither he nor his sister have dined in this house since.'

And don't much care if they never do again, was what flashed through Isabelle's mind. Suddenly it seemed as if all the frustrations and disappointments of the last few weeks, her uncle's cruel beating that still caused pain at every unwary movement, boiled up in her and spilled over.

'I knew nothing of any quarrel and even if I had, why should it affect me? Mr Holland made a generous offer that has cost you nothing. Ever since we came here, you have told me over and over that we can look for nothing from you or my uncle and that as soon as possible I must earn my own living and make a home for Guy and myself, but how am I to do that with nothing to help me – am I to be a household drudge, a scrubbing maid,

96

a servant to run at everyone's bidding?' She raised her head proudly. 'I am Isabelle de Sauvigny whether you like it or not and Guy is the Comte de Sauvigny, you cannot take that away from us and at least if I can study, then perhaps I can teach and somehow I can hold together the honour and dignity of my father's house . . .'

The words were pouring out in a fiery flood that left her trembling but still defiant.

'Have you quite finished?' said her aunt icily. 'I don't know what that tirade means but if you believe you can win over Lord Kilgour by appealing to his pity, then let me tell you that you are making a very great mistake. Robert Armitage is a reserved man, proud as the devil, and his father although he lives quietly out of the world is the Earl of Glenmuir, and certainly would not welcome the bastard daughter of a beggarly French nobleman as his son's bride.'

'Ohhh!' An impotent fury swept through Isabelle. 'That wicked lie! One day I'll prove you wrong, I swear I will.'

'How? By sending to France to have the records examined?' said her aunt pityingly. 'My dear girl, the Revolution has destroyed them long since. You and all those like you are beggars, living on Britain's charity and you should remember it. We are at war with France and will be for a very long time yet.'

The anger, the bitterness had been bottled up for too long. She had to say what was in her mind whatever wrath it brought down on her head.

'What is it that frightens my uncle so much?' she said recklessly. 'Is it because one day my brother may claim the inheritance that should have come to my mother and which he has stolen from us?'

That cut too near the bone. Augusta got to her feet.

'Be silent, you wretched girl! You are talking of matters of which you know nothing. Go to your room. I will talk to you again later.'

But Isabelle did not move.

'I've been silent too long. Why do you hate us so much? Why? Is it because of my mother? Did you hate her too because

your husband loved his sister so very dearly? Were you jealous
of her beauty and her success and her happiness when she fled
from this hateful house? Is that why you long to destroy us who
are her children?'

It was a shot in the dark but it had a frightening effect. Two
spots of fiery colour appeared in her aunt's pale cheeks.

'How dare you say such a wicked thing when but for us you
and your brother could have been begging in the streets? Your
uncle shall hear of this. He will know how to punish you.'

The words choked in her throat and she slapped the girl's
cheek so hard and with such force that the heavy rings on her
fingers left a scarlet trail behind them.

For a moment Isabelle stood there, shaking, a trickle of blood
running into her mouth, seeking some relief from the baffled
fury that still possessed her. Then she snatched up the antique
Chinese vase that stood on a side table and smashed it to the
floor with all her strength so that it splintered into a hundred
fragments. She stared at it for an instant, horrified at her own
violence, then ran from the room slamming the door after her.

She raced up the stairs and along the landing, pushing past
one of the maidservants, broom in hand, who stared after her in
astonishment.

In her own room she dipped a towel in the water jug and
held it against her bruised cheek, still trembling, still hopelessly
frustrated. If only she could bundle her few clothes together,
pick up her cloak, call Beth and walk out of High Willows for
ever. But how could she? She had nowhere to go, no friend with
whom she could take refuge, no money to take her anywhere,
and there was Guy. She could not leave her brother. Whatever
happened, they must still stay together.

She had no idea what kind of punishment Aunt Augusta
would devise for her and if she told Sir Joshua as she threatened
– Isabelle shuddered involuntarily feeling the whip biting again
into her naked flesh. But one thing was sure, she could not
endure to stay in this house a moment longer. She picked up a
shawl and hurried down the back stairs as quietly as she could
and then slipped out by the kitchen door. She called Beth who
was never far away and began to run through the gardens and

down the bridle road that took her to the seashore, the only place where she could be reasonably sure of being alone.

It was there several hours later that Robert Armitage came upon her. He was riding back from a long and interesting exploration of the marshes with Fred Howard, the engineer, who had proved to be both capable and extremely well informed.

Isabelle was sitting on a rise of the shingle, her arms around her drawn up knees, staring over the grey choppy sea. The day that had begun with sunshine had clouded over and a sharp cool breeze had blown her hair into a dark tangle around her face.

She was too absorbed in her gloomy thoughts to hear his approach. Beth lying beside her raised her head, recognised a friend and lay down again with a gentle wag of her tail. Robert dismounted and came towards her, leading his horse. The crunch of the pebbles under his booted feet roused her but she still kept her head averted.

'A mermaid should be sitting on a rock singing as she combs her hair with a golden comb,' he said smiling down at her. Then his voice changed. 'You look distressed. Has anything happened?'

'No, what should there be?'

The wind blew back the tangled hair from her face and he saw the cruel marks of Augusta's hand, the bruise on the cheekbone already darkening, the dried streak of blood.

'You're hurt,' he said with concern and dropped on one knee beside her. 'What happened to you?'

'I stumbled and fell against some stones,' she said tonelessly.

He didn't believe her. No stones had done that damage. Someone had struck her and viciously – a thrashing and then this. What on earth was going on beneath the apparently quiet surface of this country household?

He said gently, 'You should put something on that, a cold compress to take down the bruising and some liniment.'

'I will presently,' she said indifferently, and then roused

99

herself to be polite. 'What have you been doing this morning, Mr Armitage?'

'I've been making a tour of the marshes. There is a great deal of interest if, as seems only too likely, we are obliged to establish a line of defence along this coast.'

'Will everyone be evacuated if it does happen?'

'That will depend on circumstances. At present we hope Bonaparte is too occupied in Europe to pursue plans for invading Britain. I don't think there is any immediate need for alarm.'

Her own troubles loomed a good deal larger just then than the prospect of a French army sailing across the Channel. She turned to look at him.

'Why did you tell Venetia about Mr Holland last night?'

'I didn't,' he said quickly, 'at least I'm pretty sure I didn't. I did mention something about you reading Latin, but that was all, I swear it was. Why? Is it then a secret?'

'In a way,' she said wearily. 'I have known all along that my uncle wouldn't approve. Now it seems Mr Holland, who is Vicar of Snargate, quarrelled with Sir Joshua some years ago – and therefore any connection with him is strictly forbidden.'

'I see. I am sorry if I've inadvertently caused trouble.'

'Oh it's not your fault. You couldn't have known about it, and in any case why should you wish to keep anything from Venetia?'

'Why do you say that?'

'Well, you are on the point of becoming engaged to her, are you not?'

He frowned. 'Where did you get that idea?'

'I don't know exactly. Venetia certainly lays claim to you and I know my aunt it quite set on it.'

She saw his face harden and realised suddenly that he could at times look remarkably stern and uncompromising.

'If what you say is true, then I must make sure that my very short acquaintance with the young lady is not misunderstood.'

'Then it is not true.'

'It has never been true.'

She looked at him and then away across the sea.

'In that case I think I'm glad. I don't believe Venetia would have suited you at all.'

'Don't you? Why? She is very pretty.'

'She can't read Latin for one thing, and she never looks at a book from one year's end to another.'

She had the direct simplicity of a child and it both amused and pleased him.

'You know my sister said exactly the same thing in slightly more forcible terms. Marian never hesitates to say exactly what she thinks.'

Somehow, sitting on the beach with him far away from the house and her everyday life, she had felt free to say anything that came into her head but now, with her aunt's rebuke still ringing in her ears, she suddenly realised how very impertinent she must have sounded. Would he think she was deliberately trying to attract his attention to herself? It was just that his quiet friendly manner made her feel that she could say anything to him and he would understand.

'I'm sorry,' she said a little shyly. 'I should never have said such things to you on such a very short acquaintance.'

'Not so short. We are actually friends of very long standing, are we not?'

'My aunt will never forgive me. Her greatest wish is to see Venetia a Countess one day.'

'In that case I'm afraid she would have had a very long wait,' he said drily. 'My father is in excellent health.' He smiled at her troubled face. 'Don't be afraid. I shall not say a word, simply make sure I escape an awkward situation I seem to have blundered into without realising it.'

'Venetia will be very disappointed.'

'Not nearly so disappointed as if I were to make her my wife. My sister never tires of telling me how impossible I am to live with.'

'Does she? Why?'

'For a variety of reasons.'

She clapped her hand to her mouth. 'Oh dear, there I go again. I shouldn't be asking you things like that. I apologise. It is not at all proper.'

'And what *is* proper?'

She sighed. 'I don't rightly know. Mr Holland is the only gentleman I really talk to, and he is over sixty and rather like my father would have been if he had not been murdered.'

'And into what category would you put me?' he asked teasingly.

'I'm not sure.' She regarded him seriously for a moment. 'An elder brother, I think. I've always thought I would like that. You see I feel so very responsible for Guy. It would be wonderful to share the responsibility.'

'And what are your brother's ambitions?'

'Simply to get away from here and live his own life, I suppose. I think if it were not for me he would have run away long ago and enlisted in the King's army.'

'That could be a very rash step to take.'

'That's what I keep telling him, but all the same he is very unhappy and sometimes I am afraid he will do something foolish.'

She was looking away from him and he watched the lovely curve of her cheek with a queer tug at his heart. He wanted to say 'Perhaps I could do something,' but knew he should not be involved. It could alter the course of his life and might put more than himself at risk and yet he badly wanted to find out more about her.

He said gently, 'When I saw you and your brother on the ship that night I was aware that something terrible must have driven you there. Would you like to tell me about it?'

'I've never spoken about it to anyone,' she said in a whisper. 'It was buried deep inside me and there was no one who would listen or try to understand. Guy was too young. It was better for him to forget.'

'But not you?'

'No. It haunts me still.' She was silent for a moment and then went on as if the floodgates had opened, and she could not hold back. Not even to Lucien had she opened her heart. It had been he who talked and she who had listened, enchanted, but with this friendly stranger it was different.

'It all began the day the revolutionaries came to the château

102

. . . before it had all been talk and rumour but suddenly it was there all around us and terrifying . . .'

The pictures grew in his mind as she described the revolutionaries, the beloved Grandfather forced into the midst of them, blood on the white hair as they bludgeoned him to death, the frantic journey, the constant fear, and the man they called friend who had betrayed them so callously. In the months he had spent in Paris that year Robert had seen many such tragedies, husbands torn from wives, children from mothers, and even worse the evil spawned in those who saw in the guillotine a fearful and satisfying way to pay off old grudges.

'One day I would like to go back there,' she was saying, 'I would like to see the château where we grew up. I'd like to prove to all the world that Guy and I are what we say we are . . .' She turned to look at him. 'Do you think it will all still be there?'

There were tears in her eyes and he had a great desire to put his arms around her and say 'God willing, I'll take you there myself some day,' but that was impossible. Instead he said quietly, 'It's very likely, not everything has been destroyed and peace may come sooner than we believe.'

'Thank you for listening.'

She gave him a long look and then turned away. They were silent for a little, then she said suddenly, 'Have you noticed? The wind has dropped and the sea is calm as milk. It often happens at this time of the year just as the tide is on the turn. I never tire of watching it. It helps me to see my own troubles more sensibly. Those ships out there,' she went on dreamily, 'do you see? So still they hardly seem to move.'

His eyes followed where she pointed. The sea was like a ripple of grey silk.

> 'Day after day, day after day,' he quoted softly,
> 'We stuck, nor breath, nor motion,
> As idle as a painted ship
> Upon a painted ocean.'

'That describes it exactly. Did you just make it up or did someone write it?

103

He laughed. 'Alas, I'm no poet. It was written by someone called Samuel Taylor Coleridge. Have you never heard of him?'

'No, never. Mr Holland is wonderful but he is just a little old-fashioned. He doesn't think any modern poet can equal those of the past.'

'That must be remedied,' he said, 'but not now, I fear.'

'No,' she sighed, 'it must be very late and I've been here all day. I must go back.'

He gave her his hand to pull her to her feet and then took out his watch.

'Dear God, it's close on five o'clock.'

'Heavens, I must run.'

'Shall I see you back to High Willows?'

'There is no need. I know the path well. Do you return to London soon?'

'Not for some days. We shall meet again I hope.'

He collected his horse which had been cropping discontentedly at the thin tussocky grass.

She was standing very straight, looking up at him like a well-trained child.

'Goodbye, Mr Armitage, and thank you for talking to me.'

'It's been a pleasure, and it is not goodbye but *au revoir*,' and obeying an impulse as once before on that cold November morning, he raised the small hand to his lips and kissed it lightly.

She turned back from the path to watch him ride away towards Rye, the feeling of utter desolation that had possessed her all day unaccountably lightened. He gave her the same feeling of warmth and comfort as he had done all those years ago on the ship and at this wretched moment she had needed a friend desperately.

The house was strangely quiet when she returned to it. Venetia and her mother had just come back from a busy round of visits in the carriage and were resting before dinner. Sir Joshua had returned alone so the evening meal would be very quiet and Isabelle could not make up her mind whether to stay in her own room or face her aunt as if nothing had happened between

104

them. Perhaps it was the meeting with Robert Armitage that boosted her courage. She came boldly into the dining room, her face swollen now and discoloured. Although she did not realise it, she had won a minor triumph. The one thing that her aunt did not want was to rake up the painful ghosts of the past and with Isabelle in her present mood she was not at all sure that she would accept punishment submissively so, though anger still smouldered against her rebellious niece, she said nothing to her husband and it was Guy who remarked on his sister's face and stirred up more than he had bargained for.

'Good Lord, Belle,' he exclaimed, 'what on earth have you done to yourself?'

'I tripped up and hit my face against the cobbles.'

'More than likely fell over that damned dog of yours,' growled James, who was in a perpetually bad temper these days. 'The bitch ought to be put down.'

'Why?' retorted Isabelle in defence of her pet. 'Beth does you no harm.'

'She bares her teeth if I go anywhere near her.'

'If she does, it's your fault. You kicked her down the stairs once. She's never forgotten.'

'Let her get in my way just once more and I'll shoot the bitch.'

'If you do, you'll answer to me for it,' said Guy flaring up.

'Good Lord, it can actually speak. I thought the cat had swallowed your tongue,' mocked James. 'What do you suggest, cousin? A bout of fisticuffs?'

'Are you insulting me?' Guy was on his feet. 'If so, come outside and I'll show you what can be done with fisticuffs. We'll settle it here and now.'

'For God's sake!' thundered Sir Joshua, bringing his fist down on the table so hard that everything jumped. 'Stop bickering the pair of you. As for you, James, let the dog be. It does no harm. And if you've got nothing better to do, Guy, than make empty threats, then you can spend the evening helping Mr Forrest with his accounts. He is sorely behind with them.'

'I work all day, I'm damned if I'm going to work all night

too. Mr Forrest can go hang for once,' and Guy stormed out of the dining room leaving his meal half eaten.

'Damned young idiot!' mutterd James. 'Can't he take a joke?'

'Leave the boy alone,' growled his father.

'Oh for goodness sake,' exclaimed Venetia pettishly. 'Can't we eat our dinner in peace without all these stupid quarrels? Papa, do we *have* to stay here all the summer? Can't we go to Bath for a few weeks as we did last year? We went visiting this afternoon and everyone, just everyone, has gone away except us, haven't they, Mamma? It's so deadly dull.'

'Dull it may be, but a trip to Bath costs money, a dozen new gowns for the pair of you and heaven knows what else,' but Sir Joshua was already softening. Venetia had always been his pet. 'We'll have to see. Later on perhaps, before we go back to London.' He glanced at his wife. 'Your mother and I will talk it over. Perhaps we can persuade young Lord Kilgour to spend a few days with us. You'd like that, wouldn't you, puss?' and he gave her a sly look and pinched her cheek.

Venetia jerked her head away. 'Oh Papa really! You shouldn't say such things.'

'And what about Lord Kilgour himself? Would he like it?' thought Isabelle with a warm little glow. She felt she knew a great deal more about him than they did.

She excused herself as soon as possible and went off in search of Guy, but he had disappeared already as he did now almost every evening. As he lacked any other companionship, she knew that increasingly he was mixing with some of the wilder elements in that part of Kent, younger sons of farmers and some of the sporting gentry who tended to gather at the Ship and Anchor. Guy, who had been a gentle shy boy, squeamish at the sight of blood and more likely to be found poring over a book than indulging in noisy games, had been deliberately toughening himself. Cock fighting, dog baiting, rat hunting in the huge barns with their sharp little terriers that would once have terrified him, he now forced himself to take part in, and despite his denials she was almost certain that he had joined the band of smugglers who operated under the leadership of Jonty Daley. Handsome in his way, cocksure and self confident, Jonty was just the type of personality to fascinate Guy, who found it so hard to come to terms with himself.

She stood at the window very late that evening looking out across the garden. These nights were what the villagers called 'the dark of the moon', the time in between the full moon and when the first thin new crescent appeared in the sky, and it was on these nights that the boats put out to sea to meet the French luggers and land the goods along that lonely and desolate coast. They were a small group, all local men, and the secret was well kept. The Revenue Officers for all their vigilance were hopelessly outnumbered and rarely made any captures of men or of goods and even if they did, no jury would convict in the face of witnesses who would swear unblushingly that the prisoner was sick in bed or at least five miles away on the night in question. Only now and again when in despair the dragoons were called in did anyone suffer. Up at Rustinge the blackening corpses of two smugglers had hung in chains for months, a grisly reminder of what could happen to them. But not to Guy, she told herself, it wasn't possible, and yet fear still stabbed at her.

The following afternoon she was in the housekeeper's room, repairing a tapestry firescreen that had been burned by a spitting coal from one of the winter fires. It was a tedious and exacting task trying to match in the colours of the flowers from the big basket of tangled skeins of wool, and the stitches were very fine. It was one of the beautiful pieces embroidered by her own great grandmother, who had been a noted needlewoman in the days of old Queen Anne. The house was very quiet. Venetia and her mother were out in the carriage and Sir Joshua on a visit to friends in Canterbury. As she put down her needle and stretched her aching back, the footman put his head around the door.

'A gentleman to see you, Miss.'

'To see me? You must be mistaken. It's no doubt Miss Venetia he wants. Tell him she will be back about five o'clock.'

'Oh no, it's you he wants right enough, very particular he was about it too,' said Franklin, coming into the room with a sly familiarity she had always disliked from their very first meeting all those years ago.

'It's that Lord Kilgour,' he went on, 'Miss Venetia's beau.'

'Don't be impertinent,' said Isabelle coldly. 'In that case I suppose I had better see him. Tell him I'll be with him in a moment.'

When he had gone, she took off her apron and looked down with dismay at her oldest gown, put on that morning in preparation for a working day, but there was no time to change. She gave a quick glance in the mirror. The swelling had gone down a little but the blow had given her a truly magnificent black eye. Oh well, nothing could be done about that. She pushed the hair out of her eyes, retied the ribbon that held it back and ran down the stairs.

He was standing at the window of the drawing room and turned at once as she came in.

'I happened to be passing so I took the liberty of bringing you this.'

'What is it?' She took the book he was holding out and frowned over the title, *Lyrical Ballads*.

'Do you remember yesterday when we spoke of Coleridge and the "painted ship on the painted ocean"? Well, you will find it all in there *The Rime of the Ancient Mariner*, vastly mysterious and romantic, with other verses too by his friend William Wordsworth. I thought it might appeal to you.'

An unexpected gift was such a rarity that she felt almost overwhelmed by it.

'And you thought to bring it to me? How kind, how very kind.' She opened the book at random reading a line here and there and then looking up at him. 'How much I would like to show it to Mr Holland.'

'Why not take it to him now?'

'Now? Oh I don't know that I should. As I told you, it is not easy.'

'If you will permit me,' he went on unperturbed, 'I would be happy to accompany you. I'm anxious to meet as many local people as possible while I'm down here, and this would be an excellent opportunity.'

108

It was true. He had been trying to find out as far as he could about the local community not only in connection with the defence plans but also with the illegal trading and who better than the Vicar of a small parish? That there was another and more personal reason he chose to ignore.

She frowned at him for a moment and then broke into the delighted grin of a mischievous child. He was giving her the excuse she needed. It was he who suggested it and Aunt Augusta could hardly blame her for agreeing to her valued guest's request.

'It's a roughish walk across Walland Marsh. Do you mind?'

'Not in the least. I imagine one of the stable lads will attend to my horse.'

'Of course. I will speak to Jason.'

It took only a moment. His horse was led away and they set out to walk along the narrow footpath. It was an afternoon of mixed cloud and sunshine, the air fragrant with the scent of grass and water and the cow parsley that grew thickly alongside the way. They paused at the stile. He helped her mount it and then stood for a moment, leaning on the top bar, letting his eyes range across the vast stretch of pasture starred with buttercups and dotted with browsing sheep and their half grown lambs.

'Strange to remember that this was all marsh and inland creeks till the Romans came and built the first sea defences.'

'Some winters the meadows flood still. They become enormous shining lakes, the seabirds flock in and it's like living on an island. Barty has to be out night and day shifting the sheep particularly if it is at lambing time. Gwennie and I bottle-fed five of them in the kitchen one January because their mothers had drowned.'

He was so attentive and so easy to talk to that she forgot her shyness and that he was a distinguished member of the Foreign Office, and went on chattering happily of her day to day existence, revealing far more of herself and her life than she realised.

At the gate leading into the rectory holding, Mr Holland's old white mare ambled across the field towards them looking for a tasty titbit. Isabelle rubbed the velvet nose affectionately.

'Nothing today, Rosie dear, I'm sorry. She was thin as a scarecrow when Mr Holland first rescued her from the brute who was starving her, so we called her Rosinante after Don Quixote's horse,' she explained. 'But she is fattening up nicely now.'

'Have you read *Don Quixote* then?'

'Oh yes, but not in Spanish. That was too difficult.'

'You astonish me. I imagined you reading Spanish as easily as you read Latin.'

'Mr Armitage, are you making fun of me?'

'Heaven forbid.' He pulled a bunch of juicy herbage and held it out to the horse. 'I gather that sometimes when your uncle is in London, you borrow his best horse and ride it hell for leather all the way to the beach.'

She looked startled. 'Where did you hear that?'

'Never mind, but don't look so alarmed. I promise I won't give you away.'

'I suppose you think it is very improper. I know my aunt would if she knew, but it is so very tempting. It all began one day when Jason damaged his leg and couldn't exercise her so I took Juno out for him.' She looked away across the fields. 'Long ago at Sauvigny I had a beautiful mare called Romaine. I used to ride with my father.' A shadow passed across her face and she went on quickly. 'We'd better hurry. I can see Miss Holland in the garden. She'll be wondering who you are.'

Harriet Holland was bending over her flower border, a large apron around her waist and a big white sun bonnet tied under her chin. She straightened up when she saw the stranger.

'I've brought a friend to see you,' said Isabelle unlatching the gate. 'This is Robert Armitage, Viscount Kilgour, and he wishes to meet Mr Holland.'

'I daren't shake hands, my lord, I've been grubbing up weeds,' she said, a little flustered at the sight of the elegantly dressed young man who was smiling down at her. 'They grow so fast, I can't keep up with them.'

'You remind me of my grandmother,' he said pleasantly, 'she is nearly eighty and still gardens vigorously and that takes some doing when a braw wind blows across from the sea. In early March you can't always stand upright but nothing deters her.'

'I know how she feels. A garden can't wait and it is very satisfying work because you can see the results,' went on Miss Holland, wiping her hands on her apron. 'You will drink a dish of tea with us, my lord, won't you? Isabelle, take the gentleman to the vicar. He is in his sanctum, and then come and give me a hand in the kitchen.'

Mr Holland, with a strange looking plant in one hand and his spectacles balanced precariously on the end of his nose, was bent over a large volume spread out on his table and did not look up as Isabelle opened the door and ushered Robert Armitage into the tiny cupboard-like room.

'In a minute, Harriet, I'll come in just a minute,' he muttered testily. 'I'm trying to track down this extraordinary plant.'

Robert peered over his shoulder. 'I think I know that volume. Isn't it John Parkinson's *Paradisus*? My grandmother used to call it her garden lovers' bible.'

'Indeed it is and still full of relevant information after more than two hundred years, and this is a first edition,' said Mr Holland proudly. 'I found this plant on the marshes yesterday, quite new to me, and have been trying to identify the root system.'

Then he broke off and looked up.

'God bless my soul, what am I thinking of? I didn't realise . . .' He scrambled to his feet. 'My apologies, sir.'

'Think nothing of it, Mr Holland. I'm Robert Armitage,' he said and held out his hand. 'Isabelle told me how she reads Latin with you and I persuaded her to bring me to meet you.'

'Indeed she does and believe me she is a very apt pupil, a far better scholar than a number of young men whom it has been my misfortune to have to coach. Is there something about which you wish to consult me, sir?'

'In a way perhaps there is.'

Mr Holland ruthlessly swept books and papers off the only other chair. 'Sit down, my dear sir, make yourself comfortable. Isabelle, my dear, run and warn my sister that we have a guest.'

'She knows already.'

111

The rapport between them, begun in that fortunate recognition of Mr Holland's obsession, grew rapidly after Isabelle had left them and joined Miss Holland in the kitchen.

'Who is he?' she whispered setting out the best eggshell china cups and a plate of newly baked griddle cakes.

'I believe Aunt Augusta was hoping that he would offer for Venetia,' said Isabelle, spreading the cakes with cream and strawberry preserve.

'And now?'

'I think she may have mistaken his intentions. She is going to be very disappointed. His father is the Earl of Glenmuir.'

Miss Holland gave her a shrewd glance. 'Maybe the gentleman has had the good sense to prefer someone else.'

'Meaning me? Oh no, that's just silly. I think he's a little sorry for Guy and me because he did happen to be on that ship that brought us over from France, and then it made him laugh when he caught me trying to translate Virgil.'

Miss Holland grunted and carried the loaded tray into the front parlour.

'And is Venetia the only reason that has brought him down to Kent?'

'Oh no. He is someone very important in the Foreign Office and he has been talking about coastal defence to my uncle and to other well known people around here. I am sure that is what he will be discussing with Mr Holland.'

'I see,' said Harriet, setting the table and standing back to look it over, quite sure that she could worm everything out of Gilbert when the visitor had gone. 'When we are quite ready, dear, I think you had better give the gentlemen a call before I pour the water into the pot.'

Tea was an instant success. Robert won Harriet's heart at once by declaring that the griddle cakes were the best he had tasted since he was a boy in Scotland.

'My grandmother's cook used to make great batches of them and when I was home from school I ate them till they came out of my ears.'

'An iron griddle is the secret and mine has been in use for

generations,' said Miss Holland, much gratified. 'There's nothing like it for the best results.'

Isabelle brought out her book and Mr Holland, glancing through it, said he supposed that changes must come in the writing of poetry as in everything else, but he still thought that it should be majestic and sonorous, and not fantastical and rooted in the trivial.

'Didn't Catullus write verses to his mistress's sparrow and Horace compose odes about his Sabine farm?' said Robert slyly and Mr Holland laughed.

'You're so right, sir. The trouble is that the old get set in their ways and tend to dwell on the gods of their youth, forgetting that time moves on.'

When they left, Miss Holland apologised for their poor welcome and he took her hand in his.

'Never apologise, dear lady. I haven't enjoyed myself so much for years.'

'Come and see us again if you have the time,' said Mr Holland. 'I could perhaps give you further useful information about the people here, and it is a pleasure to talk to a young man whose sole topic of conversation is not prize-fighting, dog baiting or riding to hounds.'

When they returned to High Willows retribution would have undoubtedly fallen on Isabelle's head if Robert had not intervened and neatly taken the wind out of Aunt Augusta's sails.

'Wherever have you been?' she stormed. 'Franklin told me that Lord Kilgour had called and you had taken him across the fields to meet the Reverend Holland when I had expressly told you how things were with us. It is quite unforgiveable of you.'

'I am afraid that I must take the blame for it, Lady Brydges,' said Robert easily, before she had time to draw a second wrathful breath. 'For various reasons I very much wanted to meet Mr Holland, and your niece very kindly offered to make the introduction. I have spent a most enlightening afternoon.'

'I see. Well, of course, if that was the case . . .'

'It was indeed. It so happens that I called this afternoon,' he went on smoothly, 'with the intention of asking if the young ladies would care to accompany me on a trip to Dover Castle on Sunday. I've been given an invitation from the Governor and I understand it is a most interesting relic of our history, and there is the added attraction of viewing some of the French prisoners who are shut up there.'

Isabelle glanced at him in surprise. An afternoon gazing at unhappy Frenchmen like animals in a zoo didn't seem the kind of thing to amuse him, but Aunt Augusta, somewhat mollified, was smiling graciously.

'A charming notion. My husband is away for a few days but perhaps we could make up a little party. Venetia would be most interested, wouldn't you, dear? It is just the very thing she enjoys. Would you care to stay and dine with us this evening, my lord?'

'Thank you, no. I am afraid I have another engagement. Captain Durrant of the Dragoons has invited me to join him and his brother officers in the Mess at Hythe and I fear I shall have to be on my way if I am not to be very late. Until Sunday then, Miss Venetia, Miss Isabelle. I shall look forward to your company,' and he took his farewell.

'I don't know why you had to agree, Mamma,' said Venetia crossly. 'I'm sure I don't want to spend Sunday tramping around some old castle.'

'Yes, you do, dear, it will be very instructive and it is most kind of Lord Kilgour to suggest it. When your father returns, I'm sure he will be delighted.'

'What about Isabelle, Mamma? He did mention her.'

'If there is room in the carriage and if Mrs Bedford can spare her. We shall have to see when the time comes.'

Isabelle knew what that meant. She had never been included in the carriage drives, picnics and excursions around the countryside to places of interest which made up the long days of summer at High Willows. Always at the last moment some pressing reason would be found why she should be left at home. Usually she did not mind, very much preferring to be free to do as she pleased, but this time she was aware of an angry frustration. What did Aunt Augusta fear? That she might steal Venetia's thunder? That was fit only for laughter.

114

It was not until she reached her own room that she remembered the book she still held in her hand. There had been a charm about the afternoon and the memory of it soothed her ruffled spirits. She sat on the bed and looked at it more closely. On the fly leaf someone had written 'From Marian with love.' Could that be the sister he had spoken of? He had given her his own copy and she found it oddly comforting. She had had so little experience of men of his kind that she found him difficult to understand. He treated her with an easy charm, kindly and a little amused, like an uncle, or a cousin or a brother.

After a few minutes she closed the book, put it carefully on the table and went to the drawer where she had hidden the ring Lucien had given her. She drew it out and slipped it on her finger. Would he have left it for her if he had not intended to return one day? Somehow saving his life had created a special bond between them. She pressed the hand against her face and all the excitement, the thrill, the passion, the intensity of those few days came flooding back. If only she could have taken wing with him, away from all this, into the unknown. For a moment the longing was so fierce she felt dizzy with it, then reaction set in. It was done, it was finished. She drew off the ring and put it away again. Time to come down to earth, to the ordinary chores of every day. Impossible dreams could lead nowhere, as she knew only too well.

5

No one could have been more surprised than Isabelle to find herself sharing the carriage with Venetia on that fine Sunday morning. She was well aware that she would not have been there but for the quiet insistence of Mr Armitage, and the plain fact that Lady Brydges had developed one of her sick headaches and it was unthinkable that Venetia should go alone without a suitable chaperon. At the last moment James decided to accompany them, so they set out with the two young men riding each side of the carriage.

There was a brief stop for a midday collation at the little village of Folkestone perched on its high cliffs and popular with elderly visitors who valued the peace and quiet for the sake of their health. Then they were away and crossing the wild heathland of the Warren to Dover. She looked at the tall figure riding beside the carriage with grace and ease, and thought how pleasant it was to have found a friend, even if it were no more than the passing whim of a man probably bored with his present company.

She had never travelled more than a few miles from High Willows since the day she had come from France and so everything was of interest, and though Venetia yawned while James refused pointblank to accompany the sightseeing tour of the castle, Isabelle listened with rapt attention to the young Captain who was historically minded and had been appointed as their guide. Dover Castle was often called the Key to England, he told them, and there had been a fortification on this lofty hill long before William the Conqueror marched into it. The little group of visitors obediently stared up at the high stone walls, thought how cold it must be in winter and decided they would not care to live there. They gazed from the tall windows across the huddle of picturesque houses to the sea and expressed wonder at the tower of the ancient lighthouse, the *pharos* built by the Romans when they raised the first defences. Then with a sigh of relief they poured through the narrow doorway and out on to the leads of the roof where a bunch of French prisoners, obviously the most presentable and best behaved, were crowded on to benches working away at the tiny objects they were allowed to sell to visitors.

A fierce wind tearing in from the sea nearly blew Isabelle's bonnet from her head, tangling her hair into wild curls as she hung on to the ribbons laughing. It snatched Venetia's parasol out of her hand and it would have sailed over the parapet if it had not been adroitly caught by a young Naval Lieutenant who returned it to her, winning a beaming smile and murmured thanks.

James, who had come to join them, suddenly clapped him on the shoulder.

'Perry Conway by all that's wonderful! What the devil are you doing here?'

'Home on sick leave and staying with my aunt. Nearly lost a leg and look like being ordered to the Home Fleet, worse luck,' he replied.

'Do you know my sister?' went on James.

'We met in London in the spring,' said Venetia, holding out her hand to him. 'You look very much better than you did then, Lieutenant.'

'Oh I am, much better. I can not only walk now but even run at a pinch.'

Isabelle, seeing her cousin's blush and noting the intimate little smile she exchanged with the young man, wondered if this was the younger son of whom Sir Joshua had so strongly disapproved. Then she was distracted by the little objects the prisoners were offering for sale. Among them there was a tiny ship carved from the mutton bones saved from their miserable rations, most exquisitely fashioned with sails and rigging ingeniously contrived from the sacking that covered their mattress beds. She exclaimed at its perfection and the sailor, entranced

117

to hear his native French, replied with a voluble rush of information.

Isabelle said, 'I'm sorry . . . I would love to buy it but I have no money with me.'

'Permit me to buy it for you,' said Robert at her elbow.

'Oh no, no, you shouldn't . . . I can't accept it,' she protested.

'Of course you can,' and he put the money down on the table. 'It's an act of charity. The poor devil can buy himself a little luxury, tobacco perhaps or anything else he fancies to alleviate his imprisonment.'

'How is it they are so skilled?' she asked, admiring the workmanship.

'Sailors are not always fighting a battle or busy with the work of the ship. There are days, weeks, months, of boredom and since not many of them can read or write, they learn to use their hands in a dozen different ways.'

Some of the other men scenting a possible customer clustered around her. One of them, a dark gaunt fellow with a purple scar across one cheek, was proudly showing a tiny guillotine most cleverly fashioned. He displayed its ingenuity by putting a sliver of wood in place and bringing down the sharpened metal that chopped it in half.

For an instant Isabelle seemed to see again the black hideous machine in the market square of a town they had clattered through, seemed to see her father, to see him thrust forward, to hear the sickening sound as the blade descended. Then she turned away in quick revulsion and felt Robert's arm around her and her face pressed against his coat. It was only for a moment, then she raised her head.

'Are you all right?' he whispered.

'Yes, quite all right. It was silly of me.' But her hands were trembling and she moved away from him, away from them all, walking towards the parapet and into the keen breath of the salt wind and the sparkle of the sunlit sea.

'I didn't mean to distress the lady,' muttered the sailor. 'There's been a great many who have liked my little toy.'

'No doubt,' said Robert with distaste.

He was about to follow Isabelle when someone came up behind him and tapped him on the shoulder.

'The very man I want to see,' said Captain Durrant of the Dragoons.'I have received a piece of information this morning that I am pretty sure will interest you.'

'Indeed. What is it?'

Somewhat reluctantly, Robert allowed himself to be led away towards the doorway.

Isabelle had moved along the parapet, angry at herself and her involuntary weakness. At the turn of the buttress all was suddenly still and she stood for a moment staring across the harbour filled with busy shipping, but seeing in her mind's eye the grey walls of Sauvigny, the grove of chestnuts that were a glory of pink and white when they lit their candles in the spring, saw herself running across the grass and into her father's arms, laughing, carefree. Would she and Guy ever see it again or would Henri Rivage be lording it there by now, the reward of his treachery?

She shivered and leaned her head back against the sun-warmed stone, and it was then through her abstraction that she heard the voices from the other side of the wall where the narrow arrow slit opened out. Something about what was said caught her attention.

'We've been given information. It could be tonight, a goodly haul by all accounts.' There was a murmur and the voice went on. 'Not for me to name any names, but it's pretty certain and the Revenue Officers have asked for a loan of some of my men. Would you care to ride with us? You may learn something in connection with your business here.'

That was Captain Durrant, she was quite sure of that, but the other voice was a mere thread and she could not place it.

'The Ship and Anchor has always been a hotbed for them but up to now we've never had the good fortune to pounce on them red-handed. This time it will be different . . .'

The voice died away and Isabelle suddenly felt icy cold. She knew what it meant. On this dark moonless night the smugglers were expecting a 'run' from France and someone must have betrayed them. What was she to do? Should she warn them or should she let it go ahead and justice be done? Then it hit her. What about Guy? Would he be there tonight? If he blundered into the trap, what would happen to him? The others were clever at getting themselves out of trouble but Guy could so easily be the scapegoat. He did not belong, he was the foreigner, the stranger, not one of them would be willing to risk his neck to save Guy's skin.

She was suddenly terribly anxious to return home, to find him, to make sure he was doing nothing dangerous tonight of all nights. Although she knew there were hours yet before anything could possibly happen, she fretted at the delays. The privileged little party with Lord Kilgour were courteously invited to take wine and cakes in the Governor's apartments. They stood chatting idly together while the time passed and she could have screamed with impatience at the delay.

They were so late in setting out that it was well past nine o'clock by the time they reached High Willows. Robert Armitage declined to stay and sup with them but said he would be calling on the following morning to make his farewell, since he must return to London.

'Needs must,' he said with a smile and a shrug. 'The war goes on and I have my orders. I must play my small part.'

Isabelle thought he had spoken of staying longer but was too distracted to wonder why he had altered his plans. She escaped as soon as she could to go in search of Guy, but he was nowhere to be found.

'Did he say where he was going?' she asked Gwennie.

'Not exactly, Miss, but that Jonty Daley was here,' she went on disapprovingly, 'asking for Master Guy, he was. Franklin was sharp with him, told him to clear off, that he wasn't wanted round here, but later on Master Guy came down himself, told me to tell you he might be late and you weren't to worry.'

So she had been right. He was going to join Jonty and his men, and what was she going to do about it? For the moment she could not get away from the house without explanation. There was supper to be eaten and an inquisition from Aunt Augusta. Where exactly did they go? Who was there and how were they treated? With proper respect, she hoped. After all, if Sir Joshua had not been away, he would almost certainly have accompanied them.

Isabelle answered as best she could, scrupulously avoiding any mention of Lieutenant Conway until quite suddenly Venetia lost all patience.

'Really, Mamma, must you go on and on? What does it matter whom we met? It was just a day out, that's all, and we're not on trial. If you want to know, we had a simply marvellous time and I don't know about Isabelle but I'm dead tired and I'm going to bed,' and she flounced out of the room and up the stairs.

'I don't know what comes over her lately,' muttered her mother, 'she is becoming so difficult.'

'Perhaps she misses London society,' ventured Isabelle, for almost the first time feeling a hint of sympathy for Venetia. 'It can be very dull down here.'

'Nonsense!' snapped her aunt crisply. 'It's nothing of the sort. There's a great deal to do if you set your mind to it. Young people nowadays are so irresponsible, never content, always hankering after what they can't have.' She looked round at Isabelle. 'You had better get to bed too. You look washed out. There is still plenty to be set to rights tomorrow. You can't expect to go jaunting off on holiday every day, you know.'

Thankfully Isabelle hurried away. The long case clock in the hall struck eleven as she passed it. It must be now or never. If Guy wasn't here, then she must go and find him. She waited for a little until the house gradually quietened down. Doors and windows were shut and bolted. It was overcast but a mild dry night. She picked up a shawl, wrapped it around her thin dress and crept down the back stairs. She unbolted the garden door, her heart in her mouth. Beth started up from her corner but Isabelle petted and quietened her, telling her to be a good dog and stay. Then she was through the door and closed it silently behind her.

The night was very dark and if she had not known the path so well, she might easily have gone astray. As it was, the going

121

was rough and she stumbled more than once in her thin kid shoes, desperately afraid she might be too late.

She had never been out at this time before and the marshes seemed suddenly full of frightening shapes and strange noises. The abrupt screech of an owl nearly frightened her out of her wits, there was the rustle of small night-hunting creatures in the hedgerows; the eerie cry of a dog fox, the thin whistle of the wind through the tall reeds along the dykes, a sheep who lumbered across her path, a terrifying dark shadow till it gave a disgruntled bleat and she realized what it was.

At last the black shape of the Ship and Anchor loomed up before her but all was quiet, no sound, no light anywhere. They must all be down on the beaches already.

She went on bravely ploughing over the piles of shingle. Far away to the left was the outline of the light house. She paused to get her breath and suddenly out at sea a gleam of light shone like a star and then was gone. Was it an answer to a signal from the shore? Oh God, they must be there already and Guy with them. Her breath was coming in sobbing pants and it was heavy going over the loose pebbles that fell away under her feet, but she kept on till suddenly, without warning, she collided with a dark figure who seized her roughly by the shoulder, jerking up her chin to see who it was, and she was staring at Guy.

'Good Lord,' he whispered, 'it's Belle. What the devil are you dong here?'

'I came to warn you,' she panted. 'I heard of it by chance at Dover. The Revenue Officers are out after you with the Dragoons.'

'What! Are you sure?'

'Quite sure. I heard Captain Durrant speak of it.'

'Wait here,' he said quickly. 'Don't move. I must tell Jonty.'

He bounded away into the darkness and she took a few steps after him. Now she could see dark figures moving on the beaches and there was a boat, but whether it was coming or going she could not be sure. 'Hurry, hurry, hurry!' she muttered to herself, standing still, her hands clasped, praying that all would still be well, and it was at that very moment that all hell seemed to break loose.

122

There was the gleam of lanterns, the flare of torches, the flash of gunfire, men were running and shouting, she could hear the jingle of harness and a horse screamed. Then Guy was with her again pushing her back.

'Get down,' he said urgently, 'get down under cover. You could be hurt.'

He was thrusting her towards the shelter of the scrubby gorse and broom that grew at the side of the field.

'Lie down. Cover your face so that you can't be seen.'

She felt his hands on her and fell to her knees. Then he was gone again.

She crouched on the tussocky grass with fear churning inside her. They were fighting now, she could glimpse the uniform of the soldiers, guns were being fired but whether to kill or merely to warn and frighten, she didn't know. How long she stayed there in an agony of uncertainty she had no idea. Then quite near she heard a man's voice exclaim, 'Got him that time, the bastard!' There was the sound of a shot and then running feet. A moment later a body cannoned into her. She fell sideways and then realised with horror that it was Guy who had fallen beside her, face downwards.

She turned him over with shaking hands but he was not dead.

'He's only winged me,' he muttered, but there was blood on his shirt and on her hands.

She dragged him into the shelter of the bushes and the very next moment it seemed someone else was there bending over them.

'Dear God, what are you doing here?' whispered Robert Armitage.

'I might say the same of you,' Isabelle retorted fiercely. 'Was it you who shot him?'

'No, but you'd better cover him up with your shawl to hide him if you don't want to see him arrested and hanged. Keep as still as you can. I'll be back in a moment.'

He left them and she heard someone say querulously, 'I swear I nabbed one of them. Where the devil did he go?'

'Across the beach, man, towards the inn.'

She heard the crunch of the shingle, then Robert was there again.

'That no doubt was the fellow who fired at you. Now stay here and keep very quiet, both of you. I'll try to find out what's happening.'

He moved away and Guy said weakly, 'What is *he* doing here?'

'I wish I knew. Lie still. I'm going to try and stop the bleeding.'

She turned up the hem of her dress and ruthlessly tore the frill from the bottom of her white petticoat, making it into a pad. She opened his shirt and pressed the wad against the wound from which the blood was welling.

Guy gasped with the pain and she said anxiously, 'How am I to get you home?'

'I'm all right. I can walk.'

But when he tried to sit up, his head swam and she knew it would be impossible and that she was not strong enough to support him.

'Let me rest a little,' he mumbled.

She made her shawl into a kind of pillow and eased him back against it wondering where she could turn for help. The shouting and the noise had begun to die down now, but she dared not make any move yet.

It was some time later that Robert came back, and she asked him quickly what had happened.

'They have made a couple of arrests but the others got away and with most of the loot, I'm afraid. Captain Durrant is furious about it, which is not surprising after all the preparation. Someone must have warned them.'

'Yes, I did,' she said defiantly.

'You? And how did you know?'

'By accident. I overheard the Captain speaking of it this afternoon. I didn't know then that you would be riding with them,' she went on accusingly.

'I had my reasons,' he said drily, 'but I didn't shoot anyone, I assure you. So you thought you would contravene the law, did you?'

'I was not thinking of the law, it was Guy who concerned me and if you want to report me for what I did, then you can.'

'I scarcely think that will be necessary.' He looked from her to the boy, who was lying with his eyes closed. 'The real point is what are we going to do with this young man?'

'You needn't trouble,' muttered Guy struggling to sit up, 'I can take care of myself.'

'Not just at the moment you can't and what about your sister? Do you want to see her taken up and imprisoned with you?'

'Of course I don't. If you can help me to the Ship and Anchor . . .'

'That's a forlorn hope, my friend. The excise men are already swarming all over it and you would have a difficult task explaining a gunshot wound to them.'

And it would be the same if they got him to High Willows. There would be Sir Joshua's questions to face in the morning. There were a few moments of blank silence, then Isabelle suddenly sat up.

'I've been thinking. If we could get him to Mr Holland, he would help us, I'm sure.'

'It's the devil of a way,' muttered Guy.

'I've got my horse here. We can hoist you into the saddle. Are you sure Mr Holland will co-operate? It means waking him in the middle of the night.'

'Absolutely sure, and it would give me time to think what to do next.'

'Very true. Wait here while I fetch the horse. I'll be back.'

Guy was weak from pain and loss of blood, but somehow Robert got him into the saddle and he clutched the pommel, fighting against the faintness that threatened to overcome him at every step of the way.

It took a considerable time to reach the vicarage and it was Harriet Holland who responded to their urgent knock. In her white lace night-cap and red flannel dressing gown she took command of the situation with far more composure and competence than her brother, who was willing enough but nervous and apprehensive, only too well aware of the keg of brandy in the outhouse and wondering how he would face up to the

125

hammering on the door and the wrathful Captain Durrant demanding to search the house.

Fortunately nothing of the kind happened and Miss Holland and Robert Armitage between them managed very well. They half carried Guy into the parlour, stretched him on the sofa and stripped off his shirt and jacket.

'He's deuced lucky,' commented Robert examining the wound. His varied and sometimes dangerous life had necessitated a rough knowledge of first aid that had often proved useful. 'The bullet has passed through the fleshy part of the upper arm so we're not in need of a surgeon to extract the ball. Warm water, Miss Holland, and some bandages and I think we shall do quite well.'

Isabelle's offer of help was brushed aside, and it irritated her that she was obliged to stand by holding the bowl and the lint ready for them while they swabbed and cleansed, applied one of Miss Holland's invaluable herbal liniments and bandaged the arm and shoulder firmly into position. Guy was paper-white but had endured the pain stoically.

'Good man,' said Robert, washing his hands and drying them on the towel Isabelle handed to him. 'You stood that pretty well. Now a little of Mr Holland's excellent cognac and I must ask you a few questions.'

'You can't badger him now,' exclaimed Isabelle, 'you can't, not when he is faint and sick. It's inhuman. He ought to rest.'

'He can rest afterwards. There are one or two things I need to know. They are in fact the only reason I took part in this botched affair tonight.'

'I won't allow it,' she said stormily.

'I am afraid you must and afterwards he will be all yours to coddle and comfort as much as you like.'

Mr Holland had fetched the brandy and Robert poured a small measure into a glass, then banked up the cushions behind Guy.

'Now take your time and drink it slowly.' He looked around at them with a faint smile. 'With your permission I think perhaps a small measure would do us all good.'

126

'At this hour of night I don't really think it is quite the thing,' ventured Mr Holland.

'Well, I do,' interrupted his sister. 'You're looking quite shaky, Gilbert, and I'm not surprised. I could certainly do with it myself. It will give us all fresh heart.'

'How right you are, dear lady,' murmured Robert and proceeded to pour a small quantity in each of the glasses on the tray.

This was a new Robert Armitage, thought Isabelle, taking a tentative sip and feeling its warmth help to still her inward shivering. The easy charm, the light banter, the air of the elegant man about town had completely vanished. This was a man sternly in command of himself and of the situation, quietly determined to go ahead and do exactly as he intended, brooking no interference.

Miss Holland scented his resolve immediately. She drank the brandy he had poured for her and then, with a nod to her brother, quietly carried the bowl and towels out of the room. Gilbert Holland, casting an anxious look at Isabelle, followed her leaving Robert alone with the brother and sister.

He drew a chair up beside the sofa and took the glass from Guy's hand, putting it on the table behind him.

'Feeling stronger? Good. Now just one or two questions.'

'No,' said Isabelle firmly, 'no. It's not right. Why can't you let him be?'

'Keep out of this, my dear, or else I shall be obliged to ask you to leave us alone together.'

She drew back, angry with him because it seemed to her then that he had been deceiving her, professing a friendship and an interest only to worm out of her everything he could about her and about Guy.

'Go on,' said the boy wearily, 'can't we get this over and done with?'

'Certainly.' He leaned forward. 'Now, first of all, I'm under the impression that you have been going to and from France quite frequently during the last few months.'

Guy frowned. 'How do you know that?'

'Never mind about that. I have my informants.'

127

'Spies, I suppose,' said Isabelle bitterly.

'Don't interfere, Belle. This is my concern, not yours,' Guy's voice had a new firmness. 'It so happens that I went twice only.'

'For what purpose? Was it to negotiate bringing over one of Bonaparte's spies illegally into this country?'

'No, it was not,' went on Guy with angry vehemence. 'It was nothing of the kind. It was simply to work out a new system of exchange with the traders. The only member of the gang who spoke French fluently was captured last year and Jonty was hampered by a very imperfect knowledge of the language. He was afraid of being cheated. You see there were other goods they were planning to bring in besides gin and brandy and tea.'

'And were you successful?'

'Yes, it seemed to work. I've had a great deal of experience with accounts under Mr Forrest.'

'I see, and there was no mention among you of an illegal emigrant who was anxious to make the crossing in one of the free traders' ships?'

'Well, yes,' said Guy reluctantly, 'there was, but I had nothing to do with it. Jonty said the deal had gone wrong and the fellow, whoever it was, either didn't turn up at the meeting place or was drowned.'

'Drowned!' repeated Isabelle before she could stop herself. 'Did you say drowned?'

Robert swung round to look at her. 'Why do you say that? What do you know about it?'

'Nothing, nothing at all. What should I know except that it has happened before.'

'I see.' He gave her a long look, then turned back to Guy. 'I suppose it is useless to ask you to give me the names of the traders you dealt with.'

'I'm not an informer,' said Guy coldly. He paused and then went on slowly. 'But I did gather information that you might find interesting.'

'About what?'

'The threat of invasion.' Robert looked sceptical and Guy gathered his strength and went on quickly. 'It was in the tavern where I had to wait. There were some seamen, a couple of them

128

Bretons. We had a Breton stableman at the château. As a boy I could speak their lingo pretty well. They were laughing at the gullible English being taken in by a lot of bogus preparations along the shore, leaky barges that wouldn't have crossed a millpond safely let alone the Channel.'

'M-m-m, very interesting if it is true.'

'It's true enough. When I caught the drift, I asked a question or two.'

'And they'd no idea who you were?'

'Why should they? I was just any Breton lad waiting for what he could pick up.'

Robert was looking at him thoughtfully. 'Smart lad. But now for something else. I know you won't want to listen to me but I'm going to give you a piece of advice. Keep clear of the smugglers and of any dealings with the French. Quite apart from the illegality of the venture, you are in too vulnerable a position. You are French, you speak the language – the authorities if they hear of it are not likely to take any chances. You don't want to find yourself a prisoner for the duration of the war and neither, I imagine, does your sister. I can't see Sir Joshua going out of his way to save either of you if it comes to an arrest and a trial.'

'That's true enough,' said Guy. 'He'd be only too happy to be rid of us.'

Miss Holland put her head cautiously around the door.

'May we come in? Gilbert and I have been discussing what to do with our patient. Wouldn't it be best for that wound of his if he were to stay here with us at least for the rest of the night?'

'My uncle will be home tomorrow,' said Isabelle, 'and he is sure to hear all about the raid on the smugglers from Captain Durrant.'

'And he will undoubtedly want to know where and how his nephew got himself shot by the dragoons, especially if he happened to be recognised,' went on Robert. 'Am I right?'

'Yes,' said Isabelle unhappily, 'yes, you are.'

'The smugglers won't give me away. You can be certain of that,' put in Guy quickly.

'Thieves' honour, I presume,' said Robert drily. 'Supposing I tell him of my own part as an observer in this miserable affair, and that young Guy came with me as guide and maybe to see the sport.'

The boy had pushed himself up, gritting his teeth against the pain.

'We're not wild animals even if they do hunt us down. My uncle would never believe you.'

'Maybe not and your comrades, if they should hear of it, will be inclined to believe that you are the traitor who gave them away. It seems you lose out on both counts, my friend.'

'I can manage,' said Guy. 'I'm not a child. This is only a flesh wound and provided I do all the work Mr Forrest sets down for me and am willing to undertake anything else that comes up – he hates to be tied to desk work – he doesn't ask too many questions. I even stay the night at the estate office sometimes when there is an overload to get through. I could do that now and then nothing would be asked at High Willows. But there's something else you seem to forget. I've got to see Isabelle back to the house before her absence is noticed.'

'You will stay where you are, young man,' said Robert firmly. 'I will take your sister back to High Willows.' He glanced at her. 'I suppose you can still find your way in.'

'Oh yes. I left the door unbolted and you need not concern yourself. I know the path.'

'I think we had better make haste,' he went on, ignoring her. 'It will be dawn soon and the household will be stirring.'

'You must not worry about your brother, my dear,' said Harriet, picking up the shawl and wrapping it around Isabelle. 'We'll take good care of him and I'm sure no one, not even Sir Joshua, would ever dream of doubting Mr Armitage's honesty.'

'You flatter me, ma'am,' he said drily.

'You take Isabelle back to the house and if you care to stay for what's left of the night, there is a bed for you here.'

'You have been a tower of strength, both of you, but I'll not trouble you further. If you'll see to my horse for a little longer, I'll be back and take myself off. There is strategy to be thought out for the morning.'

Isabelle kissed her brother and hugged Miss Holland and

then they were outside in the chilly wind of the hour before the dawn. The sky was beginning to lighten and in the east there was the first faint streak of lemon.

They walked quickly and, though she would have been glad to avoid any contact with him, she was so desperately tired that she was grateful for the hand that gripped her firmly when she stumbled over the rough ground.

All was quiet at the house. No one was up yet though very soon they would be banking up the kitchen fire and bringing in the water for the giant kettles and pans. The door was as she had left it and she would have slipped through but he stayed her for a moment, turning her to face him.

'Don't look so woebegone. It will work out, I promise you.'

'Why are you doing all this for us?' she whispered.

'Let's say because I have a certain fellow feeling. I was seventeen once myself, and a rebel.'

'Is that all?'

She was gazing up at him, her face very pale, the eyes huge and dark and questioning. He felt her shiver in the bleak morning wind that blew across the courtyard. He bent his head and kissed her full on the mouth.

'If you must know, that's why,' he said abruptly and pushed her gently towards the door before he strode away.

She stood quite still, unable to stir because the embrace had been so strange, so unexpected. Then she went in quickly, rebolted the door and fled silently up the stairs and into the safety of her own room.

She sank on the bed utterly exhausted. So much had happened since she had crept out of the house earlier that night that she could not think straight. Anxiety for Guy, anger with Robert Armitage that he had seemed to be using her and her brother for purposes of his own, and now this. What was she to think? Was he friend or wasn't he? What had he meant by his questions? And what did he know? And then there was Lucien. Was it Lucien Robert was thinking of? But *he* was no spy, she was sure of it. Thank God she had not been betrayed into mentioning his name.

She got up wearily and began to strip off her dress stained

with blood where she had tried to bandage Guy's hurt on the shore. She dipped her face in the cold water. Too late to go to bed now. Gwennie would be up soon and she must prepare for the many tasks of the day, and pretend that nothing unusual had happened. She combed her tangled hair and touched the lips he had kissed, still wondering. She felt as if she had been caught up in something she did not understand and it troubled her greatly.

Tomorrow he would be gone back to London, to a life of which she knew nothing. With him a door in the cage had seemed to open for a little into a wider existence and had now slammed shut again. Like Lucien he had come and was now gone. She wondered if she would ever see him again.

6

In one way Guy was fortunate. Sir Joshua sent word that he would not be returning till the end of the week and Isabelle, together with the rest of the household, breathed a sigh of relief. By that time last night's affair would have died down. Captain Durrant, calling at noon with an apologetic account of the night's unsuccessful raid and a hint that someone from High Willows might have been involved in it, received a freezing reception from Aunt Augusta.

'I'm surprised at you, Captain, for even making such an outrageous suggestion. You can be absolutely sure that nobody from this household has ever had any dealings with this gang of criminals.'

'We did receive information, my lady,' he ventured unhappily.

'Lies undoubtedly. You must know as well as I that people of that class are only too ready to incriminate their betters. My husband when he returns will be most displeased.'

However afterwards she made sure of calling the servants together, told them what had happened and asked if any of them had any information concerning the night's doings. One and all they stared at her with blank faces taking good care to say nothing.

She warned them that involvement of any kind no matter how slight would be severely punished and then dismissed them before turning to Isabelle.

'Where is your brother? Why isn't he here with the others?'

'He is with Mr Forrest,' she said quickly. 'Arrangements for the sheep shearing have begun already and I know Mr Forrest is very anxious to get them finished before this fine weather comes to an end. Guy has to remain in charge at the office and

133

as they go on very late he has made arrangements to sleep there.'

'I see. Well, make sure he hears what I have been saying today.'

'Yes, of course. I will tell him so that he understands exactly what has happened.'

Fortunately Aunt Augusta did not pursue it. She had other things on her mind.

'There's something else I must tell you, Isabelle. I had meant to leave it until later in the summer but this letter from your uncle confirms it and you may as well start making arrangements now. We have found an excellent post for you. Lady Patterson is in need of a governess for her three children and I have recommended you strongly. As you are aware she has a boy of nine and two younger daughters. You will go to her after the summer holidays at the beginning of September.'

So it had come at last. Isabelle remembered Stella Patterson only too well. She had come on a visit the summer before last bringing her brood with her. Their nurse had fallen sick and Isabelle had been obliged to act as nursemaid and had not enjoyed it. Lady Patterson was one of those indulgent mothers who spoiled their children to excess and then expected someone else to remedy her mistakes. She drew a quick breath.

'What about Guy, Aunt Augusta? What will he do?'

She shrugged her shoulders indifferently. 'No doubt Sir Joshua will find something suitable for him soon, a clerkship in one of the counting houses of a business acquaintance in the city would do very well. Meantime he can remain with Mr Forrest.'

'But if I am to go to Lady Patterson who lives the other side of Dorset we would never see one another.'

'Really, Isabelle, did you expect anything else? A young woman in your position must be grateful for anything that is being done for her and if that means parting from your brother, then it is something that must be endured. I daresay you will be given a few days' holiday from time to time and maybe you can see each other then.'

She brushed the matter aside as utterly trivial, with no understanding at all of the strong vital link between brother and sister. Isabelle had known it had to come but now it was only a couple of months away she felt sick at the prospect. Somehow she had always cherished a dream that she and Guy would go on together bound by their childhood memories and the tragedy that had robbed them of everything they held most dear. Guy needed her. He was a dear boy but he was far too easily led, far too much influenced by others. He needed her strength of purpose, her determination, and then he was now the Comte de Sauvigny, the last of their house; her father would have wanted her to remember that always. To be parted would be unbearable. The last years with all their restrictions and frustrations seemed suddenly to be happy in comparison with what was to come.

' I knew it would happen sooner or later,' said Guy when she told him. 'They can't wait to be rid of us. Let's go, Isabelle, let's cut and run. We'll go to London. I can work and so can you. At least we'd be together and free.'

He paused for a moment. They were standing in a corner of the yard. In the huge barn the shearers were hard at work. They moved from farm to farm through the summer months and worked with incredible speed and efficiency. The warm air was filled with the bleating of the penned sheep and the heavy greasy smell of the fleeces.

'What about that fellow who was here, that Robert Armitage?' went on Guy slowly. 'He did us a dashed good turn that night. He might help us find something. Why not write to him, Isabelle?'

'Oh no, I couldn't. It would be too humiliating.'

'I don't see why,' argued her brother. 'He liked you, I'm pretty sure of that. I'm not a fool, you know. He didn't care a rap for Venetia but he had a way of looking at you.'

If that were true, and she was pretty sure that it was not, it was much more likely to be all in Guy's imagination, then it only made the very idea more intolerable.

'No, Guy, no, it would be impossible. I couldn't beg help from a stranger.'

'Have it your own way but we've got to do something and pretty soon too.'

'Yes, yes, I know.'

She felt as if they were in a trap and whatever way they looked at it there was no escape.

In the next few days all the local talk was of the Carnival which usually took place at the beginning of August and involved Rye and all the neighbouring villages throughout the marshes. The children decorated floats on the huge carts loaned by the farmers drawn by four shire horses, their harness glittering, the brass polished to gold and their manes and tails plaited with coloured ribbons. Despite the grinding poverty throughout the country districts, the near starvation from last year's failed harvest, despite the anxiety as to whether the peace talks would ever really come to anything or whether Boney would fulfil his threat and come swarming across the Channel with his hundreds of invasion barges, the Carnival still filled every mind, children and grown-ups alike, a kind of defiant fling in the face of the enemy.

In other years the gentry had usually remained aloof from these rural junketings, but this time Aunt Augusta decided to have a large house party before they took off for the promised trip to Bath to which Sir Joshua had at last reluctantly agreed.

'It's near enough to your birthday, Venetia, we can celebrate it at the same time. That charming Viscount Kilgour was *most* interested when I mentioned it to him before he left and promised to return if his work at the Foreign Office permitted.'

Venetia shrugged her shoulders indifferently and Isabelle was more and more convinced that she had not the least interest in Robert Armitage but only went along with her mother's enthusiasm to avoid argument, and she could not help noticing when she helped with the writing out of invitations that a certain Lieutenant Peregrine Conway and his aunt Lady Ravenswood had been added to the guest list.

There was so much to be done one way and another that the dreaded separation from her brother receded temporarily into the background till something happened that brought it back very forcibly indeed.

One night, about a fortnight before the Carnival, Guy left the estate office very late after working with Mr Forrest on the last

136

of the sheep shearing. He was carrying a leather bag of money, something between ninety and a hundred pounds. It was not more than half a mile through the park and it did not occur to anyone that he was in any danger, but he never arrived at High Willows.

Isabelle, finding his bed unslept in the next morning, was worried but did not immediately raise the alarm because he had been sleeping down at the estate office more than once since the night of the smuggling raid. However Mr Forrest, coming up during the morning to report to Sir Joshua, was horrified to find that the bag of money had not been delivered and at once began to ask questions.

What could have happened? Had the boy himself taken off with the cash? Isabelle, closely questioned, was furiously indignant at the suggestion.

'Guy is not a thief.'

'No, he's a good honest lad,' said Mr Forrest fairly. 'Could he have been robbed? It should surely not have taken him more than half an hour to walk from the estate office, so where is he?'

By midday they set out to search, Barty, Jason and the stable lads, even James condescended to go with them.

Isabelle had insisted on going with Barty, torn with anxiety. Guy would never have gone off anywhere without telling her so what could have happened to him? The men had spread out across the marshes. Barty with another shepherd took the bridle path that led through Denge Marsh to the Ship and Anchor, and it was Beth who found him. Racing far and wide the dog suddenly started barking and pawing at the ditch that ran along beside one of the dyked fields. They ran towards her and there lay Guy, half in and half out of the water, and for a paralysing heart-stopping moment Isabelle thought he was dead.

He lay in a huddled sodden heap, blood on his face and on his torn shirt, his body contorted as if in pain. She touched his cheek, fear gripping her, but it was still warm and when Barty and the other man lifted him on to the improvised stretcher a long quiver ran through his body.

'Don't 'ee fret, Miss,' said the shepherd kindly, 'he looks badly enough and someone has beat him up proper but he's still breathin'. We'll get him back to the house and Jason'll go for doctor.'

Sir Joshua frowned over him and even Aunt Augusta showed some slight concern.

Dr Meadows summoned from Rye looked down at the boy stripped of his sodden clothing by Isabelle and Gwennie, who were washing the mud and blood off the battered body.

'It's fairly obvious that the lad must have fought for his life,' he said to Sir Joshua, 'look at those knuckles skinned and bloody. They must have dragged him away and kicked him savagely to within an inch of his life. Take a look at those bruises, wonder is that he survived. If he'd fallen face downward in that muddy ditch, he'd have been beyond anyone's care. As it is . . .' He shook his head doubtfully over his patient.

He strapped up the cracked ribs, stitched a long slash from a knife and treated as best he could the cuts and abrasions.

Guy was stirring and muttering but not yet fully conscious and quite unable to answer questions about what had happened to him.

'Let the boy be,' said the doctor sharply. 'Twelve hours of exposure in that state is enough to knock the sense out of anyone, even if it doesn't give him a congestion of the lungs. You'll have to give him time.'

He administered a strong opiate, warned Isabelle of the likelihood of fever and said he would return the next day.

'And a fine expense that is going to be,' said Aunt Augusta irritably when he had gone. 'He'll be coming twice a day if we're not careful. What on earth was Guy doing walking back at that hour with a bag of money?'

'It's Mr Forrest who should be blamed, not Guy,' retorted Isabelle indignantly. 'Those robbers might have killed him.'

'Well, we shall have to see what comes of it. Your uncle will be making enquiries but I very much doubt if we'll see a penny of what's been stolen. You'd better care for your brother yourself, Isabelle. There is a great deal to be done and Gwennie can't be spared to play sick nurse.'

Isabelle was more than willing to look after Guy, especially as by the time the doctor returned the next day he was in a high fever.

'Just as I thought,' he said and drew a pint of blood from him, much against Isabelle's will as she thought Guy had lost enough blood already. He left her with a cordial guaranteed to bring down the fever and to be administered every three hours.

'No solid food, only a little broth if you can persuade him to take it,' he said before he took his leave.

There were two days of racking anxiety before the fever receded and Guy was able to speak of what had really happened to him.

He had seemed a little better that morning after a restless night and she persuaded him to swallow a few spoonfuls of the chicken soup Gwennie had brought. Then he fell into the first really peaceful sleep since he had been rescued. It was late afternoon before he woke and she was sitting beside the bed with a basket of mending on her lap. Aunt Augusta was not one to see anyone sitting idle if she could help it.

Isabelle glanced up to see Guy frowning at her as if he were trying to remember, but his eyes were no longer cloudy with fever but bright and clear.

'How long have I been lying here, Belle?'

'Nearly three days now. How do you feel? You look better and you're cooler. I think the fever is going.'

He stirred painfully. 'I feel as if a herd of elephants had trampled all over me, but my head seems clearer.'

She put down her sewing basket and got up. 'I'll fetch you some food. That will give you strength.'

'No, Isabelle, no, don't go, not for a moment. I want to talk to you first. What are Uncle Joshua and Mr Forrest saying about it?'

'They believe you were attacked by robbers who stole the money and beat you up. It's a wonder they never killed you.'

'It wasn't robbers, Isabelle.'

'Then who?'

'It was Jonty and some of the gang.'

'Are you sure?'

'Quite sure. I saw them clearly before they jumped on me.'

139

'But why, why?'

'Can't you guess? They believe I was the one who laid information about them to the Revenue Officers.'

'But how *can* they think that? It was you who warned them.'

'Yes, but much too late. Jonty believes that was just a trick on my part to make them believe I was innocent.'

'But you *were* innocent.'

'Try telling them that,' said Guy bitterly. 'You see, one of the dragoons has died so the fellow they captured could be accused of murder. It was their way of getting back at me.'

'They could have killed you.'

'Oh no, Jonty is too clever for that. Murder can mean hanging if they're caught. They went as far as they could. I fought back but there were three, maybe four of them, it's a bit muddled up in my mind. Four pairs of hob-nailed boots knocked the sense out of me and I must have passed out. I did try later to climb out of that slimy ditch but I couldn't. I remember the fearful stench and the cold but then I must have fainted again because the next thing I knew, a dog was licking my face.'

'That was Beth.'

'After that, it's just been muddle and pain and frightful dreams till now.' He tried to push himself up in the bed. 'What are we going to do about it, Belle?'

He looked so white and so exhausted that she pressed him gently back against the pillows.

'Don't talk any more now. I'm going to bring you something to eat. Afterwards you must rest. We'll talk again later this evening.'

'You'll not tell Uncle Joshua any of this, will you?'

'I ought to. Jonty and his mates should be punished.'

'No, Isabelle, no. They believed that I was the traitor and that they were justified in doing what they did.'

'In murdering you?'

'They stopped short of that.'

'Only just, and what about the money?'

'They weren't interested in that. They took it to make it look like robbery.'

'I'm not so sure.'

140

But Guy was to be proved right. Days later the money was found in a ditch far along the shore by one of the shepherds rescuing a sheep that had fallen into it. It was quite untouched. It seemed there was a kind of honour even among thieves.

But that was not till afterwards. Later that same day when Guy had told her what really happened, they spoke again, drawing close to one another and whispering in the shadowy light of the candle.

'How can I stay here now?' he said despairingly. 'They were my friends after all and now I've become their enemy, someone they no longer like or trust. It's unbearable. I felt I was doing something useful even if it was against the law. I enjoyed it and that fellow Armitage was interested in what I had to say. He was, wasn't he, Belle? I could have gone back, found out more of what he wants to know if all this hadn't happened.' He turned to look at her. 'Who is he, Belle? I know he is in the Foreign Office and mixes in political circles that Uncle Joshua would sell his soul to break into, but he's not just one of those high society fops, he's more than that, isn't he? What does he really do?'

'I don't know,' she said thoughtfully. 'I wish I did. On the surface he is so charming, so easy to get on with, and yet even all those years ago when we were on the ship and he was so kind to us – do you remember, Guy – even then I sensed that there was something different about him.'

Could he help them or would he think it an impertinence? She would find it almost impossible to ask. She tried to put the idea out of her mind. Only one thing seemed to her certain. She could not leave Guy here alone, not now. She would never have a moment's peace. She would have to find a solution to that problem. But at this moment, with Guy still so sick, she could think of nothing.

'What you must do first is to get fit again,' she said, making him comfortable for the night. After that there would still be time, but not so much after the Carnival was over, she thought despairingly, putting water where he could reach it easily and leaving the candle still burning. She could come in later to see if he was sleeping, though she thought he was well enough now to be left alone for a few hours and she badly wanted the solitude of her own room to think, to try and reach a decision. It would have been so much simpler to have stolen the money and run away together. It would have kept them for a year while they looked around for some other means of existence, and then she laughed at her wild thought. The Comte de Sauvigny and his sister were not thieves unfortunately. How much easier it was if one had no scruples.

And while she undressed and put on her dressing gown for some reason she thought of Lucien. What would he have done? Seized the main chance as he had done with James's horse and afterwards faced up to the consequences? I owe you a life. Wait for me. All those empty promises and yet how wonderful it would be if they were fulfilled, only that was like asking for the moon.

She sighed and lay down on the bed, picking up a book and leaning towards the candlelight. She would read *The Rime of the Ancient Mariner*, rock on those stormy seas, let her imagination run riot far away from the hard everyday practical side of life and perhaps out of it would come some solution she had not yet thought of, some wonderful dream like Lucien appearing at the Carnival, a Prince out of nowhere, and whisking her and Guy out of this existence into some other world. The candle guttered, the book fell to the floor and she woke up with a start. The dream like all such airy nonsense had vanished. It was time to see if Guy was sleeping soundly, to blow out his candle and return to her own bed and to the stern reality that must soon be faced.

Part Two

ROBERT
1801–1803

7

'I have had another invitation to High Willows,' said Robert
Armitage to his sister when they were breakfasting together in
the pleasant morning room of the family house in Arlington
Street. 'It appears that it is Venetia's birthday, there is a local
Carnival to attract the younger guests, and Lady Brydges has
decided to indulge in a house party.'

Marian looked up quickly. 'Will you go?'

'I rather think I shall.'

She refilled his coffee cup, added a little cream and said
carefully, 'I wouldn't have thought a rustic Carnival would
appeal to you all that much.'

'It doesn't,' he admitted frankly, 'but I do have another
reason for going down to Kent.'

'I understood that the question of coastal defence had been
shelved for the time being now that the threat of Bonaparte's
invasion seems to have receded with Nelson in charge of the
Channel Fleet.'

'That's true enough,' Robert smiled. 'Incidentally our little
Admiral is furious about it. He came back from his victory in
the Baltic looking forward to a few weeks' well-earned leave
with his beloved Emma and stormed into the Navy Office in a
towering rage, only to be told firmly by the PM that nothing
less than the hero himself would appease the nation's alarm.
That appeared to please him and I must say he is setting about
the task with a commendable energy.'

'Then what is taking you down there this time?'

Robert drank the last of his coffee, folded his napkin with
some deliberation and then looked across at his sister.

'I have something to tell you,' he said slowly. 'If everything
goes as I pray it will, I hope soon to be married.'

145

'Married!' exclaimed Marian. 'Oh Robert, not Venetia!'

He smiled faintly. 'No, not Venetia as it happens, but her cousin.'

'Cousin? What cousin?'

Marian was taken aback, scarcely able to believe what she was hearing, wondering if this was one of Robert's jests, except that his manner was quiet and serious.

'Who is she? Where did she come from? Why have they never brought her with them to London?'

'Her mother, it seems, was Sir Joshua's half sister and her father was the Vicomte de Sauvigny. Her grandfather was murdered by the mob in '93 and her father lost his head to the guillotine. She and her young brother were hounded out of France. It so happens that I was on the ship that brought them to England some years ago, two friendless and terrified children.'

'You never mentioned it.'

'Why should I? It was a common enough tragedy at that time.'

Marion frowned. 'Why have we never heard of them?'

'They weren't exactly made welcome. There had been some bitter family quarrel. As far as I could see they've been shut up at High Willows and treated an unpaid servants for the last six or seven years.'

She had a lurking suspicion that Robert was being trapped by that deep concern for the unfortunate that existed beneath his usual calm reserve and was guessed at only by those who were very close to him.

'But you can't *marry* a girl like that, just out of pity. It would be most unsuitable. You mustn't do it, Robert. It's the worst kind of basis for a successful marriage.'

'You're quite wrong, Marian. Pity may have played a small part in it, I suppose, but that's not the reason.' He paused for a moment, his mind going back to that first vision of her rising from the sea. Was that the moment when the magic began or was it afterwards, and in any case he couldn't tell Marian about that, she would think him stark crazy. 'The truth is quite simple,' he went on deliberately, 'I find I can't contemplate

146

going on with the rest of my life without her. I suppose this is what poets and romantics call love at first sight. I never thought that so absurd a thing could happen to me,' he shrugged his shoulders helplessly, 'and yet it hit me like a . . . like a bolt of lightning "that doth cease to be ere one can say it lightens."'

'Oh don't quote Shakespeare to me,' exclaimed Marian irritably, 'this is far too serious. I can't believe it. It's so unlike you and what on earth is Father going to say?'

'Seeing he is at present living with his head gamekeeper's daughter I don't think he can say very much.'

'But he hasn't *married* her.'

'True and I don't mind Jeannie. She's a nice girl and she is good for him. He's been a different man these last few years. Are you implying that I should set up Isabelle as my mistress? That is not at all my intention nor is it what I want.'

'How does *she* feel? Have you asked her? Have you spoken to her uncle?'

'Not yet and I rather fear that Isabelle may reject me. She has a dignity and a pride remarkable in such a young girl.'

'She will fall into your arms and thank God for her good fortune if she has any sense,' exclaimed Marian indignantly.

'You are too partial, my dear. I'm not exactly a young woman's dream lover, am I?' He turned to her suddenly with an appeal that was almost boyish. 'You'll like her, Marian, she has a rare charm and a good mind *and* she reads Virgil and Horace with a taste for history and literature.'

'She sounds like the very worst kind of blue-stocking,' said Marian dampingly. 'A fine basis for marriage, I must say!'

'Why? It gives us shared interests and that goes a very long way.'

'How old is she?'

'Nineteen, and her brother is a couple of years younger.'

'Oh Robert,' sighed Marian, 'are you thinking of taking on the whole family? It is quite absurd. I can't believe you are serious.'

'Never more serious in my life,' he said with decision and got up from the table. 'And now I really must go. Dealing with Bonaparte is the very devil. He is as full of tricks as a cage full

147

of baboons. Ever since we began these negotiations for peace, despatches have flown between us and Paris dealing with ever more demands on his part, and most of my staff have the most deplorable ignorance of diplomatic French, and even, I'm sorry to say, of basic English.' He turned back as he reached the door. 'By the way, I meant to tell you. David Fraser is back in town. I ran into him at White's yesterday and invited him to dine with us tonight. It doesn't upset your plans, does it?'

'Not in the least. I was intending to spend a quiet evening. London's a desert at the moment. I thought David was in Turkey.'

'So he was but now he's back and as full of outrageous tales as usual. I may be a little late. If I am, I'm sure you will be able to keep him entertained.'

He took his hat and gloves from the hovering butler and went down to the waiting carriage. For a second Marian sat staring after him, trying to assimilate this unexpected and very unwelcome news. There were a hundred questions she wanted to ask about this girl who had so astoundingly captured the interest of her difficult and fastidious brother. Then the servants came in to clear the table and she took herself upstairs to her own sitting room on the first floor.

While she dealt with her correspondence and interviewed Cook about a rather more elaborate dinner than usual, since David Fraser was very much of a gourmet, she pondered what her brother had sprung on her and realised that in one way it was not altogether surprising. She had always known that though he kept it well hidden, Robert had inherited the family leaning towards lost causes. It was what had driven him to undertake these secret missions across the Channel; it was what had sent their grandfather at eighteen to fight for Charles Stuart at Culloden in 1746. He had survived that disaster by a miracle and in flat defiance of his family, who had remained discreetly neutral, had gone with his Prince into exile. It had cost a fortune in fines before he was allowed to return to Glenmuir bringing with him a French bride.

Marian wished her grandmother was not so far away in Scotland. She would have liked to have been able to consult with her about this crazy plan which Robert seemed determined to carry out. Elise de Morney had come to Glenmuir at seventeen and ever since had greatly influenced everyone living there. She had transformed the interior of what had been a gloomy castle stronghold into something resembling the gracious château of her own youth. She had always taken the greatest possible interest in her grandchildren, talking French to Robert almost from birth so that by the time he was five he was bilingual.

She had been a tower of strength when their mother, her daughter-in-law, had died from a late pregnancy that had sadly killed both her and the baby when Marian was eighteen and Robert twelve. She had been the only one able to deal with her son who had blamed himself so severely that he had withdrawn from the world into seclusion and despair. She had accepted it philosophically when, five years ago at the New Year party for servants and tenants, he had suddenly emerged from his withdrawal and was roused to a late blossoming by Jeannie Macrae, young, exceedingly pretty and very outgoing, and had quite openly and with her consent taken her to his bed.

She had understood too that though Marian was happy to see her father recovered from the gloom of so many years, his daughter had found it very hard to accept. It had driven her to take refuge with her brother in London and content herself with yearly visits to Glenmuir. And now, she thought wryly, it seemed history would repeat itself. She was to be sent packing by a chit of a girl whom her brother had only known for a few days and was proposing to make mistress of his heart and his home. Of course he was bound to marry some day, she had always known that, but not like this. She felt it her duty to do all she could to prevent him making such a fatal mistake and ruining his life and possibly hers too.

Marian was thirty-six, an intelligent woman with many interests of her own. She was keenly interested in music, attended concerts and the opera, read a great deal and attended lectures. She had her own circle of friends and once a week went down to a settlement in one of the worst slums of London where she helped with the distribution of food, clothing and medical aid. Robert did not altogether approve but she persisted. She had always interested herself in her father's dependents at Glenmuir and though the wide open spaces, the moors and mountains around Arisaig were not like the filthy sordid conditions of Wapping, sickness, starvation and dire poverty were common to both.

It was early evening when with a quickening of the heart she saw David Fraser alight from the carriage and come up the steps. She went to greet him with outstretched hands.

'Marian, my dear,' he exclaimed, kissing her on both cheeks, 'looking as beautiful and serene as always. When I'm away and think of England, it is always you who comes into my mind.'

'Flatterer! I don't believe that for an instant.'

'It's true, I swear it is. You and Robert are like rocks of sanity in what can sometimes be a chaotic world.'

There had been a time when she had believed herself in love with him. She had been twenty-three and he nineteen when Robert first brought him to Glenmuir and he had stayed on with them to shoot and hunt the stag and make them laugh in the evenings with his crazy antics. She was young then and still cherishing illusions. She had not yet come to terms with the plain fact that although she was an Earl's daughter with a sizeable portion of her own, she was the type of young woman whom men call 'a good sort', one to whom they confide their troubles and ask for advice, but never one with whom they fall in love or seek in marriage. The pain, disillusion and heartache were now long past. With strong determination she had built a life for herself and enjoyed it. Only now and then, when a friend showed off a new baby or as now, seeing David again with his charm and his laughter, did a sudden pang of fear for the future sweep through her. Without Robert she would be so desperately lonely.

She had not intended to confide in David, knowing that to her brother this would be something deeply private, but all three of them had always been so close and the question came out almost without her thinking.

'Did Robert mention to you that he hopes to be married soon?'

'No, he didn't. You know Robert is close as an oyster about himself. Who is the girl? Do I know her?'

'It seems that no one does.' Then she couldn't stop herself and it all came out in a rush. 'She is some penniless French refugee with a very doubtful background who has probably put herself out to capture Robert. I wouldn't put it beyond that uncle of hers, Sir Joshua Brydges, trying to further the match for his own advantage. Lady Brydges has been pushing her daughter under the nose of every eligible young man for the past two years. They are the most insufferable people.'

David frowned. 'Robert is not the type of man to be pushed into anything. I would have said any kind of pressure would have quite the opposite effect.'

'He says he is in love with her, can't live without her. It's not like him to talk like that. Oh David, is it possible to fall crazily in love in just a few days?'

'My dear girl, you can fall in love in an hour. I know. I've done it myself but, fortunately, perhaps, it very rarely lasts. This, I take it, is a good deal more serious. He hasn't taken you to meet her?'

'Not yet and David, you won't mention it to him, will you? I wouldn't like him to think I'd betrayed his confidence.'

'Not a word. Silent as the grave, that's me. Where did you say these people live?'

'Sir Joshua has a house called High Willows down in Kent somewhere on the Romney Marshes.'

'Supposing I run down there, take a look around, try and find out something. When does he go?'

'Quite soon. At the beginning of August.'

'Right. I'll keep it in mind and, Marian, don't fight against it. If he's riding an obsession, opposition will only harden him against you.'

'I suppose you're right but I feel so wretchedly helpless.'

'You worry too much. These things have a way of working themselves out. I'd put my trust in Robert's good sense any day of the week.'

And with that she had to leave it. Very soon afterwards Robert himself was there and they spent a delightful evening talking over old times and listening to David relating how he had inadvertently broken into a harem and only just escaped being sewn up in a sack and tossed into the Bosporous.

'I don't believe a word of it,' said Marian laughing at him. 'They don't do things like that nowadays.'

'Don't they just! There was a strong rumour running around Istanbul that the Sultan's latest wife, very young and beautiful by all accounts, aroused the jealousy of her predecessor and disappeared one night only to be found later with her throat slit.'

'More likely she'd eloped with a lover to escape the old man's unwelcome embraces and the throat slitting was a cover-up to spare his pride,' said Robert cynically.

He seemed so relaxed, so like his usual self, discussing the latest political moves with David who was keenly interested and could himself contribute some valuable opinions he had picked up during his travels, that Marian could scarcely believe he had really meant what he had told her that morning. Perhaps it was all nothing but a 'Banbury tale', a piece of nonsense they could laugh over later when the right time came.

She went to bed at last and left the two men still comfortably talking together. When he had shut the door after her David came back to the hearthrug and stood looking down at his friend for a moment.

'Are you still flitting across the Channel on these mystery trips of yours?'

'Yes. I've just come back actually. You know what happened last December, I suppose. A few hotheads tried to assassinate Bonaparte in the rue Saint Niçaise when he was on his way to the Opera to hear Handel's *Creation*. It failed of course, just as we all knew it would.'

'Royalists, of course.'

'There has been an appalling wave of arrests and executions in consequence and what is worse, it has completely disrupted our organisation just when we least wanted it to happen.'

'And so they sent you to sort it out?'

'Something like that.'

'Do those dissident groups of rebels have any idea who you really are?' asked David curiously. 'It could be damned dangerous if they do.'

'In most cases we use code names.'

'And you go in disguise of course. I've never forgotten how brilliant you were at changing yourself in those crazy games we played up at St Andrews in our salad days.'

'With an undistinguished face like mine it's not difficult,' said Robert drily.

'Quite a number of young ladies of my acquaintance hold a very different opinion,' remarked David.

'Indeed. You flatter me.'

'I thought when Dundas resigned with William Pitt over that political crisis, you would have gone with them.'

'They begged me to remain since I do provide a sort of bridge between the PM's fumbling efforts and the opposition.'

It had been Henry Dundas, member of Parliament for Edinburgh, clever, good-natured with his red face and strong Scots accent, a close friend of the Earl of Glenmuir, who had recruited Robert into his department when he came down from the university – mainly because his fluent idiomatic French would be of inestimable value in interpreting the diplomatic nuances of the official documents and secret messages that flew between the two countries.

And then Robert had important connections in enemy country. His grandmother's family had suffered in the Terror. The head of the house with his wife had gone to the guillotine, their estates had been confiscated, but some of his cousins had survived. Jacques de Morney still lived quietly in the country, devoted to his scientific researches, but also managing to move around and provide useful information about popular reaction to the workings of the police state Bonaparte was slowly building up, and he could also provide cover for Robert in his guise as a wealthy wine merchant travelling from vineyard to vineyard in search of fine vintages. In that way he had been able to carry advice, information, encouragement and money to the royalist organisations that still existed throughout France. But not even to his oldest and closest friend was Robert prepared to give too much away.

David dropped into the armchair and grinned at him.

'You know when you marry, you'll have to give up this dangerous life of yours. Not all women are as understanding as Marian. Your wife may not stand for it.'

'Perhaps.' Robert was not to be drawn. 'We have a serious problem in the department just now. Information has been leaked at the crucial moment so that the enemy have had foreknowledge of certain moves and it has given them the advantage in their negotiations. Though we have our suspicions, so far we've not been able to lay a finger on who is responsible. However none of that is your affair. What do you intend to do with yourself now you're back in England?'

'Oh I don't know,' said David airily. 'Go up north to see Papa and Mamma I suppose. If your peace treaty materialises, I rather fancy a trip to Paris. I'd like to see what those bloodthirsty ruffians have done to the old place.'

'You are very welcome to stay here while you are in London.'

'That's uncommonly good of you but I still have my apartment in Piccadilly and now I suppose I really ought to go.'

'Shall I send for a cab?'

'No, I'll walk. It's no distance and I think I'm equal to any bruiser who may be after my money or my life.'

Robert saw his friend to the door and then retired thoughtfully to bed. Despite the firm declaration of his intention to his sister that morning, he was still greatly at odds with himself. It seemed to him that notwithstanding the nerve-racking hours he had spent across the Channel during the past few weeks, the even tenor of his life had been turned upside down and all because for some inexplicable reason he had been enchanted by a young witch, who possessed not only a most unusual beauty but also a mind that was quick, sensitive, intelligent and somehow responded to something deep within himself. He passionately desired to take her away from her narrow constricted life, so barren of love and sympathy, and see her grow and blossom with all that he could give her, and yet at the same time, absurdly enough, he felt as diffident about approaching

154

her as if he were a boy in love for the first time. Perhaps he had been content with his life for too long and, as David had hinted, he needed the shock of change. He would soon know. In a very short time now his fate would be settled one way or the other.

8

Robert arrived at High Willows late on a fine afternoon and found several guests already comfortably installed. The lawns behind the house had been shaved to green velvet. Venetia was stretched out in a long chair, Perry Conway sitting adoringly at her feet. Captain Durrant was walking in the shrubbery with Sir Joshua. The whole scene, the ladies in their light-coloured dresses with their lace-trimmed parasols, had an air of luxury and relaxation in vivid contrast to the frantic atmosphere at Whitehall all that past week, with Bonaparte again on the warpath threatening invasion if his demands were not instantly met, secret documents being despatched to the coastal districts putting them on the alert, and volunteers drilling again on village greens and parading in Hyde Park in front of King George who had miraculously recovered his wits.

He was shown to his room, washed off the dust of travel, changed from his travelling dress and went down to be greeted effusively by Lady Brydges and with rather more reserve by his host. Several middle-aged gentlemen pounced on him almost immediately, demanding how much the latest rumours could be relied on and whether it was true that the moves towards an early peace were being seriously jeopardised. He wondered what in the world had induced him to spend a weekend in such uncongenial company.

He walked in the gardens, chatting to this one and that, but saw no sign of Isabelle or her brother and a casual enquiry to Venetia brought a careless shrug of the shoulders.

'Oh Isabelle is always off somewhere. She is probably helping the villagers with the Carnival.'

In fact he did not see her until they sat down to dine rather earlier than usual so as to allow time for those who were

156

proposing to drive down to Rye and watch the procession. His keen eye noted at once that Isabelle looked even more pale than usual and that Guy walked with a limp and appeared as if he had only recently recovered from serious illness. He wondered what could have happened. Surely he was not still suffering from the effects of the smuggling raid. He regretted that his absence abroad had not allowed him to make enquiries. He had assumed that as he had heard nothing, all had been well.

It so happened that Isabelle had stolen an hour that afternoon to help Miss Holland and the children decorate the Snargate float. It was only a very small cart drawn by Mr Holland's old white mare and since there was no money to spare, it was hung with bunches of dock and corn, with clusters of wild flowers and tall feathery reeds from the meadows and hedges. The prettiest of the little girls, chosen to be queen for the day, had a wreath of white daisies on her newly washed hair and a length of old red curtain to serve as a train. She tripped over it and bloodied her nose but nothing would induce her to part with it. Isabelle had begged some bright ribbons from Mrs Bedford and plaited them into Rosinante's mane and tail. The children, all wildly excited, were perched on the cart, tucking into the jam-filled scones Harriet Holland had baked for them. The boys who would be carrying the tow-headed, pitch-soaked torches, had to be constantly restrained from lighting them now instead of waiting for dark.

'Will you be coming to watch the fun with the others?' asked Harriet as Isabelle prepared to hurry home.

'I don't think so. There won't be room for me in the carriages and in any case there is bound to be something for me to do.'

She raced back to the house only just in time to change into her white dress and earn a heavy frown from Aunt Augusta for coming late to the table.

No expense had been spared that night. Cook had excelled herself with delicious food and by the time dinner was done, lanterns had been lit in the gardens glowing like coloured fruits among the trees, and musicians had begun to play in the drawing room. A little later it would be left to James to gather

157

some of the younger members of the house party together and take them off in the carriages to view the Carnival.

The company, replete with food and wine, dispersed into the drawing room or into the garden and Robert went in search of Isabelle. He found her in the dining room beginning to gather glasses together on a tray and superintend the servants who were clearing the tables.

'Leave that,' he said, 'and come and talk to me.'

'I don't think I should. The servants are terribly overworked and the new maid is very unreliable.'

'I'm sure they can manage perfectly well without you and I want to know everything that has happened since I was last here.'

'Aunt Augusta will be looking for me,' she objected. She was a little shy of him, uncertain of herself, remembering how they had parted and what Guy had said about him.

'Then I fear she will have to look in vain,' he said, taking the tray from her and putting it safely on the table. 'Come into the garden with me. We can be alone there.'

A little unwillingly she let him take her arm.

'There's a great deal I want to know,' he went on. 'I did not hear from you so I judged everything had gone according to plan, now I'm not so sure. What is wrong with Guy? Is he still suffering from that gunshot wound?'

'No, it's worse than that, much worse.' She paused, still a little doubtful of him, but the need to confide in someone was strong and the night of the raid had brought them very close together. 'You were right,' she went on slowly, 'when you said he might be suspected of treachery. Jonty and the gang believed it was he who had given the information and they very nearly killed him.'

They had drawn away from the others, turning down a quiet avenue of neatly trimmed box. The golden light of the lantern hung high above them in a small arbour lit her face with a warm glow.

'Go on,' he said. 'Tell me exactly what happened.'

'It was terrible. Beth found him lying in one of the ditches. I thought at first he was dead. He was covered with blood and

158

had been kicked and bruised and beaten.' It all poured out then, the days of sickness and fever, what the doctor had said, what Guy had told her and the robbery that was no robbery. 'He is up now,' she went on, 'but he is still in pain and he goes nowhere except down to Mr Forrest's office. You see they were his friends, his comrades, and he feels it terribly in spite of what they did to him. I wanted them to be punished for it but he will not let me tell Sir Joshua and I suppose he is right. It would only make it worse for him but it's a terrible burden to bear and now there is something else, a problem that I don't know how to solve.'

'And what is that?'

'Aunt Augusta has found a position for me. In September I am to go to Lady Patterson as governess to her three children.'

'Oh no,' he said quickly, 'please God, not that!'

'Why? Do you know her?'

'My sister and I have suffered from those three children,' he said wryly.

'I daresay I could cope with that,' she said, 'that's not the worst. You see, she lives on the far side of Dorsct. I should never see Guy. How can I possibly leave him alone here after what has happened? He needs me. I would never have a quiet moment. Oh dear God,' she went on with a kind of quiet despair that had been slowly building up in her for so long now. 'I shouldn't be saying all this to you, I know I shouldn't. It's just that – that it's been shut up inside me and there is no one who understands or cares.'

She turned away from him, deeply ashamed of her outburst and fighting hard against the reluctant tears.

There was a momentary pause. He looked at the pure line of her averted cheek, then took the plunge.

'Listen to me, Isabelle, I could offer you a post you might find more congenial.'

'You could?' She turned back to him, her eyes glowing with sudden hope. 'One that would mean Guy and I need not be parted?'

'One where you could certainly see him whenever you wished.'

159

She frowned. 'But how? Where? I don't think I understand.'

'Marry me, Isabelle. Marry me and your problem will be solved.'

'Marry you!' Her eyes widened. She was staring up at him so taken by surprise that for an instant she was speechless, then she said quickly, 'Oh no, no, you can't mean it!'

He seized her hands in his, drawing her towards him. 'Believe me, I do mean it with all my heart.'

'But it's impossible. I couldn't . . . it would be all wrong . . . I couldn't take advantage of . . .' She pulled away from him, turning her back, catching her breath in a dry sob because in a way it was a solution, it was tempting, and yet she knew she couldn't accept it.

He turned her back to him, tilting up her face to look at him.

'Why is it impossible? Why do you say it's wrong? Do you dislike me so much?'

'Oh no, no, it's not that at all. It's just that you are – who you are – and I am nothing. I could not accept such – such kindness. I couldn't because . . .'

'Is there someone else who has already won your heart? Is that what you are trying to tell me?'

For an instant the thought of Lucien flashed through her mind. If only it could be he and not this man, whom she liked but did not love. How could she take what he offered and give him nothing in return? Everything that was proud and self reliant in her fought against it.

'No,' she said faintly, 'no, there is no one else.'

'Why then? We share a great deal and there is much I could give you and your brother.'

'I know and that is why. Don't you see? It's too much, far too much.'

He drew her close to him, fighting a desire to take her in his arms, to kiss and kiss and promise her the whole world and was absolutely certain that if he did it would be instantly and finally refused. Then before either of them could make any further move, they were rudely interrupted.

James appeared at the end of the avenue out of breath and highly indignant.

160

'We've been looking for you everywhere, Isabelle. Where the devil have you been? We're just off to the Carnival and Venetia refuses to go without you.'

She detached herself from Robert. 'Very well. I'll come, but I thought some of the other ladies were going with you.'

'They've all cried off. Mamma has been saying it's not at all proper, the company may be rough and so on, all nonsense of course, and she won't let Venetia go alone and the poor girl's set her heart on it.' He glanced at Robert. 'What about you, sir? Are you game for a lark?'

'Oh yes, I'm game for anything,' said Robert making up his mind immediately to accompany Isabelle. 'Perhaps Lady Brydges will feel happier if I'm also in charge of the young ladies.'

And so it proved. They went back to where the others were gathered around the carriages. Isabelle guessed that Venetia was anxious not to be parted from her Lieutenant and felt a certain sympathy. She was still feeling so disturbed by Robert's unexpected proposal that almost any distraction was welcome.

Sir Joshua was grumbling that it wasn't peace yet by a very long chalk and they were tempting providence by rejoicing too soon.

'Oh for God's sake, Father,' exclaimed James explosively. 'Can't we have a fling for once and forget Boney and the confounded war?'

Lady Brydges still demurred at the girls going with them on the plea that there might be trouble. You never knew what to expect from people of that class and they could not expect to be treated with proper respect.

'I am sure the ladies will be perfectly safe in my care,' said Robert smoothly. 'I will watch over their comfort and it would be a pity if they could not enjoy a little of the entertainment.'

At the very last moment Guy appeared and announced that he was coming with them.

'Oh no, dearest, you shouldn't,' whispered Isabelle.

'Why not? I've nothing to be ashamed of and I'm not going to be driven into hiding.'

'I know but you're not really fit yet.'

'Oh for God's sake, stop molly-coddling me!' he said irritably. 'I'm not a child. I'm perfectly well,' and as if to prove it he scrambled up into the seat beside Jason on the box.

Robert thought it might be rash in the circumstances but admired the boy's spirit, so he said nothing and they drove away at a rattling pace.

The carriages of the gentry were drawn up to one side of the water meadows lying alongside the river, where they had an excellent view of the long procession as it streamed down the hill on which Rye was perched. In the centre of the Salts an enormous bonfire of brushwood had been built towering to the sky with fireworks buried in its heart.

Harvests had been wretchedly poor for the past two years and the country folk here as well as in other parts of England had suffered cruelly from starvation and extreme poverty, their young men driven to enlist in the army or press ganged into the navy, but all the same that night, with the prospect however distant of peace at last, all the frustrations and anxieties were forgotten in an upsurge of excitement and enjoyment. The decorations on the floats were tawdry, bright rags and cheap tinsel taking the place of gold and silks but ingenuity went a long way. Neptune sat high up clutching his trident, a crown of silver paper on hair of seaweed, Britannia complete with towering helmet and bright flag was mounted on a scarlet draped chair and waved a majestic spear to the enthralled crowd. In the darkness of the night the marchers with their flaming torches gave the whole scene a glamour and a mystery of its own.

Near riot and threatened insurrection had haunted the country all this past year as Robert knew only too well but occasions like this acted as a safety valve. The town band sawed away at violin, fife and pipe and then came the children singing the old harvest song going back so far no one now knew its origins.

Jonty's strong untutored baritone sang the first line. . .

'I'll sing the one O'

162

And another voice took it up.

'What means the one O'

Then with a rush came the children, uneven, tremulous but very sweet.

'Eight is the bright walkers
Seven's the seven stars in the sky
Six is the provokers
Five's the thimble in the bowl . . .'

'What does it *mean*?' whispered Venetia but except for a few dusty scholars no one now knew or cared.

Isabelle, caught up in all the excitement, forgot for a little the anxieties that oppressed her. The crowd, growing larger and larger every moment, surged forward towards the bonfire.

'Can't we go and join them?' urged Venetia, her pretty face alight with the thrill of it.

'I don't think it's quite the thing, it's an awful crush,' murmured Perry doubtfully and looked to Robert for guidance.

'Provided we keep close together, I don't think we shall suffer any harm.'

He took Isabelle's arm and they moved forward in a party followed by James and his particular friends. The crowd gave way to the gentry and let them take their place in the front. A company of strolling players who had been at Hastings all the past week were flitting here and there in their gypsy costumes and one of them, a tall thin man in striped breeches and stocking cap, masked like Harlequin, danced up to Isabelle, swung her round in a merry whirl, stood still for a second looking searchingly into her face, then kissed her cheek and vanished.

'Devil take the fellow!' exclaimed Robert. 'What does he think he is playing at? Who is he? Do you know him?'

'No, not at all.' Something about him had reminded her of Lucien and she laughed: it was part of the carefree night. 'I don't think he meant any harm.'

The last float rolled slowly down the slope, creaked across the grass and came majestically to a halt lit by a dozen torches held high enough to light a huge shapeless effigy with a tricolour sash and topped by a cocked hat, unmistakeably the hated enemy, Bonaparte himself. He was greeted with a roar of derisive laughter as he was hoisted to the top of the bonfire. The mayor, resplendent in gold chain, had stepped down and while the horses were led safely out of harm's way, he looked around him before solemnly approaching their small party and asking if Miss Venetia would honour them by lighting the bonfire.

She blushed and hesitated, then as the crowd surged around her, she ran forward, thrust the flaming torch into the heart of the brushwood and was quickly drawn back out of danger by Perry Conway.

There was a pause while the crowd waited breathlessly, then the dry tinder caught fire and began to blaze up to loud cheers.

It was only then amid the dancing flames that Isabelle caught sight of Jonty again. His eyes lit fitfully by the blaze of the fire were fixed on Guy, who was unaware of him until he spoke.

'I wonder you have the damned impudence to show your face among decent folk.'

Anger flared through Isabelle at the injustice. She took a step between him and her brother.

'Let him be,' she said fiercely. 'Haven't you done him enough harm?'

'My brother is goin' to swing. Did you know that? The rope will be squeezin' out his life because of you and your brother and your fancy man who hadn't the guts to stand up and be counted.'

Guy started forward but was firmly put aside and Robert confronted the smuggler.

'Are you by any chance referring to me?' he said coolly.

Jonty was momentarily taken aback, then he took a step forward.

'Aye, it's you all right skulking behind the soldiers, kickin' the bread out of honest men's mouths.'

'I rather doubt the honesty,' said Robert ironically.

'Oh you do, do you? Your kind know how to twist words all

164

right. And what did you give her for information received? Tell me that. You're not the first, y'know, there have been others out to get what they can.'

'Is that so?'

'Aye, you ask her.' Jonty thrust his head forward, his voice low and vicious. 'You ask her who it was she met night after night down on them marshes.'

All around people were pushing forward, shouting, laughing, happy, but for an instant it was as if they were isolated, glaring at one another. Then Robert's fist shot out and caught Jonty a clean cut on the jaw with such force that he was sent sprawling backwards into the crowd, and at that precise moment the brushwood blew up into a sheet of flame enveloping the grotesque image with the cocked hat.

A triumphant yell broke from the enthralled mob as a firework exploded into a burst of stars and a flaming stave of wood flew through the air and landed on Jonty, knocking him back as he was struggling to his knees. Women screamed and drew back as the flame licked at him but with a lightning reaction Robert had grabbed it and flung it back into the bonfire before it had done more than singe the smuggler's loose shirt. One of his mates was helping the cursing Jonty to his feet.

'Better get him away before he causes more damage,' said Robert crisply and turned his back on them.

'God damn you!' screamed the humiliated Jonty but Robert was already shepherding his little flock through the crowd followed by Perry with his arm around Venetia who was protesting plaintively that she wanted to stay till the end.

'Better not. Seems a pity to spoil the evening with a vulgar brawl,' said Robert shortly.

'I can look after myself,' said Guy angrily. 'I don't need you to fight my battles.'

'It was not you I was concerned with, my dear boy, but I have never been able to stand bullies.'

They fought their way to the carriages while fireworks exploded to shouts and yells and a resounding roar as the effigy slowly sank into the molten heart of the fire.

'You're not going yet, are you?' panted James coming after them. 'The fun has only just begun.'

'I'll see the ladies back to High Willows and leave you to follow when you wish,' shouted Robert.

Jason had managed to extricate the carriage from the others and they climbed into it. Perry and Venetia were so wrapped up in each other they seemed almost unaware of anyone else but themselves. Jonty's unexpected attack had shocked Isabelle, spoiling the evening's enjoyment. Prying eyes must have seen more of her and Lucien than she had expected, and innocent as their meetings had been, they had drawn their own conclusions. She felt numb and sick that it should have been thrown into Robert's face in such a vulgar fashion. She looked anxiously across at him. He had slipped his burned hand inside his coat and she felt guilty. She leaned forward.

'Is it very painful?'

'It's nothing, only scorched.'

'You shouldn't have done it.'

'I've seen what damage fire can do.'

'When we reach the house, you must let me treat it. I have some salve Miss Holland gave me that will draw out the inflammation.'

'Very well, if you must.'

He gave her his warm friendly smile and it comforted her a little.

The drawing room, with the musicians still playing softly, Sir Joshua seated at the whist table with some of the older gentlemen and the ladies quietly chatting, seemed a haven of peace after the noise, excitement and heat of the crowds at the Carnival.

Aunt Augusta was frowning disapprovingly at the black smudges on Venetia's expensive gown of pink mousseline-de-soie but for once the girl was too excited and too elated at being chosen to light the bonfire to pay much heed to her mother's scolding.

A cold collation was being served for those who wanted it and while she and Perry were giving a spirited account of all that had happened, Isabelle hurried up to her room and returned with a pot of ointment and some bandage.

'It really isn't necessary,' protested Robert.

'Yes, it is,' she took his hand in hers. 'It will be raw by tomorrow.'

The palm and fingers had begun to blister already. Very gently she spread on the salve and then covered it with a gauzy bandage.

'Does that feel better?'

'Much more comfortable certainly. Now come and eat with me. I may need assistance.'

But she shook her head, dreading what else might be said and the questions that could be asked.

'I must go and find Beth,' she said hurriedly. 'She has been shut up all day, poor darling.'

She ran down to the yard outside the kitchens, released the dog from the shed where she had been chained and took her out into the gardens.

It was very late and most of the lanterns had already burned out. A fresh salty breeze blew across the marshes from the sea and she pulled her shawl closely around her and walked quickly, glad to be alone, to have time to think, time to make up her mind. She still couldn't believe in Robert's proposal of marriage. It couldn't be true. He must have been jesting in his ironic way, and then James's interruption and the trip to the Carnival had made any further private conversation impossible. She had thought at first he was about to suggest a post in his sister's household, companion perhaps or something of that sort, but marriage! And what was going to happen now? Would he repeat the proposal with Jonty's vile insult thrown at him and if he did, would she accept? No, no, she couldn't, she was sure of that. Her pride, the pride of an ancient family, rose up against it even though it spelled escape and meant she and Guy need not be parted. But she didn't *know* him, didn't *love* him and what did he feel for her? Compassion, pity for the poor creature for whom something must be done? It never struck her that he could be in love. He was not like Perry, all hands and feet and bumbling adoration, and why should he love a French waif when she had so little to recommend her and was burdened with a teenage brother when presumably he could take his pick of society if he chose. It was incredible, it was crazy, there must be something behind it, but what?

For one rebellious moment she saw Aunt Augusta's face if she was mad enough to accept him – the look of baffled fury, the cold rage, that she, the outcast, the despised, had won the prize she had so passionately desired for Venetia. She laughed aloud at the very idea, though she knew it could never happen.

Round and round raced her thoughts as she walked on and on till the sudden screech of some night bird woke her from her abstraction and she realised how far she had come and how very dark it was. No moon had yet risen and suddenly without any real reason she was frightened. Something, or was it someone, was moving stealthily among the shrubs bordering the path and Beth growled. The memory of Jonty's savage bitterness flashed across her mind. Was it he lying in wait for her or for Guy? Panic-stricken, she picked up her skirts and ran, arriving back in the kitchen courtyard badly out of breath, and leaned against the door a little ashamed of her foolishness.

No lights showed in the house. Everyone must have gone to bed. Then a candle wavered in the kitchen and Gwennie peered out of the door.

'Oh there you are, Miss Isabelle. I knew as you were out and I've been waitin' up for you.'

'I'm sorry. I didn't realise how late it was.'

'They'll be dancin' and singin' down at the Carnival till all hours I shouldn't wonder.' The girl sounded envious. 'Did you enjoy it, Miss?'

'The fireworks were splendid.'

'Mr James has just come in, right far gone he is. I heard him shoutin' for Jason out in the yard and falling up the steps, wonder he didn't wake the Master. That niece of Cook's, that Mary Jane was laughin' and gigglin' with him, not decent it weren't, and so I told her.'

Mary Jane was a new recruit for this busy week, a pert, saucy young woman who in Gwennie's opinion needed a good slap down.

168

'You go on up, Gwennie,' whispered Isabelle. 'I'll lock up.'

'Don't mind if I do, Miss. I shan't be sorry to see my bed tonight. It's been a day and a half one way and another.'

'You must be worn out. I'll just see that Beth has a drink of water then I'll be coming up too. Goodnight, Gwennie.'

'Goodnight, Miss.'

The girl took the candle and climbed slowly up the three flights of stairs to the servants' quarters on the top floor.

Isabelle filled Beth's waterbowl and found her a sweet biscuit as a special treat and then took her own way up to her bedroom. She paused for a moment on the landing. A door slammed on the floor above and there was the sound of a man's slurred voice swearing and protesting. Isabelle smiled. Mary Jane was not proving such easy game as some of the other girls had done. She was a provocative little piece, not above leading the men servants on and then turning her back on them just when they believed her ready for a bit of fun. Now obviously it was James's turn to get the slap in the face. Serve him right! She was just thinking she might take a peep into Guy's room and make sure everything was well with him after the night's exertions when James came lurching down the stairs. He swung her round to face him.

'What are you doing up so late, coz?' he said thickly. 'On your way to someone's bed or just come from it?'

'Oh don't be so silly, James. You're drunk.' She tried to push him away. 'Go to bed and sleep it off.'

'Not so fast, my pretty little Belle. You know how to pick 'em, don't you? A French pirate and now a high-minded Scot – you're aiming for the top this time, aren't you? What about a favour or two for your loving cousin?'

He pulled her closer and Beth gave a warning growl.

'Still got that damned bitch under my feet.'

He swung a booted foot and caught the dog a glancing blow. Beth yelped and backed away.

'Stop it, James, for goodness sake! You'll wake the whole house up.'

But now he had an arm around her waist and treated her to

a slobbering kiss that tasted of brandy and it was more than she could bear.

'Go away, James, leave me alone,' she said angrily, struggling to free herself but he persisted, one hand tugging at her dress as he nuzzled into her neck.

The landing was narrow and the stairs to the floor below only a few feet away.

She thrust him away from her. He was already unsteady. He staggered back a few paces and tripped over Beth. Isabelle made a frantic effort to grab his arm but he was too heavy for her and fell head first all the way down the stairs.

He lay in a crumpled heap on the landing below and she stood staring at him appalled. Was he dead? Had she killed him? Surely it wasn't possible. She ran down the stairs and knelt beside him. He was breathing heavily but his head fell back helplessly when she tried to raise him. Oh God, what had she done to him? She couldn't leave him lying there like that. She had to do something but what? She shrank from rousing her uncle, dreading the questions and the explanations.

She stood up trembling. All was silent around her. Everyone must be sleeping heavily after the tiring day. She was trying to think, wondering whether to rouse Guy, when her eye fell on the faint streak of light showing under one of the doors. She stared at it for a moment before she realized it must be Robert's room, one of those she had herself helped to prepare a few days before. He must still be awake. Without stopping to think and desperate for help, she stole quietly along the passage and tapped nervously on the door.

Robert in shirt and breeches was lying on the bed, the candles still burning, a book in his hand, though he was not reading. He was thinking back over the evening and cursing himself, first for blurting out a proposal without properly leading up to it, and secondly for allowing himself to lose his temper with that foul-mouthed smuggler, an action that in this small community would be bound to cause trouble and could do harm to Isabelle.

He heard the quiet knock, waited for a moment and then slid off the bed and went to the door. Isabelle's face, white and distracted in the faint light from the candles, stared up at him.

170

'Good God, what's wrong?' he whispered.

'It's James,' she faltered. 'I think I've killed him.'

'What! Ssh, quiet now.' He drew her just inside the door. 'Tell me what has happened.'

'He was trying to . . . trying to . . .' She was shaking so much she could scarcely get the words out. 'I pushed him away and he tripped over Beth – I tried to hold him but he fell headlong down the stairs and now he – he doesn't move.'

'All right, all right now, keep calm. I'll come with you. Where is he?' He fetched the two-branched candlestick by his bed and went with her along the dark passage. 'Here, hold the candle while I take a look at him.'

He knelt down, turning James to face him. After a moment or two he glanced up at her.

'Don't worry. He's not dead, far from it. Tell me, had he had too much to drink?'

'I think so.'

'Fate is kind to the inebriated,' he said drily, 'they fall easily. He's given himself a crack on the head and he'll have a filthy headache tomorrow but he'll do. Where is his room?'

'Along the passage just beyond yours.'

'Right. Here we go.'

Robert was far stronger than he appeared. He hauled James up on his feet and with Isabelle going before with the candle, he half carried, half dragged him along the corridor and in through the opened door. She whipped off the coverlet and he hoisted him on to the bed.

Together they stripped off his coat and embroidered waistcoat and pulled off his boots. Robert unwound the starched neckcloth and opened his shirt.

'What happened?' muttered James muzzily. He was semi-conscious by now and feeling extremely sorry for himself.

'You fell down the stairs and gave yourself a bump on the head,' said Robert crisply.

He took the linen towel that Isabelle had wrung out in the water jug and put it across the young man's forehead.

James closed his eyes. 'It was that damned dog,' he said irritably. 'I feel terrible. It hurts like hell.'

171

'It probably will. You're lucky not to have broken your neck. Look more carefully how you go in future.' Robert threw one of the blankets over him. 'Best put the basin handy,' he said quietly to Isabelle. 'He may very well vomit later.'

'Shall we leave a light?'

'Better not in the state he's in. We don't want him to burn the house down.'

'Will he be all right?' she asked anxiously.

'He'll wish he'd never been born for an hour or two but that won't do him any harm,' said Robert unsympathetically. 'Come along. Let's leave him to his dreams.'

He took Isabelle's arm, picked up the heavy candlestick and they went out together, closing the door quietly behind them.

Now that it was all over, she swayed, feeling suddenly weak with exhaustion.

'Steady now.' Robert put an arm around her shoulders. 'Don't fret. He won't remember much about it in the morning. He'll be too busy nursing his bruises.'

Outside his bedroom door they paused for a moment.

'I'm so grateful to you,' she whispered. 'I don't know what I would have done if you hadn't been still awake.'

'Luckily I was. I don't sleep well after days like that, and what were you doing up and about so very late?'

'I took Beth for a walk and went much further than I intended.'

He put back the damp dark hair straying across her face and kissed her forehead gently.

'Go to bed now. Tomorrow we must talk.'

'Must we?'

'Yes, my love, we must.'

He was looking down at her with an expression she could not read, love, tenderness, a touch of humour, and in her weariness she had an immense desire to yield to him, to give up, to let someone else take up the burdens, the worries and anxieties. And it was at that moment of stillness, when they were standing so close together, Robert's arm still around her shoulders, that a door opened at the end of the corridor and Sir Joshua appeared, large, formidable, in his brocaded dressing gown.

172

'What's going on?' he said in a harsh whisper. 'What's happened, what's all this commotion? Isabelle, what are you doing up at this hour?'

His eyes had gone from one to the other, taking in Isabelle's dishevelled look and Robert's state of undress. It was easy to read what was in his mind.

'I'm afraid it was your son, Sir Joshua,' said Robert easily, making no effort to move away from Isabelle. 'He had an accident. Tumbled down the stairs and hit his head. Isabelle saw the light from my room and came to ask my help.'

'Is he hurt?'

'Nothing to speak of. A few bruises he'll be sorry about in the morning. Between us we got him to his room and made him as comfortable as we could.'

'I see. Go to bed, Isabelle. I'll speak to you in the morning.'

'Yes, Uncle.'

She fled up the stairs to where Beth was still patiently waiting for her. With her hand on the latch, she heard her uncle say heavily, 'I shall also require a word with you, my lord.'

'Certainly, Whenever you wish.'

'Very well. I'll just go and take a look at the boy.'

He stalked along the passage while Robert looked up at Isabelle with a tiny humorous shrug of his shoulders before he disappeared into his bedroom.

She thought she would lie awake for hours, the day's events churning over and over in her mind, but surprisingly once in bed she was enveloped in a blanket of fatigue so deep that nothing any longer seemed to have any importance, not even the grim look on her uncle's face. Tomorrow would have to look after itself.

She woke to Beth standing on her hind legs, licking her face and asking to be let out. She scrambled off the bed, opened the door for her and realised that it must be very late. She dressed quickly and ran downstairs where all was bustle that morning.

Those guests who had stayed overnight were preparing to leave. While his aunt was speaking to Lady Brydges, Lieutenant Conway had contrived to get Venetia to himself for a few minutes. Isabelle wondered whether promises for the future were being made between them and what would come of it if they were. Last farewells were said and the carriages rolled away down the drive. Sir Joshua retired to the library and she saw Robert go with him.

'Don't stand there idle, girl,' said her aunt sharply. 'There's a great deal to be done if we are to leave for Bath by the end of the week. Tell the servants they can start work on the bedrooms immediately. Where is James this morning?'

'I don't think he is feeling very well,' she said carefully. 'Gwennie will have taken his breakfast up to him.'

'Is he sick? Should I go to him?'

'I don't think it is serious. He was in very late last night.'

'Oh and how do you know that?'

'I was still awake. I heard him.'

'I see.'

Her aunt frowned. Sir Joshua had evidently not yet told her about what had happened and dreading any more awkward questions, Isabelle made her escape down to the kitchens, passing on the orders and looking for Beth. At any moment now the summons might come from her uncle. What was he saying to Robert at this very moment? And it was all James's fault. If she had been sensible she would have left him lying there.

She slipped out into the garden calling for Beth but she was nowhere to be seen. Beth was a home-loving dog and rarely strayed far afield. It worried her and she went further down the garden path looking for her. She had not gone very far when Mary Jane came racing after her.

'The Master's askin' for you, Miss, and you'd best hurry 'cos he looks black as the devil.' The girl fell in beside her as they walked back to the house, her face alive with curiosity. 'He's on about something. Is it what happened last night? Master James was in very late, wasn't he? I heard the commotion he made – outside my door, it was,' she gave a little giggle, 'sauce, I call it, carrying on like that. What was he up to?'

'You should know better about that than I do,' said Isabelle coldly.

The girl tossed her head. 'You don't need to be so uppity

174

about it. I'm sure we're all entitled to a bit o' fun now and then.'

She went off in a huff and Isabelle nerved herself to run up the stairs and knock at the library door. She stepped inside the room and then stood still for an instant. Robert was standing with his back against the window and she could not see his face clearly. Aunt Augusta was beside her uncle's desk, thin lips compressed, a look of baffled fury on her face. It was so exactly as she had imagined the night before that she had a crazy desire to laugh.

Sir Joshua said testily, 'Come in, girl, come in.'

Something must have taken him by surprise because he was not his usual autocratic self. He glanced at Robert and then at his wife before he spoke.

'After what happened last night what I have to say may not altogether surprise you,' he said heavily. 'Viscount Kilgour has done you the honour of asking for your hand in marriage.'

And quite suddenly and devastatingly she thought she understood everything very clearly. Her uncle's detestable assumption and Robert's mistaken sense of honour had obliged him to offer marriage – or did he see it as a way of forcing her hand after she had refused his proposal yesterday? Whatever the truth of it, the Sauvigny pride, that had once sent an ancestor to the stake rather than give up his principles, now rose up in her against it. She was innocent of any wrong-doing, she was not in need of anyone's protection. She was a person in her own right, not a sinner who had to be hastily rescued.

She said firmly and clearly, 'I am grateful to Lord Kilgour for his offer, very grateful, but I could not possibly accept it.'

'Are you crazy, girl?' exclaimed Aunt Augusta. 'Don't you realise how very fortunate you are? After the way you have been behaving you should go down on your knees and thank God for what is being offered to you.'

'And how *have* I behaved? What is it I am supposed to have done, what crime have I committed? I know how much you have always despised me and Guy. I know you bitterly regret the day we were driven to take refuge in your house. Every day, every hour, we have eaten the bitter bread of humiliation but

175

not any longer. We will go our own way, we will stand on our own feet, we don't need pity from anyone.'

She was shaking with outraged pride, the words pouring out in a fiery flood leaving her breathless. Without waiting for an answer she turned sharply and ran out of the room, so flushed and so furious she hardly realised where she was going, the door slamming behind her so that she did not hear Robert exclaim 'Isabelle!' and then turn angrily on Sir Joshua, 'God damn it, did you have to put it to her like that!' before he had flung open the door and followed after her.

'I can't believe this is happening to us,' exclaimed Aunt Augusta. 'Is he out of his mind to offer marriage to that chit of a girl, to make her his wife after all I have done, to choose *her* when he could have had Venetia.' Her voice was shaking with outrage at the slight on her daughter. 'What can he possibly see in her? It is beyond me. I cannot understand it.'

'I can,' said her husband unexpectedly. 'I have seen it in her all along. She has some quality, call it witchcraft, sorcery, whatever you like, but it is there, and beside her Venetia is pretty enough but commonplace. Her mother possessed it. Clarissa had the power to bewitch and bedevil – I know that to my cost.'

His wife stared at him. 'That is absolute nonsense, and how can you speak of your own daughter like that? You should be ashamed.' Then she braced herself as if to meet a challenge. 'One thing is certain. She must be forced to marry him. If we can't have him for Venetia's husband, then at least it will be *our* niece who has captured such an extremely eligible young man. I'll turn it to our advantage, never fear.'

But for once Sir Joshua, who rarely had a thought for anyone or anything beyond the advantage of himself or his family, revolted against his wife's cold-blooded determination to rescue what she could from the wreckage of her hopes.

'It would be an excellent match for her,' he said gruffly, 'but all the same I'll not have her forced against her will. Do you understand? Go gently, Augusta,' and the note in his voice warned her that this time he was in deadly earnest.

*

Outside the library Robert paused, uncertain which way Isabelle would have gone. Would she lock herself in her own room or would she seek her usual refuge, running out of the house and down to the sea? The latter seemed to him the most likely so he went out of the door and round to the stables, taking the path that led through the gardens to the marsh. He had been steadily cursing himself for his clumsiness. In every way he had blundered, but he seemed to have been rushed from event to event without having time to consider the best method of dealing with it.

Wasn't it utterly absurd that a man who could interpret the subtlest nuances in the most delicate of foreign politics, who was accustomed to tortuous exchanges with tricky foreigners, and who had in various disguises negotiated all kinds of difficult assignments, should have failed so utterly in matters that concerned his heart and his private life?

She must have been running quickly because he was through the park gates and on to the bridle path before he saw her. She was standing absolutely still and looking up into the branches of a solitary tree growing on the edge of Denge marsh. Something dark and ominous like some monstrous fruit was hanging from it and he redoubled his pace until he could see more clearly. The sheer savagery of it shocked him. Someone had slipped a noose around Beth's neck and then strung it over the high branch of the tree. The dog hung, paws limp, her head pathetically pulled to one side, the tongue lolling.

Isabelle was staring up at it, her face so white he thought she would faint.

'Do something,' she whispered, 'Please, please do something.'

He hunted for a small knife in an inner pocket and sawed through the thick cord with difficulty. He caught the dog's body in his arms and lowered it gently to the ground. Isabelle fell on her knees beside it.

'Is she . . . is she . . .?'

He knelt beside her. 'I'm afraid she is dead.'

'Oh God, who could do such a wicked thing!' With trembling fingers she unfolded the paper that had been looped through Beth's collar.

The letters were crudely printed. 'So die all traitors.'

'It's Jonty because of his brother, but to do this to Beth who never did any harm, who loved everybody.'

She dragged the dog's head up and held it against her, shaken by great sobs.

Robert said nothing, simply waited till the first spasm had spent itself. Then he pulled out a handkerchief and put it into her hands. The tears were running freely down her face and she seemed to realise for the first time who it was kneeling beside her.

'Why are you here?' she asked.

'I followed you.' He paused and then said urgently, 'Marry me, Isabelle. Let me take you away from all this.'

The rebellious anger had vanished now, leaving her shaken and sick. She looked away from him.

'It's not just because of last night.'

'No, no. That has nothing to do with it. I love you, Isabelle, can't you believe that?'

'But why should you when I have nothing – I am nothing.'

'You are yourself, you are everything that I want.'

It was as if this last outrage, so senseless and so cruel, was pushing her towards him but she had to be absolutely honest. The thought of Lucien was in her mind, those moments she had spent with him when the very air had seemed to stand still in ecstasy. But that was over. She must not think of that any longer.

She said bravely, 'I don't love you, Robert. You must understand that.'

He turned her face towards him. There were tears in her eyes still. They spilled over and ran down her cheeks. He touched them gently with one finger.

'You will, my darling, you will.'

For an instant she could not move, filled with a kind of terror at the inevitability of what she had promised.

Then she said, 'Will you help me with Beth?'

He got up, raising her to her feet and then lifting the heavy dog into his arms.

At the stables Jason met them, shocked when he saw what

178

Robert carried, and swearing under his breath at bastards who took out their revenge on a harmless dog.

'I'll bury her, Miss,' he said gently, 'nice and proper, down by that grassy patch where she liked to lie in the sun.'

'Thank you, Jason,' said Isabelle tonelessly. 'I'll fetch her blanket so that you can wrap her in it.'

The groom watched them walk away. If that tight-mouthed chap, Ian Mackie, was right, his master was sweet on Miss Isabelle. He only hoped that if it were so, he'd do the proper thing by her. Some of these top-lofty fellows from London had funny notions. He sighed, then lifted the body of the dog into the wheelbarrow and fetched a spade.

Robert was saying, 'I'm afraid there are a great number of matters we must discuss.'

'Not now, not now please.'

All her firm resolutions had been blown to the winds in the last half hour. She had to have time to reconcile herself to it.

'Very well, so long as I have your promise.'

'Oh yes, yes.'

He took her hand, kissed the palm and closed her fingers over it.

'That is to seal it. I'm a hard man. I don't give up easily and I shall hold you to it,' he said smiling and let her go.

He turned back to the stables, intending to give that fellow Jason a few guineas and ask him to put a small stone on the dog's grave with her name on it. That would please Isabelle.

He was aware of an enormous feeling of elation, sublimely confident that he could win her to love and passion. He would have liked to take her away now, carry her to London, put her in his sister's care and marry her as soon as it could be arranged, but he knew that in his position it would almost certainly cause scandal and for her sake that was the last thing he wanted. She had suffered enough already. There were going to be problems, God knows, Marian to be reconciled *and* his father, though at Glenmuir he felt pretty sure of his grandmother's support. There was the work that so often took him away but, thank God, a peace would be signed in a few months and even if it did not last, it would give him breathing space. There was Sir

Joshua to be reckoned with and his abominable wife who, he was quite sure, would milk every advantage she could from his marriage and for Isabelle's sake he must tolerate it.

Jonty's jibes he had discounted entirely, and if just now and then a tiny thread of uneasiness stirred, he ignored it. It was only later, much later, that it would grow into significance. At that moment he refused to give it a second thought.

9

'Marry him! He has asked you to marry him!' exclaimed Guy that afternoon, and gave a long low whistle of surprise. 'By Jupiter, that's put paid to Aunt Augusta's little plans, hasn't it?'

'It's hardly a laughing matter,' said Isabelle frowning at him.

'No, by God, it isn't!' he went on, sobering immediately. 'It's dashed serious. When did all this happen? You've kept very quiet about it.'

'He asked me first just before we went to the Carnival.'

'And you refused him?'

'Yes, I did.'

'Why, for heaven's sake, it was the answer to all our problems.'

'Oh Guy, if you can't see how impossible it seemed . . .' She paused looking away from her brother. 'Then after that terrible thing happened to Beth, he asked me again.'

'I'm not going to let Jonty get away with that, I'm damned if I am,' said Guy explosively. 'Of all the filthy low-down tricks . . .'

'No, Guy, please don't do anything. There has been enough trouble already. Beth is dead and nothing will bring her back.'

'I'm sorry, Belle, I really am truly sorry. I know how fond you were of her.' He paused and then said awkwardly, 'See here, you're not marrying this Armitage fellow just because of what happened to me, are you? I mean – it's your life – and I wouldn't want you to be unhappy for my sake. It's I who should be taking care of you.'

'I know, dearest, and I know you would if you could. Oh it's not just you, it's everything that has happened here these last few months and now . . .'

'It's a way of escape.'

'Yes, I suppose it is,' she said slowly, 'and that is what worries me.'

'It's not because of something that happened last night, is it?'

She looked at him quickly. 'What do you know about that?'

'Nothing really, but I thought I heard some kind of commotion and today James is going about looking as if he were ready to kill someone and . . . I thought he might have been pestering you.'

'Well, he did come in drunk and there was a bit of a scuffle. He fell down the stairs and I had to get Robert to help me with him,' she said a little reluctantly.

'I see.' Guy had a great deal more perception than his sister gave him credit for, but he didn't press her. He simply said, 'You do like him, don't you, Isabelle? Because if you don't, you must call it off. Tell him you've changed your mind, had second thoughts. I'll back you up.'

'No, I can't, not now. I've given him my promise and I won't go back on it. I just wish we could go off somewhere far away from here and be quietly married.'

'I don't,' said Guy with a boyish glee that made her smile. 'I wouldn't miss the look on Aunt Augusta's face when you walk down the aisle on his arm for anything in the world!'

The news had spread rapidly. Gwennie was frankly delighted and so were most of the servants, always ready to champion the underdog against the unpopular master.

Venetia said discontentedly, 'My goodness, you're a sly one, I must say. Is this what you've been angling for all along?'

'No, it isn't. It came as a complete surprise.'

'You accepted him quickly enough. You jumped at it.'

'I didn't, not at first.'

'Oh don't think I blame you.' Venetia was in an awkward mood. She had not really wanted Robert despite her mother's constant pressure but she would have liked what he could give her, and she resented the fact that he had so obviously preferred the cousin whom she had been brought up to regard as inferior to herself.

182

She looked at Isabelle curiously. 'Are you in love with him?'

'I wouldn't have consented to marry him if I didn't like him.'

'You might have done. After all he is quite a catch, isn't he?'

'That's a horrible thing to say.'

'It's true though, not like my poor Perry.'

Isabelle turned to look at her. 'I've never really asked you, but how much do you care for Perry Conway, Venetia?'

'I don't know. I'm not sure,' she said doubtfully. 'When I'm with him, I care very much. You know, Isabelle, he asked Papa again and was refused. Papa actually told him that if he persisted, he would forbid us to meet or write to one another and I don't think I could bear that. You see,' she went on with a sudden burst of unusual candour, 'Perry's father died last year and his elder brother inherited the family house in Wiltshire, so he only has a small allowance and his pay as a navy officer. His aunt has promised to make him her heir, but if I defied Papa and ran away with Perry he wouldn't give me a penny, and until Lady Ravenswood dies we would have to live in a tiny cottage or in lodgings at Portsmouth or Chatham or somewhere with all the other navy wives.'

'If you love him, wouldn't that be enough?'

'Oh it's all very easy for you, you've never had anything so you would know how to manage and wouldn't miss it, but it's different for me. Oh why is life so unfair! Why couldn't it be the other way round? You'd have married Robert if he wasn't the son of an Earl, wouldn't you?'

'Yes, I think I would,' said Isabelle thoughtfully.

'And now it's you who will be rich and I who'll have nothing.'

'Don't you believe in Perry's career? He could be an Admiral one day.'

'Not now he couldn't, not when they are talking about making peace. He'll be on half pay.' For a brief moment the girls had grown close to one another, then Venetia gave a hard little laugh. 'Oh well, Mamma says there are plenty of other men and I suppose she's right. Perhaps when you're a grand lady in society, you will introduce me to some of them.'

'Don't hate me for it, Venetia.'

'I ought to, sometimes I wish I could,' then unexpectedly she burst into tears and ran from the room, slamming the door after her.

Three days later in Arlington Street, Marian was looking down at the fat package from her brother, delivered that evening by Ian Mackie, and slit it open with nervous fingers. The first glance at the closely written page confirmed her worst fears.

'My dear Marian,' Robert had written, 'I want you to be the first to hear the good news. Isabelle has consented to become my wife.'

'Oh no,' she exclaimed aloud, 'Oh no, I don't believe it, I won't believe it!' and then looked up to see the groom regarding her with grave concern. 'You'd best get down to the kitchen, Ian,' she went on quickly, 'you'll be needing food after your long journey.'

'I'm to take back an answer, my lady.'

'Very well. It's late now. You can hardly return tonight. I'll write to my brother and you can leave early tomorrow morning.'

'I'll do that, Miss Marian.'

She stopped him on his way to the door. 'How did Mr Robert seem when you left him?'

'In the best of spirits, Miss. Never seen him so pleased with himself.'

'I see. Well, go now and get yourself some supper.'

'I will that. Thank you, my lady.'

She went back to her reading with mixed feelings.

'I have enclosed letters to Father and Grandmother,' Robert went on, 'which perhaps you will be kind enough to despatch by the London Mail. I am obliged to remain here for a few days as there are certain matters to be discussed with Sir Joshua. Lady Brydges is insisting on making all kinds of preparations and talks of bringing Isabelle to London for bridal clothes when, God knows, I'd be more than willing to marry her in her shift.'

'Oh Robert, you're mad,' she murmured to herself, 'stark staring mad!'

'I'm insisting on being married by the end of September at latest. Will that suit you, dear sister? I want you to be as happy about this as I am myself.'

184

That remained to be seen but she had her doubts.

She summoned a servant and ordered him to make sure the letters for Scotland caught the night mail and was still pondering her own reply when David Fraser called, fresh from his journey into Kent and in excellent spirits.

'You're too late,' she said accusingly as he came to greet her. 'They are engaged.'

'Are they, by George?'

'And in less than six weeks they will be married.'

'I'm not altogether surprised. The glimpse I had of them together I never saw a man so besotted.'

'Did he know you were there?'

'Lord, no. It was Carnival and I've had plenty of experience in disguising myself. Some rough spoken fellow, a fisherman by the look of him, made a few jibing remarks and Robert gave him an upper cut as clean as a whistle, sent the chap sprawling, reminded me of the days when he and I used to box with the Champion.'

'But what about the girl?' she asked impatiently.

'Well, I had no actual conversation with her but she is well thought of locally: Sir Joshua is regarded as an old skinflint, the wicked uncle if you like, and she is the damsel in distress and she's got the looks all right, not pretty, not conventional at all and dressed like a schoolgirl but eyes that haunt you, a most disturbing beauty that hits you right where it hurts most and I've seen a few in my time, you know.'

How like a man, thought Marian disgustedly, not to look below the surface, even David worldly-wise as he is. The girl was undoubtedly a clever designing minx, acting the innocent victim, with her sharp little claws embedded in her infatuated brother.

Unhappily their first meeting did little to correct the opinion she had formed. It was a fortnight or so later that Lady Brydges called one afternoon, bringing Isabelle with her. Unfortunately Robert was not there. An urgent meeting had called him away that morning.

'Be nice to her,' he said to his sister before he left, 'be kind. She will be very shy of meeting you.'

'I wonder!' she said to herself, grimly awaiting their arrival in the drawing room in her elegant gown of dark blue silk with no ornament except the small diamonds in her ears, and looking so severe and so uncompromising that Isabelle quailed at sight of her. This was the sister Robert spoke of with such affection and with whom he hoped she would make friends.

She was aware of the instant dislike and it had the effect of making her stiff and tongue-tied. If Marian had already decided against her, then she was not going to crawl simply to win her approval.

She had spent a hateful week dragged from dressmaker to dressmaker, Aunt Augusta sweet as honey when they ran into acquaintances and boasting about the coming marriage till she didn't know where to look.

'These young people, you know, it was love at first sight, it's so romantic, nothing would satisfy dear Robert but an early marriage. We are all quite *bouleversé* over it, aren't we, Isabelle?'

And in private, making sure she knew how much she grudged every penny that was being spent because it was not Venetia who was the star of the occasion. Her daughter would only be the bridesmaid and it riled her unbearably.

Oh God, thought Isabelle wearily, why had she ever consented to this marriage? If only they could have just gone quietly away somewhere. The only thing that made it tolerable was that Robert seemed to dislike the fuss as much as she did. But it was easy for a man. He could disappear into his Club, escape into male society, while she had to endure the spiteful looks of undisguised curiosity, sharp little barbs from Venetia, the constant sniping of Aunt Augusta.

She was talking about Robert now so gushingly that Isabelle could see Marian's lip curl and remained proudly aloof, shrinking further and further into herself.

There was only one moment during that dreadful afternoon when a spark of sympathy might have flashed between them.

Tea was over. It was time to leave and they had already risen to their feet when a footman inadvertently opened the door and two small spaniels came charging into the room.

'Oh, aren't they darlings!' exclaimed Isabelle and regardless of her pale blue muslin gown she fell on her knees and hugged the little dogs to her, fondling and petting them. 'Robert told me all about you.'

Aunt Augusta said sharply, 'Isabelle, whatever are you thinking of! Do forgive her, Lady Marian, but my niece is so very fond of dogs.'

'Really,' said Marian as Isabelle got to her feet, smoothing her crumpled dress while the two little dogs came, frisking to their mistress's feet. 'Edward has just brought them in from their walk. I hope they have not muddied your gown.'

'It's of no consequence. What do you call them?'

'Roland and Oliver.'

'From *The Chanson de Roland* – how perfect. Papa used to read it to Guy and me when we were children.'

'It was my brother who named them.'

Insufferable girl, trying to show off her literary knowledge. The momentary spark of sympathy was rapidly extinguished.

Afterwards in the carriage as they drove away, Aunt Augusta said, 'I must say, I don't envy you. Stiff as a ramrod and not giving an inch, that sister of his. You won't have an easy time with her, my girl, I can tell you that!'

And how pleased you are about it, thought Isabelle. Her aunt was hoping everything would go wrong with her marriage, but she wouldn't let it.

'Robert is very fond of his sister,' she said easily. 'And it seems she likes dogs, so we shall find something in common.'

Lady Brydges snorted. 'Dogs indeed! Well, it will be your problem and you who will have to deal with it.'

They were married at the beginning of October in Lydd's ancient church and at the impassioned pleading of the bride, the ceremony was conducted by the Reverend Gilbert Holland in his best lace-trimmed surplice over a new black silk cassock.

A preliminary peace treaty had been signed by the Foreign Secretary a few days before. Cheering jubilant crowds were still thronging the streets of London and coaches garlanded with laurel were carrying the good news to towns and villages throughout the country.

The austere grey walls, the tomb of Sir Walter Menil who had gone to the Crusades and actually returned to his wind-blown manor on the marshes, the sun shining through tall windows, had rarely looked on a more distinguished gathering, and Augusta Brydges gazed around her with a great deal of complacency, the only bitter and rankling regret that it was not her daughter who would be shortly standing at the altar.

Even she had been surprised at the high esteem in which Robert was held. There were few Kent families who could have mustered so many notable guests at a country wedding. Across the aisle the Prime Minister, Henry Addington, as inept in private life as he was in public, kept dropping his prayerbook. Beside him Lord Hawkesbury, who had signed that eagerly awaited peace treaty, still wore a worried frown. Henry Dundas, rubicund, jolly, with a distinctly roving eye, stood beside his friend and boon companion, William Pitt, tall, spare, with his long horse face and air of kind abstraction, and greatest prize of all, the guest who had aroused the greatest envy, the hero himself, Horatio Nelson, small, frail, in his magnificent uniform, the star and campaign medals blazing on his breast, his right sleeve tucked into his coat, the black patch over one eye. One had to be grateful of course that he hadn't brought his Emma with him. Naval and army uniforms seemed to fill the church and the brilliant gathering filled Isabelle with terror as she arrived at the porch with her brother beside her.

There had been a battle over his right to be there.

'Your uncle is your guardian,' Aunt Augusta had stormed. 'It is he who should give you away.'

'Guy is the Comte de Sauvigny, he represents my father,' Isabelle had said stubbornly and it was Robert who suggested a compromise. Sir Joshua should stand at the altar while Guy led her up the aisle.

She was seized with sudden panic as she looked up the long nave to where Robert waited with David Fraser beside him. Suddenly and frighteningly he had become a stranger. The last few weeks had gone by in a blur of preparation but now she faced reality. She was giving herself into the hands of a man she didn't really know, who had made promises he might not fulfil,

188

who would own her body and soul for the rest of her life. She had a crazy desire to drop the flowers in her hand, rip off the veil and run out of the church across the marsh and down to the sea, to be alone, to be still free. The hand she placed on her brother's arm trembled so much that he turned to look at her.

'What is it?' he whispered.

'Nothing.' But panic still held her, her feet were lead, she couldn't stir.

'Belle,' he said urgently, 'it is time.'

'Yes.'

She took a deep breath and they moved forward.

A ripple of anticipation ran through the guests as they craned to catch a glimpse of her through the gauzy veil. There had been talk, scandalous some of it. Everyone knew that Lord Glenmuir had flown into a rage at his only son daring to contract a hasty marriage without asking his consent, and had refused to make the journey from Scotland to attend the wedding. Those pushing people, Joshua and Augusta Brydges, were of course making the most of it.

Whatever was Robert Armitage thinking of to marry a penniless French chit with a dubious background whom nobody had ever heard of? She'd been a kind of servant in her uncle's household, hadn't she, and her brother, a stable boy or worse, though Heaven knows, he didn't look it. Had he put her in the family way and was now paying the price for it? Robert was surely too fly for that and it didn't look like it, the girl was slim as a willow wand, but there must be something.

All kinds of titillating rumours ran from one to the other, some of them coming from a stylishly dressed woman sitting beside a tall thin gentleman of French extraction, who was eyeing the guests with wry amusement through a gold-rimmed eyeglass. Leila Vernon was the widow of Admiral Sir Hugh Vernon and had never given up hope of winning Robert back to her bed. Curious eyes under delicately pencilled eyebrows examined the face of the bride as she came from the vestry, her hand on her new husband's arm. A pale face with a cloud of dark hair, large eyes with silky lashes that swept her cheek, slender as a lily and so very young. She felt every single one of her thirty-eight years.

Marian too was watching them as they passed by and for the first time unwillingly acknowledged that David could be right. The girl in that white satin gown sewn with pearls did possess a kind of rare beauty. She thought of Ondine, the water sprite who became a mortal and brought tragedy to herself and her lover. Isabelle too was unearthly, not quite human, and then Marian shook herself angrily. This young woman was all too human and quite obviously knew exactly what effect she was creating, and she refused to admit, even to herself, that part of her dislike was rooted in a sharp jealousy of the girl who had so easily stolen her beloved brother's heart.

Outside crowded the villagers who had come tramping in from all over the marshes. This was a rare sight and they were not going to miss a single minute of it, even if a cold wind blew in from the sea and overnight rain soaked into well-worn boots. They cheered as Isabelle appeared in the doorway. The children, well primed by Miss Holland, had gathered the last of the flowers from fields and hedgerows and showered them as they came down the steps while their elders nudged one another, arguing as to who was who and gaping at people they would never have had a chance to see in a month of Sundays.

There was one minor disturbance as they jostled one another for a good view. Robert and Isabelle moved towards the carriage where Jason waited, a white satin bow on his whip. A little knot of men were waiting close by in a tight bunch and one of them shouted derisively, 'Three cheers for the French whore and her fancy man!'

For an instant there was a frozen silence followed by such a fierce outcry that the little group thought it wise to disappear into the crowd and Robert, his face stonily calm, helped his wife into the carriage. He held her hand tightly as Jason whipped up the horses and they rolled away, followed by the other carriages and a long stream of the country folk making their way to High Willows where bread, meat and ale had been spread for them on this festive occasion.

A fair number of the distinguished guests, much to Augusta's disappointment, stayed only long enough to drink a glass of champagne, toast the happy pair, clap Robert heartily on the back and, in the case of Henry Dundas, give the bride a smacking kiss.

'I've known Robert since he was in short frocks,' he said in his jovial way. 'You have won yourself a bargain, young lady, and don't you forget it.'

'I won't, believe me, I won't.'

'Good, good.'

She was finding it a good deal easier to deal with these male colleagues of her husband than with their supercilious wives whose barbed comments and curious eyes swept her from head to toe and no doubt found her wanting.

At last there was a lull in the greetings. Robert had temporarily left her side and she stood for a moment alone near the window, glad of the cool air on her flushed cheeks.

'I don't think we have been introduced,' murmured a silky voice at her elbow, 'but I feel I must congratulate you. Robert and I are such very old friends.'

Isabelle turned to see Leila Vernon, poised, elegant, exquisitely dressed, smiling down at her.

'May I present the Chevalier Raoul de St George,' she went on. 'He is a compatriot of yours and is so very anxious to make your acquaintance. Raoul, this is Robert's lovely young wife, the former Isabelle de Sauvigny.'

'*Enchanté, Madame.*' He bowed over her hand. 'This is the first time I have ventured into this part of the country but not so long ago my young nephew had quite an amusing adventure here on the marshes.'

The dark eyes in the lean face were watching her, the thin lips had a faint curl of sardonic amusement, and her heart missed a beat.

'Indeed. What kind of adventure?'

'Ah who can tell? He likes to make a mystery of it.'

Was it Lucien he was speaking of? It had to be, and what kind of a tale had he been spinning about her?

Then Robert was back beside her, saying coolly, 'I had not expected to see you here, Chevalier. I always understood that the English countryside had little appeal to you,' and she knew by the ice in his voice that Robert did not like the Frenchman.

'True, true,' was the airy reply, 'but I received a very pressing invitation to escort a dear friend of yours and I could hardly refuse.'

'Darling Robert, how could I possibly miss congratulating you and your bride,' said Leila and leaning forward, kissed his cheek. 'It's so long since you've been to see me, naughty boy.'

For the very first time Isabelle saw Robert slightly disconcerted. He said stiffly, 'As you know very well, my work leaves me little time to spare, and now if you will excuse us, some of the guests are leaving and we should bid them farewell.'

He took Isabelle's arm and firmly led her away.

'Were those two annoying you?' he asked brusquely.

'No, not really, but I'm not sure I liked them very much.' She looked around her at the assembled guests, a little flushed now with food and wine. 'Robert, could we go now? Could we run away from all this?'

'Is that what you want?'

'Oh yes, yes please.'

She suddenly dreaded what she knew would follow. The old custom of bedding the bride and groom had long since been abandoned, but James and his friends would inevitably drink too much, there would be ribald comments, coarse jokes, rowdy laughter to be endured before they could leave.

Robert was more than ready to do as she wished, having no love of these country customs.

'If that's what you really want, then I'll look for David. He will find the carriage for us.'

'I'll change,' she said eagerly, 'Gwennie will help me. We can slip out through the garden door near the kitchens.'

'Won't we be seen?'

'Gwennie will make sure that we're not.'

They planned it like two conspirators.

'You didn't ought to be runnin' off like this,' whispered Gwennie, laying the white satin dress down carefully over a chair and helping her into the new gown of fine blue corded silk with lace ruffles at neck and sleeves. She picked up the heavy hooded velvet cloak and as she put it around her shoulders, Isabelle turned and hugged her tightly.

'Gwennie,' she said breathlessly, 'if my husband agrees, would you like to come to me later as my personal maid?'

'Me! Go up to London!' gasped Gwennie. 'Whatever would I be doin' in a grand place like that?'

'Just the same as you do here but much better.'

'That Lady Marian, his lordship's sister, she wouldn't like it,' said Gwennie doubtfully.

'I am his wife now. It will be for me to decide. Now I'll have to run. He will be waiting for me. You'll not say a word?'

'Trust me, Miss?' said Gwennie stoutly.

Never at a loss in circumstances of this kind, David was ready for them outside.

'I've got the carriage waiting half way down the drive. Come on, the pair of you, through the shrubberies or else you'll be seen.'

It was not the family carriage which had brought Robert and Marian but David's own small cabriolet with Ian Mackie in the driver's seat.

'Where to, sir?' he asked.

They were more like an eloping couple off to the Scottish Border, he thought, than two who had been decently and properly married only a few hours before. Good for Mr Robert.

'I may never come back here again,' whispered Isabelle. 'Would you think me crazy if I ask if I can take a last look at the sea?'

It was where she had always taken refuge, where she had run free with Beth, where he had seen her first like Aphrodite rising out of the waves. He smiled at the romantic notion.

'Why not? Ian, drive down to the Ship and Anchor and wait for us there. We are going to walk a little.'

'Very good, sir.'

The wind blew cool and salty but there were still a few rays of October sun and there was that warm amber glow that comes sometimes in the early autumn with a nutty smell of rotting leaves and a fragrant hint of wood smoke.

They walked hand in hand not speaking until she paused.

193

Far beyond the light house she could see the outline of the black hut where she had spent those rapturous hours with Lucien. She seemed to see him standing there with that handsome devil-may-care look of his and she felt again the kisses, the glow, the intense excitement. For a fleeting moment she was tempted to tell Robert, to pour out the whole story, but she still knew so little about Lucien or indeed about that other and darker side of the man she had married, and the words would not come. She did not realise then how much she was to regret her silence. She turned resolutely to Robert.

'Shall we go?'

'Happy?'

'Of course.'

He looked down into her face, a little troubled though he did not know why, then he bent and kissed her, a long searching kiss, before they turned back to the waiting carriage.

10

It was nine o'clock by the time they reached Canterbury, having changed horses at Ashford and galloped through the gathering dark. The Golden Lion was an old well-established hostelry that back in the middle ages might have welcomed Chaucer's pilgrims. Robert chose it deliberately. It was not on the direct route to London and no one would dream of following them there. The proprietor knew quality when he saw it and, if for a fleeting moment noting the small hand luggage he did wonder if they were perhaps an eloping couple, he asked no questions, simply showed them into a private sitting room with an adjoining bedchamber and enquired respectfully if they would be requiring supper.

'Are you hungry, my love?' asked Robert.

And Isabelle, who had scarcely eaten anything since six o'clock that morning and had endured a long wearying day, suddenly realised that she was starving.

A fire had been lit against the chill of the evening and the room, with its dark panelled walls and deep red curtains, was cosily welcoming. They supped simply on a dish of tender veal, a roasted chicken with home-grown vegetables and a luscious fruit pie topped with cream and drank the finest claret the cellar could provide that satisfied even Robert's discerning palate. Isabelle ate and relaxed, laughing with him over the events of the day, the humorous comments he made on some of the people she had met for the first time and idle speculation on Aunt Augusta's reaction to their sudden disappearance. Then the chambermaid came to say the fire was burning nicely in the bedroom, she had unpacked my lady's hand-luggage and did she require her services in preparing for bed.

'No,' said Isabelle quickly, 'No, thank you. I will look after myself.'

'Very good, my lady.'

The girl bobbed a curtsey and left with a sly glance at Robert and a giggle with the Boots outside in the passage.

'You go ahead,' said Robert, opening the inner door for her. 'I'll come later.'

She undressed slowly, meticulously folding each garment, shivering a little in her thin shift before dipping her face in the basin of water. The white lawn nightgown edged with lace made her look like a schoolgirl, young and innocent and virginal, and that was how Robert saw her when he came in, standing by the huge four-poster bed, shaking and frightened. He had undressed in the adjoining room. The dressing gown of brocaded silk hung open. She had seen Lucien naked and now in sudden panic she shut her eyes against Robert. He had seen that look of fear once before on the face of a young girl, not fear of himself but of the brute who had ravished her, and it was something that still occasionally haunted him. He shut the door and crossed to her, putting an arm around her shoulders and tilting up her chin to look at him.

'You don't need to be afraid. I won't hurt you.'

He lifted her on to the bed, then pinched out the candles, dropped the dressing gown across a chair and slid beneath the linen sheets beside her. He caressed her gently till the shaking stopped and she relaxed against him. Highly sensitive to her every mood, he was well aware that he aroused in her no answering response so that he held himself in check deliberately, not giving way to the urgent desire that surged within him lest he should frighten or distress her, not realising that she had once experienced the heady rush of passion and it might have been better for both of them if he had let his feelings sweep them away to the heights of fulfilment.

The next morning they set out for London and during the four days they spent at Arlington Street, Marian having discreetly arranged to stay in the country with friends, he realised ruefully that their present relationship was more like an elder brother indulging a much loved young sister than a newly

196

married couple on their wedding trip. She was nervous and unsure of herself, explored the house and made tentative advances to the servants who eyed her curiously, puzzled by this young girl so unlike the self-possessed fashionable young women to whom they were accustomed.

Robert was far more attached to his father than he was willing to admit and was determined that his bride should be both accepted and acknowledged by the head of the family. So they set out for Scotland after having spent a few days in which he had indulgently allowed himself to be dragged around the Tower of London, viewing the headsman's block with a suitable shiver, feeding the ravens and gaping at the lions, explored all the dusty tombs in Westminster Abbey, climbed to the very top of St Paul's with a horrible feeling of vertigo at the panorama spread before them and stood for hours on a draughty evening in St James's Park watching a firework display, which was decidely premature since there was a long way to go before the peace treaty would be finally ratified.

In many ways they dealt very happily together. They had the same interests, laughed at the same things and every day discovered new things about one another. Isabelle soon began to realise that Robert's quiet reserved manner hid an inner strength that commanded and received instant respect which extended to her as his wife. Living so restricted an existence and constantly humiliated, it was little wonder that she revelled in those first days in the care and attention he lavished upon her.

Ian Mackie was to travel with them to Scotland but Isabelle had refused absolutely to accept the lady's maid Marian had engaged as a suitable person to attend on her brother's wife.

'I'm not some grand lady,' she said, 'I can do everything for myself. Besides she looks down on me, Robert, because I am different and my father was not a duke. You can see it in her eyes. I would never feel free. If I must have someone to wait on me, then I'd like it to be Gwennie. When we come back to London, do you think Gwennie could come to us?'

He was doubtful of how the simple country girl would fit in with his supercilious London servants.

'Do you think she would want to leave High Willows?'

'She would come anywhere with me. She has been my friend ever since I first came from France. Please, Robert.'

She usually asked so little from him. 'You shall have anyone you please, my love. I will ask Marian to arrange it while we are away.'

For the first time since they had been driven out of their home, she could forget her anxieties about her brother.

There had been a fraught few minutes before they were married when Guy had proved unexpectedly difficult.

'You may shortly be my brother-in-law, Viscount Kilgour,' he said bluntly, 'but I've no intention of being a burden on your generosity and hanging like a millstone around your neck. If you take care of Isabelle, that's good enough for me. I can make my own way.'

'I've no intention of permitting you to become a burden,' was Robert's crisp reply, 'but neither am I prepared to allow your sister to worry herself to death over you as she has been doing for the last few months. If you'll pardon my saying so, you're too young and too ill-equipped for the kind of responsible post you might hold and I believe I can provide an answer to that.'

So Guy had been left in David's charge to take a crash course in languages and political history, and after that Robert was pretty sure of obtaining a minor government post for him which would give him the independence he longed for. He did not altogether approve of handing out sinecures to friends or relatives but on the other hand he had recognised the boy's touchy pride and thought he saw in him a potential for useful work in his own department.

'Go easy with him,' he said privately to David. 'If you try to patronise, he'll jump down your throat.'

'Never fear. I'll keep a light hand on the reins.' David looked at his friend curiously. 'I never quite saw you in the role of family man.'

'No? Well, there comes a time for everything,' he said easily and left it at that.

The long tedious journey to Glenmuir, which Robert had to endure at least once a year since his father refused to visit him in London, turned into weeks of unexpected pleasure chiefly due to Isabelle's delight in every new experience. She was so eager to see and explore and wonder that it had the effect of making him view the most ordinary events with new eyes. She never grumbled if the day's journey was long and tiring, if there were frustrating delays or if the inn was not so comfortable as it might be, the bed hard and the food not up to scratch, but accepted it all with gaiety and laughter as part of a new adventure.

They spent a couple of days in York to look over the Minster and wander in the city's ancient streets, and stopped at the border because Isabelle was curious to see where so many runaway couples had plighted their troth defying English law, sometimes with disastrous results.

'Venetia once said that she and Perry had thought of making a dash for it but I don't think she really meant it and Perry is far too sensible.'

'She would have had Papa storming at her heels if I know anything about your uncle.'

'Poor Venetia, she might have had you and now she has nothing. Robert, can't you do something for Perry Conway? Couldn't he be appointed Captain with a ship of his own?'

'My dear child, I'm not omnipotent and I have no influence so far as navy appointments are concerned. Henry Dundas might have helped for the sake of old friendship but he's out of office at the moment.'

'Perhaps she could marry David,' she went on thoughtfully.

Robert laughed aloud. 'Never! David is a born bachelor. He would never be induced to give up his freedom. Why worry yourself over your cousin, my love? She is very pretty and she will have a sizeable portion when she marries. She will never lack for suitors.'

'But she may not *like* them.'

He was already aware that Isabelle had a great fund of sympathy and thought for others. Maybe it was one of the qualities that had drawn him to her, and he had another and not altogether amusing example of it when they reached Edinburgh.

They stayed there for a few days, partly because he had business with the family lawyers and partly because it was a city he knew well and he wanted to show it to her.

On the last day of their stay he came in from a session in the lawyer's office to see Isabelle on her knees in their sitting room, an enormous apron tied over her walking dress, up to her elbows in lather and scrubbing away at a small, very grubby object in a large tin bath.

'What on earth is going on?' he demanded.

She didn't reply at once but lifted out a dripping little creature, enveloped it in a large towel and began vigorously to rub it dry. A maid-servant and a kitchen boy eyed him nervously and then began to drag the bath away between them.

Isabelle looked up at her husband a little shyly, cheeks flushed, eyes sparkling, determined to put a brave face on it.

'It was early this afternoon,' she said defensively, 'after you went out. I thought I'd take a walk down the Lawnmarket and in one of those narrow alleys they call wynds, I saw him. He was so small and so terrified, Robert, and two boys had him cornered and were pelting him with stones. I saw one of them give him a great kick and I couldn't stand it. I called to them to stop but they only laughed at me so I threw them all the money I had and while they snatched at it, I picked him up and ran. I had to – he looked so miserable. I couldn't just leave him, could I?'

The small squirming object had now turned into a white rough-coated little dog with pricked ears and a pair of soulful brown eyes. Some kind of highland terrier, he guessed, with a somewhat doubtful ancestry.

'And what do you propose to do with him?' he asked.

'I thought we might take him with us,' she ventured hesitantly. 'You see, I do miss Beth so terribly. I must have something of my own to care for and to love.'

'And what about your husband? Doesn't he need to be cared for and loved?'

It was spoken jestingly but there was a deeper meaning in it.

She looked up at him quickly. 'Oh but I do, I do. I'm so

terribly grateful to you. You give me so much. But, you see, this
poor little scrap has no one.'

'God forbid that I should look for gratitude,' he said
brusquely. 'If you really want a dog, I'll buy you one. What
would you prefer? A spaniel like Marian's Roland and Oliver?'

'I don't want a pampered lap dog,' she said obstinately, 'I
want this one. He needs me so badly.'

'Very well.' He sighed. 'Keep him if you must. We'd better
find out first if he belongs to anyone and I warn you that my
father's dogs will probably eat him.'

'I won't let them,' she said firmly.

So Rory as he was called after some discussion, went with
them in the carriage on their journey through the mountains to
the West Coast of Scotland and though she did her best to hide
it, she became more and more apprehensive of the ordeal that
lay before her.

They came to Glenmuir by way of Fort William and Glenfinnan.
The road sometimes ran along beside the waters of the loch and
sometimes climbed into the mountains turning and twisting.
Here and there sheep strayed across the road and they were
forced to slow down till they condescended to move away. She
was looking out of the carriage window at the magnificent
landscape of hills folded into one another in every shade of blue
and brown, while down below they could glimpse the bright
saffron weed fringing the loch turning a deep burning gold
under the October sun. They ran down through a forest of firs
and came again in sight of the sea where, separated from the
road by a waste of marshy bog, there rose a huge cairn of stones.

'This is Glenfinnan and it marks the spot where Prince
Charles landed in June 1745,' said Robert in answer to Isabelle's
question. 'My grandfather used to tell me about it when I was
a child. He was eighteen and he defied his father to join the
Prince on what seemed to him a great adventure. There were
only seven men with the Prince. They had rowed ashore from
the *Doutelle* weary and disheartened by the storms that had
ravaged them and the desertion of their French escort. They
were hungry and desperately tired. He told me how he helped

them to catch fish, how they cooked it over the white ash of a peat fire and ate it with their fingers. Six months later and the Prince was dancing in triumph at Holyrood and in a year it had all ended in tragedy at Culloden.'

'Would you have gone to join the Prince as your grandfather did?' she asked curiously.

'Perhaps, who can tell? There are no adventures like that nowadays. We are all too practical and level-headed,' and she thought he sounded regretful. Then the carriage jolted to a halt and he leaned from the window. 'Here is Bruce Macrae with the horses.'

They were to ride the last part of the journey while the carriage with their baggage took a more circuitous route by the only practical road.

Isabelle, warned by Robert, had dressed suitably in her riding habit. Bruce Macrae was a big rawboned man, sturdily independent, but the rugged face broke into smiles as he greeted Robert. Keen eyes under bushy eyebrows turned to her questioningly.

'Will your lady ride, sir, or will she be taking to the pillion?'

'Oh she will ride, Mac, you can be very sure of that.'

'Will she now?'

Macrae grunted as he led the mare forward and held out his hand.

'Welcome to Glenmuir, my lady,' he said as he lifted her into the saddle, and absurdly Isabelle felt that perhaps she had passed a minor test successfully. The next would be more formidable.

The first glimpse of Glenmuir almost took her breath away. On that desperately unhappy day when Beth died so horribly and Robert had asked her to marry him, it had all seemed so simple and uncomplicated. Now it hit her leaving her panic-stricken. One day, however distant, he would be Earl of Glenmuir and she would be expected to take her place beside him, chatelaine of this great castle, a position she felt woefully unfitted to fill.

She was looking down at a scene of remarkable beauty. The Atlantic came rolling in through creeks and small bays, meeting the waters of the loch in a swirl of white-tipped waves. The

202

castle was set on a spur of rock that seemed to thrust itself into the sea, its three towers topped with conical turrets, graceful, fairylike but immensely powerful. It was a clear bright day. Beyond the castle she could see the shapes of scattered islands, the hills of Eigg, the sharp ridge of the mountains of Mull.

'If the weather holds calm,' Robert was saying, 'we'll sail around the islands. I want to show you Iona . . . it is a place of ancient worship with a magic beyond anything you can imagine.'

The courtyard seemed to swarm with people when they rode into it, men and women, all surging forward to greet Robert and gazing at her with a frank and lively curiosity as he dismounted and lifted her from the saddle. Then through them came a tall young woman, her reddish hair wound into a coronet on her shapely head, wearing a plain but well-cut gown of deep green wool, and stretching out a hand to Robert.

'Welcome home, my lord.'

'Why so formal suddenly?' he said and laughed, bending forward to kiss her cheek. 'How are you, Jeannie, and how is my father?'

'Himself is in splendid health and looking for you all this past week. You'll find him in the library.' She turned to Isabelle. 'And is this your bride?'

'Aye, it is. Isabelle, this is Mistress Jeannie Macrae, my father's housekeeper and a dear friend.'

'Everyone at the castle has been looking forward to meeting you, my lady. You must be weary after so many days of travelling. Shall I be showing you to your room?'

'Go with her, my dear,' said Robert. 'I'll come as soon as I've spoken with my father.'

He was immediately engulfed in a sea of people and he pushed his way through them cheerfully, shaking a hand here and there and exchanging greetings, leaving her feeling bereft till Jeannie took her arm.

'It's always the same. He comes so rarely, you understand. Shall I lead the way?'

Isabelle followed her under an archway, across another

courtyard and then up a flight of stone steps and through a massive door, bolted and barred, that, like the whole castle, had once been built to withstand a siege. But within the atmosphere was very different.

The enormous stone hall had a high raftered roof, its walls hung with weapons and the heads of giant antlered beasts, trophies of long past hunting exploits, but a glowing fire of great logs burned in the fireplace while there were huge bowls of purple heather and clusters of late flowers with scarlet berries scattered on the oak tables.

'This is the oldest part of the castle,' said Jeannie, 'most of the other rooms were redecorated by the Earl's mother.'

'Does the Dowager Countess live here?'

'Oh aye, she has her own apartments in one of the turrets. You will meet her this evening.'

Robert's grandmother of whom he spoke with so much affection: she must brace herself to meet the challenge.

Up the great staircase they went, down a panelled passage and into a bedroom where the walls were hung with French tapestries. There were pieces of fine furniture and a huge bed spread with a patchwork quilt of exquisite colour and design. Curtains of deep rose velvet were looped back from the deep window embrasure and persian rugs were spread on the polished floor.

'What a beautiful room,' she exclaimed.

'It's the one always given to the heir and his bride,' said Jeannie. 'Is there anything you need? The carriage will be here soon and the men will carry up your luggage. Shall I be asking Kirsty to bring you a tray of tea?'

'I think I will wait for my husband.'

'As you please. He'll not be long I'm thinking.'

She went out, shutting the door quietly and Isabelle crossed to the window kneeling on the cushioned window seat. They overlooked a little cove almost entirely shut in by rocks and the sea came rolling in over seaweed-covered boulders. She opened the casement a little and the wind blew in, sharp and keen with a salty tang and she breathed deep, thinking how much she had missed it.

Until their luggage arrived she could not change her dress but she took off her hat and riding jacket, washed her face and combed her hair. The London hairdresser had cut it skilfully so that it curled around her forehead and neck. She looked in the mirror. Her white high-necked blouse with its lace cravat was not as fresh as she would have wished but it would have to do. A little cluster of golden roses had been put in a blue bowl on her dressing table. She could smell their fragrance and wondered if it was Jeannie who had put them there. She wandered around the room examining the tapestry with interest. It depicted the medieval romance of Aucussin and Nicolette. The lovers strolled through an imaginary landscape of flowers and mythical beasts, the colours faded but still beautiful. She opened a further door and found it led into a small room probably formed out of the thickness of the stone wall. In it was a narrow bed, a washstand and a gigantic wardrobe and she thought it might once have served as a dressing room for the bridegroom when he had drunk too deeply to share the marriage bed.

Robert did not come and after a little while she wondered if she dared to go in search of him. She opened the door cautiously hoping she remembered the way down and saw two men manhandling their heavy trunk along the passage, followed by a boy holding a struggling indignant Rory who had been left to finish the journey in the carriage and objected to it strongly.

'Give him to me,' she said quickly as the boy gave a yelp of pain. 'He hasn't bitten you badly, I hope.'

'Nay, my lady, 'tis nothing, just a nip on my thumb. He's a fine wee dog with a great fighting spirit in him,' he said as he relinquished the little dog into her arms. 'He'd have gone into battle with his lordship's hounds so he would if I'd not snatched him out of their path.'

He gave her a broad grin and ran after the two men sucking his bloodied thumb.

Rory was energetically licking her face. She tucked him under her arm and went down the stairs and into the great hall. There were several doors leading off and she chose one that was partly open. Jeannie might be there and she could ask her where to find the library. She raised her hand to push it open further and then stood paralysed at what she heard. The argument must have been going on for some time and there was anger in the raised voices.

'Well, where the devil is this kitchen maid of yours, Robert? Bring her down here. Let me take a look at her.'

'Once and for all, Father, she is not a kitchen maid,' said Robert wearily. 'She is half French and comes from a family with a history longer than ours.'

'That remains to be seen. Oh for God's sake, boy, isn't it far more likely that that bounder, Sir Joshua Brydges, has sold you a pup? She's probably some by-blow of his own. I wouldn't put it beyond him or that abominable wife of his.'

'Do you take me for a fool?'

'You're not the first man to be besotted by a pretty face and dainty manners.'

'I'm hardly a boy, Father.'

'No, you're not and that's just the trouble. All these years living like a monk wrapped up in this damned mysterious work of yours and then in a matter of days you're head over heels in love,' he gave an indignant snort. 'Love indeed! What did you do, take her to your bed and feel in honour bound to wed her,' he went on with a wealth of contempt, 'when I've no doubt that uncle of hers would have settled for cash.'

'I take that very badly,' said Robert icily. 'I did nothing of the kind and talking of bed, what about you and Jeannie Macrae?'

'What about it?' said the Earl dangerously. 'Jeannie is a good girl.'

'So she is, one of the best, and I've accepted her, but not in my mother's place.'

'Be careful what you say about your mother . . . and I've not married her.'

'No, you've not, but what happens if she becomes pregnant?'

'We'll face that when we come to it and you remember this, my boy, whatever child she bears will not succeed me here, but you will and so will your son with its kitchen-maid mother . . .'

And suddenly Isabelle could stand listening no longer. She flung open the door.

She just had time to take in the room, the walls lined with books, the great oak table with its massive silver inkstand and tall candelabra, the Earl himself straddling the hearthrug as tall as Robert but much bulkier, a mane of grey hair tied back with a ribbon, a sweeping moustache, carelessly but richly dressed, both men turning to look at her as she took a step inside the room. Then Rory, fighting to free himself, gave a shrill squeal of rage, the two large dogs stretched on the rug leaped to their feet and came charging down the room to repel the invader, jumping up at her, growling fiercely. She nearly lost her balance, but still held on to the struggling Rory whose fighting spirit was ready to meet any challenge.

'Stop those damned dogs!' yelled Robert.

'Fergus, Hamish,' thundered the Earl, 'down, boys, down. To heel!'

Amazingly the two wolf hounds, their excitement dashed, dropped to the floor and at a further stern command slunk back to their master's feet, still growling hoarsely at the back of their throats.

'For God's sake, Father,' exclaimed Robert, 'can't you keep those great brutes of yours under control?'

'Gentle as lambs, wouldn't hurt a fly,' muttered the Earl.

'That what *you* say.' Robert had his arm around Isabelle. 'Are you all right, my love? You're not hurt?'

'You told me they'd eat him and they very nearly did,' she whispered shakily.

'Here, give the dog to me.' A manservant had appeared in the doorway, alerted by all the commotion, and Robert put Rory into his arms. 'Take good care of the pup and bring him to our room.'

'Aye, my lord, I will do that.'

Robert turned back to Isabelle. 'Now come and meet my father.'

She felt both furiously angry and horribly humiliated, but before she could summon up the courage to refuse, the manservant had moved back respectfully and another figure appeared in the doorway.

'Will someone kindly tell me what is going on?' enquired a gentle voice with a touch of asperity.

The Dowager Countess of Glenmuir still retained the remnants of former beauty, and her full-skirted black silk dress with lace at neck and wrists, the richly coloured Paisley shawl around her shoulders, were worn with all the elegance only a Frenchwoman can achieve.

'*Grand'mère!*' exclaimed Robert with relief and took the hand she stretched out to him, kissing it and then her cheek.

'Robert, my dear, how good it is to see you after all this time and what is your father doing, frightening everyone to death with those great beasts of his? Really, Francis, is this the way to greet your new daughter-in-law?' and she held out both her hands with a gracious gesture. 'So this is Isabelle. Come and kiss me, my dear.'

The girl was drawn into a warm embrace and kissed the thin papery cheek that smelled faintly of some rare perfume.

'I was so sorry to miss your wedding, but these old bones don't travel easily these days and even writing a letter can become a sorry burden.' She raised her right hand. 'See, rheumatism has twisted and gnarled it like some old claw, but now we shall talk French together and be very comfortable. Come my dear, you must meet my son and receive his apologies for his rude reception.'

So Isabelle was led forward, the Earl took her hand, muttered a few words of regret and enquired politely about her journey, wondering uncomfortably how much she had overheard. It was the Countess who brought the stiff formal little conversation to an end.

'We are all longing to hear everything about you both but you must be weary and longing to wash and rest before we dine. Take care of your wife, Robert, she looks exhausted. Afterwards we shall look forward to a really long talk. We eat at seven and Jeannie will come and remind you.'

Back in the bedroom she had admired so much, Robert said a little awkwardly, 'You mustn't mind too much everything my father says. He often speaks without thinking and regrets it afterwards.'

208

'He is angry with you, isn't he, very angry because you married me instead of a girl of his choosing.'

'I'm not a boy any longer, Isabelle. For some years now I've lived my own life and gone my own way. He doesn't like it, he never has, we quarrelled over it years ago when I left to live in London, but he has to accept it.'

And accept her too. That was going to be the problem and it made her feel guilty, it was something she should have foreseen, but she was not going to argue about it now. It was already late and she was determined to show the Earl that his son's kitchen-maid wife was no bread-and-butter miss. Her trunk had been partly unpacked and the gowns grudgingly provided by Aunt Augusta laid out and hung up. There was one in a rich moiré silk the colour of flame. Cut in the latest fashion, it was high waisted and hung sheer to the floor with ruches of velvet at the hem. The square neck was cut low and she took from its case a necklet of filigree gold set with amber which had caught her eye when they were walking in York and Robert had surprised her with it the next morning. She took two of the yellow roses from the blue bowl on the dressing table and fastened them into the dark hair with a velvet ribbon.

When Robert came in from the dressing room shrugging himself into his dark blue evening coat, she turned to face him.

'Will your kitchen-maid do?'

'So you heard that, did you?' he said wryly. 'Oh yes, you'll do, a tawny tiger kitten, all claws and ready to do battle.'

But she didn't feel at all like that, only helpless and not a little frightened, wishing she could stay in the safety of their room and not go down to face hostile and critical eyes, but that would be the act of a coward and she must not let him down.

'Where's Rory?' she asked suddenly, looking around her.

'Being fed to bursting in the kitchens, I shouldn't wonder,' he said. 'Don't fret, he'll be safe enough. Now come along, my father is a stickler for punctuality.'

It was just as intimidating as she had feared it might be. The dining room was massive, darkly panelled, the long table impeccably laid with glass and silver, candles burning in many branched sconces, the Earl magnificent in black velvet, lace and diamonds at his throat. So much splendour for a simple family dinner. Servants hovered as they took their places with Jeannie anxiously making sure everything was as it should be.

The Earl suddenly looked up frowning.

'What do you think you're doing, standing at the back there, girl?' he said irritably. 'Come and take your place with us.'

'I thought tonight you would prefer to dine *en famille*,' Jeannie murmured hesitantly.

'Rubbish! You *are* family, aren't you, for God's sake?' He snapped his fingers at one of the footmen. 'Lay another place.'

'Very good, my lord.' He hurried away while they waited uncomfortably.

Isabelle knew it was being done for her benefit. The Earl's mistress was to be treated in the same manner as the son's kitchen-maid bride.

When the footman returned and stood uncertainly for a moment, she took the bit between her teeth.

'Lay the place here beside me,' she said, smiling sweetly at the embarrassed Jeannie, and felt heartened by her husband's nod of approval.

The conversation during dinner was mostly between Robert and his father with a few shrewd comments from the Countess about the political situation. How long would it be before Bonaparte's inordinate demands were satisfied and the peace treaty finally ratified and was it likely to be lasting?

'I doubt it,' said Robert. 'In my opinion it will merely provide breathing space, something the French need just as much as we do. From information gained from closest observers in Paris, Bonaparte is a very ambitious man. When he has consolidated his position in France and it is hinted he will soon be made First Consul for life, he will look for more power, crowning himself Emperor maybe, seeing himself Master of Europe and it may take a very long time to convince him that his dream is something Great Britain will never tolerate.'

'I don't think your colleagues at Whitehall would agree with you.'

'That's because they don't want to. It will be too hazardous a future, but then they have not met him.'

'And you have?'

'Let us say I have spoken with those who know him intimately,' said Robert evasively.

The Earl grunted. 'When are they going to reward you for all this work you do?' he said drily. 'I thought to see you in the Cabinet before now.'

'I've no wish for high ofice, no wish at all. I should refuse it if it were offered to me.'

'Perhaps that's just as well,' commented the Earl with a sour glance at Isabelle. 'In the circumstances you're hardly likely to be given the opportunity.'

When the Countess rose to lead the way from the table, leaving Robert and his father to their wine, Isabelle excused herself, not feeling up to small talk in the drawing room.

'Will you forgive me, Madame? I really am very tired. We were up at five o'clock this morning and it has been a very long day.'

'Of course, my dear, and you must call me *Grand'mère* just as Robert does. Tomorrow when you are rested, you must come and see my garden while the fine weather still holds. We are fortunate here. The Gulf Stream flows along the West Coast giving us a milder climate than the rest of Scotland. It is remarkable what tender plants we can grow. I still have roses blooming in sheltered spots.'

'Was it you who put them on my dressing table?'

'I thought they would provide a welcome in a strange house and you have used them to very good effect. You look very beautiful tonight, my child.'

'You are very kind.'

It helped to calm the storm inside her and impulsively she leaned forward to kiss the faded cheek before she made her escape.

When Robert came up to their room an hour or so later she was in her dressing gown, sitting on the rug close to the brightly burning fire, a sleepy well-fed Rory stretched out against her.

'You're not feeling ill, are you?' he asked as he came in. 'Grandmother told me you'd gone to bed.'

211

'Not ill, just too tired to try and make polite conversation.'

'Poor darling, what a day it has been for you. Tomorrow you will begin to enjoy it up here. There is so much I want to show you.'

She looked up at him frowning.

'Robert, are you very rich?'

He stopped in the act of peeling off his coat. 'Good God, what a question! What is it you want me to buy for you?'

'I don't want anything. You have given me far too much already. It's just that – I don't know – I never thought about it till tonight.'

He dropped his coat on the bed and began to unfasten his neckcloth.

'That display this evening was put on for your benefit. We don't always dine in such style when we are alone.' He smiled down at her. 'Do you want a potted history of the family finances? We're not really Highland gentry, you know, we've only been at Glenmuir for a little over two hundred years, not like most of them up here who like to believe they are descended from Fionn MacCumhaill.'

'Who is he?'

'They call him Fingal down south and he sleeps in the mountains of Appin with three thousand warriors around him and when Scotland is in need of them, they will rise again at the sound of Fingal's horn.'

'Is that true?'

'It's one of the myths, they cling to,' he said drily.

He pulled up a chair beside her and she knelt up, putting her hands on his knee and looking up at him.

'Shall I go on?' he asked smiling indulgently.

'Please.'

'Back in the days of old Queen Bess one of my ancestors was only a simple border laird living in his ancient keep of Kilgour, that's where the title comes from. Then by a stroke of luck he met and fell in love with an heiress, the last of her line, and better still he actually married her. That is how we came to Glenmuir. His son rendered some rather shady services abroad to Charles II and received an earldom for his pains, but he was

212

a canny man. He didn't intend to rely on his mountain pastures and thousands of sheep. Instead he invested in shipping in the newly discoverd islands of the Pacific, sugar plantations and spices and, I rather think, black slaves. Fortunately for us, he prospered and though we have gone up and down since then, we've still hung on to our profits. My grandfather was a romantic and lost a good deal of it because of his attachment to the Stuart cause, but my father is an astute man and has a very capable business manager, so I should say we're not millionaires but rich enough to buy you anything you fancy within reason.'

She sighed. 'I wish you weren't. I wish you were poor because then I could work and give *you* something.'

'My little love, what nonsense you talk. You give me all I want which is yourself.'

She knelt upright, looking earnestly into his face. 'What did your father mean when he said you should have been offered high office?'

'Oh he would like to have seen me Prime Minister at twenty-four like Billy Pitt,' he said lightly, 'and I can't convince him that it is the very last thing I've ever wanted.'

'Do I make you happy?'

'Blissfully. Now stop fretting and come to bed. My father can be an old bear but stand up to him and he'll soon begin to crumble, forget to bite and be at your feet, just as I am.'

'Why doesn't he marry Jeannie?'

'You guessed about her, didn't you? That was why you acted so cleverly at dinner. The fact is he loved my mother very much and fell into a black despair when she died. It was Jeannie who lifted him out of it, but I don't think he could ever bring himself to put anyone else in her place. When the Armitages love, they love for life and after.' He drew her to him, tapping her lightly on the nose, half smiling and yet serious. 'You remember that, my girl, you are stuck with me for all eternity.'

Did he mean what he said or was he jesting? She never quite knew how to take him and she lay awake a long time that night thinking about it, very conscious of what she had taken on when she had married him and wishing passionately that she could repay him in the way he most desired. And yet she could not pretend to a love she did not honestly feel. One day, she thought in a kind of desperation, one day perhaps when she bore him a child, it would be different. He stirred beside her and murmured something. She touched his hand and the fingers closed around hers even in sleep and somehow she was comforted.

11

The Countess's flower garden was almost entirely surrounded by a high wall protecting it from the cold winds of winter sweeping in from the sea. There she grew all kinds of rare plants and from his childhood Robert remembered it as a place of secret delight full of scent and colour during the long days of summer. This year the warmth seemed to linger for longer than usual and there was a gentle October sunshine when, the morning after their arrival, he found her in the herb garden superintending the work of the gardener. Andy Rufus, as the children used to call him though the fiery red of his hair had faded now to grey, had begun as gardener's boy when Elise de Morney had first come to the castle as a bride and though now as gnarled and bent as an old tree root he jealously guarded his privilege, and felt himself as capable of a day's hard work as the young man who had been promoted to sweep and carry and push the loaded wheelbarrow.

'He don't know no more than a monkey on a stick,' he grumbled 'as soon pull up one of my lady's valuable plants as some stinking weed.'

A few fat bees still hovered over a bed of thyme and Robert could smell apple mint and lavender as she came to meet him.

'Ah dear boy,' she said, 'I have been hoping you would come and talk to me. How is Isabelle this morning? More rested now, I hope.'

He smiled as he took the hand outstretched to him. She was a dear familiar figure, still contriving to look elegant even wrapped in a huge plaid shawl with a hat rather like a giant mushroom tied under her chin with a rakish bow.

'We thought of going across to Mull, and if the sunshine

215

holds take the ferry to Iona. Jeannie is packing a picnic basket for us.'

She gave a little shiver. 'Your grandfather took me there once. It's an eerie place, full of ghosts. I didn't care for it.'

'Isabelle will,' he said confidently. 'She feels as I do about so many things.'

He had drawn her arm through his as they walked slowly to the old stone seat set against the wall where it could catch every vagrant ray of sunshine.

'We shan't be able to sit here much longer,' she said regretfully. 'Winter comes so early and in all the years I've lived here, I've never quite grown used to it.' She drew him to sit beside her. 'Now tell me all about this girl wife of yours. It has come upon us so suddenly that your father simply cannot reconcile himself to it.'

'I know it has made him angry but certain circumstances made it necessary.'

She gave him a quick look. 'She is not *enceinte*?'

'No, she is not,' he said emphatically. 'That is what Father hinted – that I'd got her with child and then felt obliged to marry her. It was not like that at all and I can't make him understand that there were other and far more pressing reasons why we should marry quickly.'

She had taken his hand in hers and was stroking the long fingers.

'You love her very much, don't you?' she said gently.

'Yes, I do. It sounds ridiculous and I was not expecting it but it hit me like a – like a – '

'*Coup de foudre?*'

'A bolt of lightning. Yes, I suppose it was rather like that,' he admitted wryly. 'Absurd, isn't it, for me to say that, when in a few weeks I shall be thirty.'

'I think it hits all the harder when one is no longer very young.' She paused. 'I don't think it was quite the same for her, was it?'

'Why do you say that?' he said quickly.

'Forgive me if I am wrong. I have known her for a few hours only and yet – there are certain things – impressions – she

216

admires you, she is grateful – perhaps a little afraid – but she is not – what is it you say in English? – not head over heels in love.'

'No, to my regret. You're right as always, but you must not think she has deceived me. She has always been utterly and scrupulously honest.'

'And you were still prepared to marry her on her terms?'

'Yes, on any terms.'

'Have you thought that one day she may meet someone else with whom she may fall in love? It happens, Robert, you know that as well as I do. You are taking her back to London and into a society that will be new to her, a fashionable heartless society fully of temptations to a young inexperienced girl. She is unusually beautiful and other men, unscrupulous men, will desire her. What will you do then?'

'I trust Isabelle implicitly.'

'And if she fails your trust?'

'I'm not sure. If she takes a lover, I think I will probably kill him.'

He was smiling and yet it was said with such intensity that she feared for him. She closed her hand over his.

'Let us pray that it never happens, that her respect and affection will be sufficient to withstand all temptations.'

'Not respect, *Grand'mère*, not affection but love.'

She touched his cheek gently. 'Dear boy, I can only hope you're right. Now be off with you or the best of the day will have vanished. That channel is notorious for sudden squalls.'

She watched him walk briskly away and could not quite still her anxiety. Robert was far more vulnerable than he appeared on the surface. His cool air of detachment, his ironic turn of humour, were a shield against the passion that drove him into danger for causes in which he believed. Though he had never confided in her, she knew that once years ago he had failed tragically to save a life entrusted to him and had never quite forgiven himself. She wondered if it had played a part in driving him into this hasty and perhaps ill-judged marriage. With her practical good sense she knew very well that many marriages were based on no more than convenience, the desire for a home of one's own, for children, companionship, perhaps even affection, and proved perfectly satisfactory, but she had an uneasy conviction that Robert was one of the few men who looked for something more, for a union of mind and spirit, and for that very reason could be the more easily hurt. She sighed and got to her feet picking up the basket in which she had been gathering a few herbs, rosemary, dill, sage, coriander, which over the years she had painstakingly taught their stout Scottish cook not only to use but to appreciate. She walked slowly towards the house. It was one of those days when an oppression of the heart made her remember her seventy-seven years.

Robert and Isabelle ate their picnic on the beach at Mull, wafer-thin oatcakes and fish caught by Ian Mackie and grilled over the fire he had built in an angle of the rocks of red granite that sloped down to the long stretch of pure white sand. There was a fruit tart and creamy cheese with little sweet apples, a bottle of wine and whisky, not forgetting a dram for Ian. The relationship between Ian and his master was quite unlike any she had known at High Willows. The Scot was respectful but at the same time independent and never afraid to speak his mind, a frankness Robert appreciated and only very rarely rebuked.

It was one of those perfect days with which the Atlantic occasionally blesses the Western Isles during early autumn. When they rowed across to Iona, the water was so clear a green that leaning over the side Isabelle could see the darting shoals of small silver fish and the deep purple streaks of the drifting weed.

Robert had been right, she thought. There was something magical about this tiny island set in the shimmering sea with its miniature mountains whose fretted peaks rose against a brilliantly blue sky. It was to this island that Columba had come from Ireland, that fiery Celtic monk with his tremendous voice, his quick temper and the driving force of his faith that had brought him to convert the pagan Scots at much the same time as Augustine landed on the shores of Kent and carried Christianity to the powerful King Ethelbert, baptising him and all his court at Canterbury.

218

Only a small number of crofters eked out a poor living on the island and they met no one as they climbed up to the lonely ruins of the Cathedral and monastery which had once housed a community of Celtic monks.

'The ancient kings were all buried on Iona, most of them Scottish, a few Norwegian,' said Robert, painting the picture for her. 'The royal barges came by night across the sea to the music of the harps and the monks met them, the torches blazing as they carried the coffins up the path which is still called the Street of the Dead.'

The chapels that had once held them had long since crumbled to dust, but the stone coffins were still there, fretted and worn by the winds and the fierce storms of winter, Hrolf and Thorkin, Finn and Erlend, the forgotten names went back to some fabulous past. Macbeth was here lying beside the murdered Duncan. She shivered as she put out a hand and touched the sunwarmed stone.

'I read the play once,' she whispered, 'Mr Holland used to say that it contained some of the saddest lines Shakespeare ever wrote. Do you remember? "Life's but a walking shadow . . ."'

'"A poor player,"' went on Robert finishing it for her,

> '"That struts and frets his hour upon the stage,
> And then is heard no more; it is a tale
> Told by an idiot, full of sound and fury,
> Signifying nothing"'

'I think I rather agree with him. Does it frighten you? Grandmother says the island is full of ghosts and Ian flatly refuses to leave the shore. He is firmly convinced that if you stay too long, you will become a ghost yourself.'

'I don't think I am afraid,' she said slowly, 'but I have a queer feeling of being nothing in a vast void of timelessness.'

'I know what you mean.' He had moved a little away from her, staring out across the sea. 'I came here once to be alone and to make a decision that ultimately changed my life.'

'Tell me about it.'

'It was years ago now when I was very young, not long after

219

I came down from St Andrews. I was asked to undertake a mission to France that would be both lonely and dangerous but which for family reasons was well within my power to accomplish. My father had always wanted me to follow him into the army, and David and I saw it as a grand lark and had been thinking of taking up a commission and thoroughly enjoying ourselves, when suddenly I was faced with making a choice. I came here alone and somehow, in this most holy of places, the life I had been planning seemed utterly trivial and I knew that if I could play my part in a battle against oppression, against an evil tyranny, then I must do it at whatever personal cost.'

'And you've been doing that ever since.'

'In a way perhaps I have.'

She felt as if for the first time she was being given an insight into something deep and hidden in him and wondered if that first meeting on the ship all those years ago was when he had returned, the mission accomplished, but the atmosphere of danger and secrecy still clinging to him.

She would have liked to question him further but abruptly his mood had changed.

'My God, how unbearably pretentious and solemn one can be at twenty-one. As if my decision could make the smallest difference to the world's suffering. Look,' he went on, pointing out to sea. 'See that black cloud out there towards the south. A squall is coming up. We must go back before it reaches us. It's no picnic to be marooned on Iona. We'd probably end up by becoming two of *Grand'mère*'s ghosts. Come on. We must run.'

He grabbed her hand and they raced down to where Ian was waiting anxiously by the boat and only narrowly escaped a soaking. The squall caught up with them as they landed, dragging the boat up the beach out of the force of the wind and then running across the sand, taking refuge in one of the crofter's stone huts where they were received with true Highland hospitality and offered giant mugs of scaldingly hot tea laced with whisky.

That day on Iona was one of the moments that Isabelle remembered most vividly from the weeks they spent at Glenmuir, though they enjoyed many excursions together. She went fishing with Robert and Ian on the loch, thrilled when she caught a fish only to have Ian pronounce it too small and then throw it back much to her chagrin. They rode up into the mountains on sturdy little ponies so that Robert could show her where he and David had stalked the deer. Once as boys, he told her, they had scaled the snow-tipped peak in search of an eagle's nest.

'It was one of the most terrifying experiences of my life,' he confessed. 'The great bird was of course defending its fledgling from marauders like us. You've no idea of the huge span of the wings when they are hovering just above you. I could almost feel the cruel beak tearing out my eyes. David fell about ten feet out of sheer terror and I dropped on top of him. It was a mercy we were not both killed. We never tried that again.'

She spoke French with the Countess and, under her gentle probing, revealed more to her than to anyone. She would take chocolate with her in her pretty room in the West Tower and speak of her life at the château and her worry about her young brother while Elise de Morney stitched calmly at her tapestry frame and realised there was a depth of hidden fire and passion under the seemingly quiet self-contained young girl. She wondered how much of it Robert had guessed at or whether he was blind to the load of trouble he had taken on himself.

Jeannie, who was inclined to be prickly at first, was won over by Isabelle's genuine interest in the household management of the castle. Over the years, despite impatience and boredom, she had learned a great deal from Mrs Bedford and, though on a much grander scale, Glenmuir's problems were not unlike those of High Willows.

Only the Earl still remained stiff and unyielding. Time and time again in his presence she would feel his eyes on her critically watching, ready to find fault. The very fact that he was always scrupulously courteous only made it worse. Robert frequently argued with his father on a variety of topics, sometimes quite fiercely, but she was aware of the strong bond between them and it made her feel guilty as if she was failing him in some way.

So the days went by and then one morning the Earl mentioned

that he was riding up into the hills to see a tenant of his who had recently had a bad fall and broken his hip in a couple of places.

'Climbing up into the mountains after a lost sheep at his age,' grumbled the Earl, 'the old fool should have had more sense. His daughter works in the castle kitchens and could well look after him down here, but will the old devil budge from his cottage, not he. He says he manages well enough with his eldest grandson looking after him.'

'I remember Donald,' said Robert. 'He must be over eighty by now. We used to go fishing together. He taught me to cast my first fly, when I was about seven. Isabelle and I will ride up with you.'

'Better not,' muttered his father, 'it may not be a pretty sight. The doctor has done what he can, but I gather the poor chap is practically bedridden.'

'You needn't worry. Isabelle is not one of these nervous females.'

They set out together with Ian riding behind them carrying a basket filled with extra delicacies from the castle kitchens put together by Jeannie.

The Earl need not have been afraid. The one-room stone hut with its beaten earth floor and whitewashed walls was clean and tidy with a strong reek of peat smoke from the smouldering fire and the sharp tang of some herbal liniment used on the old man's damaged hip.

A tall thin man, he was stretched on a low bed banked up by pillows with a plaid thrown across him. He made a strong effort to struggle up from his bed when the Earl came in, stooping his head under the low lintel. He waved him back impatiently.

'How are you keeping, man? How's the hip going along?' he said brusquely. 'Has the doctor I sent up been looking after you?'

'Aye, my lord, he's been very good. God willing, I shall be on my feet again soon.'

'You'd better make sure you are,' said Robert gently, coming close to the bed and drawing Isabelle with him. 'I'm relying on you to teach my wife how to cast a fly properly. She's a pretty poor hand at it just now.'

The old man's brown face cracked into a smile of pleasure. 'I'll be doin' just that, Master Robert. Many's the fine day we've had together. It's a bonny wee lass you've chosen for yourself and she'll be making you a fine wife.'

'My husband has told me all about you,' whispered Isabelle, taking the thin hand in hers. She paused a moment and then leaned forward and kissed the wrinkled cheek.

'Aye, well, you take care of yourself,' went on the Earl gruffly, 'and if there's anything you're wanting, you send that grandson of yours down to the castle and Jeannie will make sure it's brought up to you.'

'I'm grateful to you, my lord, very grateful indeed, but Duncan is a good lad and he brings me all that is needful,' said the old man with a quiet dignity.

'Stubborn old devil,' muttered the Earl impatiently as they waited outside for Ian to bring their horses. 'Too damned proud to admit that he's come to the end of the road. He'll never walk again and he knows it. Lying up here like some wounded beast. I'm thinking it would be best for all of us to have him carried down to the castle whether he likes it or not.'

'No,' exclaimed Isabelle quickly, 'no, you can't do that. You mustn't. It would be cruel.' The Earl turned to stare at her. She felt the hot colour rush up into her cheeks but she went on bravely. 'Can't you understand? It isn't his pride. He knows he's nearing the end and he wants to die in his own place with all the things he has loved best around him. You'll kill him if you shut him up in a room, however well he's cared for.'

She stopped, abruptly aware of the Earl's heavy frown as he turned away from her, taking the bridle of his horse.

'That wife of yours has a sharp tongue in her head, Robert,' he said stiffly. 'You'd be wise to watch it.'

He heaved himself into the saddle and went trotting ahead.

Robert was looking amused. With flushed cheeks she let him help her to mount. If she had offended his father, it was just too bad. She was right, she knew she was right and she wasn't going to apologise.

They rode in silence for a while and presently were making their way in single file down a long narrow mountain path when

223

a hare suddenly loped across the road right under her horse's nose. The mare took fright and bolted. She managed to hang on but hadn't sufficient strength to pull her up. They careered on together past the Earl and on down the twisting path, thin overhead branches whipping into her face. She was clinging on for dear life when at last a low hanging bough swept her from the saddle. She rolled over and over, bruised and breathless, ending up face downwards in a mass of soft earth, pine needles and dead leaves. Robert had come racing after her. He leaped from his horse while she was already struggling to her feet.

He caught her up in his arms and she leaned against him.

'I'm all right,' she gasped, 'quite all right. I'm not hurt, only winded.'

There was blood on her face where the sharp twigs had struck her. She found she had badly bruised her ankle when she tried to stand on it, while a shooting pain ran up her back, but she would have died rather than confess it as the Earl caught them up and sat on his horse calmly waiting.

'Better send back for some sort of conveyance to carry her home, Robert,' he said with a touch of scorn at anyone being so foolish as to fall off in mid gallop.

'No!' she was fierce in rejection. 'No, it's not necessary. Robert, help me back into the saddle.'

Ian had gone after the mare and brought her back looking rather ashamed of herself.

Robert was anxious. 'Are you sure you're not hurt? We've still a fair way to ride.'

'Of course I'm sure. What's a tumble? I've had plenty of them.'

It was worth all the agony of the jolting ride home to hear the Earl's gruff comment when they dismounted in the courtyard and servants came to take the horses.

'She's a plucky lass with a will of her own, that kitchen-maid of yours, Robert, I'll say that for her.'

As she limped painfully into the castle she felt as if she had received an accolade.

Then there came the night of the party. Robert had been talking about returning to London before the snows came and travelling south became impossible.

'Father would like to invite our neighbours and friends to meet you, since it may be a year or more before we come back to Glenmuir.'

'Why should they want to meet me?' she asked rebelliously.

'You are my wife, remember, and one day you will be Countess of Glenmuir.'

'I know and that is what terrifies me. They will all be sitting in judgment.'

'They'll be far more likely to envy me my good luck in finding such a jewel of a wife.'

'Don't laugh at me, Robert.'

'I'm not laughing. I mean it. Make yourself beautiful to please the old man. He'll never admit it but I'm pretty sure he is looking forward to showing you off.'

She had grave doubts about that. He was far too stubborn to yield so easily. It was more likely to be pride. He would not care to admit that any son of his could have made a mistake. But she had her pride too and she would do as Robert wished. She wore her wedding dress, the sheer white satin sewn with tiny pearls at neck and hem. Kirsty had pressed it with loving care and brought her a cluster of white roses with a note from the Countess.

'These are the very last of the year. It would please me so much if you would wear them tonight.'

But the greatest surprise was still to come.

Vast preparations had been going on in the castle for several days. There was to be an informal buffet supper, salmon cooked whole on silver dishes, fresh lobsters, lamb roasted on the spit, venison pasties, an immense array of delicious food laid out in the dining room. Guests began arriving in the early afternoon, some by carriage, some on horseback. She could hear the servants bustling to and fro as she dressed. The musicians had begun to play. By now they would all be assembling in the drawing room. She must make haste. She stared in the mirror and thought she looked pale and washed out. She rubbed her cheeks hard to bring back a little colour.

Robert came up behind her putting a hand on her shoulder.

'No need to tremble, my love. You look radiant.'

225

He lifted a curl of dark hair and kissed the nape of her neck.

She swung round on him. 'Don't try to comfort me. I look just as scared as I feel.'

'Scared of what?' he said smiling down at her. 'Ghosts?'

'Yes if you want to know. Ghosts of your ancestors, of all those other Countesses of Glenmuir.'

He touched her cheek gently. 'None of them could hold a candle to you.'

'I wish that were true.'

A knock on the door startled her but it was only the Earl's personal servant who came in carrying a long narrow box.

'His lordship would be happy if you would consent to wear this tonight, my lady.'

He bowed and went out leaving Isabelle staring down at the jewel case he had handed to her.

'What is it?'

'Open it and see.'

Half afraid, she fumbled with the clasp and lifted the lid. On a bed of purple lay a slender collarette of pearls and diamonds with a matching bracelet, both of a very fine and delicate workmanship. She looked at them with awe.

'Does your father really wish me to wear them?'

'He couldn't have paid you a greater compliment,' said Robert drily. 'They belonged to my mother.'

'Robert, I shouldn't be wearing them,' she sounded distressed, 'not when he loved her so much.'

'You can and you must. It is his final acceptance.'

He took the necklace and fastened it around her throat and clasped the bracelet on the slender wrist. He kissed her firmly on the lips and then took up the long gauzy scarf embroidered with silver stars, draped it around her shoulders and pushed her towards the door.

'No more prinking, no more doubts, no more holding back. Into the fray we must go.'

Walking down the staircase and into the great hall ablaze now with a hundred candles, her hand on Robert's arm, she faced the eyes of thirty or more couples all turned towards her and knew a moment of pure triumph when the Earl himself came forward to take her hand, to kiss her cheek and present her to the assembled company as his son's bride.

For the first part of the evening the euphoria supported her, but then slowly it began to fade. With Robert constantly at her side, it had been easy. The men crowded around them congratulating, complimenting, laughing, full of charm and admiration. There was dancing in which she could take her part with ease and accomplishment but as the evening wore on, it changed.

Robert was more and more engulfed by friends of long standing, boys he had grown up with. To some of them who were marooned for long months in the Highlands, he brought the sophistication of London society, and their elders sought him for the very latest news of the political situation. She was left among the wives and daughters whose attitude was very different. Robert in his quiet way had been a very eligible young man, and rumour had attached him to this one and that, so that now they eyed her with envy and an undisguised curiosity. Many of them had spent months among Edinburgh society; they had accompanied relatives to London for the season and they spoke with ease and familiarity of people and events about which she knew nothing, the opera, the theatre, concerts and the very newest romance from the circulating library. They giggled behind fans at the shocking details of the latest scandal and she found she was withdrawing more and more into herself, remaining silent unless directly questioned.

'You're French, aren't you?' said one. 'I daresay Robert will be taking you to Paris to meet your family soon.'

'I have no family, only a brother.'

'How long have you been in England?'

'Since I was twelve.'

'Really, all that long time and living down on the Kent marshes. However did you survive it?'

They made it sound somehow disgraceful, as if she had been shut into a prison. In a way High Willows had been a prison, but she resented the slur they seemed to put on it.

'However did you meet Robert?' asked a girl with deep red

227

hair, who had been introduced as Fiona, a distant cousin of the family and who appeared to know everyone.

Isabelle bit her lip.

'He came to visit my uncle.'

'And fell in love at first sight. How very romantic and not at all like Robert. We always used to say he'd never marry, didn't we?' And she looked around at her companions, seeming to draw them together into a conspiracy against the newcomer. 'Do you remember how we used to tease him and David about it?'

Isabelle was very aware of a streak of malice. Maybe Fiona had wanted him for herself. She felt cut off from them, a freak from an alien background, different from everyone else, almost as if she were really the slut from the kitchens, and it became increasingly hard to bear.

'How do you get along with Marian?' asked Fiona, still relentlessly probing.

'I scarcely know her yet. We have only met once or twice.'

'Is she going to live with you in London? I must say I wouldn't care for that. Marian rules the house and would like to rule Robert if she could. If I were you, I'd ask her to move out and set up her own establishment.'

'I couldn't do that. She is very fond of Robert.'

'Much too fond.' Fiona exchanged a significant look with one of her cronies. 'I expect you are acquainted with a number of the other *émigrés* who are taking refuge over here?'

'No, none at all.'

'How very odd. All those I have met seemed to know one another.'

'I did meet the Chevalier de St George at my wedding,' she said defensively.

'You *were* honoured. I understand he never went out of town. Was his nephew with him?'

'His nephew?'

'Lucien de Vosges. Oh my dear, you must *meet* him. He really is something, so handsome and so exciting, quite, quite *ravissant*.'

'Has he been in England long?' she asked in a stifled voice.

'Oh no. July it was. The Chevalier brought him to a reception

228

at Carlton House given by the Prince of Wales, you know.' Fiona gave a little giggle. 'He kept us all enthralled with tales of his adventures, just like a romantic novel. All nonsense, I expect, but he told them so well and with such an air.'

Indeed he did. She remembered it all too vividly, and he was there in London. She would be meeting him soon. He would recognise her. She felt so dizzy at the thought that she turned her face away in case anyone should notice. Somehow she had never thought of him as cutting a dash in society. He had been her castaway whom she had rescued, fed, found clothes for and with whom she had shared all she had. Was he really the nephew of that arrogant Frenchman? If so, why hadn't he sent to him immediately for assistance? There was something mysterious about the whole affair that puzzled her.

By now the guests had both eaten and drunk well and the evening had begun to grow a little wilder. The formal set dances were over and the musicians had begun to play reels and strathspeys.

Robert was being urged to take part in them and refused at first.

'It's years since I danced a reel. I'm too old for such things. I shall fall over my own feet.'

'You've only been married a month. You're not a family man yet,' urged Fiona.

'I'll join in if my wife will come with me,' he said to Isabelle.

She shook her head. 'I don't know the steps. I shall only spoil it for everyone.'

'You're looking very pale,' he said with concern. 'Are you sure you're feeling quite well?'

'Of course I am. Don't worry about me. They're your friends, Robert, not mine. You go and join them.'

Cousin Fiona had taken his arm. 'Benedick, the married man!' She was mocking him, the others joining in, so that laughing, he let them lead him into the group forming up in the centre of the room.

Isabelle watched for a time while the dancers moved in and out, the music growing louder as the pace quickened. She felt deserted, alone in the midst of a crowd. She knew she was being unfair, but couldn't help feeling hurt that he had not chosen to stay with her. The Countess had already retired and Jeannie was busy elsewhere. Those who had not joined in the Highland dancing were sitting together in small friendly groups in which she would certainly not be welcome and suddenly it was all too much for her. No one took any notice as she slid quietly around the room and made for the stairs. A footman coming with a tray of fresh glasses paused to ask if he could bring her anything.

'No, nothing,' she said. 'If anyone should enquire, I am going to my room.'

'Very good, my lady.'

She went quickly up the stairs and into the bedroom. The fire had already been lighted and Rory, stretched out on the rug, raised a sleepy head to greet her as she shut the door quietly and leaned back against it. She was aware that she should not have run away but was infinitely glad of a few minutes of peace in which to gather herself together and face the fact that shortly she would be meeting Lucien again. That in itself was disturbing enough, but now she was Robert's wife and if, out of mischief, out of sheer devilment, Lucien spread the tale of their meeting, the few days they had spent alone together on the deserted beaches, she trembled at the thought. She could imagine too well how much that scandal-loving sophisticated London society would make of it and the harm it could do.

Slowly she began to reason with herself. Of course he would not do any such thing. What had been between them had been warm and real, hadn't it? Lucien would never wish to harm her.

She lit the candles and began to undress, putting the jewelled necklace and bracelet carefully back into their casket. The evening that had begun so happily had come to a disappointing finish.

When she was in her nightdress she blew out all the candles but one and climbed into the large bed. Thinking she would not be retiring until later, Kirsty had not yet brought the warming pan and the touch of the icy linen sheets made her shiver. She could still hear the distant sound of the music, fast and furious now with shouts of laughter, and she felt shut out from it, lonely and neglected, forgetting it was by her own choice. She knew

230

that some of the guests who came from a long distance would be staying the night in the castle while others who were young enough not to fear a moonlight ride home would be leaving soon.

It seemed a very long time before all sounds gradually died away and the castle lay wrapped in silence, and even longer before she heard the footsteps coming along the corridor. Robert came in quietly, shutting the heavy door with infinite care. She heard Rory give a shake and patter to greet him and his quietening voice. Out of sheer perversity she pretended to be asleep, lying with her eyes tightly closed and her face turned away from the door. She knew he came to bend over her, felt his hand gently touch her cheek, then still very quietly he took the lighted candle and went into the adjoining room. Her eyes wide open now she stared at the door firmly shut behind him and felt cheated.

What did she want him to do? Rouse her, sit on the bed and talk to her about the evening in his usual humorous companionable way? She wasn't sure, only that she felt utterly miserable and her eyes pricked with unshed tears in the thick darkness.

The night passed very slowly. She must have drowsed eventually because she woke very early when it was barely light. Everything was very quiet as if the castle was still sleeping after the late night. One curtain had been drawn back. Up here in the north, light came earlier and stayed longer than on the marshes. She slid out of bed, shivering a little as she crossed to the window. The sky was suffused with a rosy glow that just touched the shimmering grey silk of the sea and she could see the waves far out gently creaming over the rocks in the little cove. The beauty of the morning almost took her breath away and she had a sudden longing to go down there, breathe in the salty wind, let it blow away the misery of the previous evening as she had done so often before at High Willows. She dressed very quickly, putting on her thick riding skirt and soft kid boots and taking up a warm woollen plaid to wind around her shoulers. Then tucking Rory under her arm she opened the door quietly and tiptoed down the corridor.

*

Robert was awakened by a pounding on the door and a frightened voice calling his name. He struggled up through a heavy sleep, cursing himself for having drunk more than usual the night before and now suffering from the effects of it.

The hammering shot through the pain in his head. 'What is it?' he shouted irritably.

'It's my lady, sir.' Kirsty half opened the door. 'It's the Lady Isabelle. She is . . . Oh come, sir, do please come.'

'What's wrong? Is she ill?'

He was out of bed now, pulling on his dressing gown. In the bedroom Kirsty grabbed him by the arm.

'I came to light the fire and she wasn't here . . . and then I heard the wee dog barking . . .' she was gabbling as she dragged him to the window. 'Look, my lord, look!'

Rory was perched on a rock far out to sea, whining and barking, too terrified to move, while the tide came sweeping in with strength and ferocity as it did in these narrow coves. Isabelle, balanced on sea-weed covered stones, was desperately trying to reach the little dog. Even as he watched, her foot slipped and she fell into the water that was swirling breast high around her.

'Christ!' exclaimed Robert, knowing with a chill at his heart that at any moment a bigger wave could carry her out to sea, and she could be drowned before anyone was able to reach her. She had no knowledge of the power of the sea and its currents on this coast.

Frantically he dragged on breeches over his nightshirt and pulled on boots, staying only to speak urgently to Kirsty.

'Get a fire lighted as quickly as you can and prepare something hot, coffee, tea, anything!' and then he was gone racing along the corridor, down the stairs, across the hall and through the long passages that led to the outer door. Even as he came through onto the beach, he saw Isabelle stumble again and the water closed over her head. He ran down the shingle shore splashing through the shallows.

Isabelle had struggled up again and reached the dog. She grabbed hold of him and looked back in terror at the depth of

232

water and the wild crashing waves that lay between her and safety.

'Don't try to move,' Robert was shouting. 'Stay where you are and hang on to the rock. I'm coming to fetch you.'

She did as she was told. Another wave broke over her head but she came through it, flattening herself against the wall of rock until Robert could reach her.

The waves were bouncing in higher than ever and it took all his strength to fight his way through them.

Isabelle felt her numbed fingers begin to slide. She could not hold on any longer. A huge wave swept her into darkness. She came through it spluttering and choking, then Robert was there, the water receded and she was leaning against him.

'Give me the dog,' he gasped, 'and then hang on to me.'

With Rory under one arm and the other around her waist, Robert struggled back with Isabelle, slipping on the slimy seaweed, falling and then fighting their way up again, until at last they reached the shallows and collapsed together on the narrow strip of shingle beach.

'Whatever were you doing down here at this time of the morning?' he gasped breathlessly.

'I didn't realise the sea came in so fast. It's not like the marshes . . .'

'In winter it reaches the castle walls. I thought for a moment I'd lost you.' He began to recover his breath and got to his feet. 'Come along. You're soaked to the skin. You mustn't stay here in this wind. You'll catch your death of cold.'

His arm around her, he was hurrying her along and through the door. Servants were up and about now. They stared at the master and his lady, water dripping from them on to the newly swept floors and rugs in the great hall and up the stairs. Kirsty met them on the landing looking concerned.

'The fire's burning up lovely, my lady,' she said, 'and I'll be bringing the hot coffee this very minute.'

'Bring the brandy with you too,' said Robert.

'Aye, my lord, aye, I'll do that.'

Kirsty had not only built up a roaring fire but had also thought to fetch the big bath towels and hang them by the

233

hearth to warm. Robert put down Rory who immediately shook himself violently, spraying water all over them.

'I could murder that little beast,' he exclaimed feelingly.

Now that it was all over, Isabelle was laughing and shivering helplessly.

'For heaven's sake, don't just stand there, girl, strip off those wet clothes,' he said, relief from tension making him impatient.

'You too,' she said, fumbling at her skirt with numbed fingers.

'In a moment. Here, let me.'

He pushed aside her frozen hands and began to undress her, throwing aside the soaked skirt and shawl, wrapping the huge warm towel around her and then kneeling to pull off the sodden boots one by one, and chafing her icy feet.

'I'm all right. I'm warm now,' she protested.

It was only then that he peeled off his soaked nightshirt, kicked off his breeches and boots and rubbed himself down vigorously. He wrapped the towel around his waist and turned towards her.

She had begun to dry her hair, her arms upraised so that the towel slipped from her naked shoulders and back, the painful marks where she had been whipped now almost vanished.

For a moment it was as it had been on that morning when he had seen her first. She was Aphrodite rising from the foam of the sea, and a violent desire rose in him quickened by the danger, by the agonising fear that had shaken him when he thought he wasn't going to reach her in time.

He came towards her slowly, taking the towel from her hands and tossing it aside. Her body glowed rosily in the light of the fire. He ran his hands up the long slim legs, across the flat stomach to the finely rounded breasts and his kisses followed his hands burning like fire. She trembled as they reached her throat and then her mouth. He teased her lips open, his tongue seeking hers and finding it, and she was shaken by a curious sensuous feeling of languor and weakness. She swayed towards him murmuring something, a word of protest, almost of fear, but now he was beyond control. He lifted her in his arms and carried her to the bed. He had never made love to her like this before, his hands seemed to be everywhere, exploring her body,

234

arousing feelings she did not know she possessed. She was shaking, half afraid and yet longing for him to go on and on.

Kirsty coming with the tray, knocked and then opened the door. She took one look at the couple on the bed, then put down the tray and fled. They had not even heard her.

This time he held nothing back. He could not. He was carrying her with him into realms she never knew existed. It was as if something inside her had burst open and he was deep within her. Then she could no longer think or reason, but only give herself up to it.

Presently they lay quiet, his arm still around her, his head on her breast.

'Your hair is still damp,' she said dreamily, 'and you smell of the sea.'

'Hardly surprising. I must have swallowed a good deal of it.'

'Oh wind from the sea, blow my lover to me . . .'

'What's that?'

'An old song Gwennie used to sing. The boy she loved was captured by the Press Gang.'

'Poor devil.'

'Perhaps he'll come home now that we are going to have peace.'

'Very probably, if we do and if it lasts.'

He shifted a little and she sat up suddenly in consternation.

'Robert, there is a tray by the hearth. Kirsty must have brought it and seen us.'

'Does it matter? You're my wife, you know, not my mistress.'

But she could not accept it with quite the same indifference he did.

'Yes, I know, but . . .'

He was not sure whether his precipitate action had distressed or pleased her and wisely did not enquire.

'Let's see what she has brought before it grows cold,' he said, getting off the bed and reaching for his dressing gown.

He knelt by the fire pouring the coffee and putting in a little brandy. When he brought it to her she was sitting up, her damp hair tousled into ringlets, the blanket pulled around her.

'You look about ten years old,' he said, amused. 'I shall be accused of cradle snatching.'

He fetched his own cup and sat beside her. They sipped for a little in silence.

'You've put brandy in it,' she said suddenly. 'You'll make me drunk.'

'Not on a teaspoonful. It will counteract the chill from this morning's dip.'

'Robert, were you angry with me last night?'

'Angry? No, I don't think so. Should I have been?'

'Because I left the party so early.'

'I didn't blame you. The trouble is I've known some of these youngsters since I was a boy, only I've grown up and they haven't. They still feel it's the thing to act like lunatics and drink themselves into a stupor and I don't any longer. But it's not so easy to escape on occasions such as these.'

'Were you drunk?'

'Not so as you'd notice, but I didn't want to disturb you. I woke up with a confounded headache but the sea has cured that.'

'I feel so guilty.'

'So you ought,' he said teasingly. 'Thank God Kirsty woke me in time or you wouldn't be here with me now and nor would that abominable little dog.'

They were back to their old loving friendly relationship, but were they? She knew now of a deeper, darker side of her husband, a trembling realisation of it that made her doubt her own feelings. She did not think anything would ever be quite the same again.

The next day Robert began to make preparations for their return journey to London and to her surprise she regretted it. It meant a new life, another set of rules. It meant Marian who disliked her and Lucien who perhaps liked her too much. All problems Robert would have dismissed as trivial but which loomed large to her: she braced herself to face them.

12

It was a cold blustery March morning and the fire in Marian's sitting room was burning sulkily. Every now and then the variable wind would send little puffs of smoke into the room making her eyes sting, while a cold draught chillingly crept up her back. In exasperation she put down her pen and crossed to the hearth, poking the coal vigorously into fitful flames that died almost at once. It was really too bad when the chimney had been swept just before Christmas. Nothing seemed to have gone right ever since her brother had brought his young wife back to Arlington Street, which was not really fair, but then Marian felt she had cause to feel aggrieved. She had just suffered a most annoying interview with Cook.

Mrs Pratt was a formidable woman who knew her value. No employer would willingly have seen her go to a rival with her superb soufflés, her exquisite sauces and her truly magical ice pudding. She had knocked and come in folding her arms across her ample bosom, her starched white apron impeccable, her manner respectful but stubbornly independent.

'May I have a word with you, my lady?'

'Yes, of course, Mrs Pratt. What is it?'

'It concerns that country girl come with young Mrs Armitage, Gwennie Foster.'

Marian's heart sank. It was not the first time. She had known there would be trouble, she had warned Robert but he had paid no heed. Isabelle had asked for her and that was all that mattered to him, she thought with a tinge of resentment.

So Gwennie had come to them in the New Year and had been immediately unpopular in the kitchen. She was an outsider for one thing and for that reason on the defensive. She was far too outspoken, even daring to criticise Mrs Pratt's famous recipe for

237

pork and beef galantine as being too rich and what was worse she had a most irritating way of hinting that she knew a great deal more about the new young mistress and yet refused absolutely to satisfy their very natural curiosity.

'I'm not one to carry tales as you well know, my lady,' said Mrs Pratt virtuously, 'but I feel bound to report that Gwennie has been stealing food from my pantry.'

'Stealing food!' exclaimed Marian. 'Whatever do you mean? Isn't the girl being given enough to eat?'

'Indeed she is and more than enough,' said Mrs Pratt indignantly. 'None of my staff go short and I must admit that it is apparently not just for herself. The scullery maid reported to me that she was seen carrying it out late in the evening and giving it to one of those dirty beggars that seem to be under our feet wherever we go nowadays.'

'Many of them, I'm afraid, are men who have been discharged from the armed services and they're unemployed with nowhere to live,' said Marian placatingly. 'Perhaps the girl feels sorry for one of them.'

'That's as may be,' said Mrs Pratt, 'but that's not the worst of it, not by a long chalk. Last night and the night before that, she was seen bringing one of these wretches into the scullery and letting him sit and eat his food there if you please and I have reason to believe that last night he actually slept in a corner of the stable.' She paused as if the enormity of it took her breath away. 'It's not right, my lady, he could be a robber or worse. We could all be murdered in our beds. What with the Master being away in France and Mr Mackie with him and Mr Hawke off for a few days visiting his sick sister, who is there left to defend us against some villain and his confederates, I'd like to know? It's as good as opening the door to them. The young maids are terrified already and Kitty reported that the new child just come from the orphanage was shivering and crying all the night through. I don't like it, I don't like it at all, my lady.'

'No, I can understand that.'

Marian sighed. She was not easily alarmed and thought Mrs Pratt's tale had a good deal of exaggeration in it. However it

238

could not be allowed to go on. Something had to be done about it.

'Leave it with me,' she said at last. 'I will speak to Lady Isabelle and then talk to the girl myself.'

'Very good, my lady. I'm sure I'm not one to start up any trouble but I felt it was my bounden duty to come and tell you. I'd never forgive myself if anything dreadful were to happen.'

'No, of course not, and thank you. I will deal with it.'

Left alone, Marian rang for Kitty and sent her to find Isabelle only to be told that she had gone out early riding in Hyde Park and had not yet returned.

That was another source of irritation. Robert had bought his wife a beautiful and expensive mare and made sure she was properly schooled. He had ridden out himself with Isabelle as often as his work permitted.

Ever since his return from Scotland he had been continually called in to Whitehall to help deal with the terms of the peace treaty that still hung fire due to Bonaparte's persistent arguing over every tiny point at issue until at last, in exasperation and aware that the country was becoming more and more impatient, Lord Cornwallis and Lord Hawkesbury had been despatched to Paris with an ultimatum. A final settlement must be made and the treaty signed and ratified within eight days or the whole fragile structure would be scrapped and the two countries would be once again at war, a situation neither Britain nor France wanted, and Robert had gone with them as someone who had been familiar with it from the outset and could be relied upon to interpret the subtle nuances which the cunning and unscrupulous French might insinuate into it. He had been quite uncertain when he would return.

It was not until an hour later that Isabelle came in glowing with health after her morning ride but inwardly apprehensive. A summons to Marian's room nearly always meant a reprimand or a reproach delivered in the sweetest possible way but extremely irritating for all that. She wondered which it would be this time.

Rory came bouncing in with her and the two spaniels lying on the hearth rug sat up stiffening and then slowly subsided again. There had been a battle royal in the first few days which had ended in Oliver with a torn ear, Roland ignominiously taking refuge under the sofa and Robert, who had valiantly separated them, with a badly bitten hand. Now there was a kind of armed peace with the two aristocrats demurely trotting beside the Highland ragamuffin when Edward took them walking.

'I'm sorry if I've kept you waiting, Marian, but I'm only just returned,' said Isabelle breezily. 'There was such a wind in the park this morning, it blew all the cobwebs away.'

'You shouldn't be riding out alone,' scolded Marian. 'I've told you before and you know Robert doesn't approve of it.'

'Well, Ian is with him and Edward rides like a sack of potatoes. If I could go alone all over the marshes without harm, I'm sure nothing could happen to me in the park in the midst of a crowd.'

'That's just the point. It's not at all proper and you could receive some very undesirable attentions.'

'Oh proper! What does that mean?' said Isabelle impatiently. 'Nobody has accosted me yet. It might be fun if they did.' Marian looked scandalised and she went on quickly. 'What did you want to see me about?'

She listened to the story of Gwennie's misdeeds in silence.

'I'm sure there must be some simple explanation,' she said at last. 'I'll speak to her about it.'

'Please do so as soon as possible. I can't afford to lose Mrs Pratt. She is one of the best cooks in London.'

'I'm sure it won't come to that.'

'Let's hope not.'

Summoned to the morning room, Gwennie was at first highly indignant.

'I never stole so much as a crumb. I wouldn't never do such a thing. I went without myself and only took what would have been my share, pieces of pie and some bread and cheese. It's a wicked lie to say I stole.'

'I believe you, Gwennie, don't upset yourself. But why did you take the food? Who is this man?'

She stared at Isabelle for a moment and then it all poured out.

240

'It's Tom, Miss, Tom who was took up by the Press Gang all those years ago. He's served in the same ship all this time, rose to gunner's mate he did and now with the war coming to an end, he's been discharged with all the others. But he'd never forgotten, never for one minute, he said. He went to High Willows and they told him I was up here in London so he trudged all the way 'cos, you see, he never really learned to write proper. A week ago it was when I saw him outside on the night I took Rory for his last walk. Half afraid he was to knock, it all looking so grand, but I knew him at once. He didn't look no different except he's lost three fingers off his left hand, blown off they were, and his arm still so stiff he can't hardly lift it, and that makes it hard for him to get any labouring work. He hadn't eaten a morsel for two whole days so I had to do something. He didn't want to take it at first, thinking I might be blamed.'

'Why did you bring him in?'

Gwennie hesitated. 'That were two nights ago. It were blowing that cold, a wind to cut you in half and raining with it. I let him just come inside and eat the food and then with Mr Mackie being away I thought he might just bed down in the stable with the horses and it wouldn't do nobody any harm, just till he finds something for himself, and I don't know why that Mrs Pratt has to go running to Lady Marian about it and getting you into trouble.'

'I'm in no trouble, Gwennie, but my husband is away and I'm not sure what to do for the best . . . perhaps I'd better come and talk to Tom.'

'Would you, Miss, would you?' said Gwennie eagerly. She could never get used to calling Isabelle Madam or my lady, try as she would.

So that evening the kitchen staff had the unusual pleasure of seeing young Lady Kilgour dressed for dinner, and looking lovely as a dream in the dazzled eyes of the youngest maid, going through to the scullery and talking to the disreputable beggar who, it now appeared, was Gwennie's fancy man. In actual fact Tom was neat and clean enough in his sailor's canvas trousers and jacket, awkwardly turning over and over in his hands the straw hat that still wore the name band *Arethusa*.

'I never meant no harm, Miss – my lady – it were just wantin' so bad to see Gwennie again. It be nearly six years now since I bin at sea.'

'I know, Tom. I do sympathise. What did you do before the Press Gang took you up?'

'I were workin' with horses, my lady,' he said eagerly, 'at the George in Rye it were. I grew up on a farm, see, and I were used to 'em, doin' nicely I were, and then . . . well, 'tain't no use goin' on about what's past. I thought with all them coaches and carriages up here, it would be easy to find work but seems there be too many of us lookin' out for it.'

'Listen, Tom,' said Isabelle, making up her mind. 'I can't promise anything, but when my husband comes back from Paris, I will ask him if he can help you to find something and in the meantime Gwennie will bring you some food and – and if it will help, you can go on sleeping in a corner of the stables.'

'I'm not askin' for charity . . .' he began stiffly.

'Tom, you never ought to say such things,' whispered Gwennie.

'It's all right. I understand,' went on Isabelle, 'and I daresay there are plenty of little jobs you could undertake for us if you would.'

'Anything, my lady, anything. You just tell me and I'll do it but I wouldn't want to cause you no bother . . .'

Despite his brave words, Isabelle thought he looked woefully thin and half starved.

'It's only temporary,' she warned. 'It depends on what my husband says about it.' She cut short Gwennie's fervent thanks. 'Don't worry about it any longer. I'll speak to Cook.'

Up to now she had left all household management in Marian's capable hands, not daring to interfere. Now she summoned all her dignity and gave the astounded staff a short lecture on being kind to those who had fallen on hard times.

'Tom has fought and been wounded in the defence of all of us,' she said, 'so we shouldn't grudge a little to help him now. I'm sure I can rely on your goodness of heart.'

'Well, I never,' said Mrs Pratt when she had gone. 'I never thought she had it in her, not for one minute, I didn't. She's always been quiet as a mouse up to now. If the Master hasn't realised it already, I dare swear he has got himself a handful there, and Lady Marian too!'

'Didn't she look a dream?' murmured the youngest maid, still wrapped in wonder.

'You'll find yourself in a dream if you don't get on with peeling those vegetables,' said Mrs Pratt sharply. 'Talking like that about your betters indeed!'

Marian was outraged when at dinner Isabelle confessed to what she had done and Guy, who had joined them that evening, glanced from one to the other in silent amusement.

'Do you realise what you have done, giving a man of that kind the run of the house?'

'He is coming no further than the stables.'

'That's what you believe but who knows what he can work through that serving girl of yours. He could be up to any trick. You should have waited till Robert returns before taking it upon yourself to make such a decision.'

'Is that what you would have done? Tom could be dead from cold and hunger before then. What about that hostel of yours in the East End you are always talking about? Do you turn them away to die in the streets?'

'That's entirely different,' said Marian stiffly.

'Why is it different?' Isabelle paused a moment before she said deliberately, 'I know you have lived in this house for a great many years and I've only been here for a few months but I *am* Robert's wife and I think I ought to be allowed to have some say in how things are done.'

'You'd like me to go, wouldn't you? That's been the trouble all along. You want to drive me away.'

'No, no, I don't, indeed I don't. I've never thought of such a thing. I want us to be friends.'

'Friends! I'm afraid I find that hard to believe when you've tricked my brother into a marriage he should never have made. I find the whole situation intolerable, quite intolerable.' Marian got to her feet, trembling with anger. 'And now if you'll excuse me . . .' and she hurried from the room, nearly colliding with

243

the servants who had come to remove the first course and bring fresh plates.

'It's about time you showed her who is mistress here,' said Guy when the door closed behind them. 'She doesn't like her nose to be put out of joint, that's obvious. Why don't you ask Robert to send her packing?'

'I couldn't, Guy, I simply couldn't. She did offer to go, you know, when we came back from Scotland but I knew Robert didn't really wish it, though he left the decision to me, and I felt I had to ask her to stay on. This is her home. It would have been cruel. She really loves him and he is very fond of her. I couldn't interfere between them. I just wish she didn't dislike me so much.'

'You know why, don't you? He is all she has and she would dislike anyone who took him so completely away from her.'

'But I haven't taken him away, not really.'

'Oh yes, you have, my dear. I don't think you realise how very much he thinks of you.'

'You're talking nonsense.'

'Indeed I'm not. I see a good deal that you don't so I warn you – look out for squalls. Now I must go.'

'Oh must you?' she said wistfully. 'I was rather hoping we might have a quiet evening together for once.'

'Sorry but I'm promised at the theatre, the new farce at the Haymarket actually.'

'You'll be very late.'

'I'll be in time for the last act.'

'Guy,' she stayed him with a hand on his arm, 'you don't visit the gaming houses with those friends of yours, do you?'

'My dear girl, what have I to gamble with?'

'Robert gives you a generous allowance.'

'And David doles it out as carefully as if I were a schoolboy. He's a high flyer, you know, Belle, but he makes quite sure I don't follow. He keeps tight hold of the reins. I'll be glad to be free and responsible for myself.'

'Oh Guy, it's barely six months since . . .'

'I know, I know. Don't mistake me. David is a good fellow and Robert has been extraordinarily generous and I'm an

244

ungrateful pig, I do realise that, and one day I'm going to pay him back every penny. Stop worrying about me, Isabelle, I'll fall on my feet.'

'Make sure you do.'

'I will.' He dropped a kiss on the top of her head and went off cheerfully.

Isabelle looked after him wondering if she was simply being foolish to be so concerned about him. Guy had taken to his new life like a duck to water. At the crammers he had met other youngsters studying like himself, sons of good families who took life lightly and were out for a good time even if it was on limited funds. Guy was welcomed into their midst and having a good grounding in history and languages naturally did as little work as possible. He had already tasted the heady pleasures of the gaming tables, not amongst the great at Crockfords, but at smaller establishments, and with beginner's luck had made several small wins. But for David's watchful eye he might have plunged a good deal deeper.

With good clothes, money in his pocket and the prestige of his sister's marriage, life presented him with dazzling prospects and an absolute blind confidence in his own ability to avoid all the pitfalls lying in wait for the inexperienced.

Marian did not come down to the drawing room, so Isabelle spent a lonely evening with Rory on her lap and a pile of new books beside her but she did not find them nearly so thrilling without Robert to discuss them with and point out what she should study and what she should avoid.

In the weeks since Christmas they had not gone all that much into society, partly because Robert did not particularly care for dining out except with chosen friends and partly because he thought a good many of the invitations came out of sheer curiosity, and he considered it wiser that she should be given time to settle into her new life before being launched into the maelstrom of London society.

It did not mean that she did not have a great many other pleasures. He took her to the theatre and while he sat yawning a little at Kemble's heavy periods and Mrs Siddons' high drama as Lady Macbeth, Isabelle sat entranced, dazed with wonder at

245

her first play and hungry for more. They went to the opera and to concerts and he drove her down to Brighton in a high-flying phaeton with a pair of blood horses, even letting her handle the reins on a quiet section of the road. Brighton was all the rage since the Prince of Wales had bought a house there and was having it transformed into the semblance of an Eastern fairy tale. After they had duly admired it they tramped along the shore to Black Rock in a tearing wind that set Robert's teeth on edge but which Isabelle adored, her cheeks flushed, her hair blown into an enchanting tangle and Rory dancing along ahead of them.

Sometimes, watching them on a quiet evening reading to one another, arguing over some knotty point or laughing at some jest she did not understand, Marian had to admit that her brother had changed, seemed to have become younger, more irresponsible, less serious.

She spoke about it one day to David.

'I don't understand it,' she complained. 'He is so different. He takes things so lightly.'

'He's happy, that's all, not carrying the burden of the world on his shoulders as he has been for the last few years and he's very much in love. It changes a man.'

'But they're not like lovers – not really,' she objected, 'more like brother and sister. I don't like it, David.'

'For God's sake, stop fretting about it, woman. People are different. They don't all follow a pattern. She is a rare and lovely creature. I tell you, if it weren't for Robert, I'd willingly take a fling with her myself.'

The Treaty of Amiens, as it was called, was signed at last at three o'clock in the morning on March 25th after a gruelling session of five hours with Bonaparte and his astute and unscrupulous foreign minister Talleyrand exacting concessions till the very last moment. The peace mission returned utterly exhausted to a Britain seemingly going off its head in celebration. As the news spread through the country, bonfires flared and fireworks exploded. In London happy crowds surged through the streets almost as bright as day with rows of candles blazing in the windows and flaming illuminations outside the French Consulate in Portman Square. Even the gaming houses in St James's Street were resplendent with lamp-lit crowns and gaudy patriotic inscriptions.

Robert was received rapturously by his wife and his sister but refused flatly to go out and join the cheering multitude.

'All they're thinking about is the price of bread coming down and Hollands gin and French brandy flowing across the Channel,' he said drily.

'And will that happen?' said Marian.

'I doubt it, I doubt it very much.'

'You don't believe this peace will last, do you?' said David later when they were waiting for the ladies to join them before dinner.

'To be honest, I don't. I talked with a great many people in Paris and drew my own conclusions. It will last just as long as Bonaparte wants it to last and not a moment longer. After that there is going to be hell to pay.'

'Do the others in the government agree with you?'

'Pitt does and Dundas, Cornwallis too. After it was all over he remarked, "We've signed a treaty not for peace but for war!" It's a gloomy outlook but I'm afraid he is absolutely right.'

However he said nothing of this to Isabelle or his sister especially as Mrs Pratt had excelled herself with a truly magnificent dinner, despite the kitchen staff being in as much a state of rapture as the rest of the country.

Guy joined them when they were half way through, his hat lost, his hair tousled, his coat nearly torn off his back. He had been out in the rejoicing streets and had seen the French Envoy, who had brought the news, greeted by a hysterical mob who took the horses out of his carriage and dragged it triumphantly to Downing Street.

In all the excitement of that evening, Isabelle completely forgot about her protégé who much to Gwennie's gratification had been invited to partake of a glass of wine and join the kitchen staff when they sat down to their own dinner.

The noise, the cheering, the surging crowds, the popping of fireworks went on till the early hours of the morning so she slept a good deal later than usual and she was only half dressed when Robert came into the bedroom.

'What's all this Marian has been telling me about some poor wretch who has been bedding down in our stables and frightening Cook and the maidservants into fits?'

Isabelle bit her lip in vexation. How like Marian to get her story in first.

'She said something about you being responsible. Is that right?' he went on.

'Yes, it is. I told him he could sleep there.'

'A little rash, wasn't it?'

'I didn't think so.' She swung round on the dressing stool to face him. 'Marian has only told you the half of it. He is Tom, Gwennie's Tom. Do you remember me telling you about him?'

'The fellow who got himself picked up by the Press Gang?'

'Yes. He had been wounded, his left arm and hand are practically useless so when he was discharged he walked all the way to London to see her again and he looked so thin, so desperate, I couldn't see him turned away. I said he could stay but only till you came home. You see he had nowhere to go and I thought, I hoped, that perhaps you could do something for him. Could you? You know so many people.'

He looked down at her, frowning a little and wondering how many more of the homeless and abandoned he might be asked to take on.

'I don't exactly choose their servants for them, my dear,' he said half humorously. 'Am I expected to provide for all the poor wretches discharged from the Navy?'

'Oh no, not all of them, just for Tom. Please, Robert.'

'Well, perhaps. I'll have a word with Ian and then see him for myself. There may be something.'

'I knew you would. I knew everything would be all right when you came home. I told Marian so.'

'Did you miss me?'

'Every moment.'

'I had it in mind to bring you something as a memento but I was shut up every hour of the day arguing my head off with Talleyrand who has been royalist, exile, revolutionary and now seems set fair to be an ardent Bonapartist. When all this excitement has died down, we'll take a pleasure trip to Paris. Would you like that?'

'Oh yes, more than anything.'

He touched her cheek and smiled and then went in search of Ian Mackie.

'The fellow certainly seems to have a way with the nags,' said Ian cautiously, 'there's no doubt about that and he's a decent cleanly body too. You could have eaten your dinner off the stable floor.'

'That's navy discipline for you. Can we do with an extra hand in the mews?'

'Aye, we could now with your lady's mare and the new pair of carriage horses.'

'Very well. I'll speak to him and if I think he is a likely choice, we'll try him out for a month or so and see how we go on. At least there'll be one less begging on the streets.'

'I think you're being quite ridiculously generous,' said Marian irritably when she heard of it. 'You're bound to regret it. We'll have that girl running off to the mews every tiff and turn, you mark my words, and probably getting herself pregnant into the bargain.'

'We'll cross that hurdle when we come to it,' he said equably and brushed away Gwennie's fervent gratitude.

That spring fashionable London, which had been as it were holding its breath wondering which way the cat would jump, began to celebrate more decorously but no less extravagantly, beginning with the Countess of Wincanton's ball. Everybody who was anybody, and some who were nobody, were angling for an invitation and it was strongly rumoured that the Prince of Wales himself would look in later in the evening.

'Do we go?' asked Robert at breakfast passing the gilt engraved card across the table to his wife and his sister.

'Of course we must go,' said Marian. 'If anyone is responsible for the success of this treaty, then you are. You must be there.'

'You exaggerate, my dear. I did little but interpret a word or two here and there. What do you say, Isabelle?'

'I've never been to a real ball,' she said a little wistfully.

'Then that settles it. It will be hot, noisy and quite unbearably crowded but we will go. You'd better look to your finery, ladies.'

It was the first major event of the season and also the first grand affair Isabelle had attended as Robert's wife. As the days passed she began to think of it with a certain degree of apprehension. She had a new gown she had chosen for herself, ignoring Marian who thought the sheer satin of palest green with an overdress of organza embroidered with golden stars far too theatrical. Her brother's wife should look more dignified, more in the current matronly style, not like a will-o'-the-wisp blown by a wind. She complained about it to David who wisely made no comment. Women must fight these battles out between themselves.

Gwennie helped her to dress that evening. She had turned into a very passable ladies' maid, caring for all Isabelle's new gowns and underwear with a loving attention. She was threading a gold embroidered ribbon through the dark hair when she saw Robert come in from his dressing room and at his nod quietly vanished.

Isabelle had taken out the gold filigree necklace he had given her in York and he came up behind her and took it out of her hands.

'Not that bauble. I have something more fitting.'

She looked up at him in surprise. 'I thought you said you didn't bring anything from Paris.'

'Neither did I. I chose this for you before I went away.'

He put the necklace around her neck and busied himself with the clasp.

It was emeralds and diamonds skilfully wrought into the shapes of tiny flowers and so exquisitely beautiful that she gave a little gasp.

'Like it?' he asked.

'Oh Robert, it's – it's fabulous.'

'My wife is going to put all the other society beauties in the shade.'

'You shouldn't say such things. Something terrible is bound

250

to happen. I shall probably fall flat on my face when I make my curtsey to the Prince.'

'I doubt if that will worry him. He will forgive anything to a beautiful woman.'

She turned round to face him.

'Robert, I don't know how to say this. You are so good to me and I'm so terribly grateful.'

She saw the quick frown.

'A fig for gratitude! I do it because it pleases me and for no other reason. And now we must go. Marian will scold us if we keep her waiting.'

The road leading to the imposing Wincanton house in Piccadilly was a river of light as the coaches rolled up one after the other, disgorging a galaxy of silks and satins, of jewels and flowers and ostrich plumes, the red and gold of uniforms, the black, green and plum of handsome evening coats, satin breeches, white silk stockings and buckled shoes.

For one panic-stricken moment she wanted only to turn and flee, then the carriage had pulled up, the door was opened, Robert was helping her out and she was somehow walking calmly up the grand staircase, her hand on his arm, followed by Marian and David totally unaware that the joyous evening before her would change and disrupt both Robert's life and her own.

To say she caused something of a sensation was putting it mildly. There were a number of people who had attended that country wedding in Lydd Church alive with curiosity. Then to their disappointment the couple had vanished into Scotland and since their return little has been seen of them. Spiteful rumours spread among the gossips that Viscount Kilgour was keeping his kitchen-maid wife well hidden.

If that was true then it was to some purpose for she certainly surprised them that night, and most of the younger men were of the opinion that Kilgour might be a sober high-minded intellectual but he certainly knew how to pick 'em! They noted he kept close by her side for the early part of the evening but after a time when she had lost her shyness and began to enjoy herself, they discovered she was no dumb beauty but had a pretty wit spiced with a faintly foreign accent that was decidedly intriguing. French, they said she was, which they found easy to believe for she had style and was different. She said what she thought with a simplicity that appealed to jaded appetites. The women however were not so easily conquered. They felt a certain resentment that she should so easily monopolise not only her husband but that seasoned man of the world, David Fraser, together with most of the other more attractive young men and she had a pretty way of glancing at her husband and waiting for his nod before letting herself be carried away into the dancing.

'Play-acting! That's what it is!' remarked one dowager who had two unmarried daughters to another who had three and one still in the nursery. 'There is something artful about her and where, I ask you, where has she been all these years?'

Isabelle, unaware of the effect she had made, was thoroughly enjoying herself and said so to Venetia whom she met for a moment in the supper interval.

'I didn't even know you were in London. Why haven't you been to call on me?' she asked reproachfully.

'We've only just come up from High Willows.'

'Is Perry here?'

'No.' Venetia had a sullen angry look. 'You might as well know though it's not been announced yet. I'm going to be married.'

'Married! To Perry?'

'Heavens, no.' For a moment Ventia looked so savagely unhappy that Isabelle was startled. 'He's not even in London. I'm going to marry Sir Hugo Dexter. Do you know him? He is over there talking to Papa.'

Isabelle looked and gasped.

'But he's so *old*, Venetia.'

'Not really, only fifty-five,' she went on in the same cold, bitter voice. 'And he's a widower with two daughters. He's very, very rich and has a great deal of influence which is just what Papa wants.'

'But you can't marry a man like that, you can't, Venetia. You can't care for him.'

252

'What does that matter? Hugo wants me and he wants a son and I'm dead tired of fighting Mamma. At least I shall escape. I shall have my own home. I shall be free.'

'But you won't be free . . . not really.'

'Oh yes, I shall. I shall make sure of that. He's beckoning me. I must go.'

Isabelle put a hand on her arm. 'Venetia, will you come and see me? Will you? Please do?'

'Perhaps. I will try,' and then she had pulled away smiling sweetly at the grey-haired man who had taken her possessively by the arm and was leading her away.

Isabelle looked after her, puzzled and distressed, wanting to help and not knowing what she could do.

The Prince arrived at last. Running to fat though he was only just past forty, he was still handsome in a florid kind of way. He smiled at the new Lady Kilgour graciously when she made her curtsey.

'I gather your husband has been doing great things for us in Paris,' he said.

'You are too kind, sir,' said Robert as he bowed over his hand. 'My wife and I recently had the pleasure of seeing the remarkable rebuilding of your country house at Brighton.'

'Isn't it splendid?' said the Prince obviously much gratified. 'Those two new wings and the exquisite shell canopies over all the windows . . . I'm having the interior remodelled too in a Chinese style. The Music Room will really be something, dragons, you know, and wallpaper that has to be seen to be believed. Does your wife care for music – Haydn, Mozart?'

'Oh yes, yes, indeed, your highness,' murmured Isabelle.

'Good, good, then you must both come to one of my musical parties at Carlton House.'

'We should be honoured, sir.'

Robert led his wife away, smiling down at her.

'You didn't fall flat on your face after all. In fact you have made an impression. They fight for invitations to his musical evenings. You know, my dear, the Prince really possesses quite good taste – if only he wasn't so easily led astray by those around him who are only interested in filling their pockets at the expense of his. Are you weary of all this yet?'

'Oh no, not in the very least.'

So he stifled his boredom and stayed on, indulging her as he might have done a child at her first grand party.

It was some time later and Robert was leaning against one of the flower-garlanded pillars when Marian abandoned her partner and came to join him. The dance had just come to an end. Across the ballroom Isabelle was standing under a blaze of candles in a shimmer of gold and green.

'Oh! she doth teach the torches to burn bright,' murmured Robert almost under his breath.

'What did you say?' exclaimed Marian, not sure she had heard aright.

'I always thought that line exaggerated till now but old Will knew exactly what he was talking about.'

'You are no Romeo,' said Marian tartly.

'True, true,' he smiled. 'Not like me at all, is it?'

He is far deeper in love than I ever imagined, thought Marian with a sudden sharp pang. Please God don't let her hurt him too much.

Frowning, she followed the direction of his eyes.

'Who is that with Isabelle?'

'The Chevalier de St George whom I don't particularly care for, nor his so-called nephew. I have a grave suspicion they are not all they pretend to be.'

'How do you mean? Spies? Emigrés, but in Bonaparte's pay?' Marian sounded shocked.

'I don't know, Marian. We have nothing specific against either of them, just doubts, that's all, and maybe now we are at peace, it is of little importance. I think perhaps I'll go across and rescue her.'

Isabelle, exhilarated by the dancing, had been thanking her partner and preparing to return to her husband when someone spoke her name.

The silky voice of the Chevalier was saying, 'May I present

254

my nephew? He has been longing to meet you from the moment he arrived.'

She turned quickly and was unexpectedly face to face with Lucien, slim, graceful, fashionably dressed, the long dark hair now cut short and curled, but beneath the air of elegance it was the same Lucien, the olive skin, the rakish charm, the faint impression of some wild creature who walked alone and dangerously, the same dark smouldering eyes now fixed on her, alive with recognition. The surprise, the shock, were so intense, she could not take in the words that were being said, only knew that he had taken her hand in his, that he was kissing it, holding it too long, the very touch seemed to scorch her skin.

He was saying something complimentary but she felt so confused she could find no reply and then Robert had come up beside her and had taken her arm.

'Forgive me but I fear I must take my wife away. There are friends who wish to say goodbye.'

'You are not leaving yet surely,' said Lucien. 'I had hoped so much that your lady would do me the honour of dancing with me.'

'Later perhaps. Come, my dear,' Robert was turning away when the Chevalier stopped him.

'I understand we must congratulate you on the successful conclusion of the treaty.'

'You are mistaken, sir,' said Robert stiffly. 'Any congratulations are due to Lord Cornwallis. I did nothing.'

'I think you choose to underrate yourself.'

Robert shrugged. 'If you say so,' and walked away taking Isabelle with him.

The two Frenchmen stood looking after them before the Chevalier said quietly, 'You are quite sure she is the girl?'

'Oh yes, undoubtedly. I had not looked to see her married to *him* of all people.'

'It could be a stroke of good fortune for us when the time comes. Follow it up, Lucien, but go cautiously. If Robert Armitage is who we think he is, he could be formidable.'

'Trust me. I'll have her eating out of my hand,' said Lucien confidently. For once the task assigned to him was one he could pursue with pleasure as well as profit.

Isabelle was saying, 'I suddenly feel quite desperately weary. Do you think we could go now?'

'I am afraid it is not etiquette to leave before the Prince. You've exhausted yourself, my dear, with too much dancing. Come, sit quietly for a while. I'll find you a glass of champagne.'

She let herself drop on the gilded chair with a little sigh while Robert went in search of a footman. It was ridiculous to feel so disturbed. It was nearly a year ago now. She was Robert's wife, she had put all memory of him behind her, and yet the moment he had touched her it was as if the intervening months had been swept away and they were standing again on that deserted beach, the wind blowing around them, the taste of salt on his lips, her castaway, whose life had belonged so entirely to her . . . She leaned her head back wearily closing her eyes. Of course it was all nonsense, it was only the shock, it would pass.

She sensed rather than saw him sit beside her, his breath on her cheek as he leaned towards her.

'Come, dance with me, Isabelle, we've so much to say to one another, haven't we? I've waited so long for this moment.' He gave a little chuckle. 'Our last meeting – do you remember? Your poor cousin worsted by a rascally Frenchman and a dog . . .'

'Beth is dead,' she said tonelessly.

'How sad! Your guardian, your protector! She never quite trusted me, did she?'

She shivered as his hand ran caressingly down her bare arm.

The musicians had begun to play again, a dreamy waltz. It was a dance from the Continent, only just beginning to creep into England but fiercely resisted by the more staid and respectable assemblies as indecent. However the Countess had always been a little daring so now, at three o'clock in the morning with comparatively few couples left, she had given way to the urging of some of the younger set.

'Come,' said Lucien and like someone hypnotised, she let him pull her to her feet, take her in his arms and glide among the dancers. She could feel his hand burning through the thin silk of her gown and then they were swaying into the rhythm of the music.

'We must meet soon, we must talk. Where, Isabelle, where?' he was murmuring above her head.

She pulled herself together. 'I am married, Lucien.'

'Does that matter? Is your husband such a tyrant that he does not allow you even to talk to another man?'

'No, of course not, only . . .'

'Only nothing. When I saw you tonight, it was a dream come true.'

'Why did you never come back?'

'Sadly I'm not always my own master, but now it will be different.'

There was a sensuous pleasure in the feel of his arms, in the contact of their bodies, in the sheer joy of seeing him again and with a sigh she gave herself up to it.

Robert came back with the champagne and was joined by Marian. It was very late and the Prince had already left. He looked around him, puzzled for a moment.

'I left Isabelle here. She said she was tired.'

'Not too tired to be dancing it seems.'

Marian was scandalised. She did not approve of the waltz and to see Isabelle cavorting around the room in the arms of a man she had only just met – it wasn't decent.

Robert frowned but said nothing. No doubt that pushing young man had over persuaded her but all the same he didn't like it.

The music ended and Lucien brought her back to him, thanked her for the honour bestowed on him, smiled winningly at them both and strolled away.

'Such impudence!' muttered Marian.

'I thought you were exhausted,' said Robert briefly.

'So I was but I've never waltzed before.' It was a lame excuse.

'And I hope you never will again unless it is with your husband,' said Marian sharply.

Isabelle ignored her. 'Are you going to scold me, Robert?'

'Not this time.' He took her arm. 'Come along, it's late and high time we went home.'

They spoke very little in the carriage and the journey was not long. In the house one of the servants was waiting with biscuits and hot coffee but she shook her head.

'I think I'll go straight to bed, Robert.'

'Very well, my dear. I'll be up in a moment.'

'Good night, Marian.'

In the bedroom Gwennie was waiting for her.

'Shall I help you undress, my lady, and get ready for bed?'

'Not tonight, Gwennie. I can manage. It's so very late. You go to bed.'

'Was it very grand?' asked the girl a little wistfully.

'Yes, it was, quite wonderful and the Prince of Wales was there. He invited us to one of his parties and I've danced so much I've practically worn my shoes through.' Isabelle was a little impatient. 'Good night now, Gwennie.'

'Good night, my lady, sleep well.'

She went reluctantly. She would have liked a few minutes of interesting gossip.

Isabelle was in her petticoat and fumbling with the clasp of the new necklace when Robert came in.

'Let me do that for you.'

He came up behind her, loosened the clasp and as she dropped it on her dressing table he let his hands wander across her bare shoulders, pushing aside the satin petticoat and bending to kiss her neck.

For the first time she stiffened against him.

'No, Robert, please. I really am quite exhausted.'

He sensed her withdrawal at once and wondered what had disturbed her but he was too proud a man to force her to come to him against her will.

'It has been a very long and tiring evening for you and you did marvellously well. Good night, my love, and make sure you sleep late tomorrow.'

He went out closing the door behind him and she knew he had gone to the room where he sometimes slept when working late or called away early. Oh God, she thought, now I've hurt

258

him and I don't want to do that now or ever – it's just that tonight I can't seem to think straight. It's just that I thought now that we were at peace, Lucien would have gone back to France and I'd never need to see him again.

But it wasn't like that. He was there, overwhelmingly alive and her treacherous body had responded to him at once. If only it had not happened so quickly, if only she could have had time to prepare herself but seeing him so suddenly before her, that powerful animal magnetism had drawn her to him as quickly and irrevocably as it had done on the beaches of Dungeness. She must fight it, she must drive it out of herself and yet she knew with a frightening conviction that he was not going to allow her to escape. Fashionable society was comparatively small. They would inevitably meet frequently and if she deliberately shunned him, it would have the very effect she wanted to avoid. The curious and the scandalmongers would wonder why.

She lay awake for a long time planning her strategy. She would behave normally, laugh and talk with him as she did with David and the other young men, never refer to the past, never forget for one moment that she was Robert's wife. Lying in bed and planning it was easy and she did not yet know that the reality was going to be very different.

Lucien also had his plans. He found her eminently desirable, far more so than the waif on the seashore. She represented a challenge he was prepared to fight for and win for a variety of reasons and it would be a very long time before she realised just how frightening and dangerous some of those reasons would prove to be.

13

April that year was a magical month, the trees dressed in the tenderest green, the chestnuts ablaze in candles of pink and white, daffodils blowing in the wind, the air smelling fresh and new-washed, even the occasional showers had a brightness and a sparkle as if everything had sprung into new life at the coming of peace, with only a very few gloomy enough to prophesy it would not last.

Riding in Hyde Park two days after the ball, Isabelle was aware of a lightness of spirit that matched the spring morning. Seven o'clock was not the fashionable hour when society gathered to show off its fine horses, elegant riding habits or handsome carriages. That was why she liked it so much. It was the nearest she could come to those stolen mornings when she had ridden Juno down to the sea which occasionally she still remembered with regret, though Zara, the chestnut mare, had won her heart from the very first moment Robert had taken her to the mews and introduced them to one another.

He guessed at her reason and much to his sister's disapproval raised no objection to her riding out in the early morning, only advising her to take Ian with her when he was unable to accompany her himself. At this early hour there were very few ladies and she had a nodding acquaintance with admiring army officers, with dashing riders bent on displaying their equestrian skills, and elderly gentlemen who found an early morning canter did wonders for their overworked livers.

She urged Zara into a gallop outstripping Ian and thought how foolish she had been to let the unexpected meeting with Lucien disturb her so much. It had just been the shock, the vivid memory of their last evening together in the little black hut, the intimacy between them. Who knows what might have happened if James had not come between them, something for which she was now deeply thankful. Of course Lucien had no hold over her. It was ridiculous to think he had. She was worrying herself about nothing.

Zara leaped forward exhilarated by the fresh breeze. Isabelle had let her have her head when she became conscious that someone else had come up beside her. They were riding neck and neck and with one swift sidelong glance she saw with a sudden dread that it was Lucien, Lucien on a raking black horse laughing as he stretched out a hand and caught at her bridle.

'Slow down, my beauty, don't run away from me. You'll have us in the Serpentine if you don't take care.'

She knew he was right. She could see the sun glinting on the water and the people who strolled along the banks. She slowed down to a trot and Lucien kept pace with her.

'You've given your groom quite a shock. He thought your horse had bolted.'

'Ian knows me better than that,' she said coldly and turned to look at him.

He was smiling wih that same devil-may-care rakish charm and despite her resistance, despite all her brave defiance, the spell he had woven around her during those long hot days of summer was as potent as ever. He drew off a glove and leaned across, his long, lean fingers seeking and caressing her wrist and she shivered at his touch.

'I made some discreet enquiries. I guessed I would find you here. It's like the old days, isn't it? Have you forgotten them already? Ever since the ball I've been waiting for this moment.'

'I am not alone,' she said in a stifled voice.

'Send your groom away. Tell him I will make sure you come to no harm.'

'No, no, I'd rather not.'

'What are you afraid of?' He summoned Ian with a careless wave of the hand. 'Here, fellow, I'm an old friend of your mistress. I will escort her safely home.'

'That's as may be, sir, but I have my orders,' said Ian stubbornly.

'I'm sure you have, but not to hold your mistress prisoner surely?'

'It's all right,' said Isabelle quickly. 'I know this gentleman well. You need not wait. Go back to Arlington Street and if Lady Marian should ask for me, I will be returning within the hour.'

'Very good, my lady, if you say so,' but he went reluctantly, pausing to look back with a long stare before he rode away.

'He obviously doesn't trust me an inch. What does he think I'm going to do, run off with you for an hour, a day, a week?' Lucien's eyes sparkled dangerously. 'It's an idea. Don't you ever long to escape from that very proper husband of yours?'

'Don't speak of Robert like that. He is the kindest man in the world.'

Lucien grinned. 'Is he indeed? And rich into the bargain. Is that why you married him?'

'Oh you're impossible.' She turned away from him angrily. 'I don't have to answer to you for what I may have done.'

'True, but don't scold me. You know my rash tongue only too well. I swear I shall burst into tears if you do.'

'Now you're being ridiculous.' But despite herself she began to smile.

'That's better. Let's walk together like old friends. I have a tale to tell and so have you.'

He pulled up and slipped from the saddle. Then he put his hand on her bridle and lifted her to the ground. He tethered the horses to one of the white posts that bordered the drive and with an easy familiarity took her arm so that she felt as if the intervening months had rolled away and they were walking together in the bright dawn with the sea wind blowing around them.

He began to tell her of his adventures on that night when he had stolen James's horse and ridden away.

'Was your cousin very angry?'

'He was furious!' She smiled a little at the memory. 'Especially when the ostler at the White Hart brought the horse back with your message.'

'I must have cut a sorry figure in those borrowed plumes,' he

262

went on ruefully. 'I think the landlord at the inn believed me to be a rascally cutpurse who had relieved some unfortunate traveller of his gold. At my last stop I was forced to share lodging with some country bumpkin who smelled as if he'd lately left the pigsty and would have helped himself to what was left of my cash if I hadn't had the good sense not to drink too deep and to keep a wary eye open.'

'What did you do to him?' she asked curiously.

'Never you mind.'

He had a way of spinning a tale so that it was amusing and yet showed him in the best light.

'And is the Chevalier de St George really your uncle?' she asked.

'Well, perhaps not quite, the cousin of a cousin if you must know,' he replied evasively. 'You should have seen his face when I turned up on his doorstep looking for all the world like a mummer from a Christmas pantomime and none too clean either, but all is well with us and we run along very comfortably together. But what of you? I could not believe my eyes when I saw you at the Countess's ball more radiantly beautiful than ever and married to no less a person than the son of the Earl of Glenmuir. Did you uncle ever find out about our meeting?'

'Yes, he did, but not till after.'

'And was he very angry?'

But she could not bring herself to tell him about that horribly humiliating beating.

'He did question me but I told him nothing in case he would send after you. It was only after you had gone that everything seemed to go wrong.'

She paused and he pressed her arm against him. 'Tell me about it.'

And because she could not help herself she began to speak of Guy, his involvement with the smugglers, the loneliness, the separation that had threatened their life together.

'I know it was childish but I used to dream that somehow you would come back and like a miracle everything would come right.'

'I know. I thought of you too so often,' he said remorsefully.

263

He took her hand, urging her to sit beside him on one of the white painted seats near the lake. 'But I have something to confess.'

'Confess? I don't understand.'

'How should you?' He paused for effect skilfully weaving a tissue of lies and truth that in her innocence she believed utterly. 'I could not tell you before because I was so ashamed. You see I never knew my father.'

'You mean he died before you were born?'

'No, worse than that. It was in Martinique and it seems he abandoned my mother when she was pregnant. She never spoke of him and it was not until I was leaving her and the island perhaps for ever that she at last told me his name.'

'What did you do?'

He looked away. 'I was foolish. I realise that now but I badly needed a friend. I sought him out in Paris and he repudiated me, refused to believe that I was his son, spurned me from his door like some stinking beggar . . .' That at least had been true and he stared bleakly into a memory he would rather have forgotten.

'Oh Lucien, I am sorry.' Her sympathy was all the greater recalling her own bitterness at the slight Aunt Augusta had once put upon her and Guy.

'Well, it is over,' he said bravely, 'all my hopes, all my dreams, and I must learn to live without them but what had I to offer my princess, my lovely Isabelle? You did well to turn to your Robert.'

'He came when I was desperate,' she whispered.

'And won the prize that could have been mine,' he said bitterly.

'You must not say that, Lucien.'

'Maybe but you can't stop me believing it and regretting it.'

She shivered suddenly and got to her feet. 'It must be growing very late. I should not stay any longer.'

'No, you're right. It's blowing up for rain too.' He took her arm as they walked back to the horses. 'What does he do, this Robert of yours?' he asked casually. 'He gives me the impression of being a man of parts.'

264

'Oh he is. He is attached to the Foreign Office. That was one of the reasons he came to High Willows. He was concerned with the defence of the coast against Bonaparte's dreaded invasion and he has been in Paris with the peace delegation. Most of his work is very secret. He never speaks of it.'

'Not even to you?'

'Certainly not to me.' She looked up at him as he untethered the horses. 'Will you be going back to France now that the war is over?'

'If it is over,' he said drily. 'No, I don't think so. There is nothing for me there. The Chevalier has been kind enough to say he enjoys my company and he prefers to remain in a country where you are free to live and speak as you will without police spies reporting your every word.'

'Is that what happens in France?'

'So it seems. That is why he got out when he could. If Bonaparte grants an amnesty to all émigrés, will your husband try to recover Sauvigny for you?'

She frowned. 'How do you know about Sauvigny?'

'You must have told me when we first met.'

But she hadn't told him. She had never spoken of her own childhood. It had been he who talked and she who listened. He must have heard it from someone else.

'No, I don't think so,' she said at last. 'It is over and my memories are cruel ones. I try not to think of it any longer. My home is here. If Robert does anything, it would only be for Guy's sake.'

He helped her into the saddle and then took his place beside her as they rode out of the park and made their way to Arlington Street through a Piccadilly thronged with handsome carriages, high-flying phaetons and riders like themselves making their way impatiently through butchers' waggons, coalmen's drays and bakers' carts amid the shouts of street pedlars and the shrill whine of itinerant musicians. It had taken Isabelle a long time to grow accustomed to the incessant clamour of the London streets but on this particular morning she hardly noticed it. The chance meeting with Lucien was too disturbing, a feeling of guilt mingled with a heady delight that he had not forgotten

265

her, that they were back to last summer with the same spice of danger. She could not deny the tiny thrill that went through her whenever he turned to look at her with that small intimate smile of his.

Marian saw Isabelle from her window riding quite brazenly beside the Frenchman. She saw how he held her hand just a moment longer than was decent before he kissed it and was filled with a hot wave of anger. Someone ought to warn Robert, but of what? She knew only too well how he would despise such tittle tattle and her for conveying it. Was it possible that she went to meet this young man on those other mornings when she insisted on riding alone? It was an unworthy suspicion and she tried to banish it but it remained in her mind.

It was the start of an extraordinary summer. It seemed as if the rejoicings would never cease. Balls and masquerades followed one another nightly, the theatres and the opera were crowded, almost every performance ending with a patriotic song bellowed out by a standing audience. The King, recovered temporarily from his madness, went sea-bathing at Weymouth, the Prince drove down to Brighton, watching the growing magnificence of his fantastic palace and taking care to forget his mounting debts, while important members of the government thankfully closed their portfolios and retired to their country estates or took the children to play on the beaches of Eastbourne or Folkestone. Certain that they had secured a notable victory, Parliament set about disarmament with an almost indecent haste. Only ten days after the treaty was signed, the Prime Minister stood up in the House and abolished Pitt's unpopular income tax, halved the army, disbanded the Volunteers and reduced line-of-battle ships from over one hundred to forty. Perry Conway, like a great number of other naval officers, was reduced to half pay with little or no possibility of promotion.

Only in the inner depths of the Foreign Office and down at Walmer Castle where Pitt was taking his vacation were there uneasy feelings that Bonaparte had made peace only to prepare for war and while Britain carried on enjoying herself in her

266

usual heedless fashion, he was quietly developing his plans to conquer the world.

Robert held much the same opinion but kept it to himself and in the meantime was finding it both amusing and gratifying that after her début at the Countess's ball, Isabelle had suddenly and unexpectedly become the rage. The Prince had smiled upon her, had invited her to one of his eagerly sought-after musical parties, she had *arrived* and in its unpredictable way London society had taken her to its fickle heart. Invitations poured in to balls, concerts, musical evenings, routs and garden parties so that she was quite overwhelmed by the flood.

'How do I know which to accept and which to refuse?' she said helplessly.

'There are scarcely enough hours in the day for all these,' remarked Robert rifling through the gilt engraved cards, but under his tuition she began slowly to learn how to deal with them.

The very fact that she had few of the affectations, the little hypocrisies and sly coquettish manners of most fashionable young ladies only seemed to make her more attractive. She was new and she was good fun.

'Farouche!' said one dowager disparagingly, 'no proper sense of occasion!'

'A dressed up country miss putting on airs!' muttered the disgruntled.

Her candour, simplicity, her instinctive courtesy towards the old, the undistinguished, the humble, only added to her charm.

'She is a child still in many ways,' said Robert to Marian, who grumbled about her extravagance and complained that now they were expected to be out and about every night of the week, completely disrupting their quiet tranquil life, but all the same on the few occasions when he did not accompany her himself he always made sure of leaving White's or the gaming tables or the peace of his library in good time to be there and escort her home.

Everywhere she went that hectic summer she seemed to meet Lucien and without making it too obvious it was difficult to avoid it. He was dancing with her, appearing in the box at the theatre, slipping into the empty seat beside her at a concert, talking with her, laughing with her, bringing her ices, teasing, amusing, fascinating. They grew more and more intimate and all the time there was that constant spice of danger. She seemed to be living two lives, one that made her blood race, filled her with guilt and excitement, and those other more serene, peaceful hours she spent with Robert.

Of course it was noticed, of course it was talked about, but very little of it reached Robert. He was not the kind of man to whom scandal was repeated. Whether it affected him personally or referred to another, he would dismiss it with contempt.

On her birthday her two lives were to clash in a way that frightened her. She was breakfasting in bed after a late night and thinking about that other morning only a year ago when she had woken with the certainty that something was going to happen and she had been only too right. It had come with such swiftness that sometimes she could scarcely realize it.

She was sipping her chocolate when Robert came in, bent down to kiss her and put a red leather casket into her hands.

She looked up at him. 'What is it?'

'Look and see.'

She opened it swiftly and gave a little squeal of surprise and pleasure. It was a bracelet with earrings to match the diamond and emerald necklace he had given her before the ball.

'Oh Robert, they're so – so exquisite!' and overcome with affection, gratitude and a small pang of guilt she flung her arms around his neck and kissed him to the imminent danger of the breakfast tray which he rescued only just in time.

'Come, come, you are twenty now, an old married lady,' and he smiled down at the flushed face, the tousled hair. Was it only a bare year since he had seen her on that deserted seashore, barefooted in her faded cotton gown, and without realizing it had fallen hopelessly and maybe foolishly in love?

He sat on the edge of the bed pushing aside an indignant Rory. 'What would you like to do today?'

'I don't mind so long as I spend it with you.'

'Very well. Get up and dress, lazybones. I have a plan.'

'What kind of plan?'

268

'You'll find out in due time.'

He stood up as Gwennie knocked and came in. She was carrying a huge bouquet of dark red roses and a small gilt wrapped package.

'For you, my lady, just come by special messenger.' She put them on the bed. 'And many happy returns from me and from all of us downstairs.'

'Thank you, Gwennie. Will you take the tray? Then come back and help me to dress. I'm getting up now.'

'Very good, my lady.'

She picked up the tray, bobbed a curtsey to Robert and went out, shutting the door with special care instead of her usual cheerful slam.

'Our Gwennie is learning city manners,' said Robert amused. 'Which of your many admirers has sent you the flowers?'

'I don't know and I don't think I care very much.'

'Don't be such an ungrateful baggage. Some luckless youngster has probably spent his all to please you. Open up the package and let us see.'

She fumbled over the wrapping with a tiny spasm of uneasiness. It was a beautifully engraved silver comfit box and inside on blue velvet lay four large antique buttons.

She knew at once where they had come from. They had adorned that old coat she had found for him in the attic and she knew he had sent them here to her own home in a pure spirit of mischief, knowing full well how they would be remarked on and how difficult it would be to explain them away.

'Is this some jest?' asked Robert frowning down at them. 'Surely an extraordinary gift. Is there a note?'

'None. Oh it's just some stupid joke. It must be one of Guy's friends,' she improvised quickly. 'I remember now. The other day I was laughing at their extravagant coats and waistcoats. You know how they favour the very *dernier cri* of fashion. They must have wanted to tease me about it.'

She knew she was babbling on, not really making much sense, and she buried her face in the flowers to hide the colour that rushed up into her cheeks. She was tempted to tell Robert the whole story there and then but if she did, what would he think?

Wouldn't he wonder why she had kept it secret for so long? Then the moment had gone before she had time to gather her wits and come to a decision.

'I don't altogether care for some of those youngsters Guy is going around with,' he was saying thoughtfully. 'I think I'll have a word with him about it.'

'Oh no, don't! . . . I mean you know how badly he takes any criticism and they're quite harmless, only young and silly.'

'Don't worry. I'm not going to play the heavy guardian.' He glanced at his watch. 'Now, Miss, I'll give you an hour to dress and make yourself beautiful. Then we're going to a match.'

'What kind of a match?'

'Wait and see,' said Robert and left her to dress.

The Gentlemen of the Marylebone Cricket Club were playing a match against the Gentlemen of Hampshire for a stake of five hundred guineas, and when Isabelle and Robert arrived at the open fields beyond Marylebone there was already a considerable crowd of spectators of every social class from Lord Winchilsea who was one of the Club's patrons down to the local butcher's boy. Robert as a member of the Club had privileged seats in the front amongst the élite and Isabelle, who had never seen more than a scratch match played by villagers on the town green, was fascinated by everything from the stately players in their white nankeen trousers, coloured coats and tall hats to the intricacies of the game which Robert painstakingly tried to explain and which seemed to her so absurd that she went off into gales of laughter.

It was a noisy gathering, bets being made and taken, with roars of applause at some lucky strike and boos and catcalls from the opposition when a fortunate catch caught out some favourite batsman.

Afterwards Robert introduced Isabelle to the victorious Captain of the MCC and the tall, bearded player bowed over her hand.

'Honoured to have you with us, Ma'am. You should come and watch one day when your husband is playing. He wields a nifty bat.'

270

'Did, Fred, did, but not any longer. My cricketing days are over.'

'More's the pity. Lost him to politics, Ma'am, and they're not played by the same rules,' he said disapprovingly. 'A grievous loss to the Club.'

Isabelle, in white muslin with a large shady hat tied under her chin with cherry coloured ribbons, was a charming enough sight to strike envy into the heart of any lady who was lamenting the loss of her first youth, and Leila Vernon was no exception. She came towards them all smiles, with the Chevalier in close attendance and with a sharp desire to take that prinked up miss down a peg or two.

'Well, if it isn't the little bride,' she said gushingly. 'I'd no idea you were an *aficionado* of cricket, my dear.'

'I'm not,' said Isabelle flatly, 'but I am learning fast.'

'Under you husband's tutelage of course. But where is your usual faithful admirer? Isn't he at your feet today?'

'I'm afraid I don't know what you mean,' said Isabelle coolly.

'Oh come, my dear. Maybe he doesn't care for cricket,' she went on dripping poison, with one eye on Robert. 'Foreigners seldom do, especially the French. You know, my dear Robert, you two present a charming picture of innocence and experience. She looks so wonderfully young, she could almost be your daughter.'

'Really. My wife happens to be celebrating her twentieth birthday,' he replied icily, 'and I am not yet quite in my dotage. Good day to you, Lady Vernon.' He nodded to Leila and her companion and took Isabelle's arm. 'Come, my dear, we should not keep the horses waiting any longer.'

As they moved away the Chevalier said smoothly, 'Quite a set-down, dear lady. The gentleman does not appear to care for you.'

'He once cared far too much.'

'Is that so? But not regrettably any longer, I fear. Does the child know?'

'Not yet, but she will. I'll make sure of that. I understand that the little nobody has your nephew on a string.'

271

'Oh no, my dear Leila, there you're quite wrong. It is she who dances to his tune.'

She looked at him with a little doubtful frown. She had an uneasy feeling that the two Frenchmen with all their polished manners were using her for their own purposes. Well, more than one could play that game. She shrugged her shoulders and took his proffered arm.

Marian had decided that as it was Isabelle's first birthday after her marriage, it was her bounden duty to make it a family affair, so dinner that evening included Sir Joshua and his wife with James and Venetia and her dour fiancé, Sir Hugo. Despite everything that had happened and though she presided as hostess at the dinner table, Isabelle quailed beneath the hard stare of Uncle Joshua and Aunt Augusta. It had the effect of reducing her and Guy to the silent children who had suffered night after night at High Willows. It would have been a leaden evening without David and Robert, who contrived to toss the ball of conversation from one to the other with such expertise that Sir Joshua unbent and even the glum Sir Hugo brightened up.

When the ladies withdrew to the drawing room, Isabelle managed to draw Venetia away under the pretext of showing her the new costume she had ordered for the forthcoming masquerade. It was in the style of a Dresden shepherdess with hooped skirts and laced bodice, very pretty indeed, though they spent very little time admiring it.

Isabelle said bluntly, 'It's weeks and weeks since the ball, why haven't you come to see me?'

'I don't know.' Venetia was fiddling with the gold topped bottles and jars on the dressing table. 'Because I'm jealous, I suppose. You have everything and I seem to have nothing.'

'That's not true. It hasn't been all that easy for me, you know. Robert's father was terrifying. He called me the kitchen-maid bride.'

'To your face?'

'More or less. You know, Venetia, you don't have to marry Sir Hugo.'

272

'Don't I? Who else is there? I prefer him to some of the lumpish boys with rich fathers and precious little else that Mamma keeps pushing under my nose. Maybe when I've given him the son he wants so much, I shall be free to please myself.'

'You don't mean . . . take a lover?'

'Why not? Other women do. It happens all the time. You can't pretend you don't know.'

'But you can't do that, Venetia, not you,' said Isabelle distressed. 'It isn't decent, besides Perry would never consent to such a hole-and-corner affair.'

'Oh Perry! Sometimes I wish I had never met him. He doesn't want anything more to do with me. He wrote me a hateful letter and when I didn't reply he called one day and Mamma had the servants shut the door in his face. Since then there has not been a word from him.'

Her voice was hard but Isabelle saw how her lips trembled.

'Oh Venetia, I'm so terribly sorry. If only I could do something to help.'

'Well, you can't,' she said with an angry vehemence, 'nobody can unless war breaks out again and they make Perry an Admiral and even then . . . oh what's the use of thinking about that?'

'When are you going to be married?'

'Not till next year. I've held out for that. Hugo is annoyed about it and so is Mamma. I think she is afraid he will cry off. She is longing to get me off her hands. She has never cared for me as she does for James, and Hugo has influence. He's obtaining a post for James in the Admiralty where he will be paid a good salary for doing nothing, I suppose.' Venetia was gazing at herself in the mirror, tucking away a curl that had come adrift. 'Oh well, perhaps I'll be left a widow, then I shall be able to do as I please, like your friend Leila Vernon.' She gave Isabelle a quick look. 'Wasn't your Robert her lover at one time?'

For a moment Isabelle was shocked. Then she recovered herself.

'If he was, it was a very long time ago and she's certainly no friend of mine. And anyway Sir Hugo may live till he is ninety.'

273

'In that case he will be in his dotage and beyond worrying about me anyway.'

They laughed but it had a hollow unconvincing sound.

'Isabelle,' went on Venetia slowly, 'I wasn't going to tell you this but now I think perhaps I should. It's about Guy.'

'What about him?'

'Well, James frequents one of those expensive gaming houses that are privately run. Papa would be furious if he knew but the point is that he meets Guy there and that Frenchman you're so friendly with.'

'Do you mean Lucien?'

'Who else? Isn't he one of your most devoted admirers? Everybody has noticed it.'

'Noticed what?'

'The way he follows you around everywhere. Oh I don't blame you. He's very attractive and why shouldn't you have some fun while you still can. Robert can be so very serious, can't he?'

'I've no idea what you are talking about,' said Isabelle coldly.

'Oh come, I think you have,' went on Venetia with a little secret smile. 'You know who Duncan House belongs to, don't you? Leila Vernon with the Chevalier de St George holding the bank for her night after night. Rumour says she has run through the fortune Sir Hugh Vernon left her and this is a fashionable way of recouping her losses.'

Isabelle frowned. 'How do you know all this?'

'I got it out of Hugo when he declared he didn't want me to attend any of her parties. He didn't consider it quite the thing for a young woman. But it's all very exclusive, I believe, gentlemen of the very highest standing go there apparently and play for very high stakes. I thought perhaps you ought to warn Guy that he could be playing with fire.'

'Yes, yes, I understand. I didn't know. Thank you for telling me.'

Robert and Leila Vernon, could it be true? It did explain why she disliked her so much. But she had no wish to discuss any of this with Venetia, and the opening of a door and the sound of voices downstairs gave her an excuse.

274

'I think I can hear the men leaving the dining room, we'd better go down or they will be wondering what has become of us.'

'Oh dear God, must we?' whispered Venetia. 'If you knew how miserable I feel.'

'I do know.' With a friendly impulse Isabelle gave her cousin a quick hug. 'Don't despair. Something may still happen. It did to me when things were at their very worst.'

'Perhaps.' Venetia brushed a hand across her eyes. 'Do I look all right? Hugo notices things.'

'You look lovely. Good enough to eat. Come on.'

They went down the stairs and into the drawing room hand in hand.

The masquerade was to take place at Vauxhall in the famous pleasure gardens and was ostensibly in aid of the wives and children of the servicemen so summarily dismissed, many of whom were starving. All fashionable London wanted to take part in it and were fighting for the expensive tickets. Marian was strongly against it.

'Vauxhall is not what it used to be,' she said austerely. 'No decent well-bred young woman would dream of going there nowadays, only actresses, women of the streets, people of that sort.'

'But this is different,' argued Isabelle. 'It's a special event and I've heard so much about Vauxhall and I've never been there. Besides I've got the loveliest costume and it's such a dreadful pity to waste it.'

Robert had somewhat reluctantly agreed to go with her but refused to dress himself up like a popinjay at a fair, and then at the last moment he was forced to withdraw. He had been invited to dine with his old friend and patron, Henry Dundas, in order to meet other members of the opposition who held very different views about the peace from those held by the Prime Minister. The invitation was also in the nature of a command and he felt he ought to accept it. David was out of town and Robert did not altogether like trusting Isabelle to the protection of her brother but she begged and pleaded so he ultimately gave in and saw them into the carriage in the early evening, Isabelle looking particularly enchanting in her shepherdess costume with a black velvet mask embroidered with sequins and a tiny straw hat with a wreath of cornflowers.

'All you need is a lamb on a blue ribbon,' remarked Robert drily.

'I did think of it,' she said seriously, 'but the poor creature would be frightened to death by the fireworks.'

Guy had dressed himself as a gypsy, slouch hat, blue choker at his throat, white shirt and scarlet cummerbund, black breeches and soft leather boots.

'As soon as I can decently take my leave,' said Robert, 'I shall come and collect you. Look after her, Guy.'

'I will, sir, don't you fret.'

They were like two children delighting in the frolic ahead and it had the effect of making him feel old which was ridiculous, he told himself. After all he had only just turned thirty. But this whole crazy summer of parties and balls celebrating a very shaky peace when more than half the population of Britain was on the point of starvation seemed to him rather like dancing on the lip of a volcano which could erupt at any moment and bring disaster with it.

He went back into the house and was on his way up to his dressing room when Marian stopped him.

'What is it?' he said a trifle impatiently, coming back to her.

She drew him with her into the drawing room and closed the door.

'You know whom Isabelle hopes to meet at this wretched masquerade, don't you?'

'Naturally I know,' said her brother frowning. 'Guy has made up a party of his friends, most of them youngsters, but entirely respectable.'

'Oh I am not referring to them. It's the Frenchman, Lucien de Vosges. I've not spoken of it before but she is seen everywhere with him. Whenever you are not with her, he is at her side. People are talking about it. I find it most distasteful wherever I go to hear such remarks being made about my brother's wife. Why do you shut your eyes to it, Robert?'

'I'm not shutting my eyes to anything. If my wife's beauty

276

and charm are such as to draw the attentions of men who are not entirely desirable, that is hardly her fault. Isabelle has never behaved in any way to cause me the slightest anxiety. Should I forbid her a few simple pleasures because of idle gossiping tongues?' He put his hand on hers for a moment. 'Marian, my dear, I know you mean well but do stop fretting yourself about a situation which does not arise. If it ever does, believe me, I shall know how to deal with it. And now I really must go and dress or I shall be late for my dinner appointment.'

He went out of the room leaving her wishing she had not spoken, a little distressed in case he despised her for it, and yet sure that something had to be said. She wished she could believe that Robert was right, and that Isabelle would not betray his trust.

The twelve acres of Vauxhall Gardens lay across the river from Westminster Abbey and had been a place of amusement and pleasure for more than two hundred years. There was a magnificent rotunda in the Gothic style where concerts were held and an organ played, there were the flower beds, long shady walks, little pavilions where a cold collation could be served, rose-covered arches opening onto vistas of ponds and fountains and charming arbours hidden in copses of trees for secret assignations and other such delights.

The evening began well with a concert where Madame Antonelli sang soulful Italian ballads and the orchestra played Handel's Water Music followed by dancing with a merry throng in every conceivable costume, medieval ladies jostling cowled monks, punchinellos, Greek athletes in golden tunics and even a Bacchus draped daringly with bunches of grapes over a tiger-skin.

But after a little Isabelle was forced to admit that Marian had been right. Despite the expensive tickets there was a certain vulgarity. Although Guy's young friends behaved towards her with the utmost propriety, there were a great number of other very noisy parties. Once she saw a scantily dressed young woman run screaming down a path followed by two men hallooing like huntsmen and she heard the scuffle and the muted laughter when they caught her.

Their supper of cold chicken with oyster patties, cream syllabubs and a liberal supply of champagne was served in one of the pavilions and presently Isabelle who was not hungry moved away up the path to look at the pond where water lilies bloomed and fish darted to and fro as she scattered crumbs on the water. Nearby another group begun to dance on the shaven grass and one of the revellers suddenly detached himself to seize her by the arm and try to drag her among the rowdy dancers. She resisted strongly but was unwilling to scream or make any kind of fuss, when suddenly someone else had grabbed her tormentor by the shoulder and flung him aside so roughly that he fell backwards into the pond emerging dripping with green weed to roars of laughter and would have hurled himself at his attacker if his friends had not restrained him.

It was only then that she realised that her rescuer was Lucien. He was masked but she knew him at once, Lucien in doublet and hose, all brown and gold, looking for all the world like a young Florentine Prince of the Renaissance. She caught her breath with surprise and a kind of guilt. She had not expected to see him there and in fact had been trying to avoid him every since her birthday.

'You are surely not here alone,' he said.

'No, of course not. I am with my brother. We were supping together and I got up to scatter crumbs for the fish.'

Guy leaped to his feet when he saw what was happening and Lucien smiled at him.

'May I borrow your sister for a little?' he said easily. 'These gardens are new to me as I believe they are to her. I will return her to you safe and sound, I promise you.'

Guy hesitated and Isabelle said quickly, 'We'll just take a little stroll while you finish your supper.'

'Guy and I are old friends,' said Lucien, 'didn't you know? He will trust you to my care, won't you, Guy?'

'Of course, only don't be too long. We shall wait here for you to come back.'

They walked away together and the evening instead of

278

proving a sad disappointment suddenly blossomed into delight. The air was filled with the sweet night scent of the flowers and coloured lights had been hung among the trees. He had drawn her arm through his and she wondered why it was that his very presence, the pressure of his arm against her side, had the power to make her heart beat faster but somehow it did.

After a little they reached the bank of the Thames. Wherries still plied back and forth, some of them with lighted lanterns that bobbed across the darkening water like small stars.

She said suddenly, 'It was very wicked of you to send me those buttons. I did not know how to explain them away.'

'It was a small jest I thought you might appreciate. Haven't you told your husband of our first meeting?'

'No.'

'Why, Isabelle, why? Do you fear his anger so much or is it because you must know by now that I am fathoms deep in love with you?'

'You mustn't say that.'

'You can't stop me and it is true.'

'No, Lucien.'

She began to walk away from him and he followed after her.

'I've wanted to say that to you for a very long time but you have been avoiding me.'

'I won't listen.'

'You must listen.'

He had caught at her hand and swung her round to face him. They had reached one of the pretty devices in which the garden abounded, a small stone seat under an Italian cupola raised on slender pillars and he drew her to sit beside him.

'We fell in love on that lonely seashore when you saved my life and it is still there between us, isn't it?'

'I don't know, Lucien,' she said desperately, 'I don't know.'

'You do know, only you are afraid to admit it even to yourself.'

'I am married, Lucien, to a good man. I can't betray him. I can't do anything that might hurt him.'

He was silent for a moment before he said deliberately, 'Not

279

even if he betrays you? Do you know that he was the lover of Leila Vernon?'

She turned to look at him before she spoke. 'I have been told so but if he was, then it was a very long time ago.'

'Are you so sure of that? He's not a boy, Isabelle, nor is he a saint. He may need more, far more than you can give him.' It was something that had troubled her more than once and she drew away from him in an agony of doubt and indecision while he drew closer, whispering, his voice low and urgent.

'You say you can't deceive him but hasn't he deceived you? What do you really know of him? What about those trips he makes in secret? Does he tell you of those? Haven't you wondered what he does? He is an agent of British Intelligence, Isabelle, a spy with murder and death dogging his steps wherever he goes.'

'I don't believe you,' she said vehemently, 'I know the men he works with, I have met them. How can you possibly know such a thing about him?'

'Oh we know. You can be quite sure of that.'

'Who is we?'

'The Chevalier has friends in Paris and now there is peace he exchanges letters with them.'

'Is the Chevalier a spy too that he pretends to have so much secret information?' she said angrily.

'How can you say such a thing? He lost everything he held most dear in the Revolution and afterwards, but he was once in a position to know about these things.' He put an arm around her, drawing her close against him. 'Believe me I did not want to tell you but now I must. What can you feel for a man who must plan murders and assassinations? Is that where your heart would be? I can't believe it. Don't you remember what you shared with me in that little black hut? Those moments of bliss that belonged to us alone? Heart and soul with only one thought, only one desire.'

His voice, low and seductive, was in her ears. He turned her face towards him and kissed her gently at first and then with increasing strength and for a moment the magic was there,

280

warm and urgent, till with a sudden reaction she thrust him away from her.

'No, Lucien, no, we must not.'

But he felt her tremble, had sensed the response in the lips under his, believed that he could now make her wholly his and he followed up his advantage.

'Did you never wonder why he married you so suddenly, so unexpectedly? You are French, you have links with the past, when war comes again and it will come, he will use you just as he has used others,' he murmured pouring out the poison, seeing the tears in her eyes and the trembling of her mouth.

He drew her close against him and she felt her senses swim as he kissed her neck, the swell of her bosom above the muslin fichu and came back to her lips, teasing them open, mingling breath, tongue touching tongue . . . But he had underestimated the strength of her integrity, her loyalty to the man who had given her so much when she needed it most. She was suddenly afraid, horribly afraid, not only of him but of herself.

With a violent revulsion she pushed him away from her so forcibly that he almost lost his balance on the stone seat. Then she was on her feet, running blindly down the path, her breath coming in sobbing pants till she collided with a man coming swiftly towards them and fought to free herself from his arms till she heard Robert say reassuringly, 'Don't fight me, Isabelle, you're quite safe with me.'

Robert had left the dinner party soon after eleven o'clock and Dundas had smiled benevolently as he excused himself.

'I fear our friend has a beautiful young wife and has not been married a year yet,' he said jestingly to the assembled company, 'he must be forgiven for deserting us.'

He had taken a boat across the Thames, alighted at the water steps and entered the gardens. He ran into one of Guy's young friends who told him that Isabelle had gone for a stroll with a gentleman she had seemed to know very well.

'Do you know who he was?'

'I'm afraid not, sir. He was in costume and masked like the rest of us but I am sure that Guy knew him.' He waved his hand vaguely. 'I think they went down that way towards the river.'

'I see. Thank you.'

It could be any one of their many acquaintances. There was no reason why he should feel uneasy and yet somehow he did. He walked up and down several paths impatiently glancing over little bands of revellers he met by the way and he was coming up the path from the river when he noticed the cupola with its stone bench and, despite the poor light, thought he recognised the shepherdess costume. He saw the two figures melt into a passionate embrace and quickened his steps. Then she had thrust the man away from her and was running towards him.

She was clinging to him shaken and breathless and he held her tightly against him.

'What is it? What has happened? Was that fellow assaulting you?'

'Yes,' she gasped, then shook her head. 'No, no, not really. Oh I don't know what I'm saying. I think he was a little drunk.'

'Who was he?'

'I don't know,' she said distractedly, 'just someone in our party. I don't think he meant any harm. I know it was foolish but he frightened me.'

The man had already vanished into the shadows before Robert could reach him and he thought she was possibly shielding one of Guy's more rowdy friends.

She said in a choked voice, 'Marian was right. This is a horrible place. I wish I'd never come. Can we go home now?'

'I don't see why not. I'll leave word for Guy that we have left.'

Although the night was warm she was shivering so he took off the dark red cloak he had worn as a concession to the masquerade and wrapped it around her.

She was silent in the boat, her face very pale in the lantern's dim light. As they crossed the river the fireworks exploded into a shower of golden stars followed by others so that the whole night sky was filled with a blaze of colour.

There were chairmen waiting at the Westminster steps for returning revellers. Robert summoned two of them with a flick

282

of his fingers and they hurried forward ready to carry them back to Arlington Street.

The servants were still up and had a tray of coffee waiting for them.

'I think I'll go straight to bed,' she said wearily.

'Wait a moment.' Robert poured the coffee, put in a little brandy and brought it to her. 'Drink this first. It will revive you. I have something to tell you.'

She sipped the coffee and was glad of its comforting warmth.

'What is it?' she asked.

'Something which I hope will please you. We are going to Paris.'

'Paris!' It somehow linked up with everything Lucien had been implying. Had the men he had been dining with given him his marching orders? She went on quickly, 'Pleasure or business?'

'Purely pleasure I hope,' he replied surprised. 'I've no sort of business in France at the moment. Do you like the idea?'

'Oh yes, very much.'

She put down her cup. The thought of going right away, escaping from Lucien, from the delightful but disturbing social round that had been filled with so many mixed feelings of pleasure and guilt was like opening a door into a calmer safer world.

She said, 'Will Marian be coming with us?'

'I hadn't thought of it but I suppose I ought to ask her,' he said a little doubtfully.

'Must you? I would so much rather it was just you and I.'

'She might be very disappointed.'

'Please Robert.'

He smiled. 'Very well, so be it. A second honeymoon in the country of your birth.'

'Wonderful!' She ran to put her arms around his neck and hug him. 'Thank you, Robert.'

He kissed the top of her head and, as they went upstairs together, could not help wondering how much she had really told him and who the fellow was who had held her in that passionate embrace. He had dismissed Marian's remarks as nonsense, now uncomfortably they came back into his mind.

But he would not question. If it had been Lucien de Vosges, then she had repulsed him with some violence, let that be sufficient.

That same night in the Chevalier's small elegant apartment just off Half Moon Street, Lucien dropped wearily on to the sofa and accepted gratefully the glass of cognac offered to him.

'She knows nothing,' he said flatly, 'nothing at all. He obviously doesn't confide in her. I used shock tactics that I'm pretty sure would have provoked a reaction if she'd been aware of his real work.'

'He was dining tonight with the opposition, men who would far rather be at war with France than at peace.'

'I know but he still left early to meet her there.'

'Did he, by God? Did he recognise you?'

'No, he couldn't have done. It was dark already.'

'Will she tell him?'

'I doubt it. She's not even told him about our first meeting.'

The Chevalier gave him a quick look. 'Is she your mistress yet?'

'No.'

Lucien got up and began to pace restlessly up and down the room.

'A holier-than-thou prude, I take it,' said the Chevalier drily.

'Not at all, on the contrary hot as mustard, but unlike most women too damned loyal to her husband to go whoring after other men,' said Lucien coarsely. 'But there's still time. I gather he fancies her more than most and men in love can talk unwisely.'

'Maybe but you'd better make sure of it before Bonaparte smashes this fragile peace. He is a hard master and there is no such thing as failure in his book, nor is he the only one we have to satisfy if we are to earn what we have been promised.'

'My God, do you think I don't realise that?' exclaimed Lucien and repressed a shudder at the thought of that other who commanded them both, the man who under Fouché, Bonaparte's Minister of Police, was the most relentless of all those who carried out his orders and was rapidly turning France, that country of culture and charm, into one vast police state.

14

By the end of the following week they were on their way to
Paris. Ian Mackie was to go with them to look after the luggage
and make himself generally useful, but Isabelle flatly refused to
take Gwennie with her.

'She'd be lost and bewildered in a foreign country and I am
well accustomed to looking after myself. Besides someone must
stay to care for Rory.'

Privately Robert breathed a sigh of relief, having seen himself
burdened with a noisy small dog and a travel sick country girl.

Isabelle packed feverishly for both of them with a firm
resolution to put every thought of Lucien out of her mind, but
all the same there were moments when she would stop what she
was doing and wonder again why he had spoken of Robert as
he had. Was it true or was he simply using it in an attempt to
put her against him and if it *was* true, then how did he come to
know so much unless he was himself involved in some way? Up
to that moment she had trusted Lucien absolutely. He had worn
a kind of halo of romantic adventure. Now suddenly it had been
torn away. Behind all that charm lurked something else, some
dark purpose that frightened her.

She had always known that Robert's reserve hid a part of his
life he confided to no one except perhaps David. He had given
her a glimpse of it on that day they had spent on Iona. She
wondered if she dared question David and then drew back. It
would seem like prying into secrets he did not want to reveal
and anyway it must be all nonsense. Ever since their marriage
he had never left her side except to accompany Lord Cornwallis
and the peace mission in the early spring.

Lucien called one day during that week and in a panic she
refused to see him, afraid not so much of him as of herself,

knowing too well how he could beguile her. He sent her flowers and she looked at the white roses for a long time, held the scented flowers against her cheek for a moment and then gave them to Gwennie.

'You take these. I have no use for them.'

One thing that did worry her a little was the friendship that had sprung up between Lucien and and Guy. That autumn her brother was to take up a post in the Foreign Office where it was hoped he could use his knowledge of languages to good effect.

'That should keep him out of mischief,' Robert had said. 'His immediate chief is a man who does not tolerate shirkers.'

He would be let off the leading strings and responsible for himself in future. She remembered Venetia's warning and one evening when they were alone together she tackled him about it.

'I gather that you and James and Lucien are in the habit of visiting one of the private gaming houses.'

'Now where on earth did you hear that?'

'Oh I don't know. People talk about these things.'

'If you must know, Lucien put me up for membership.'

'Surely you're far too young.'

'There are ways of getting round that.'

'Guy, do be careful, won't you? I remember how reckless James can be. Uncle Joshua was always quarrelling with him about his debts and another thing, I don't think you should put too much trust in Lucien de Vosges.'

'What makes you say that? He is devoted to *you*.'

'Oh nonsense!'

'Is it nonsense? It's been pretty obvious, you know, Belle. Has Robert noticed? Is that what's troubling you?'

'Of course not. Don't say such stupid things. Don't plunge too deep, that's all. You can't expect Robert to pay your gambling debts.'

Guy gave her a speculative look. 'I'm not such a fool. I *am* grown up now, you know. You go off to Paris and stop worrying your head about me.'

*

They travelled by easy stages going down to Dover in their own carriage, with Isabelle aware of how selfish she was, but feeling enormously grateful that Marian had decided to spend two months at Glenmuir with the Earl so there was no question of her accompanying them.

They went on board the packet boat on a fine summer morning and four hours later were in Calais passing through Customs with the minimum of trouble due to Robert's status and a little judicious bribery and were met by Ian Mackie who had booked accommodation at the Hotel d'Angleterre and arranged with Monsieur Dessin, the proprietor, to hire a postchaise that would carry them to Paris.

It was a vivid contrast to that other painful journey eight years before when she and Guy had been bundled into the rickety cart among the sacks of potatoes with Jean Pierre whipping up his patient horse, terrified when they were stopped at the barriers lest the guards would recognise them for what they were and send them back to Paris and death. Abbeville, Amiens, Clermont, Chantilly, she remembered them all. How different it was now. Welcomed at the inns with bows and smiles, boys racing across the yard, falling over their sabots in their haste to change the horses, excellent meals produced at the drop of a hat, nothing was too much trouble for the English Milord and his lady who surprisingly both spoke such fluent French.

There were other aspects not so pleasant of course, swarms of beggars everywhere, crippled, maimed, blind, children in filthy rags holding out skeleton hands, emaciated babies staring at them with huge reproachful eyes from their mothers' arms. Twenty or thirty of them would be gathered in the street as they entered their carriage, scattering like wild animals to grab at the handful of coins Robert threw to them, shouting '*Bon voyage*' after them as they drove away. At the city gates there were still iron barriers with armed guards who scrutinised their papers word for word before waving them on.

'Was it always like this?' asked Isabelle when one guard took so long that Robert became impatient, till he realised the man could not read. 'I thought the Revolution had changed everything for the better.'

'It does not always work out that way. After chaos comes tyranny, how else could order be restored? They will pay lip service to the old watchwords – Liberty, Equality, Fraternity,' said Robert drily, 'but you must still watch your step. Fouché's henchmen are every bit as ferocious as any royalist secret police and Bonaparte is horribly sensitive to criticism, all the more so because he hasn't a thousand years of tradition behind him. If any artist dared to caricature him as Rowlandson does the Prince of Wales in some of our broadsheets he would be very lucky to escape hanging.'

Entrance into Paris meant more iron barriers, more armed guards and even more Customs officials searching every corner of the postchaise as if they had hidden something subversive under the cushions, only Robert's title and a cautious bribe preventing them from turning out Isabelle's most intimate garments and even plunging dirty hands under her travelling cloak and feeling all down her body for suspicious and forbidden articles. Then thankfully they were through and bowling through the streets to the Hotel Impérial in the rue du Dauphin. Once established there it was different. The city might be shabby, still wearing the scars of the last tumultuous years, but Isabelle was enchanted with it and Robert who knew it intimately was only too happy to show it to her.

Their hotel was crowded with English tourists but they avoided them as much as possible, preferring to visit the show places alone and without the French guides with their raucous voices and execrable English. They did all the expected things of course. One night they were invited to dine at the British Embassy in the rue du Faubourg St Honoré. Under the blaze of a thousand candles some seventy guests sat at the long tables and Isabelle saw for the first time Bonaparte's Foreign Minister, Charles-Maurice de Talleyrand now in his early fifties, lamed almost from birth but fastidious in his manner, supremely elegant in dress and 'with the morals of an alley cat', whispered Robert wickedly under his breath, causing Isabelle to smother a giggle. Directly opposite him in vivid contrast sat Joseph

Fouché, Minister of Police, and a bloodstained revolutionary with an intimate knowledge of the Paris underworld, shovelling in his food, grubby ruffles falling over hands with blackrimmed nails, stains on his handsome velvet coat, loud-voiced and vulgar. It was like the meeting of two worlds which had once been separated by an impassible gulf.

It was much the same curious clash of cultures when they attended a reception at the Tuileries. The gardens, once famous for their beauty, had been trampled and devastated by the invading mob and were now being hastily restored. When they entered it, the palace ballroom lit by a dozen enormous crystal chandeliers dazzled them with its splendour and a richness that bordered on vulgarity with the gilded furniture, the overstuffed sofas, the tables of onyx and alabaster, the velvet curtains heavily embroidered with gold, nothing at all like the refined elegance of the London drawing rooms with which Isabelle had become so familiar.

It was almost impossible to believe that a bare twelve years before, the raging crowd had wrecked and looted it, smashing, burning, destroying. The room was crowded with English visitors, with French aristocrats returning from exile in the vain hope of regaining their lost inheritance, mingling uneasily with the *nouveaux riches*, the parvenus rapidly climbing higher and higher in the wake of their new idol, Napoleon Bonaparte.

With a fine sense of timing he made his entrance in the grand manner, the dance abruptly coming to an end, a fanfare on silver trumpets, the doors flung open by footmen in resplendent livery with powdered wigs. Then he was rapidly walking through the centre of the room, the ladies curtseying, the men bowing their heads as he paused to say a gracious word here and there.

Isabelle watched him with fascinated eyes, remembering the description Lucien had given her on the beach in Kent, a small man with lank black hair, almost insignificant until you saw his eyes and heard him speak. He wore a plain green uniform with white lapels to the coat, in direct contrast to his marshals who followed him resplendent in scarlet and gold with jewelled orders glittering on their breasts.

289

He stopped when he reached them, piercing eyes under frowning brows, fixed on Robert.

'I know you, do I not, Monsieur le Vicomte!' he said with a rasp in his voice. 'As I remember it, you caused us a great deal of trouble with the treaty, a word here, a sentence there, Talleyrand was not pleased with you, my friend,' he went on emphasising each word with a jab into Robert's chest with a short stubby finger. 'He does not care to be put in the wrong by a damned Englishman.'

'I am sorry, sir, if my zeal was unwelcome, but surely it is far better to look for the exact phrase if argument is not to come later.'

'You certainly did your utmost to prevent that,' he commented drily and turned to Isabelle. 'Is this lady your wife?'

'Yes, General, the former Isabelle de Sauvigny.'

'Sauvigny, Sauvigny . . . now why is that name so familiar?' Then he snapped his fingers. 'I have it, my physician, Dr Henri Rivage de Sauvigny, a very clever fellow, cured me of a wretched imposthume not so long ago. Sadly he is not here this evening, he does not care for social gatherings. Is he your father perhaps, Madame?'

'My father died under the guillotine,' said Isabelle in a choked voice.

Bonaparte looked taken aback for a moment. 'That is part of the past, Madame, a past we must now learn to forget and put behind us. Let me be the first to welcome you back to a Paris that is rising from the ashes to a new life.'

'Thank you, sir,' said Robert quickly, seeing the rebellion on his wife's face and dreading what she might say next. 'We are extremely happy to be here at such a momentous time.'

'Good, good,' he gave them his flashing smile that could be so charming and yet could hide so much, and moved on.

'Did you hear what he said?' Isabelle's voice was filled with angry indignation. 'Henri Rivage betrayed my father to his death and would have done the same to us if we had not escaped and now not only has he ridden high at this – this usurper's hands but he has stolen our name and Guy's inheritance.'

One or two people had turned to stare and Robert drew her quietly to one side.

'Be careful, my dear, in what you say. The very walls have ears and Henri Rivage is not the only one to profit by his treachery. There are a great many others in Paris today. Be thankful he is not here tonight and that you do not have to meet him.'

'I wouldn't stay one moment longer if I thought that was possible.'

'No doubt but in the meantime you must learn tact. In one way at least Bonaparte is right. The past is gone and can never be brought back.'

'You're so calm, so reasonable,' she raged. 'If I had my way, I would shout it aloud, I would shame him for the vile traitor he is!'

'And where would that land you? In prison or at the very least deported, and speaking for myself, I have no wish to crawl home with my tail between my legs,' he said humorously.

'Oh Robert!' she exclaimed half exasperated, half smiling, and he pressed his advantage.

'That's better. Now come, drink a glass of champagne with me and let us find something to laugh at together. There's plenty here tonight, God knows, laughable and also a little pitiable. Too many hankering after a lost world.'

Her indignation slowly subsided and the rest of the evening passed pleasantly enough with some of their English acquaintances, but Robert remained thoughtful. Dr Henri Rivage, according to the latest secret reports to reach him, was almost certainly linked with French intelligence and had an unenviable record of murder and assassination among the royalists and other dissidents. Paris, on the surface so gay and so welcoming, had its own underground world of suspicion and dark intrigue.

Robert, who had spent a year at the Sorbonne with one of his cousins when he was seventeen and the Revolution only a dark shadow in the future, was familiar with the old city, with the university and the *Quartier Latin* and the narrow streets where the houses almost met overhead, where people lived out their lives in attics and cellars, ancient, beautiful, picturesque and mostly filthy. When Isabelle tired of the elegant shops in the rue de Rivoli and the Palais Royal, the fashionable drives up the Champs Elysées and into the Bois de Boulogne, he took her on a literary tour showing her the dark alleys where François Villon had lived out his poverty-stricken violent life, forever out of pocket, in and out of prison, pouring out his witty scathing verses, the house where Abelard had wooed Héloïse, writing lyrics that still breathed a touch of their fiery tragic love –

> Take thou this rose, O rose,
> For love's own flower it is
> And by this rose
> Thy lover captive is . . .

'How do you know that?' she asked him curiously and he laughed.

'Results of a misspent youth. The verses of the medieval scholars were part of my study course.'

She was happy he shared so much with her and the dazzle of Lucien began to fade.

She saw where Danton had lived and the house from which Robespierre went to his death, and shuddered at the door through which Charlotte Corday had gone to murder the blood-stained Marat in his bath.

One day he showed her the house where Pierre Ronsard, most famous of lyric poets, had come to die.

'Papa was a great lover of his poetry,' she said. 'He used to read them to us. Guy was quickly bored and only wanted to run off and play but I loved them even if I didn't always understand what he meant.' She sighed. 'I suppose Henri Rivage will have all those books now.'

'If the mob didn't burn them with the château. Books provide useful fuel when you are freezing.'

On the way back to their hotel he bought her an old leatherbound copy of Ronsard from a bookstall on the Quai d'Orsay and much later that night, he leaned on his elbow watching her sitting cross-legged on the huge old-fashioned bed reading him snatches of her favourites, looking very young and lovely and innocent . . . but was she? He was not quite so immune from spiteful gossip as he appeared. Some of it had reached his ears. Marian had made sure of that. He had already guessed that more lay between her and that handsome rogue Lucien de Vosges than appeared on the surface. Was he the castaway to whom she had wanted to give everything? Was he the man she had ridden down to the seashore to meet as that damned smuggler had hinted? He had waited for her to tell him with her usual candid simplicity, and the very fact that she had said nothing and indeed shied away from the subject was all the more disturbing.

'One of my favourites,' she was saying, 'is the sonnet he wrote to his last love. Do you remember? The one that begins –

'*Quand vous serez bien vielle, au soir, à la chandelle* . . .'

'Translate it for me,' he said lazily.

'Robert, you are teasing me. You understand it perfectly.'

'Maybe I do but I'd like to hear you try.'

She frowned over it, groping for words.

'When you are old, at evening, candle-lit,
Beside the fire, bending to your spinning wheel
Read out my verses and say "Ronsard wrote
This praise for me when I was beautiful . . ."

'Oh I can't, it's too difficult, and it doesn't sound the same in English. But if someone wrote such lovely verses for me, I think I'd fall into his arms.'

'My dear, Ronsard was seventy at that time and Hélène was a beautiful young woman.'

'I know but still . . .'

Robert sat up.

'When thou returnest will tell me,' he quoted with mock solemnity,

'All strange wonders that befell thee,
And swear

293

No where
Lives a woman true and fair.'

'Oh that's a beastly thing to say. Women are not like that. Who wrote it?'

'A man called John Donne who ended up a respected Dean of St Paul's but he had a riotous youth and he knew all about love.'

'I don't know so much.'

Robert laughed. 'Alas, I'm no poet. I can't pen a sonnet to my mistress's eyebrow. I have to rely on other men's words.' He leaned across and took the book out of her hands. 'For God's sake hold your tongue and let me love!'

'Did he write that too?' she asked, wide-eyed.

'He did and I can't think of anything more apt.'

He pulled her into his arms. She came willingly enough but he still had a despairing feeling that the flame was not yet lit for him. Had that bounder whom he distrusted with every fibre of his being succeeded where he had failed? He tried to dismiss the tormenting thought but in spite of everything it persisted.

They had been in Paris for over a month and in the early morning mists had begun to gather over the Seine but the weather still remained fine and warm. One afternoon Isabelle came back to the hotel with her arms filled with parcels after a shopping spree in the famous Palais Royal. She dropped one as she came into the hall, the porter leaped to pick it up for her and the man at reception held out a sealed note.

'For Monsieur le Vicomte, Madame,' he said. 'It came this morning by special messenger.'

'I will take it. He will be in later.'

She took it with her parcels up to their suite and dropped them all on a chair. The note fluttered to the floor and the seal broke. She picked up the fallen sheet and read it without thinking. There was only a single sentence. 'The devil is on the prowl so take care.' That was all, no signature, no indication as to whom it had come from. She stared at it. What did it mean? Could it be a jest or did it link up with what Lucien had told her about Robert? Was it a warning of danger but from whom and why? Paris was filled with English who were welcomed everywhere. A cold wind seemed to blow through the room and she shivered. Then without quite knowing why she did it, she lit a candle, softened the wax and resealed it. She could not bear him to think she had broken it open on purpose and read something meant only for his eyes.

It was early evening and all the candles had been lit by the time he came in. She had spread out her purchases on the daybed and was looking through them.

'What are you trying to do? Ruin me?' he asked, eyeing them with raised eyebrows.

She had thrown a shimmering silver scarf over her head and shoulders. 'How do I look?'

'Bewitching but we must hurry. We're going to the opera.'

'Oh lovely! I only have to change my dress. There is a note for you. Someone left it downstairs. It's on the table.'

He picked it up, broke the seal and for a moment stood very still, frowning down at it.

'Is it anything important?'

'No, no, not at all.'

He held it to the candle flame until it crumbled to ashes before he turned back to her.

'Come along, my pet, don't just stand there. No time to waste if we're to dine before the theatre.'

At intervals during the evening watching his face totally absorbed by the glorious music, she wondered what the message had meant and if he would confide in her, but in the interval some of their acquaintances joined them in the box so that neither then or later when they returned to the hotel did he speak of it.

Robert had hired a carriage for their stay and the days passed very pleasantly with so much still to see and enjoy that she frequently forgot about it.

They went to the races in the Bois, they dined one night at the Café Procope, haunt of artists, writers and actors for the last two hundred years. She dragged him unwillingly to the Jardin des Plantes to look at the wild animals and he retaliated by

295

taking her out to Saint Denis where the kings and queens of France had been buried since the thirteenth century, but sadly the revolutionaries had desecrated the bodies and scattered the bones so that only their monuments remained, mutilated and filthy in the ancient abbey.

One evening a few days later they came out of a concert hall in the Champs Elysées. It had been extremely hot and the cool night air was more than welcome.

Isabelle said impulsively, 'Let's walk a little,' so Robert told their driver to follow them slowly and they found their way to one of their favourite walks along the river.

The moon was up already and lit a silver streak across the dark water. Isabelle leaned on the parapet looking along the Seine to where she could see the glimmer of lanterns and the faint outline of Notre Dame etched against the night sky. The ravages of destruction that marred the city by day were all hidden, the night was filled with beauty and with magic.

She heaved a long sigh and said, 'How lovely it is and how peaceful.'

A little gust of wind stirred her hair as she smiled at Robert, and at the same moment a black faceless shadow seemed to rise from the ground, so unexpected, so menacing that she had no time to move or cry out before it struck. She saw a glitter of steel, saw Robert stiffen against the sudden onslaught, saw the arm plunge down and down, then came the clatter of horses' hooves, the shadow raised its head and was gone into the darkness as noiselessly and as terrifyingly as it had come.

Robert had fallen back against the parapet, gripping it with one hand to stop himself falling.

'What is it?' she whispered. 'Are you hurt?'

He thrust a hand inside his coat and it came out black with blood.

'My God, he has killed you!'

'It is nothing,' he muttered through clenched teeth. 'The carriage, Isabelle, it can't be far . . .'

In the dim light his face looked greenish white and she was afraid to leave him.

'Go,' he said, 'now . . . please . . .'

Terror lent her wings. On the other side of the road two people stopped to stare curiously and then hurried on, seeing what they supposed to be one of the street walkers with her drunken lover. She waved frantically and the driver of their carriage quickened his horse and pulled up beside them.

'You must help me,' she said. 'My husband has been brutally attacked. He is badly hurt.'

'It happens. He won't be the first nor the last,' he grumbled, climbing down from his high perch. 'Take my arm, Monsieur, lean on me.'

Between them they hoisted Robert into the carriage and he leaned back against the cushions with his eyes closed. Before he climbed back to his seat the driver picked up the knife from where the assassin must have dropped it in his haste.

He handed it to Isabelle, long and thin and deadly. 'Better keep it, Madame, show it to the *flics* though I've never known them to catch one of these night birds yet.'

The next few hours merged into an unbearable nightmare. At the hotel when the driver went in to fetch assistance, Robert roused himself to grip her hand.

'No police,' he whispered.

'But we should report it. He could have killed you.'

'No . . . no . . . no police.'

The porter came out with the driver and together they assisted Robert up the stairs and into their rooms. He lay back on the day bed, his eyes closed, the dark stain spreading ominously on his coat.

'Fetch a doctor,' she said urgently to the porter, 'quickly and then find our servant. Tell him he is needed here now at once.'

The man hurried away and she turned to the driver of their carriage.

'I am very grateful to you,' she said. 'Come tomorrow and I'll see you are properly rewarded.'

He held out the knife, horribly stained with blood, and she took it from him shuddering and put it on the table.

Dr Rainier arrived within half an hour and by that time Ian had come running up the stairs and with a grim and silent efficiency, as if murder were only to be expected in this barbarous country, helped Robert to strip off his coat and blood-soaked shirt. Isabelle caught her breath when she saw the jagged wound but the doctor was maddeningly calm about it, as if knife wounds and attempted murder were too frequent to cause undue concern.

'You are fortunate, my dear sir,' he told Robert. 'A few inches to the right and it could have pierced the lung and you would have been coughing blood. As it is, provided no infection sets up, you should do well enough.'

The fact that his patient was by now suffering intense pain and had lost a considerable amount of blood seemed not to worry him at all. He swabbed and bandaged and left a tincture of laudanum with Isabelle.

'Use it sparingly, Madame,' he said and showed her how to measure the drops. He eyed the knife on the table curiously. 'A wicked and vicious weapon, a surgeon's knife, it would seem that your husband's assailant knew well where and how to strike. I take it that Monsieur le Vicomte is English, Madame, though he speaks such excellent French. We may be at peace now but old enmities are slow to die. I will call again in the morning.'

It was Ian who took over the painful task of getting Robert undressed and into bed. By this time his endurance had reached its limit and he was close to fainting with pain and exhaustion when Isabelle brought him the carefully measured dose of laudanum. She raised his head a little to swallow it and he caught hold of her hand.

'Don't worry too much. I have come through worse. You must ask them downstairs to find you another room so that you can rest. Ian will stay with me.'

'No, Robert, no. Do you think I could sleep for a single moment? I am staying here with you and Ian will be at hand if we need him.' She put a finger on his lips. 'Now don't argue. You will only tire yourself. I shall be perfectly happy here in a chair beside you.'

'There is no need,' he whispered painfully.

'There is every need.'

All through that long night, getting up at intervals to wipe the sweat from his face with a damp towel, to bring him water when he asked for it, persuading him to take a few more drops of the laudanum to deaden the pain, she was slowly realising something about herself. Lying back in the chair with time to think, she knew with a devastating certainty that if he were to die she would be utterly bereft. It came upon her with an unexpected force how much he had crept into her heart and mind, not because of what he had given her, not the gifts and the jewels and the rich life, but he himself. She did not yet completely understand it but she felt somehow that she had taken everything and given nothing in return, and knew now with a clutch at her heart that if he were no longer there, the loss would be utterly unbearable.

Towards morning he grew more and more restless, tossing on the bed, sweating with pain and fever so that when Dr Rainier called surprisingly early he lost the complacency of the night before and was considerably more concerned.

'I fear there is grievous infection there,' he said, drawing her away from the sick man and into the other room. 'Either it has come from the weapon itself or from some substance entering into the wound. It was a savage blow, Madame, your husband must have a vicious enemy who did not only seek to kill but to cause as much suffering as possible. He is young and healthy so we must hope for the best. No food except for a few mouthfuls of a clear bouillon if he will take it and a little fruit juice, orange or lemon, if you can procure it. If there is any sudden change, then send for me, otherwise I will call again this evening.'

He offered to send a nurse from the hospital but she refused absolutely, knowing how Robert would loathe a stranger tending him in his weakness. She and Ian could manage it between them, she said, and if the doctor thought it strange that a fashionable young wife should be so willing so spend hours by the bedside of her sick husband, he put it down to one of the odd quirks in which the English were so prone to indulge themselves.

As the day wore on, Robert grew worse. The fever increased and he was in a great deal of pain. Isabelle wished passionately she had one of Miss Holland's herbal potions instead of the nauseous draught Dr Rainier sent round intended to bring the fever down and which he shuddered away from. During the afternoon Ian with great difficulty persuaded her to lie down for an hour or two on the day bed.

'It won't help the Master if you break down, my lady, it will only fret him.'

With great reluctance she gave in and much to her surprise did fall into a light sleep for an hour or so and afterwards, bathed and refreshed, she was able to face Dr Rainier when he came in the early evening and shook his head over his patient with a face like doom.

He redressed the wound and frowned at the inflammation and how Robert flinched at the slightest pressure.

He wanted to draw a pint of blood from him on the plea that it was a sovereign remedy to bring down the fever but she refused to allow him to do so. Robert had lost enough blood already and it would only weaken him in the fight against infection.

'The mounting fever and the irregular pulse could be dangerous, Madame. If it breaks before morning then we can perhaps hope but if not . . .' he shrugged his shoulders, 'then I fear we are all in God's hands.'

She wanted to scream at him but knew that any protest would be useless. When he had gone she sent Ian to supper and to rest for a few hours.

'I'm not leaving you here alone, my lady,' he said stubbornly.

She was aware of his devotion to his master and also that there were certain attentions Robert would prefer to receive from him rather from her so she said, 'I should be very glad of your company, Ian, but we may have a long fight before us. Come back in the early morning.'

It was shortly after midnight and she must have dozed a little in the chair when she was aroused by a cry so sharp, so agonised that it startled her. Although she had shaded the candles, she could see that Robert had pushed himself up in the bed and was staring in front of him.

'No, no,' he muttered in a strangled whisper, 'No, not Cécile, oh my God, not Cécile,' and he put up a hand to his eyes with

300

a gesture of horror as if what he saw was too unbearable to watch. He was obviously in the throes of some frightful nightmare probably induced by pain and the laudanum.

She crossed to him quickly putting her arms around him and holding him close, trying to soothe him.

'It's all right, dearest, it's all right. It's only a dream.'

He leaned against her, shivering violently though he still burned with fever.

'What happened?' he muttered. 'What was I saying?'

'You were having a bad dream, that's all.'

She piled up the pillows and eased him gently back against them. Then she fetched a towel and wiped the sweat from his face.

'Could I have something to drink?' he murmured. 'My mouth is like an ash pit.'

She brought him lemon water that the hotel had supplied and he drank thirstily.

'It's a very long time since I had that dream,' he said. 'Once it was nearly every night.'

'It's the pain and the drug,' she said soothingly, taking the glass from him. 'Tell me about it. It may ease you.'

'I don't think I can.'

'Try. To share pain is sometimes to halve it.'

At any other time, she thought afterwards, he would never have spoken of it, it was buried too deep within him, but he was sick and feverish, still partly drugged by the laudanum, still lost in some haunting memory. It came at last in murmured fragments as if he were reliving the past, but she slowly pieced them together.

'It was two years after the war had broken out. There were pockets of royalist resistance all over France, in the Vendée, in Lyons, in the south. My cousin Jacques was in the thick of it. The war was going badly for us. We needed all the help we could get. It was necessary for someone to liaise with them, get them organised, supply guns and gold and bring back information.'

'And that was what you were doing?'

301

'Yes, for a time. It was easy for me. I knew the country. I had the connections.'

But dangerous, she thought with a shiver, terribly dangerous.

'What happened?'

'I suspected that one amongst us was a traitor, an informer for those bloodthirsty devils in Paris, but I was not sure who it was until one winter's night.'

He paused so long that she thought he had fallen into an exhausted doze but then he went on, his voice so low she could scarcely hear the words.

'Jacques' niece, Cécile, carried messages for us from one group to another. I didn't want to use her. She was a child, only fifteen, but he said, "It is safer. Who will suspect a schoolgirl going to and fro through the streets?" None of us used our real names. We were all known by the names of birds. I was Rossignol, the man I was to meet that night was known as Le Hibou, the owl. I was to contact him in a barn outside the village with gold and with information of a shipment that was to be landed secretly on one of the Brittany beaches.'

'The smugglers,' she breathed.

He smiled faintly. 'Yes, we used them sometimes.'

He paused for a moment, then drew a painful breath and went on so quietly she had to bend close to hear the whispered words.

'When I reached the place I knew at once that something was wrong because he was not alone. Cécile was with him. It was bitingly cold and a small brazier burned inside the barn. I said at once, "What is the girl doing here?"

'And he laughed. "What fools you are to trust your secrets to a child. That pretty head holds all the information we so badly want, my dear Rossignol, and before the night is out you and she will sing together." I saw then in the flickering light of the fire that Cécile's hands and feet were bound so that she could not move easily. She had backed against the wall and I could see the stark terror in her eyes. God knows what he had already done to her.

'We did not carry guns mainly because if stopped by Fouché's thugs it meant imprisonment and death. I waited for a moment,

302

calculating my chances of taking him by surprise and I saw him draw an iron bar from the brazier glowing red at one end.

'"I want them now," he said, "the names, the meeting places. I know you have them between you. Now quickly or else the little Cécile will lose all her pretty looks." He moved nearer the girl so that she could feel the heat of the red-hot iron and I saw her cringe back and stifle a scream. I knew what they could do. I'd seen men hung over a slow burning fire till their feet blistered and blackened. I'd seen women tortured. He moved a step nearer to her exulting in his power, certain of victory, and I took a chance. I leaped at him.'

She could see it all so clearly, the shadowy barn, the trembling child, the terrifying glow of the fire.

Robert was staring in front of him, his eyes filled with a dark horror.

'It was a mistake,' he went on in a hoarse whisper. 'In falling he kicked over the brazier, the straw caught fire. The flames licked across the floor and Cécile cried out struggling to free herself but helpless to run. He had got to his feet and launched himself at her. I grabbed the fallen iron bar and swung it at him. The fiery end struck him across the face and he yelled in pain clawing at it desperately as it burned his hair. The flames had reached Cécile's thin dress and it flared up. She screamed and screamed in terror. I tore off my coat, wrapping it around her, trying to smother the flames. I carried her outside into the cold night air, but I was too late, hopelessly too late. I ran as if the devil were after me to a house where I knew I could get help and shelter. They did what they could but she died a few hours later . . .' He closed his eyes wearily. 'Jacques did not blame me, nobody blamed me, but I have never been able to forgive myself.'

'What happened to the man who tortured her?'

'At the time I thought only of Cécile. Afterwards we knew he must have died in the fire.'

He had fallen back against the pillows, his face grey with pain and exhaustion. Isabelle was filled with such a flood of tenderness, such a strong desire to give comfort that she could not

303

speak. Instead she took his hand in hers and after a moment felt his fingers return her pressure.

A little later when she would have moved away, he whispered, 'Don't go. Please don't go,' so she stayed sitting close beside him, his hand in hers, until after a time he drowsed into a shallow restless sleep.

She grew stiff and cramped but was unwilling to move, her thoughts going over and over what he had told her. It had been a frightening glimpse into that secret life of his, of which he had spoken so little. That cryptic message 'The devil is on the prowl' – had that been a warning from one of those with whom he had worked in the past? Were there enemies who dreamed of revenge? She shivered as if somewhere in the shadows danger still lurked.

She could not sleep and as the hours crept slowly by she learned something about herself. Ever since that terrible time in France when the happy world of childhood had been ruthlessly destroyed, she had longed to love and be loved, to be needed, to belong. It was what had drawn her so close to Guy and had spilled over recklessly to Lucien, helpless and dependent on her. She had saved his life and in a mood of wild generosity had wished to give him everything, even herself. All these summer months in the first flush of success it had been there, his glamour, the excitement, the thrill of belonging, till that last meeting in the gardens of Vauxhall when the handsome boy, the adventurer with his charm and appeal, had suddenly worn a different and frightening face. She had been living in a dream, an illusion. Now she was away from it she seemed to see it all with a cold clarity and felt deeply ashamed to have been so deceived.

With Robert it had been different. He had come to her from another world outside the dull dreary round, sure of himself, independent, giving everything and asking for nothing and now suddenly she was seeing another side of him, one she had never dreamed of, sensitive, vulnerable to pain and loss. All her values had turned upside down. For the first time she felt he needed her, that she had something to give, and her heart went out to him. She remembered a poem she had read somewhere . . .

True love is a durable fire
In the mind ever burning
Never sick, never old, never dead,
From itself never turning

and felt that for the first time she understood it.

The next morning miraculously Robert seemed a little better. It was as if the torment of the night had purged the flush of fever. He was still in great pain, he still looked utterly exhausted and sick, but his eyes were less clouded and he was more himself.

Dr Rainier when he came was so pleased with his patient and with himself at the success of his treatment that Isabelle could have hit him.

He re-examined the wound, sniffed approvingly at the bandages and after causing Robert what she thought was a great deal of unnecessary pain, he turned to her.

'I think we may allow ourselves to hope, Madame, the infection I feared has lessened and our patient appears to be holding his own. But we must take care, great care. Perhaps he may be allowed a little food today, a few mouthfuls of chicken broth and maybe a glass of wine, but only one, mark you. I felt sure that the draught I sent across would do the trick in reducing the fever,' he went on complacently, 'and we will continue with it today. Send your man for it as soon as possible and follow the instructions exactly.'

'Pompous ass!' muttered Robert when he had gone. 'There is nothing I dislike more than being talked about over my head as if I were an idiot. Chicken broth indeed! And what is this miracle draught of his which has had such a striking effect?'

'It smelled so disgusting,' confessed Isabelle, 'that I only gave you one dose. I threw the rest away.'

Robert ventured a laugh and gasped with pain. 'Thank God for an intelligent wife.' He paused for a moment, gathering strength before he said, 'Listen, my dear, you've been caring for me quite long enough. You mustn't exhaust yourself. Go out into the fresh air away from this stuffy sickroom. Ian can supply all I need.'

'I shall do no such thing,' she said firmly. 'You may be a little better but, as Dr Rainier said, we have to be very careful and I wouldn't trust you two together for a single moment. Ian is your willing slave. You could probably persuade him to let you get up.'

'Don't lecture me. I'm not strong enough to argue.'

'A good thing too. I wouldn't listen to you even if you did.'

She felt as if a huge weight had been lifted from her shoulders. Of course he might suffer a relapse but she would not let herself think of that and he was still very weak, the least exertion making him sweat but despite the pain he refused to take any more laudanum.

'It clouds my mind. I dislike not being in full possession of my senses,' he said when she tried to persuade him.

He said nothing of the night before and of the haunting revelation he had made to her so that she wondered if he remembered it or if it had all been part of his nightmare. He rested for most of the day, drifting into half sleep, a low fever still hanging about him intermittently. He ate very little but was glad to share the tray of tea brought to Isabelle during the afternoon, something which ordinarily he didn't care for.

Fortunately there was no relapse and each day he improved a little more, much to her relief, and at the end of that nerve-racking week they had an unexpected visitor.

One afternoon she was sitting in the big chair by the bed dozing a little in the warm sunny room. She had been reading to him from a book of English verse, such an unlikely find on a Paris bookstall that they had not been able to resist it.

One of the verses still hovered in her mind as she lay back with closed eyes –

My true love hath my heart, and I have his
By just exchange, one to the other given . . .

She wondered if that might ever be true of her and Robert.

She was roused by a door being flung open. A cheerful voice called 'Hallo there!' and David came striding into the adjacent sitting room.

306

For a moment she stared, unable to believe her eyes, then the relief of seeing him, of being able to share her anxiety with someone so close to both of them, overwhelmed her. She stumbled to her feet, the book falling to the floor, and ran to meet him.

'Oh David, I'm so glad to see you, so very glad!'

He put his arm around her, holding her close. 'Here, here, what's all this? I never knew I was so popular.'

'You don't know, you just don't know.' A little ashamed she tried to free herself. He kissed her cheek while still keeping an arm around her waist.

'What's all this I've been hearing downstairs about Robert being at death's door?'

'He very nearly was, but thank heaven he is a little better now.'

'May I take a look at him?'

'Of course.'

Together they went through into the bedroom.

'Well, well,' he said looking down at his friend, 'this is a fine thing, I must say! Laid low in the midst of what should have been a second honeymoon! You've not been fighting a duel with some impertinent fellow who's been making sheeps' eyes at your wife, I hope.'

'Nothing so gallant, I'm afraid,' said Robert wryly. 'A mere knife thrust from some night prowler.'

'Money or your life?'

'Something like that. Luckily he didn't get either. Isabelle would you ask them to bring up something for David, a tray of tea – coffee?'

'Coffee for me, please. I'm no lover of the ladies' gentle brew.'

He gave Isabelle a broad grin and she went off to order it, feeling sure that Robert wanted to have a few words with his friend alone and making up her mind to worm it out of him afterwards.

She had her opportunity about a week later. Robert had made great strides but, though permitted to be out of bed for a few hours, he was strongly advised not to attempt to ride a horse or even take a carriage drive.

'It is ridiculous that your stay here should be spoiled because of me,' he said one morning when Isabelle was breakfasting with him. 'What's David here for? He can escort you wherever you would like to go.'

She protested that she had no particular desire to go anywhere but Robert had made up his mind and the next day David presented himself in mid-morning, dressed for a country excursion.

'I'm under orders to take you out,' he said cheerfully. 'Where would Madame like to go?'

'It's too bad of Robert. You must have plenty of plans of your own.'

'None of any importance. I'm at your service.'

She laughed and gave in so after they had had a delicious luncheon at Frascati's, the afternoon found them strolling in the gardens of Versailles, sadly neglected since the appalling day when the enraged citizens had rampaged through them in a frenzy of destruction. It was a mellow September day with gentle hazy sunshine, and a shade of melancholy lay across the great lakes where the fountains no longer played, where nymphs and cupids lay as they had been hacked down, forlorn and mutilated.

David was a charming companion and she felt at ease with him. They chatted pleasantly and presently he drew her to sit beside him on one of the marble seats looking across at le Petit Trianon where the young Marie Antoinette had entertained her closest friends and pretended to be a simple country girl.

'In his youth my grandfather was often at court,' said Isabelle dreamily. 'He was high in favour with the King and he used to tell Guy and me about the wonderful fêtes champêtres, the plays and ballets and masqued balls. It all sounded to us like some gorgeous fairy tale.'

'Do you never regret that it is all gone?'

'Not really. Why should I when I never knew any of it. At Sauvigny it was quite different. My father lived simply. But it

308

does seem sad that so much that was beautiful has been wilfully destroyed and nothing better has come in its place.'

It was very quiet in this secluded garden and she leaned back, taking off her bonnet, letting the gentle breeze blow through her hair and feeling rested for the first time since Robert had been struck down.

They were silent for a little and then David said quietly, 'Isabelle, may I ask you a very personal question?'

She looked up at him a little startled. 'What is it?'

'How much do you care for Robert?'

'Haven't I shown how much I care?'

'Oh you've been a very loyal and dutiful wife these last weeks, no doubt about that, but are you in love with him?'

'Why do you say that?'

'Because he cares for you very much indeed.'

She was staring down at her hands, pleating and repleating the ribbons of her bonnet.

'When Robert first asked me to marry him down at High Willows,' she said in a low voice, 'I refused him. Then something happened, unexpected and horrible, and he asked me again and . . .'

'And you accepted him as a way of escape.'

'It sounds hateful when you put it like that,' she said in quick defence. 'I told him the truth. I said I liked and respected him but I was not in love with him, but he still . . .'

'Pressed you to marry him.'

'Yes.'

'I see. And now?'

'I don't know, David, I don't know,' but she couldn't go on. Her feelings were too new, she was too confused, too unsure of herself and she turned on him almost angrily.

'Why are you asking me all these questions?'

'One hears things.'

'Robert doesn't listen to gossip.'

'No, I don't think he does, but I'd not like to see him deceived and hurt.'

'You need have no fear of that,' she was quick in denial.

'I'm glad to hear it.'

309

She looked directly at him. 'Now may I ask you a question and will you tell me the truth?'

'Is it about Robert?'

'Yes.'

'What is it you want to know?'

And quite suddenly she knew she couldn't proceed with her questioning. Whatever was secret in Robert's life, he must tell her himself. She would not discuss him with anyone, not even his friend. She looked away.

'It doesn't matter.'

'Are you sure? I've known him for a long time.'

'It wasn't important.' She began to put on her bonnet. 'It's beginning to grow rather cold. Shall we go?'

'As you wish.'

He got up and gave her his hand. They walked away together talking of other and more trivial things.

As soon as Robert was strong enough to make the journey they would be returning to England, but there were one or two matters to be settled first. He had insisted on her portrait being painted, a miniature on ivory, to be framed in a silver case that could be closed for travelling.

'It flatters me,' she said, a little dissatisfied when it came back from the silversmith. 'Why did you want it so much?'

'To remind me of my will-o'-the-wisp of a wife when she flies away from me,' said Robert lightly.

'I shall never do that.'

'I hope not.'

She had one unpleasant experience in those last few days. She had been at the opera with David and the music of Monteverdi's *Orfeo* was still ringing in her ears. In the crowded foyer they were momentarily separated and suddenly she was pushed up against a man she knew instantly. It was only a glimpse, the hat shaded much of his face and he was older, thinner, but there was no mistaking the lean dark features, the short black beard, the eyes that met hers for an instant, so filled with bitter hatred that she stopped breathless, swept back to childhood, unable to move or speak. Then he had vanished and David was again at her side.

'What is it? You look as if you'd seen a ghost.'

'I think perhaps I have.' With an effort she shook the memory away from her. 'It was just someone whom I thought I once knew.'

When she was packing for them both, she came upon the assassin's knife, a long thin blade used with a devilish skill – that was what Dr Ranier had said, and Henri Rivage was a surgeon. The hilt was finely wrought in silver, no ordinary kitchen or butcher's knife, but it was ridiculous to think of such a thing. What had Dr Rivage to do with Robert? It was the Sauvigny inheritance that he had coveted and had now won for himself. She was tempted to throw the knife aside, then suddenly buried it deep in the bottom of their trunk.

It was the beginning of October when they travelled down to Calais by easy stages and took the packet boat to Dover. It was the first anniversary of their marriage and they celebrated it with champagne and drank to the future, not yet aware of the web of hatred, revenge and jealousy that was being woven slowly around them and would threaten to tear them apart.

Part Three

ISABELLE
1803

15

It was a morning in late May and Isabelle was standing at the long windows of the drawing room looking out on Arlington Street. It had been raining earlier but now a watery sun glittered on the puddles and on the fresh green of the plane trees opposite. It was strangely quiet for mid morning, no clatter of carriages and very few pedlars, only the Indian with his black turban and his tray of exotic spices, a gypsy in her bright rags selling white heather for luck and the organ grinder with his thin pathetic monkey which usually sent Rory into a frenzy of barking. The latest news seemed to have kept everyone within doors. It was only a few days since the fragile peace treaty had finally collapsed and Britain was once again at war with France.

It had been hanging in the balance for a couple of months now with Bonaparte raging at the stubborn British who refused to yield to certain of his demands. He was said to have screamed in fury at the Ambassador, raising his cane threateningly, which Lord Whitworth endured with stolid calm while inwardly wondering what he would do if this violent Corsican actually attacked him. It was nearly a week since he had thankfully withdrawn from Paris and returned to England with his staff. But Robert had not come with him.

He had gone to Paris in early April urged by his Chief in the Foreign Office and privately by Henry Dundas who had been very forthright about the ineptitude of the present government.

'For God's sake, get over there, Robert,' he had said. 'Let's have the truth of the matter. Find out exactly what's going on and whether the mass of the people are solidly behind Bonaparte if he drives them into war or whether the whole sorry business is mere bombast in a final attempt to get his own way.'

Isabelle had implored him not to go.

'It's too dangerous,' she urged. 'They tried to kill you a few months ago, they could succeed next time.'

'But this is entirely different, my dear. This is politics. I'm not going as a private person. I shall have diplomatic immunity. And if I can find out something useful, then I must do what I can.'

'Is that all you think about?' she said tempestuously. 'What you can do for Britain? What about us? What will happen to Marian and me if you get yourself murdered?'

'History doesn't usually repeat itself and you'll be well provided for,' he said smiling. 'I shall take the very greatest care I promise you.' He gently turned her to face him. 'You wouldn't want me to refuse, to stay cowering in my kennel like a beaten dog because once I ran into trouble. I'm not a soldier, Isabelle, never fancied it somehow, and I've no head for navigation but this is something I can do and must do even if it is only for my own peace of mind.'

'Oh Robert,' she leaned against him. 'I shall not have one easy moment till you return.'

And he had not come back with the embassy party and there was no word for her, so where was he? She felt sick with anxiety. He would not be pleased if she were to badger the Foreign Office or go weeping to Henry Dundas. Wives of men like Robert did not do such things any more than did army and navy wives left at home with their men far away. They were expected to show more fortitude. The memory of that terrible night in Paris when the assassin had leaped on him came back night after night to torment her.

She felt very young and helpless alone in this great house with only the three dogs and the servants for company. Marian had gone to spend some weeks with an aged relative in Oxfordshire who had been taken ill and could not cope with noisy little dogs so Roland and Oliver had been left in her care.

She felt foolish tears prick her eyes and brushed them away angrily. It was no use standing there moping. She would dress and take the dogs for a brisk walk in St James's Park. That would help to blow away the megrims of anxiety and help her to think clearly.

As she turned from the windows, the butler knocked and came in.

'What is it, Hawke?' she said a little impatiently.

'A gentleman to see you, my lady, a naval gentleman.'

'A naval gentleman!' She took the card from the silver salver and gave a little squeal of surprise. '*Captain* Conway! It must be Perry. Show him in, Hawke, at once.'

It was several months since she had seen him and when he came through the door in full panoply of naval uniform, she thought he had grown in dignity. He was no longer the impulsive boy, he had matured over the past year. She went to meet him with outstretched hands.

'Oh Perry! This is wonderful. You've been promoted. You have a ship of your own. Aren't you pleased?'

'Well, yes, I am of course very pleased. One should not be thankful when it means that we are at war again but it has pushed me up the ladder, not very far but it is a start. It's not a ship of the line of course, only one of the smaller sloops, but it's my very first command and it's all due to Lord Nelson's recommendation when I was with him at Copenhagen and in the Channel Fleet. Of course the peace knocked it on the head but now, when every seaman is urgently needed, it was remembered and here I am, Captain of the *Sirius*.'

'It couldn't have happened to anyone more deserving,' she said warmly. 'Is your aunt pleased? Come and tell me all about it. I'm afraid Robert is away. He is still in Paris.'

'In Paris? But haven't you heard?'

'Heard what?'

'Two French ships were captured in the very first naval action and Bonaparte was so furiously angry that he has ordered the arrest and imprisonment of all English travellers in France.'

'Oh no, it can't be true!' she looked at him aghast. 'He can't do such a wicked thing. Are you sure?'

'Quite sure. I've just come from the Navy Office. They were full of it. To treat civilians so savagely is contrary to all decent behaviour and it could be a very long war.'

'Robert in prison!' She let herself drop on the sofa feeling as if

317

the bottom had suddenly fallen out of her world. 'I can't believe it.'

He sat down beside her. 'You must try not to worry too much. He is so familiar with the country and he speaks the language so well, I'm sure he will find a way to escape the worst.'

'Yes, yes, of course he will, he must. He has friends over there too.' She tried to pull herself together. 'Will you take some refreshment, Perry? Coffee – a glass of wine?'

'Thank you, no. I must not stay. I have to go down to Chatham where my ship is being refitted. There is a great deal to be done before I sail.' He paused and then went on with an effort. 'Isabelle, I really came to ask a great favour from you.'

'What kind of a favour?'

'It's about Venetia.'

'Venetia? But Perry, she is to be married in the early autumn.'

'I know all about that.' He got up and began to pace up and down the room before he turned to face her. 'I'm afraid I behaved very badly when she told me about Sir Hugo. I was so hurt, so sick and angry – and I wrote her a terrible letter. I regretted it as soon as it was sent. I wrote again apologising. I wrote several times. The letters were all returned unopened. I called and the door was shut in my face. But now this has happened. I shall be going away for months, perhaps years, and I must see her again. I want to tell her how sorry I am but however I try I can't get anywhere near her.'

'What do you want me to do?'

'You are good friends,' he went on eagerly. 'Couldn't you ask her to visit you and then let me know when she will be here so that I could call as it were unexpectedly?'

'Oh Perry, how can I?'

'If then she turns her back on me, I'll accept it but if not, if she will just meet me and talk for a little so that we can part friends and not enemies, that's all I want, nothing more I swear.'

'I don't know,' said Isabelle doubtfully, 'I don't know. My aunt will be very angry and so will Uncle Joshua.'

318

'They needn't know. Please Isabelle. Is it so much to ask, and you've always been such a good friend to both of us.'

She looked at the distraught young man. 'I can't promise but I'll try. Leave your address so that I can send to you.'

'Oh thank you,' he said seizing her hand and pressing it warmly. 'Thank you a thousand times.' He took out one of his cards and wrote the address of his lodging on the back. 'This will always find me.'

He took his leave, still protesting his gratitude and she looked after him doubtfully, very uncertain as to whether she had acted wisely. She was almost sure that Venetia was still in love with him but was that love strong enough to break her engagement to the wealthy Sir Hugo and face all that would inevitably follow, the scandal, her parents' anger? It would need great courage. She felt pretty sure that if they did meet, Perry would do his best to persuade her to marry him and the responsibility lay heavy on her. Although she and Venetia had remained on friendly terms over the last few months, they had never really been close. Oh well, Perry would have to take his chance as any man in love had to do. She sighed and went upstairs to dress and get the dogs ready for their walk.

If Marian had been there she would have insisted that Isabelle must not walk alone in the Park. She should at least take Gwennie with her, but Isabelle had a scorn of conventions. In times of stress she needed to escape and be alone just as she had once fled to the seashore. So she set off through the narrow back streets, walking briskly, the three dogs on their leashes, and far too absorbed in her gloomy thoughts to notice the surprised glances that were thrown at her.

In the Park people were strolling along the grassy walks now the rain had stopped. There were nursemaids with their small charges and as the three dogs released ran joyously in all directions, one of the toddlers ran with them and fell flat on his face on the wet grass. She hurried to pick him up but he had already scrambled to his feet staring solemnly, uncertain whether to cry. Then he suddenly gave her a gap-toothed smile and charged off again. She wondered if Robert was disappointed that she was not yet pregnant. He had never spoken of children but she knew his father had mentioned it more than once. Inadvertently she had seen one of his letters – 'Isn't that kitchen-maid of yours breeding yet? Get to work, boy, or I swear Jeannie will overtake you.' She had laughed at it but still felt that somehow she had failed him.

It had been a very quiet winter. It had taken Robert longer than they had expected to recover from the knife wound. It had struck deeper and done more damage than Dr Rainier had supposed and, being a man who had rarely suffered any sickness other than an occasional cold, he was an exceedingly bad patient, refusing to take proper care and impatient of his physician's good advice. And now he could be in prison or at least under some kind of restraint, maybe for the duration of the war, but was it true? He could well have been sent on some secret mission and she felt a rage of anger against all the politicians sitting comfortably at Whitehall and letting Robert and others like him run the risk of treachery, danger and a knife thrust in the back.

She had crossed the Park by now and come to the pretty ornamental bridge that crossed what they used to call Rosamund's Pond. She leaned on the rail for a few minutes looking across to Duck Island. Pelicans, unwieldy and corpulent, wad-dled along the shore. There were slim grey secretary birds and glossy green mallards, a few screaming gulls that had come up from the river in search of rich pickings, and half a dozen swans, stately as galleons in full sail, reminding her of Perry and his new command. Perhaps she and Venetia could go down to Chatham to see him before he sailed. He would be so proud to show them over his beloved *Sirius*.

Her thoughts were rudely interrupted by a loud hissing, a dog's frenzied squeals and the beating of powerful wings and to her horror she saw that Oliver, always the most daring of the three, had ventured into the water in pursuit of a low-flying seagull and was being savagely threatened by a swan defending her three grey cygnets. Isabelle raced across the bridge and down to the water's edge, calling Oliver frantically but, fright-ened by the bird with its spread wings and vicious outstretched neck, the little dog swam on instead of turning back. She was gathering up her skirts and preparing to plunge in after him when she was abruptly thrust back and a young man strode into the shallows, smacked the angry bird smartly with his riding crop and snatched up the wildly struggling little dog. He deposited Oliver at Isabelle's feet.

'There he is, a disgusting object, but sound in wind and limb,' he said laughing.

The dog shook himself vigorously, spraying them with a shower of mud and blood where the cruel beak had struck at him. She snatched him up holding him close, turned to express her gratitude for the rescue and to her dismay saw that it was Lucien, that same maddening, charming, lying Lucien whom she had done her best to avoid ever since that hateful evening in the Vauxhall Gardens.

For a fleeting moment the old spell still worked its magic and she trembled, then abruptly it vanished. He was two people, she realised that now. Behind the laughing boy lurked someone darker and more dangerous. During these winter months she had taken good care to keep him at a distance and at first it had been easy as up to Christmas they rarely went out socially and afterwards she had heard through the usual gossip that he and his so-called uncle had gone to Paris where she hoped devoutly they would stay.

'I am very grateful to you,' she said stiffly, pulling herself together, 'especially as it has ruined your coat.'

Lucien must have been riding as he was in breeches and boots but his handsome green coat was liberally bespattered with splashes of mud.

'N'importe,' he said gaily. 'I am only too delighted to have been of assistance.' She made to move away and he stopped her. 'Don't go, please don't go, not for a moment. I want to know why you have been avoiding me all these past months.'

'Avoiding you? I'm not aware of doing any such thing,' she said quickly. 'It is true my husband's health has not been good and so we have spent a very quiet life during the winter, but I really mustn't stand here talking. Oliver is shivering and he has been hurt too. He'll catch his death of cold if I don't take him home.'

'Are you on foot? I will walk with you.'

'There's really no need.'

But as she walked away, he kept pace with her and when they approached the gates and she stopped, anxious to put the other two dogs on their leashes, he calmly took them from her, snapped them on the collars of Roland and Rory and continued to walk beside her.

'Despite his ill health there is a strong rumour that your husband was in Paris when war was declared once again and has been trapped with the other unfortunate Englishmen loitering in France. Is it true?'

'It may be,' she said cautiously.

'You're heard from him of course.'

'Why are you asking all these questions?'

He shrugged his shoulders. 'No reason, merely friendly interest.'

By now they were threading their way through the narrow streets and the unsavoury mews that lay between the Park and Arlington Street, carefully avoiding muddy puddles and piles of horse dung. She felt him close behind her, his breath on her neck.

'Why are you still angry with me, Isabelle?' he was whispering. 'Is it such a crime to love you? All through these long months you have never been out of my mind, only to find myself utterly rejected. Can't you forgive the madness of that last night at Vauxhall? Am I to be banished for ever from your friendship, from your affection?'

Once the honeyed voice would have carried her away, even now it made her heart beat faster, but this time with anger. Did he think her so easily tricked, so quickly won over? The mist of enchantment, of illusion had been swept away. How could she have been so ready to trust, so foolish as not to recognise the falsity? She did not believe for a single moment in his protestations of love but why was he so persistent? What lay behind it?

It was purely unhappy chance that brought Marian back

from Oxfordshire at almost the same time as they reached the house. She stepped from the carriage to see her brother's wife on the steps with that abominable Frenchman so close together it might almost have been an embrace.

'Aren't you going to ask me in?' Lucien was saying. 'Offer me a glass of wine and something to repair the damage?' He leaned closer, one hand fonding the little dog which she clutched against her breast.

'I'm afraid not. You must forgive me but poor little Oliver must be bathed and attended to immediately.'

'Excuse me.' Marian was coming up the steps as the footman opened the door.

'Marian!' exclaimed Isabelle in surprise. 'I did not expect you home yet.'

'Obviously. Good day to you, Monsieur de Vosges.'

She swept by him with a freezing glance and Edward went down to the waiting carriage to collect the luggage.

'I've been given my *congé* with a vengeance,' said Lucien ruefully. 'Lady Marian doesn't approve of me, I fear, but I shall call, Isabelle, and enquire after the sufferer.'

He gave Oliver a little pat on the head and ran down the steps, turning at the bottom with a jaunty wave of his hand.

Oh God, she thought as she went into the house. Why did it have to happen like this? Heaven knows what Marian will read into it.

She very soon knew. She was on her knees by the bath tub with Gwennie in attendance, sleeves rolled up, bathing an indignant and very smelly Oliver while the other two dogs looked on with smug faces since they didn't have to undergo the indignity of soap in their eyes and up their noses. She knew that Marian had come in but chose to ignore her.

'Hand me the big towel, will you, Gwennie?'

She lifted out the dripping Oliver and began to rub him vigorously.

'Perhaps you will have the goodness to tell me what all this is about,' said Marian stiffly.

'It's quite simple. I was walking the dogs in St James's Park and silly little Oliver chased a seagull into the lake. One of the swans attacked him. He might have been killed if Lucien had not rescued him.'

'And does Monsieur de Vosges usually accompany you on your morning walks?'

'No, of course not, as you very well know. I met him by chance and very luckily as it turned out. Gwennie, I think we've finished with all this now. Will you call the maids and have it cleared away? What has brought you home so soon, Marian? I thought you were to stay for another month.'

'Oh it was all a storm in a teacup. My great aunt thought she was dying and it was nothing worse than a bad attack of indigestion brought on by over indulgence. I couldn't stay away when I heard the news. Where is Robert?'

'He went to Paris very soon after you left for Oxfordshire. He has not yet returned.'

'Didn't he come back with Lord Whitworth?'

'No, it seems he may have been arrested along with the other English who were still in France. Come up to my sitting room, Marian, and I will tell you all I know.'

In her anxiety for her brother Marian seemed to have forgotten about that chance meeting with Lucien. At Robert's insistence they had made very little of the attack in Paris but she was always a little jealous in case he might have confided more to his wife than he did to her.

As the days passed with still no word, Isabelle grew more and more anxious until one morning she could bear it no longer. She summoned up all her courage and called upon Henry Dundas in his fine new house, now that he had been created Lord Melville. After some delay she was ushered into the great man's office with its fine desk, its handsome bookshelves and rich Aubusson carpet.

The statesman, a little stouter, a little more rubicund than he had been at their wedding, came to meet her.

'My dear young lady, you come into my dusty room like a breath of spring. What can I do for you?'

'I think you know, my lord,' she said bluntly. 'I want to know what you have done with my husband.'

'Ah well, now,' he retreated behind his desk. 'Come and sit down, my dear. Let me offer you some refreshment.'

'No, thank you,' she said firmly holding her ground. 'I just want to know about Robert. Has he been arrested? Is he in prison? Or where is he?'

He looked at the charming face framed in dark curls under a really enchanting straw hat, thought what a lucky dog Robert was and then wondered if he'd been fool enough to confide in his wife or if she had simply made a lucky guess.

'I can only tell you one thing for certain,' he said slowly, 'he is not among those Bonaparte has had arrested. He is in no danger but it may be a little while before he returns. In the meantime, my dear lady, I would counsel the utmost discretion and if that is what the majority of your acquaintances are believing, then don't undeceive them. Do you understand me?'

'I think so. I'm not quite a fool, you know, my lord. I know what you wish everyone to believe. Robert has told me nothing but all the same I have realised that the man who attacked him in Paris last year was no ordinary sneak thief, was he?'

He smiled wryly. 'The less said about that the better.'

'I realise that too. When will he return, my lord?'

'I wish I could tell you but I can't. Soon, very soon, that's all I can promise you.'

He was courtesy itself. He came with her to the door, pressed her hand warmly, gave her his genial smile and said, 'Have a care to your friends, my dear. There are listening ears everywhere and chance words accidentally dropped can add up to a great deal when pieced together.'

'Is that how spies gather information? Is that what you are trying to tell me?'

'Maybe. There is something else I would say to you. Warn that young brother of yours to keep away from a certain fashionable gaming house. He could lose more than his money.'

Alarmed she said quickly, 'What has Guy been doing?'

'Nothing as yet so far as I know, but a word in season would not go amiss. These young men, you know, heedless, thoughtless, and I happen to know a great deal about the company who

325

are in the habit of gathering there. I'm sure I don't need to say any more.'

He was a cautious man but she wondered if he was deliberately warning her against Lucien and the Chevalier, though she had had so little to do with them during the winter. Isabelle had eyes and ears. She heard the latest political gossip. She guessed that now that war had broken out again, the opposition with Dundas and William Pitt would seize every opportunity to discredit the present government and bring them back into power. Any secret information Robert could bring them would be a strong weapon in their hands.

All during this past winter with her attention centred on her husband Isabelle had not thought to enquire too much as to how Guy amused himself, but now the warning Venetia had given her last year came back into her mind. What was going on in Leila Vernon's discreet and expensive supper rooms under the guise of gaming tables for gentlemen? Without wishing it she had an uneasy feeling that she might soon be caught up in something dark and mysterious when Robert was not here to advise and protect her.

What had happened in Paris, the sudden realisation that it was Robert who meant all the world to her, still overwhelmed her, yet she was shy of confiding it to him in so many words. Instead she had tried to show it by the tenderness and care she lavished on him, so that occasionally even Marian had wondered if she had been mistaken in her sister-in-law. Now she took the first opporunity to tackle Guy about his gambling and he dismissed it lightly.

'For God's sake, Belle, what do you take me for? I do go there sometimes with some of the other fellows from the Foreign Office. What harm is there in that? Leila Vernon is a dashed good sort and she certainly serves some splendid suppers.'

'What do you do there?' she asked curiously.

'Eat, drink, talk, take a hand at whist or hazard or faro. The Chevalier usually holds the bank.'

'Is that all?'

'What did you expect? Orgies? It's very respectable, you know.'

326

'Is it? Leila Vernon has a certain reputation.'

'If you mean what I think you mean, then I can assure you, she acts with the greatest discretion.' He gave her a boyish grin. 'A fellow like me wouldn't stand a chance with her.'

Isabelle frowned. 'I should hope not.' He might be right but she had her doubts. Rumour said Leila Vernon could be free with her favours. 'Could you take me there?' she went on.

'Good God, no! It's not the place for someone like you. Robert would have my blood for it.'

'Well, do be careful.'

'Don't be a goose, Sis,' he said affectionately. 'I know what I'm doing.'

'I hope you do.'

Perhaps she ought to play along with Lucien for a little, try and find out why he was so persistent, what it was he and the Chevalier wanted with her and Robert. When a day or so later he called as he had promised, she was gracious, offered him refreshment and accepted his invitation to take a turn with him in his fine new phaeton. She earned a black look from Marian as she came down the stairs in her prettiest bonnet and new spring gown but she ignored it, feeling happily that she was doing something that could help Robert in that secret work of his and never realising how easily her behaviour could be misinterpreted.

A chance meeting with Venetia when they were both choosing gloves in the new shop recently opened by a certain Mr Swann reminded her of her promise to Perry which she had been in danger of forgetting.

'Mamma keeps telling me I really must choose my wedding gown,' said Venetia listlessly, deciding on pale lavender kid with tiny pearl buttons.

'But the wedding is months away, isn't it?'

'Early in October.'

'I brought back some charming fashion plates from Paris last year. Would you like to take tea with me and look through them? They are full of lovely new ideas and some of them were actually designed for Josephine. I saw her when we attended a ball at the Tuileries and she looked ravishing.'

It was arranged for the following Tuesday and when she went home, she sent Edward with a note to Perry's lodging. She had done her part. Now it was up to him.

Tuesday afternoon duly came and they were drinking tea and poring over the drawings when she heard the sharp knock at the front door and had a sudden spasm of panic. Suppose Venetia turned on her in anger, suppose she just walked out or created a scene? Then Hawke had come in.

'Captain Conway is asking if you will receive him, my lady,' he said and before she could remark on the strange coincidence, Perry was in the room, looking handsome and distinguished in his new uniform. Venetia had risen, the papers in her hand falling to the floor. The two were staring at one another, their eyes locked together, in another minute they could be in each other's arms. Isabelle muttered some excuse and slipped out of the room. There was nothing more she could do except leave them alone to fight it out between them. She went up to her own sitting room and stayed there till she heard the front door slam and saw Perry come out and walk quickly down the street with a spring in his step that had certainly not been there before. Then she went down to the drawing room. Venetia was standing at the window looking after him. She turned as Isabelle came in.

'Why did you do it? Why? Why?' she said accusingly.

'I did nothing. I never expected such a thing to happen.'

'I think you did. Oh Isabelle, I'm so wildly happy and so wretched all at once but thank you all the same, thank you a thousand times,' and she flung her arms around her cousin and hugged her.

'What happened?'

'I don't know yet, but all this time when I thought he hated me, he's been trying desperately to see me.' She pressed her hands against her hot cheeks. 'I must go. I mustn't stay any longer.'

'What are you going to do?'

'Don't ask me, but it's wonderful and frightening, and you'll still be our friend, won't you? If he writes to me and sends letters here, you will see that I get them, won't you, and the other way round.'

'I don't know,' she began doubtfully.

'But you can't turn your back on us now, you can't, please, Isabelle.'

'Very well,' she sighed, 'if I must.'

'I knew you would. I told Perry so, and now I really must go.'

She was such an entirely different person from the girl who had not even been able to summon up interest in the enchanting Parisian fashions, that Isabelle wondered if love had woven its magic spell and they were willing to defy parents, convention and the righteous anger of Sir Hugo Dexter if jilted at the last moment by his young bride. She hadn't bargained that she would be part of the conspiracy but if she must, then she must, and she had a spasm of anxiety as to what Robert might say about her rash decision to act as postman between the lovers.

May moved into June and Isabelle hid her consuming anxiety about Robert, put on a cheerful face and began to accept some of the invitations that up to now she had resolultely refused. Britain had been swept into war fever. Henry Dundas had gone down to Walmer and persuaded William Pitt to take up his seat once more in parliament. He made a speech that resounded throughout the country, inspiring his friends and infuriating his enemies. So many men from every walk of life volunteered that recruitment had to be closed. They drilled every day in the park before scattering to their offices or the theatre or to the clubs and the sound of bugles and drums rose above the roar of London traffic. There was talk of invasion but no one seemed to care any longer. Defiance filled the air. Let Boney do his worst, Britain was prepared for him.

In the midst of all these hectic preparations Isabelle continued to invite the company of Lucien and he found to his dismay that the simple country girl so easily dazzled by his charm had learned in her turn to be both fascinating and tantalising and a great deal more clever than he had ever expected, seeming about to yield to his urgency but always holding him off, so that there were times when he forgot his mission and its importance in sheer frustration.

'She is playing a game with you, my friend,' said the Chevalier to him one day in June. 'She has you running around her in circles and not a word are you getting out of her. She knows just what that husband of hers is playing at but is she confiding it to you, not a chance.'

'She will, she will, just give me time and I'll have her falling into my arms like a ripe plum.'

'You said that last year and look where we are, not one step forward. Have you forgotten so quickly? Our paymaster wants the girl and the boy, but above all that precious Robert Armitage, Lord Kilgour, in his own hands as soon as possible and quietly with no political overtones. They failed to get him in Paris last year and wherever he is lurking in France just now, they can't lay hands on him.'

'I know, I know,' said Lucien impatiently.

It was not easy to forget the bitter icy voice in that shadowy room giving him his orders, accepting no excuses. For a moment the sweat broke out on his face as it had done then only a couple of months ago. What a strange quirk of fate it was that the father he had sought so eagerly, so hopefully, had turned into a monster who befriended him only to use him.

The Chevalier was looking at him curiously and he said quickly, 'I think I've got the boy hooked. Guy will be easy game if my little plot works.'

'See that it does,' said his companion sourly.

But Lucien had underestimated the deep affection between brother and sister.

Isabelle's twenty-first birthday had come and gone with still no Robert. She felt too wretched to celebrate it. Parties, the opera, the theatre, all seemed dead without him at her side, and one evening in late June she was curled up on the sofa with Rory beside her and a book in her hand when Guy came into the drawing room and threw himself down in one of the chairs.

'You're home unusually early,' she said smiling at him and glad of his company.

'I know.' He looked across at her uncomfortably. 'Sorry about

your birthday, Belle. I meant to bring you something special as
Robert is still away but I'm afraid I'm cleaned out. Not a penny
to whistle with.'

'Oh Guy, I did warn you, didn't I?'

'I know, I know. Like a damned fool I staked the lot on a
number that has always been lucky for me and lost it.'

He looked so worried, so unlike his usual airy nonchalance,
that she sat up.

'Is it so serious?'

'Yes, I'm afraid it is.' He paused. 'You couldn't lend me a
couple of thousand, could you?'

'Two thousand pounds!' she was aghast. 'Oh Guy, why? Do
you owe it? Is it a debt of honour and he won't wait for it?'

'Not exactly.'

'What do you mean – not exactly?'

'Well, it's not a gambling debt. I suppose you might call it
blackmail.'

'Blackmail!'

He got up, walking away from her to the window, standing
with his back to her, staring out at the calm summer evening.
All that Dundas had hinted at came flooding back into her mind
and she was suddenly afraid.

'Guy, hadn't you better tell me about it?'

'I suppose I must. I'm not exactly proud of myself. I've been
a fool, Isabelle, but it was just a chance, just a damnable
accident. I never dreamed . . . Oh well, you'd better know the
worst. You see, I went along to Duncan House with some of the
fellows I work with and I had a portfolio with me, some
documents and letters to translate. They weren't important, I
swear they weren't, nothing highly secret, but we're forbidden
to take anything out of Whitehall . . .'

'Then why did you?'

'Oh you know how it is. I was in a hurry to leave with the
others and thought I could work on them later.' He stopped
and then went on with an effort. 'We had a jolly evening
actually and went on somewhere else . . .'

'Where?'

331

'Oh a house one of our group knew – with girls – you know . . .'

'Do you mean a brothel?'

'I suppose you could call it that. Anyway the fact is I forgot the portfolio and when I did remember and went back for it, it had gone.'

She turned cold as she thought what it could mean.

'Did you ask about it?'

'Of course and Leila said someone else had found it and promised to return it to me.'

'Who was it?'

'No one you know, a man called Scatchard. He used to work as a clerk in our deparment and was dismissed a few months ago. Leila employs him in some way. He's quite familiar there. The fact is, Belle,' he went on despondently, 'he will return it with the papers but he wants two thousand for it and if I refuse to pay up, he'll tell everyone concerned where he found it and why. You know what that will mean. They'll throw me out, labelled untrustworthy. It'll be the end for me and worst of all, I shall be letting Robert down so horribly.'

'This wretched man could take your money and still spread word about.'

'He could but I don't think he will and so long as I've got the papers back, I could brazen it out. It would be my word against his. Isabelle, you must help me, you must.'

'I haven't got that kind of money. Oh I can draw on Robert's bank for expenses and I have my allowance and he pays the bills without question but not to that amount. He would want to know why.'

'He's not back yet and I'll get it somehow. I will, Belle. I'll pay you back, I swear I will.'

'How? By gambling with borrowed money and losing far more than you're ever likely to have?'

But she had always helped him. Guy was her little brother whom she had loved and cared for ever since she could remember. She had some jewellery, perhaps she could pledge it or sell it. Her mind was in a whirl.

'When does he want the money?'

332

'Very soon, in a couple of days.'

'That's not very long. I'll try, Guy, I can't do more than that.'

'Oh Isabelle, you've saved my life.' He fell on his knees and put his arms around her waist. 'What should I do without you?'

'I'm sure I don't know,' she said tartly. 'Oh Guy, why are you such a great fool!' but she gave him a quick hug and then pushed him away.

'If I do get it for you, it will be on one condition.'

'What's that?'

'That you don't go to Leila Vernon's den of iniquity ever again.'

'Oh I say, isn't that pitching it a bit strong? Duncan House is nothing of the kind.'

'Promise,' she went on sternly, 'I mean it.'

'Oh very well, I promise.'

'And mind you keep it. I have a strong feeling that place is a den of spies.'

'Now where did you hear that?'

'Never you mind. You keep away from there in the future.'

Although Lucien's name had not been mentioned, Isabelle remembered the warning Dundas had given her and wondered if he could possibly have been involved in it in some way and then dismissed it from her mind. Surely even he would not stoop so low as to use blackmail.

That night in her bedroom she opened the casket in which she kept the jewellery Robert had given her. There were already a number of pretty trifles but the diamond and emerald necklace with its matching bracelet and earrings was among the most valuable. She had very little notion of their real worth or how to go about selling or pawning them. She didn't know whether such places existed or where they were to be found and there was no one she could ask without revealing the reason. But she did remember the jewellers – a very select establishment in Bond Street with the partners, Mr Carruthers and Mr Abernethy. She had smiled at the names when Robert had taken her there once. Would they buy the bracelet back? She could say she didn't altogether like the design and would choose another when her husband returned. It didn't sound very convincing but it might be worth a try. She hated to part with it, remembering how Robert had clasped it around her wrist on her last birthday before they went to the cricket match, but it was essential that Guy got the papers back before their loss was discovered and he was disgraced. Perhaps with any luck Robert need never know anything about it.

There was no time to be lost so the very next day she set out for Bond Street taking the carriage and telling Ian to wait as she would not be long. She was shaking with nerves when Mr Abernethy came to greet her, all smiles and bows for the wife of Viscount Kilgour and asking her how he could help her. Only the thought of her brother's distraught face spurred her on as she took out the bracelet asking in faltering tones if they would be prepared to buy it back, explaining how she had never really liked the design and when her husband returned from abroad she would choose another more to her taste. If Mr Abernethy was taken aback, he concealed it admirably.

'I am afraid it is not usually our custom, my lady,' he began cautiously. It did not do to offend these high-born ladies. 'However in this case perhaps . . . I really think it best if you would kindly step into the private office and speak to Mr Carruthers since it would of course ultimately be his decision.'

'If you wish,' she said and followed him into the sanctum where Mr Carruthers usually dealt with his more aristocratic customers. He was a tall thin man dressed in a style gone out of fashion these twenty years and with a neat wig covering his bald head. He ushered her to a chair and listened courteously, noted how nervous she was and glanced at the bracelet which he knew well.

'As Mr Abernethy will have already mentioned, Madam, it is not our usual custom to buy back articles of value but only to sell them. However to oblige such distinguished clients as yourself and your husband, I think we might perhaps make an exception in this instance.'

He wondered privately what the young woman had been up to in her husband's absence necessitating the urgent need of two thousand pounds in cash. She had been more than likely gambling at one of these discreet gaming houses as he knew a great many titled ladies did, and was now afraid of revealing her losses when her husband came back, or was she having to pay blackmail to some wretch who was threatening to reveal her liaison with some lover? His puritanical soul heartily disapproved of such goings-on but dealing with the aristocracy one grew accustomed to it, and the bracelet was worth far more than she was asking. She was obviously unaware that the necklace had come out of Paris, sold by its luckless owner during the Terror, and at her husband's request they had gone to considerable trouble and expense to trace the matching bracelet and earrings. However it would be doing a favour and obliging a customer who would no doubt prove useful in the future.

He said, 'I think we can assist you, my lady, as a special case of course. I will ask Mr Abernethy to deal with it and he will send the agreed sum to you by special messenger later today if that will suit.'

She was so relieved she felt almost faint. He accompanied her to the carriage, handed her in and smiled to himself as Ian drove away.

'That young woman has got herself into a pretty pickle,' remarked Mr Abernethy when he came back into the shop. 'The Lord only knows what tale she'll come up with when Lord Kilgour comes back from wherever he is.'

'Maybe and the less said about it the better,' said his partner austerely. 'Discretion when you are dealing with the aristocracy, Mr A., discretion and remember to keep your mouth shut. Put the bracelet away. We'll not sell it. It would be a pity to break up such a valuable set. We'll wait till my lady's husband returns. There may be some interesting developments.'

A day later and Guy came to see her, triumphant and deeply grateful.

'I've got it back all intact and no one even noticed the papers were missing. There's too much furore over some new scare that Boney has three thousand landing barges lined up at Calais all ready to come charging across the Channel.'

'Is that true?'

'About as true as that he is planning to bring his army by

335

balloon or that he is already starting work on a tunnel under the sea,' laughed Guy. 'There's a fresh crop of rumours every day. You're an angel, Belle. I'm in your debt forever. All's well that ends well, eh?'

'If it has ended well.'

She didn't feel so sure. Guy's promise of paying the money back was probably genuine enough but the crucial point was what she would say to Robert if and when he noticed. Lie to him? Say she had lost the bracelet? She tried to put the disturbing thought out of her mind.

'God damn that money-grubbing little rat, Scatchard!' raged Lucien to the Chevalier when he at last discovered what had happened. 'He was told to hold the threat of disgrace over that young idiot's head until he was ready to do anything – just anything – to save his own skin and what happens? What does that scheming wretch do? Seizes the chance of making a quick profit and then does a disappearing trick. By God, if I can lay hands on him I'll wring his damned neck!'

16

Robert landed on the south coast at the end of July after an uncomfortable journey in a small boat savagely battered by a summer storm and made his way to Rye, where Mr Lambe at the Salutation Inn was not at all surprised to see Lord Kilgour in the rough disguise of a Breton fisherman, bronzed face, grimy hair, dark stubble of beard with an unmistakeable reek of rotting fish about him, and soon had a bath ready and a change of clothes which Robert kept there for just such emergencies.

Bathed, shaved, looking once more like himself and with a comfortable meal inside him, reinforced by several glasses of Mr Lambe's excellent French claret, he set out for London.

It had in fact been a most tiring and harassing few months. Part of the time he had spent with his cousin, Jacques de Morney, in a strenuous effort to reorganise the dissident bands that had flourished ever since the early days of the Revolution and had become sadly scattered during the brief peace. They had been useful to Britain, not only by supplying information but also by providing a running sore in Bonaparte's back especially in those districts still actively republican and hostile to one man's despotic rule, but his efforts had not met with the success he had hoped for. He found several of the groups had degenerated into bands of terrorists and were in consequence being hunted down ruthlessly by Fouché's secret police involving several honest partisans in their downfall. Robbery, treachery and murder were rife on both sides, Jacques told him, destroying the pure flame of patriotism that had burned so brightly.

For the last few weeks he had toured the coast trying to assess the preparations for invasion and finding them far less successful than Britain had believed. He could not see any such force being ready to break through the blockade of the British fleet for this year at least, quite apart from venturing through the hazards of the Channel during the winter months.

He caught a glimpse of Bonaparte himself visiting the invasion ports and in a towering fury that his boat-building programme was so desperately behindhand. He had promptly given the order for another fourteen hundred barges to be set in hand but it was one thing to order and another for it to be carried out. That did not mean of course that England must not be prepared and it might be just as well to resurrect the scheme already suggested to build a canal along the vast stretch of the marshes. He would put that forward very forcibly when he returned.

This time it had been far more difficult to move safely around France even though his disguises were good and the papers he carried as authentic as a skilful forger could make them. Ever since the attack in Paris he had wondered if his identity was known and one of Fouché's henchmen was even now upon his track. Once or twice he had only escaped by a hair's breadth. He had made up his mind that when he married he would give up this dangerous work, in which he had at first only reluctantly become involved but which he was forced to admit satisfied something deep inside him, a desire to fulfil himself in some way, to pit himself against danger and win. He had only agreed under pressure to undertake this last mission. Now that it was over, he hoped his peculiar talents could be used in some other way to serve his country.

He arrived at Arlington Street shortly after nine o'clock, tired, hungry and very muddy, having ridden post from Rye through showers of summer rain.

Edward opened the door, welcoming him with a broad smile and Marian, who had seen him from an upper window, came running down the stairs accompanied by three wildly excited dogs and threw herself in his arms, hardly knowing whether to laugh or cry with relief at seeing him safe after weeks of anxiety.

'I can't believe you are here at last, Robert. We've been nearly out of our minds believing you shut up in prison and wondering how they were treating you in those vile places.

What happened? How did you escape? Wasn't it fearfully dangerous?'

'Dangerous enough,' he said lightly, 'but here I am and that's what matters.' He kissed her cheek and bent to caress the little dogs still frisking round his feet. 'Where is Isabelle?'

'She has gone out.' Marian's tone was sharply disapproving. 'Some musical soirée.'

'Indeed and where is it being held?'

'At Duncan House if you please.'

He frowned. 'Isn't that Leila Vernon's place? I was not aware she indulged in musical evenings.'

'I told Isabelle plainly that it was most unsuitable. It's raffish company not fit for people like us but she would have her way. "The music is from the Italian opera and Madame Antonetti is singing," she said, "and that's a rare treat I don't want to miss." Such affectation! That Frenchman, Lucien de Vosges, called for her in his carriage.'

'I see. Perhaps I'll go along later and pick her up.'

'But you must be exhausted,' protested Marian, 'and what about food? Knowing you, I don't suppose you've eaten all day.'

'Oh a bite of something cold and a glass of wine is all I need. See to it, will you, Marian, while I change out of these wet clothes.'

An hour or so later when Robert was freshly shaved and wearing an elegant black evening coat and crisply starched neckcloth, there was little left of the bourgeois French wine merchant or the sunburned fisherman who had slouched along the beaches of France and drunk sour wine in the shoreside taverns, except for a slight darkening still showing at the roots of his hair. He sat down to a hasty meal.

'Has Isabelle ordered the carriage to fetch her?'

'No. She said Monsieur de Vosges would bring her home.'

'Very well. Tell Ian to put up the horses and have them ready for me in half an hour.'

'Do be careful,' breathed Marian, suddenly fearful for him.

'Careful of what? I'm not going into battle, my dear, simply collecting my wife from a fashionable party,' he said jestingly.

All the same, though he took care not to let Marian see it, he was not pleased. He knew all about what went on at Duncan House in more ways than one and did not regard it as a suitable place for his wife to visit. She should have known that by now. She might have gone in all innocence of course but why with that damned Frenchman? If Guy had anything to do with it, then he would have something to say to that young man. Irresponsible he might be, but he should take care where his sister was concerned.

The concert was nearing its end by the time he got there. The footman took his hat and cloak and he stood at the back of the drawing room while Madame Antonetti poured out her soul in a final aria. He ran his eye over the company, many of whom he knew. Isabelle was sitting near the front, Lucien just behind her leaning familiarly over the back of her chair and whispering something that made her turn to him and smile. Robert had a sudden and violent desire to wipe the dazzling charm off the handsome, impudent face.

The music was over now. People were chatting to one another and rising from their chairs. He was being recognised by one or two acquaintances who shook him by the hand, congratulating him on a lucky escape from the enemy's clutches. Leila Vernon sailed up, all welcoming smiles.

'Robert, by all that's wonderful! And we have been imagining you languishing in some vile dungeon.'

He made some polite reply, his eyes still searching for Isabelle. He saw the startled look on her face, then she came running to him, pushing aside gilded chairs, forgetting all rules of decorum, to throw her arms around his neck and hug him like a schoolgirl.

'Oh Robert, Robert dearest!' She was murmuring ecstatically. 'If you only knew how anxious I've been all these weeks.'

'Have you, my love? I doubt that in your busy round of pleasure. Well, it's all over now.' He disentangled himself gently. 'Bid your friends goodbye. I've come to take you home.'

'Do forgive me,' she said, smiling around her in a dazzle of tears. 'It's all been so unexpected, I've forgot all my manners.'

'Such unusual devotion in a wife,' murmured Leila Vernon. 'You're a lucky man, Robert.'

'I know I am,' he replied coolly, gave a slight bow to her and to the company and took Isabelle's arm. 'Come, my dear.'

She bombarded him with questions as they drove home but he said little until they were in the privacy of their own room and Gwennie had been dismissed to bed. He came in from his dressing room and stood watching her for a moment. She looked so young, so touchingly innocent, but was she? He was tired and unhappy at seeing her in such company, otherwise he would not have spoken as he did.

'What in God's name made you spend an evening at Duncan House?' he said brusquely.

And because she had only gone there for his sake to try and find out what really went on there, she flared up at the injustice.

'Why shouldn't I? I was curious and Guy always describes Leila Vernon as a dashed good sort.'

'Does he indeed? You should know by now that it's not at all a fit place for my wife.'

'Oh Robert, don't be so sanctimonious. You sound just like Marian. Lucien told me you were very fond of visiting Duncan House yourself at one time.'

'And what else does Lucien de Vosges confide to you in your little tête-à-têtes?' he said icily. 'What other confidences do you share?'

'Nothing. We don't have tête-à-têtes, as you call them. He just happened to mention it one day.' She had spoken jestingly without much thought and his reaction made her angry. She turned to face him. 'He is not the only one who has spoken of it. Were you her lover, Robert, were you?'

'What has that to do with it?'

They were glaring at one another. It had never happened before and suddenly she could not bear it. She looked away.

'If you really want to know, Henry Dundas warned me against Lucien and the Chevalier and I thought if I appeared friendly I might learn something about them and about what goes on there that might help you in your work.'

'Dundas!' he repeated. 'You've been running to Dundas and asking questions about me.'

'Only because I was so desperately anxious. I felt sure that

341

all those weeks you were working for him and weren't in prison at all. I kept on thinking of what happened to you in Paris and I wanted to know the truth. I have a right to know. I am your wife.'

He seized her by the shoulders, turning her to face him. She had never known him so angry.

'What did Dundas tell you about me, and did you go babbling all this to that damned Frenchman? Did you, Isabelle, did you?'

'No, of course I didn't. Why are you treating me like this? What have I done?'

'For God's sake, how could you have acted so stupidly? Don't you realise how much harm you could do to me and to others?'

'I've said nothing about it to him, nothing at all. I swear I haven't.'

'Simply let him make love to you, I suppose, when I was out of the way.'

'No, Robert, no. How can you think that of me, how can you? Don't you trust me any longer?'

His grip on her shoulders tightened. He was staring down at the large hazel eyes that met his fearlessly. Then he released her suddenly, disgusted with himself.

'My God, what am I doing? Months apart and quarrelling over a triviality.'

'I don't want to quarrel,' she said tremulously.

'Listen to me, Isabelle, I was once fond of Leila Vernon but it was a long long time ago and it meant nothing, nothing at all compared with what I feel for you. Surely you must know that.'

'Yes, I do know, but you still won't trust me, Robert. You tell me nothing, not even after what happened in Paris. It's as if you lead two lives and I'm only in one of them.'

'I don't tell you, or Marian for that matter, because it could be dangerous for you,' he said wearily. 'It is better that you know nothing.'

'A word here and a word there and it can all be pieced together into valuable information.'

'Is that what Dundas told you?' He smiled faintly. 'It is true. You can never be too careful.'

342

'I'm sorry, I didn't realise . . . I shall never go to Duncan House again.'

She turned back to the dressing table, her hands trembling so much she could scarcely unfasten the diamond and emerald necklace. He watched her as she put it with the earrings into the casket.

'Didn't I give you a bracelet to match those?' he said idly. 'Why aren't you wearing it?'

She was so taken by surprise that everything flew out of her head and she came out with a stupid lie that she regretted almost immediately.

'The clasp was weak. I thought I might lose it so I took it back to the jewellers.'

He frowned. 'I must have a word about that with Mr Carruthers.'

'No, Robert, no, don't. It doesn't matter. I'll get it back soon. I'm not at all worried about it.'

'Very well.'

She ran her comb through her loosened hair and the gesture tautened her breasts under the low cut satin petticoat. The pent-up anger inside him exploded into an overwhelming desire and with a sudden movement he caught her up into his arms, crushing her against him, seeking her mouth with a violence not usual with him. She stiffened against him but he lifted her to her feet, slipping the satin undergarment from her shoulders and carrying her to the bed. She wanted to punish him but instead found him irresistible, forgetting their quarrel in a surge of passion that carried them away together.

Afterwards when she lay close in the shelter of his arm, he lay for a long time wakeful. Ever since last winter it had seemed to him that they had drawn closer together, that she was no longer the frightened, unhappy girl he had befriended but a woman who loved him for himself and not simply for what he could give her. He had felt so sure of it that now he regretted the anger and the spasm of jealousy that had shaken him. Soon when he had delivered his reports and they had been discussed, he would be free for a little and he had a gift for her which he had been

343

planning all this past year. She stirred beside him and he turned to kiss her.

'You're not still angry with me, are you?' she murmured drowsily.

'I ought to be, foolish child, but I'm not.'

'I'm not a child and you'll tell me everything in future? You won't leave me wondering about you?'

'I shall tell you precisely what you ought to know and no more.'

She half sat up. 'That's not fair.'

'Go to sleep. I've a long hard day tomorrow but after that I have a surprise for you.'

'What is it? Shall I like it?'

'I hope you will.'

His hands ran down the slender body and she trembled. Her mouth found his, desire flared again between them, rich and slow and fulfilling.

For the next few days Isabelle scarcely saw him. He was at the Foreign Office immersed in discussions resulting from all he had seen and heard.

It was an amazingly beautiful summer. Every day it seemed the sun shone and families basked in the heat. It was difficult to believe in the threat of invasion and war even though tarred beacons had been set up at strategic points as in the days of the Armada to give warning of the enemy's approach. French prisoners interviewed at Dover boasted that Bonaparte would be feasting at Whitehall by Christmas while the British Fleet kept strict vigil up and down the Channel and Nelson sailed for the Mediterranean, bottling up Villeneuve and the French navy at Toulon.

Henry Dundas came to dine with them one evening that week and was afterwards closeted with Robert in his study. What they discussed that night was meant only for his ears and those of William Pitt.

'There is a plot to assassinate Bonaparte,' said Robert. 'I have it on certain authority that now he has been confirmed First Consul for life he intends to crown himself Emperor sometime next year. That has roused Republican enmity to the highest pitch but as yet I could only find out very little.'

'Will it succeed?'

'I doubt it. There are far too many fools involved, too many who do not know how to keep their mouths shut. All I know for certain is that if it is likely to involve many of the royalists and our own groups, and if Fouché gets wind of it, then he will clamp down with a flurry of imprisonments and executions and worst result of all, it will unite all these dissident elements against us. They may hate and fear Bonaparte's strict rule but he has done much to restore order after the chaos and horrors of the Revolution and for that they are grateful. If he is murdered anarchy will come again.'

'And the last devil is as bad or worse than the first, eh? Would you be willing to return later? Find out more from those relatives of yours?'

'No, not this time,' said Robert firmly. 'For one thing I believe my disguise has been blown. There were too many occasions this time when only the thinnest chance saved me from discovery. Then again as I told you before, I am a married man, my lord, I have the hope of children, it would not be fair on my wife. I would be glad to serve my country in other ways you may ask of me.'

'And do you think that will satisfy you, my friend?' said Dundas drily.

'Why shouldn't it?'

'I know you as I know your father and once knew your grandfather. There is an element in you, Robert, for all your quietness, that is not satisfied with what pleases most men. You are not made to live content with the quiet domestic happiness sought by others.'

'You're wrong, sir. This time I have made up my mind. I have found that I have sought and I am happy with it.'

'Well, we shall see. But now I'm afraid I must go. I mustn't wear out the hospitality of your wife and your sister.'

'There is one further point, my lord, before you go. I have reason to believe that this foolish plot is being furthered and encouraged from Downing Street.'

345

'Oh my God!' exploded Dundas. 'I have always thought the PM little better than an idiot but just think how they could exploit it if it became known! And the King still refuses to recall Pitt back into power. We can only pray that he suffers another fit of madness before it is too late!'

The statesman was jovial with them before he left, taking Isabelle's hand and smiling down at her.

'You see, my dear, I kept my promise. He has come back to you quite unharmed.'

'Until the next time,' said Isabelle drily. 'I don't altogether believe in your promises, my lord, I know Robert too well.'

'Maybe there will not be a next time,' he replied cheerfully. 'We might even win the war.'

It was during that week when Robert was so occupied that a fat packet arrived addressed to Isabelle and she guessed at once it was from Perry with an enclosure for Venetia. She had already acted as postman more than once. She sent it on by Edward with an accompanying note and he came back with a letter which she duly sent on to Perry's lodging, not without a qualm of anxiety as to what the lovers might be planning between them.

At last Robert was through with commitments at Whitehall and free to carry out what he had been planning for some time.

'Dress yourself suitably,' he said one morning, 'we are going to spend a day in the country.'

'Are we? Where are we going?' she asked curiously. 'Is it far?'

'No, not far. It's on the river. We'll take the phaeton and I'll drive myself.'

'May I bring Rory?'

'If you wish but make sure he doesn't fall in the water. I refuse to dive in and fish him out.'

'I wouldn't dream of asking you,' she said loftily. 'I will dive in myself.'

'In which case I shall be obliged to rescue both of you. No, thank you.'

346

They looked at one another and laughed with vivid memories of that terrifying morning at Glenmuir.

'Don't keep me waiting too long, my love. It's not a grand party. It's just you and I.'

She was very quickly dressed, choosing a simple gown of flowered cotton, a wide-brimmed hat tied under her chin, and a Paisley shawl in soft rich colours which were all the rage that summer.

Robert was waiting for her. He handed her up into the high seat, dumped Rory on her lap and climbed up beside her. Ian released the horses and they were away at a good rattling pace.

By noon they were clattering through Maidenhead in fine style and then took the road to the small riverside town of Henley with its ancient church and almshouses where the old men and women came out to stare. Robert pulled up at the coaching inn to rest the horses and bring her lemonade and a draught of home-brewed ale for himself. Then they were off again driving carefully through the narrow winding street and out on to the Oxford road. After about a mile Robert turned off into a grassy lane and then through a pair of wrought iron gates. They trotted up a long sandy drive with woodland on each side until they could see the white house, one wall hung with a late flowering rose.

'Are we visiting someone?' she asked mystified.

'No.'

An elderly man had appeared, touched his forehead respectfully and came to the heads of the horses.

'Very happy to see you, my lord,' he said in a strong Scots accent.

'Everything in good order, Angus?'

'Aye, my lord, well enough, though there's a deal yet to be done in the garden for one pair of hands.'

'We shall be remedying that now.'

Robert lifted Isabelle down, the horses were led away and they mounted the wide shallow steps. The door was open and the housekeeper in her neat black dress was curtseying.

'Welcome, my lord,' she said, 'everything is ready for you as you ordered.'

347

'Thank you, Morag. I knew I could rely on you. Isabelle, this is Mistress Morag Kinsey who long ago was my nurse at Glenmuir and has been looking after everything here for me.'

'You've chosen a bonny bride, Master Robert,' said the old woman peering at Isabelle. 'Welcome to Sabrina House, my lady.'

'Have you some food prepared?' asked Robert. 'We are peckish after our long drive.'

'In the dining room, sir. Perhaps your lady would like to refresh herself.'

'Oh, not yet,' said Isabelle. 'I want to see everything first. What is this house, Robert? Why did you never tell me about it?'

Rory had already raced across the wide hall. He disappeared at the further end and she went after him.

'We'll eat a little later,' said Robert hurriedly and caught her up as she went into the drawing room that stretched along the back of the house and opened out on to a long stretch of lawn with a distant silver gleam of the river.

The house had been built possibly a hundred years before. It was cool and spacious with grace and distinction, and not yet fully furnished. Isabelle had stepped through the long windows and stood looking back at it.

'It's so beautiful. Is it yours, Robert?'

'No.' He smiled down at her. 'It's yours.'

'Mine?' she stared at him in astonishment. 'Mine, but it can't be.'

'Why can't it?'

'I don't know. It doesn't seem possible.'

'It's yours as snug and tight as lawyers can make it. I am afraid it's only partly furnished. I thought I would leave it to you to choose the final details.'

'I still can't believe it,' she said wonderingly. 'Did you buy it especially for me?'

'Not exactly.' He put an arm around her shoulders. 'I'm starving. Let's go and eat and I'll tell you all about it.'

Morag had provided a simple luncheon of cold chicken, beef and ham, with a little fresh salad, newly baked bread and country butter with creamy cheese and some late fresh peaches. Robert filled her wine glass and told her the story as they ate.

'It belonged to a great aunt, an old tartar she was, I remember how we hated her occasional visits to Glenmuir. She would box your ear for the slightest thing. She lived to a very great age, growing more and more cantankerous and then when she died a few years ago, to my great surprise she left me this house and all she had. At first I thought I would sell it. I asked Marian if she would like to live here and she hated it from the first. She has a prejudice against living anywhere near water and it is true that the Thames floods occasionally but never as far as I know has it reached the house. It had been very neglected so I had it put in order, installed Morag and Angus who had been pensioned off by my father and were living in a tiny cottage in Arisaig and then was too busy to do much about it until I married you.'

'You never told me about it,' she said reproachfully.

'Because I was still undecided but last winter I realised something. Marian is not the easiest of people to live with.'

'I've never complained,' she said swiftly.

'No, but it occurred to me that Glenmuir is a long way away and can only be visited occasionally, while Sabrina House could be a very pleasant refuge from life in the city for both of us.'

And for our children. She guessed that was in his mind though he didn't say it.

'What do you think?' he asked, peeling a peach and putting it on her plate. 'Would you like to spend time here?'

'I think it's the loveliest house I have ever seen and I want to go all over it, every tiny bit from kitchen to attic.'

'Go with Morag. She will love to show it all to you while I finish the wine and sleep it off in the garden.'

'I warn you. I shall start to make lists.'

'Very well. Later on we'll go over them together.'

She paused for a moment looking at him with a worried frown.

'Robert, are you sure Marian doesn't want to live here? She won't be . . . jealous because you are giving it to me?'

'Of course not,' he said easily. 'She had the chance and refused. She's never mentioned it since.'

She was not quite so sure but was too happy to let it worry her. So while Robert lazed in the garden keeping a weather eye upon Rory, who was scurrying about in the reeds on the river bank making a great to-do about hunting a rat, Isabelle explored every nook and cranny, finding the house larger than she had expected with ample room for the occasional guest and perhaps one day for a nursery. The rooms were mostly unfurnished except for the master bedroom where the handsome four-poster with its embroidered linen curtains had already been made up.

'We always kept it ready,' explained Morag. 'Sometimes when Master Robert came down to see how the work was progressing, he slept the night here.'

The old woman, with a lifetime of experience in service, and the young girl had taken to one another instantly. Isabelle had been well schooled by Mrs Bedford. She asked all the right questions.

'She's not like one of those fine young ladies with naught in their heads but pretty clothes and dancing and such like,' said Morag approvingly to Angus later. 'Trust Master Robert to choose the right lass even if he has taken so long about it.'

Robert was lying on a rug close beside the riverbank when Isabelle dropped down beside him.

'Well,' he said lazily. 'Does it please you?'

'Oh yes, immensely. I'm bursting with ideas.'

'Let them simmer for a while.'

She trailed her hand in the cool water gently lapping at the bank under an arching overhang of green willow.

'It makes me think of those lines from *Comus* – do you remember them? Mr Holland made me learn them by heart . . .

Sabrina fair
Listen where thou art sitting
Under the glassy, cool translucent water
In twisted braids of lilies knitting
The loose trails of thy amber-dropping hair . . .'

350

'Sabrina, my love, was the river Severn not the Thames.'

'Oh don't be so pedantic. They're both rivers, aren't they? Is that why it was called Sabrina House?'

'Great Aunt Hester had some quaint notions but I doubt if reading Milton was one of them. She didn't approve of poetry. She didn't approve of anything come to that.'

'Except you.'

He laughed. 'Maybe she disliked me one degree less than anyone else.'

Presently as shadows began to lengthen and a fresh breeze blew along the river, he stirred and sat up.

'We had better think of starting for home or it will be dark before we reach London.'

'Robert, couldn't we stay here?'

'My dear, it would be very uncomfortable and poor Morag would be at her wits' end to provide for us.'

'No, she wouldn't. She will love it. She always keeps the bed made up for you and there's plenty of food for supper. We could have a picnic.'

She was kneeling beside him and put her arms around his neck. He had taken off his coat and his shirt was damp and warm from the heat of the afternoon.

'Please, Robert. It's my house. You have just given it to me and you shall be my first guest . . .'

'Your husband and your lover.' His arm had gone around her and he kissed lightly the mouth raised to his.

She giggled. 'It makes me feel deliciously wicked.'

'We will be deliciously wicked together.' He got up pulling her to her feet. 'At least we shall be spared being held up by highwaymen on Hounslow Heath.'

'That could be rather exciting.'

'For whom? My darling, they're not all handsome rogues ready to dance a coranto with a fair lady on the wayside verge.'

She laughed and they went into the house arm in arm.

Far from being put out Morag excelled herself in providing for them. She prodded Angus out of his easy chair by the kitchen fire.

'You go on up to the farm,' she said, 'they were shooting

351

along there in the woods this past week. There'll be a partridge or two and a cock pheasant hanging in the larder like as not, and don't you forget to bring back a pint of cream.'

So they ate luxuriously and afterwards sat by a fire of scented apple wood and pine cones and presently went upstairs to share the great old-fashioned bed.

Isabelle woke early, surprised by the quiet after the incessant noise of the London streets. There was only the sound of birds, the occasional tinkle of pails as the outdoor boy brought in the water and someone was singing softly, reminding her of Gwennie and those far off mornings at High Willows. How different everything was now. For some inexplicable reason she felt a quiet content deep within her, a certainty that their night of love would have given her the child she longed for, and she hugged the thought to herself.

Robert was still sleeping, his hair ruffled, looking somehow boyish and vulnerable. She leaned over and kissed him very gently.

'I love you,' she murmured and knew it was true. Not just the ecstasy of passion but also a profound and deep affection. Lost in the sheer wonder of it, she forgot that when you reach the heights, there is only one way to go and the fates that rule our lives sometimes take a malicious pleasure in preparing a pitfall for the unwary.

17

Trouble began almost immediately with Marian, who had not wanted the riverside villa but deeply resented Robert spending a fortune on having it splendidly restored and then handing it over lock, stock and barrel to his young wife.

'You might have at least consulted me first,' she said acidly.

'I didn't think you were interested. When I drove you down there to look it over, you told me very firmly that nothing on earth would induce you to live in such a place.'

'That was years ago, soon after Great Aunt Hester died. It was in a shocking state. It would be different now.'

'It's still close to the river and still liable to floods,' said Robert drily. 'Isabelle doesn't mind that. She's prepared for death by drowning, aren't you, my love?'

'Now you're being ridiculous,' said Marian stiffly.

'Perhaps you'd like to help Isabelle with the furnishings and so on,' said Robert somewhat tactlessly, 'I'm sure she would welcome your able assistance.'

'I very much doubt it,' Marian was still aggrieved. 'Our tastes in such things are far too different.'

It was all so trivial but it made Isabelle feel uncomfortable and took the edge off her pleasure.

There was worse to come. In the relief of Robert's home-coming and the renewed happiness between them, she had completely forgotton about the bracelet and Guy's involvement with it until one day about a week later when it blew up in her face.

Robert, finding himself in Bond Street that morning, strolled into the jewellers with the intention of buying some pretty trifle for Marian to patch up the stupid little argument between them. He chose a diamond ornament in the shape of a butterfly which could be worn in the hair or on a dress and suddenly remembered what Isabelle had told him.

'By the way I believe my wife left her bracelet with you because the clasp was unreliable. If it is now repaired, I might as well collect it for her.'

The two elderly partners exchanged startled glances.

'There was nothing wrong with the bracelet, my lord,' said Mr Carruthers cautiously, 'in actual fact Lady Isabelle told us she did not care for the design and asked if we would take it back.'

'Take it back?' repeated Robert in surprise. 'I'm afraid I don't understand.'

'It would appear that while you were out of the country, your wife was in need of a large sum of money in cash. It is, as you know, not our custom to buy back articles of jewellery nor do we act as pawnbrokers,' went on Mr Carruthers with dignity and not relishing the stony look on his client's face. 'However you and your family have always been valued customers and so we agreed to oblige your wife as a special case.'

'How much was she asking?'

'Two thousand pounds.'

'Good God, that's far less . . .'

'Far less than it is worth, my lord. I know that. It is part of a set of great rarity and that is why we have kept the bracelet. We felt sure that it would be redeemed in due course.'

Robert frowned. 'I see. In that case you had better return the bracelet to me now and I will arrange for my bankers to forward the amount of two thousand pounds.'

'Certainly,' said Mr Carruthers in some relief. 'Would you fetch it for his lordship, Mr Abernethy?'

'At once.'

His partner scurried away returning almost immediately with the jewel in its case and handing it to Robert.

'Thank you. I will make sure that you don't lose by it.'

'Very grateful, my lord, always happy to oblige a customer and I assure you that you can have complete confidence in our discretion.'

Mr Carruthers bowed him out and he strode down Bond

Street extremely annoyed at the implication that he might have left his wife unprovided for and even more disturbed because she had told him nothing about it, leaving him to make the discovery in this unpleasant and humiliating fashion. What in God's name could she have wanted two thousand pounds for in such a tearing hurry?

Later that day he came into their bedroom when she was dressing for dinner and put the opened case on her dressing table. He saw the startled look on her face.

'Where did you get it?' she asked in a stifled voice.

'Mr Carruthers handed it over to me at the cost of two thousand pounds. What did you want the money for, Isabelle?'

'I . . . I . . .' She looked up at him pitifully. 'Oh Robert, are you very angry?'

'Not yet. I'm still in the dark. Oh come now, Isabelle, what is all this ? Why didn't you tell me? Why invent some silly lie? You knew I would find out sooner or later. What have you been doing? Gambling at Duncan House and ashamed of your losses, is that it?'

'No, no,' she said indignantly. 'No, I haven't been gambling. I would never do such a thing. I think it stupid.'

'Very well, then what was it? It must have been something urgent if you wanted the money in such a hurry.' Then the idea flashed across his mind and he seized upon it with relief. 'It was Guy, wasn't it? What has the young fool been up to? Plunging too deep, I suppose. I thought he had learned more sense.'

'No, it wasn't a gambling debt,' she blurted out and then wished she hadn't. It would have been safer to let Robert believe that.

'Then what was it?' he said a little impatiently. 'Has he got himself involved with some . . .' He was about to say whore and changed it to 'some bit of muslin and had to pay through the nose to get rid of her?'

Perhaps that was safer than the truth. 'Something like that.'

'It's about time he grew up and learned responsibility. Now don't upset yourself over it.' He put out a hand and turned her face to him. 'The only quarrel I have with you is that you still

355

don't completely trust me, do you? Why not tell me when I came home? Am I such an ogre?'

'On no, no, no! It's just that . . .'

'Guy is still your baby brother, is that it?' She nodded miserably. 'I thought so. If we weren't at war, I'd pack him off abroad with a fixed allowance and tell him he must manage on it, sink or swim. As it is there is not much I can do. I thought he liked what he does at the Foriegn Office.'

'Oh he does. That's why . . .'

'That's why what?'

'Oh, nothing, only I think he'd welcome more responsibility.'

'When he has shown he can deal with more serious matters, then he will be asked to undertake them,' said Robert. 'If he is at home this evening I'll have a word with him and you'd better take care of that bracelet. Mr Carruthers went to great trouble to match it up for me even if you don't care for the design.'

'Oh, but I do, I love it, I only said that because . . .'

'You couldn't think of another reason for selling it. I'm afraid you'll never make a jewel thief, my dear.'

'Oh Robert, don't laugh at me.'

'If I do, it's a very costly laugh,' he said ruefully.

'I'm sorry . . .'

'It's Guy who should be sorry and he will be when I've dealt with him.'

'Don't be too angry with him,' she said quickly.

'Well, he's not a schoolboy. I can hardly administer a beating. Stop fretting about him and leave it to me.'

They dined *en famille* that night and were joined by David who had dropped in and was asked to stay. When the men rejoined Isabelle and Marian in the drawing room and after the tea tray had been brought in, Robert got up, nodded to Guy and went out of the room. The boy gave his sister a hunted look and followed after him.

Believing Isabelle had revealed the whole sorry story to her husband, he burst impetuously into a spirited defence to which Robert listened in silence.

'I'm glad to know you're not a liar as well as a damned fool,' he said when Guy had faltered to an end. 'In actual fact Isabelle

356

told me nothing of this. She was only too ready to find excuses for you.' He then proceeded to tell him exactly what he thought of him in a scathing set-down that was all the worse because the boy knew it was deserved.

'In future when you get into a scrape I should be grateful if you would come to me and not plague your sister.'

'You were not here and I do intend to pay her back,' exclaimed Guy, goaded into protest.

'Do you? What with? Are you proposing to rob a bank or turn highwayman?' remarked Robert drily. He sat back in his chair and studied the young man thoughtfully for a moment before he went on. 'I suppose you realise that those papers you carried would have been closely examined by people not friendly to this country.'

Guy looked startled. 'But who? Do you mean de Vosges and the Chevalier?'

'Maybe. We can't be sure. Something has been going on for some time but we can't lay our finger on it.'

'Couldn't I do something?' said Guy eagerly.

'I wonder. Since you are already known at Duncan House, go there occasionally, act the simpleton if you can and in that way watch and listen. If anything strikes you, report it to me. Only for God's sake, be careful.'

Guy emerged feeling rather as if he had been flayed mentally, but with a strong determination to prove himself. By God, he'd let his brother-in-law realise he was not dealing with a callow boy any longer. He had learned his lesson painfully and intended to profit from it, a resolution that later would have an effect neither of them could have foreseen.

The fine weather still continued. Those living near the south coast would look anxiously across the Channel in the early morning but Bonaparte's army still didn't appear and September came in with golden sunshine. Isabelle busied herself happily with looking at suitable furniture, pondering colour schemes, choosing silks and velvets and even succeeded in persuading Marian into taking a reluctant interest. Robert was immersed in the revised plans for building a canal barrier across the Romney Marshes. The work would be entrusted to Colonel John Brown, a Scottish engineer of great experience, and early in the month Robert went down to Kent with him to look the ground over and this time make detailed plans. When he came back Isabelle asked him if he had called at High Willows.

'Certainly I did. Your uncle as a considerable landowner is deeply concerned. Actually there was something of a crisis brewing. It seems that Venetia has rebelled and is refusing absolutely to marry Sir Hugo.'

'But I understand the wedding is only a month away.'

'Exactly and I fear your aunt is in a rare taking over it.'

'What will happen? Did you see Venetia?'

'No. She has shut herself up and refuses to see anyone. It was extremely awkward. I backed out of it as soon as I decently could. Has she ever confided in you?'

'I know she and Perry are in love and that he is still in England,' she said carefully, unhappy at the thought of the frequent letters that had gone back and forth in these last weeks. 'There has been some kind of a hold-up in the refitting of the *Sirius* but I believe he is due to sail very soon now.'

'You seem to know a great deal about it.'

'Perry has always kept in touch.'

'I don't know that I altogether blame the girl. There's a wide gap between a handsome young Naval Captain and an elderly widower with two daughters a month or so older than herself, no matter how rich,' remarked Robert. 'Thank Heaven I'm not involved.'

But he was and far more deeply involved than he would have wished, as he found out almost a fortnight later when an outraged Lady Brydges arrived on the doorstep of Arlington Street and, brushing rudely past a highly indignant butler, demanded to see Isabelle immediately.

'I will find out if her ladyship will receive you, Madam,' said Hawke frigidly and showed her into the morning room.

A few minutes later he returned and led the way upstairs to the small sitting room where she did not wait to be announced but pushed past him and confronted a startled Isabelle.

'She's gone!' she announced dramatically,' 'She has gone

358

away, eloped with that penniless good-for-nothing Perry Conway and it is all your fault.'

'I . . . but what have I done?' began Isabelle with a horrible feeling of guilt.

But Aunt Augusta swept on. 'Don't dare to deny it. I know it was you who arranged for them to meet here, it was you who helped them to correspond. Oh, Venetia denied it over and over but at last I got it out of her. I believed then that she realised her wickedness, her folly, the disgrace, the outrage, what it would mean to Sir Joshua if she insulted her future husband in this shameless way. I left her weeping, begging forgiveness, promising to obey, but she was lying. She defied me. When I went to her room this morning, she was gone and there was only this.'

She held out a letter. 'Read that, read it and realise what you have done, you wicked, wicked girl.'

Temporarily she ran out of breath while Isabelle tremblingly took the letter which had obviously been hastily scrawled and was blotted with tears.

Robert on his way down the stairs had heard the raised voices and turned back. He came into his wife's sitting room to see Isabelle white-faced and shaking and Lady Brydges, standing like an avenging angel, her bosom heaving, breathing fire and slaughter as he told David later, and he took in the situation at a glance.

'Good morning,' he said courteously. 'I thought I heard your voice. What can we do for you?'

'Read that,' said Aunt Augusta again, 'read that and find out what a sly, conniving, lying creature you have taken as your wife.'

'Allow me, my dear.'

Robert took the note from Isabelle's hand and glanced through it.

'I see nothing so very disturbing in this,' he said calmly. 'It would seem that Venetia and Captain Conway were married by special licence at St Bride's church in the city a week ago and she has now gone to join her husband in Chatham.'

'Married, married!' repeated Lady Brydges in a kind of

359

shriek. 'Don't you realise that the wedding with Sir Hugo would have been in less than a fortnight's time! Invitations have been sent out, presents have been received, all the preparations have been made. My God, when I think of the shame, the scandal! What will be said of her, what will be said of us?'

'I admit it is very unfortunate and my sympathy must go to the bridegroom abandoned almost at the altar steps,' went on Robert, 'but think how much worse it would be if they had simply run away together. Perry Conway is a very able young man and will doubtless rise high in the service. There will be ample opportunities in the next few months and no doubt Lady Ravenswood will be only too happy to provide a home for her favourite nephew's wife.'

'I suppose I have you to thank for this as well as your wife,' said Lady Brydges scaldingly, 'encouraging Venetia to rebel against what her father and I had planned for her future.'

'No,' said Isabelle quickly,' 'no, you're wrong. Robert knew nothing of this and neither did I. I did not know of their marriage. All I did was to let their letters come through me as you had refused to allow them to meet or correspond. I didn't know what they were planning, I swear I didn't, but now it has happened, I'm glad of it,' she went on sturdily. 'I always knew that Venetia was very unhappy and that all along she had not wished to marry Sir Hugo.'

'She was perfectly happy about it till you encouraged her,' said her aunt bitterly. 'All this ridiculous nonsense about love. How long will love last in dingy navy lodgings in Portsmouth or Chatham? Married to Sir Hugo she would have moved in the very cream of society.'

'Perhaps that was not what Venetia wanted,' said Isabelle.

'Oh yes, it was, till you persuaded her. Is this the way you repay me, repay your uncle, who took you and your brother into his home, brought you up, fed you, cared for you when you could both have been begging your bread on the streets?'

'My wife acted in what she thought to be Venetia's best interests,' said Robert trying to stem the torrent of words, but Aunt Augusta was not silenced so easily.

'Everyone knows that you are so besotted with your wife that

360

you don't see her for what she is. Ask your sister, ask anyone. She has always been wilful, disobedient, yes and wanton. Ask her whom she used to meet down on the marshes till Sir Joshua brought her to her senses and put a stop to it. Ask her how she and her brother consorted with the lowest kind of smugglers bringing shame on our name, ask her what happened while you were away, how she has been seen everywhere with a certain young Frenchman who no doubt is laughing at you behind your back. Don't imagine for one moment that I don't know . . .'

'Silence!' thundered Robert striving to stem the flood of spite and venom. 'Are you out of your senses? I will not listen to such vile accusations. If you continue to slander my wife in this fashion I must ask you to leave my house.'

His anger so forcibly expressed brought her up short. For a moment she glared from him to Isabelle.

'Don't be afraid. I am going. I would only say one more thing. When you see Venetia, as no doubt you will, you can tell her that we no longer have a daughter. Neither her father nor I will receive her or her husband. She will be cut off as if she never existed and if that worthless young man thinks to gain from this ill-advised marriage, not one penny will go to her now or in the future.'

'Oh no,' exclaimed Isabelle, 'Oh no, you can't be so cruel, so unfeeling. Venetia has always loved her father dearly.'

'She has a very strange way of showing it,' said Aunt Augusta sourly. 'Ingratitude is all I have ever expected from you and your brother and now you have corrupted my daughter. As for you, my lord,' she went on, turning to Robert, 'you would do well to remember what I have said.'

She gave a sweepingly contemptuous glance from one to the other and stalked from the room.

'Thank heaven she's gone!' said Robert with relief. 'I thought at one time I would be obliged to call the servants and have her forcibly removed.'

For one frightening moment Isabelle felt she was going to faint. The room swung alarmingly around her and she dropped on the sofa, shutting her eyes and trying to hang on to her senses till the giddiness faded and the room steadied. She opened her eyes to see Robert looking at her with concern.

'Are you all right, Isabelle? You're white as a ghost. You mustn't let that wretched aunt of yours distress you so much.'

'I'm quite recovered. It's just that it has been rather a shock. You don't . . . you don't believe all those horrible things she was saying, do you?'

'No, of course not. She has no one but herself to blame, so hurling brickbats at you is a way of giving vent to her outrage.' He frowned. 'Are you sure you wouldn't like me to send for Dr Merridrew. You still look very pale.'

'No, of course not.' She managed a little laugh. 'He would think me one of those silly young women who are always ready to go off into the vapours. I thought you had an important appointment this morning.'

'Yes, I have, and I'm very late for it. Colonel Brown has produced some really remarkable plans for this new canal and earthwork on the marshes and we are to examine them in detail today. All highly secret of course at this stage and I daresay Bonaparte would dearly like to take a look at them. Now you take care of yourself. You've been doing too much lately with all this refurbishing of Sabrina House.'

He dropped a kiss on her forehead and hurried away. She sat for a little and then went slowly up to her bedroom. The news about Venetia and Aunt Augusta's vicious attack had shaken her, bringing back the memory of those few days of enchantment and Uncle Joshua's furious anger which she had hoped was now safely buried. Why had she never told Robert about her folly, laughed with him over it? Wasn't it because all last summer she had still been caught up in its magic, till Lucien himself had destroyed it and the veil of illusion had been torn from her eyes in Paris when for a terrifying moment Robert seemed lost to her and she realised where her heart lay. Now there was something else, something a great deal more important if it were to prove true: for some few weeks she had wondered if she might be pregnant. She had certainly missed her last period and there had been one or two slight changes in her condition but till this morning she had felt perfectly well with none of the unpleasant symptoms that other young women had complained of. She looked in the mirror still feeling rather shaky. Perhaps she should consult Dr Merridrew. He was a kindly middle-aged man who had shown good sense and ability in treating Robert when he had come home from Paris last winter.

The only thing was if he came to the house, everyone would be asking why and if it were true, she wanted to hug it to herself and tell Robert in her own good time. Gwennie must be her only confidante. She could send her to the doctor's house to ask for an appointment for the following day. Then if it all proved to be nothing, Marian and Robert need never know. Best get it over and done with now. She rang for the maid and told her what she had decided. Gwennie's eyes sparkled.

'Oh Miss Isabelle, isn't that just what you've been hoping for all along and won't his lordship be pleased?'

'Maybe, if I'm right,' said Isabelle, 'but not a word yet, Gwennie, not to the servants, not to anyone. Just go along to Dr Merridrew and ask if he will see me at a convenient time tomorrow.'

'I will that and don't you fret, my lady. I'll not say a word. Wild horses wouldn't drag it out of me.'

Dr Merridrew said, 'I would have been pleased to call, Lady Isabelle. You need not have come to me here.'

'I know but I did not want everyone in the household asking questions.'

The doctor nodded. It was not easy for a young wife to share a house with her husband's dominating sister.

'You are a healthy young woman,' he said with his genial smile. 'There is no reason why you should not go on very satisfactorily. I am sure your husband will be delighted.'

'I know my father-in-law will,' she said ruefully. 'Every letter from Scotland asks the same question.'

The doctor smiled. 'No doubt the Earl is looking forward to his first grandchild now that Lady Marian has failed him by remaining unmarried.' He escorted her to the waiting carriage.

'Don't forget to call me at once if you should suffer any inconvenience.'

'I will and thank you.'

Gwennie was waiting. She looked at her mistress expectantly and Isabelle nodded.

'But don't say a word, Gwennie, not yet, not till I have told my husband.'

'You can be quite sure of that,' said Gwennie, happy and proud to be sharing a secret with Miss Isabelle of which neither that stuck-up Lady Marian nor any of those high and mighty servants had the slightest inkling.

18

It was October but still that remarkable summer lingered. There were mellow days of sunshine and though the nights were cool, there had been so far no frosts or harsh winds to blight the flowers in the garden or tear the leaves from the trees that still flamed in gold and russet and crimson.

Sabrina House was finished and Isabelle was proud of it.

'Let's spend a few days there,' she said to Robert one morning. 'I want you to see everything. Last time you came with me it was only half done.'

'Why not?' he said indulgently. 'I don't suppose the war effort will fall to pieces if I take a holiday.' He smiled across at her. 'Why not this weekend? Let Ian drive you down in the carriage and I will follow the next day.'

Marian said, 'You'll be lucky if it doesn't rain and take care you don't catch a chill. I've never trusted rivers, nothing but dank wet mists and squelching mud underfoot.'

'It's not at all like that,' said Isabelle indignantly. 'The house is dry as a bone and very comfortable. You must come and stay some time.'

'We'll see. Next summer perhaps.'

Isabelle had it all planned. She and Morag would make sure there was plenty of delicious food. She would walk in the gardens with Robert and out into the lovely countryside. They would talk and laugh together and she would have him entirely to herself and would tell him the joyful news about the baby so that the feeling of failure that sometimes still nagged at her would be gone forever. She set out joyously with Rory on her lap, happy to be alone without Marian's critical eyes always ready to pass judgment and looking forward to showing Robert how she had transformed the lovely house he had given her.

*

On the following morning very early Lucien de Vosges took the same road. He debated whether he should ride or drive the spanking new tandem with the pair of matched bays which had stretched his credit to the limit.

The Chevalier had grumbled at his extravagance and he had brushed aside his argument airily.

'If you want to know what the aristocracy of Britain is thinking of, working at or planning to do, then you must meet them on their own ground.'

'And where is that getting you? Precisely nowhere,' said the older man obstinately. 'Time is running out let me remind you and the powers-that-be are growing impatient.'

'I know, I know, but I must work at this in my own way and not be dictated to by those who have never set foot in this confounded island nor met its damned obstinate and pig-headed inhabitants.'

Lucien was suffering from a bitter and angry frustration. He had found Isabelle utterly fascinating. The attraction had been there at the start, but conquest had proved unexpectedly tantalising. His masculine pride was piqued. What hidden quality did that dull, sober-minded intellectual, Robert Armitage, possess that she remained so obstinately loyal to him? Other women had succumbed easily to his special blend of charm and intense sexuality. And not just light women either. There were one or two society wives with disappointing husbands who had found a few hours of intense excitement and pleasure in one of those houses of assignation, fearful of discovery, but trembling and breathless with a fulfilment that only left them with a hunger for more, but not Isabelle. Oh no, she could rouse him to something like frenzy and then turn her back on him and lately when they had met, she had treated him with the casual indifference extended to mere acquaintances, a rejection that set his teeth on edge.

He knew all about Sabrina House. There could not be a better *rendez-vous* for what he intended. He knew Isabelle was there and her husband was trapped in the Foreign Office, his spies had told him that, so the way was clear. He rode through the cool October morning filled with the most delightful and titillating anticipation. This had nothing to do with the mission set him by his French paymasters, as Raoul de St George had taken pains to point out.

'You're stuck in a rut,' he had retorted, 'with your snivelling spies and scraps of information. I have a wider vision,' and with that he had stormed out of the apartment, but all the same he knew the Chevalier was right. This was something personal that riled him unbearably and demanded satisfaction.

Isabelle had spent a busy morning going all over the house, pleased with the results of her work and spending a little time in the spacious room on the second floor looking out on the gardens and river, which she had decided she would turn into a nursery for baby and nurse when the time came.

She ate a light luncheon and consulted Morag about dinner. There would be fresh salmon, duck roasted to a turn with a well hung pheasant, followed by fine creamy cheeses from the farm and fresh fruit. Robert was a sparing eater but a discerning one and she made sure his favourite wine was brought up from the cellar and the dry Chablis cooled in ice. Now in the early afternoon she was lying on the sofa in the drawing room, with Rory stretched out in front of a small merrily burning fire after a strenuous morning teaching the house cat who was master here and only winning a very dubious victory as was proved by the deep scratch on his nose. Isabelle was half asleep when Morag knocked and came in looking troubled.

'There is a gentleman asking for you, my lady.'

'A gentleman?' She didn't think any of their friends knew where she was. 'Who is it, Morag?'

'He's a foreign gentleman and he says . . .'

And before she could get out another word, she was firmly put aside and Lucien appeared in the doorway, looking remarkably handsome and debonair.

'No need to announce me, old woman, the lady knows me well.'

Isabelle had risen to her feet and was staring at him in consternation.

'Why have you come here like this, Lucien? How did you know where I was?'

'That's no way to greet an old friend, is it now?' Lucien had come further into the room, looking around him with lively interest. 'Very pretty, I must say. I heard about your riverside villa and find it a palace. Does it remind you of Sauvigny? There is a river there, I believe.'

'What do you know of Sauvigny?'

Morag had been looking from one to the other with a worried frown.

'Shall I fetch Angus here, my lady?'

It might come to that if he would not leave, but not yet. He had so taken her by surprise that she couldn't think straight.

'It's all right, Morag. I'll deal with this gentleman.'

As the door closed behind the old servant, Lucien said pleasantly, 'Is she your watch-dog? Surely Robert doesn't put a guard on his wife, or does he?'

Isabelle ignored this sally. 'I don't know why you have come here but you are not welcome, Lucien. I'm here alone. It's not at all suitable. I should be grateful if you would leave now, at once.'

'Oh dear, we've become very *comme il faut* all of a sudden, haven't we? Don't be silly, Isabelle. I'm interested. Won't you show me round this lovely new house of yours? There has been quite a lot of talk about it, you know. A love nest but only for husbands it seems. What a waste! Isn't it time we changed all that?'

She knew that teasing manner. Once she had found it delightful but now she had a desperate feeling of being trapped in a situation not of her own making.

'I'm not in the mood for company,' she said austerely. 'Or for entertaining an uninvited guest. I shall withdraw and shut myself in my own room till you leave the house.'

'Oh no, you can't do that, I'll not allow it.' He caught at her hands as she moved purposefully towards the door and swung her back against him. 'I've waited a long time for this and you are not going to escape.'

'Escape what? You're talking nonsense,' said Isabelle, 'and

you know it. You have come here uninvited and I am asking you to leave. To any gentleman that should be quite sufficient.'

'But then I'm not a gentleman, I'm only a fascinating rogue of a Frenchman,' said Lucien, 'and I've no intention of going, not yet awhile. Oh come, Isabelle, let's sit down and be comfortable together. Let's talk as we did during those lovely days on the Romney Marshes. I'm your castaway, don't you remember? Your castaway whose life you saved.'

He came to her then taking her hand and drawing her towards him but she pulled herself free and pushed him away from her.

'That's all over. It's finished and done with long ago.'

'Is it?' he said teasingly.

'You know it is. Are you going, Lucien, or do I have to call my servants and have you put out?'

He laughed at her with a confident amusement that chilled her.

'Put out by whom? A parcel of maidservants and an old man doubled up with rheumatics? Don't be a goose, Isabelle. You'll not get rid of me so easily.'

It was true. Ian had returned to London and except for old Angus there was no other man within call. How was she to free herself from a man who obstinately refused to leave? And Robert would be here very soon. Would he understand that this guest was uninvited? Of course he would but there was bound to be a great deal of unpleasantness with Lucien in this teasing, tormenting mood. Why had he come here? What was in his mind? She could only make a wild guess and it terrified her. It was stupid but she had never felt so helpless. Was it her own fault? Had she been playing with fire? But she had surely made it quite clear . . . he could not think her willing to . . . he was standing between her and the door with that maddening smile of his. If she could make a dash for the door into the garden, she could run around the house to the kitchen quarters where she would be safe. The idea no sooner shot into her head than she was at the door fumbling with the latch but the bolts were new and stiff and in a moment Lucien was beside her, strong hands on her shoulders.

369

'Oh no, my dear, you are not running away from me, not this time.'

She fought against him and he pulled her away from the door as Rory, small and defiant flew to her rescue, trying to sink his teeth into the elegant booted leg and receiving a ferocious kick that sent him across the room yelping pitifully.

Isabelle realised then that fighting him was a mistake. It had only inflamed him further. His hold on her tightened. He half carried, half dragged her across the room. She screamed but the servants' quarters were far away and the walls thick. He put her down none too gently on the sofa and half knelt beside her. For months he had dreamed of this moment and now it was here and he was determined to enjoy it. She would learn what it meant to tease and tantalise Lucien de Vosges.

She fought gamely but for all his slender build he was far stronger than she was. He had her pinned down beneath him while one hand tore at the neck of her thin silk gown. His fingers closed on her breast. She cried out in pain and fear staring up into the hot brown eyes, then his mouth had come down on hers with a bruising strength. His weight was crushing her back against the curved end of the sofa and a terrible despair welled up in her. This couldn't be happening to her, it couldn't. In a desperate attempt to dislodge him she brought up her knee with a painful jerk but it only had the effect of bringing his body down more heavily on hers. His hands were fumbling at her, she opened her mouth to scream again but the sound was strangled in her throat as a cool incisive voice cut through the overcharged atmosphere.

'May I ask what is going on?'

It couldn't be true and yet it was. Robert was standing just inside the door, his riding crop still in his hand. To any casual observer it must have appeared like two lovers enjoying all the excitement and pleasure of a romp on the sofa that could only have one end, and she thought afterwards with despair that that was how it must have seemed to Robert, but at the time she was only conscious of an overpowering relief.

'Thank God you're here, thank God!' was all she could gasp while Lucien slowly straightened up.

370

Robert ignored her for the moment. 'What the devil are you doing here, Monsieur de Vosges?'

His voice was still controlled but Isabelle, who knew him so well, was aware of the icy rage that possessed him.

'I would have thought it obvious,' said Lucien recovering his wit and his impudence, 'and vastly enjoyable it was. What a pity you arrived so soon, my lord. Just a few more minutes and it would have been all over.'

His insolence cost him dear. Robert raised the whip in his hand and slashed it twice across the young man's face with such force that he stumbled back almost into the fireplace.

'Get out,' he said, 'get out before I have you kicked out.'

Lucien had recovered himself. Blood trickled down one cheek.

'You fool, you blind fool,' he whispered. 'Don't you know your own wife? Tell him, Isabelle, tell him about the hut on the marshes, tell him about all those other occasions last summer . . .' Robert took a threatening step towards him, but Lucien went on, his voice rising viciously. 'You would like to destroy me, wouldn't you, as you destroyed that other one on the night you can't forget, the night that haunts you still and the girl your clumsiness couldn't save, the girl who died a horrible death screaming in agony . . . it sickens you still, doesn't it?'

Robert was staring at him. How could he know? How could he possibly have known if she hadn't told him? He was suddenly possessed by a blinding rage, a red mist seemed to swim before his eyes. He let it carry him away and he hit out catching Lucien on the chin so savagely that the young man was spun across the room and fell bruisingly to his knees. He struggled to his feet, all the airy charm wiped away, his face a livid mask of fury and outraged pride.

'By God, I'll kill you for that,' he said through stiff bruised lips, 'I swear I will.'

'I've no doubt you will try,' Robert was suddenly icily calm. 'When and how you like, the sooner the better. Now go – for the love of God, GO!'

Isabelle was huddled into a corner of the sofa. She had found the shawl she had been wearing around her shoulders earlier in

371

the afternoon and dragged it over her torn gown. Rory, shaken and miserable, crawled to her feet, still whimpering a little.

The door slammed behind Lucien and she looked at Robert imploringly. 'I didn't ask him to come here, Robert, you must believe me. He came and he refused to go . . . and then . . . and then . . .'

The words died away. Robert was looking at her, his face stony. She went on desperately stumbling over the words.

'I don't know how he knew about . . . about what happened to you that night . . . I don't know . . .' her voice caught in a little sob.

Robert was looking down at her, his feelings a chaotic mixture of love, anger and despair. His love for this girl had been absolute. He had never allowed himself to doubt. All the gossip, the hints, the occasional poisonous anonymous letter, he had put aside as no more than jealous spite, certain that one day she would tell him everything and they would laugh about it. These last weeks he had believed himself unutterably happy, wonderfully content, and now this – this ultimate betrayal – the one tortured and painful moment in his life only forced out of him through fever and pain and she had told it all to that lying renegade Frenchman – how they must have laughed together over it, finding it exquisitely amusing that a grown man of experience should be still tortured by a moment in his past.

He had loved and trusted her utterly, still loved her, God help him, and she had betrayed him, not only personally but in that secret work of his that he kept from everyone. On what kind of terms do you have to be to tell such a story and find enjoyment in the telling? He couldn't endure to stay and listen to more excuses, more lies.

'I'm going back to London,' he said abruptly. You had better return tomorrow. I will send Ian with the carriage for you.'

'But Robert please, please – you must listen to me.'

'Not now, later perhaps.'

'What will you do?'

He shrugged his shoulders. 'What I must. Your lover will no doubt send me a challenge.'

'He is *not* my lover,' she said fiercely.

'He would seem to believe differently,' he said drily.

'But you can't fight him. He would kill you.'

'I shall do my utmost to kill him first.'

He had a sudden memory of a herb-scented garden and himself saying lightly to his grandmother, 'If she takes a lover I shall probably kill him,' and now that hideous moment had come.

He left the house within an hour, refusing to take any food though Morag tried to persuade him even if it was only a glass of wine. At the last moment he leaned from the saddle to say brusquely, 'Take care of her. She is very distressed,' and then had ridden away before she could question.

The dinner prepared with such loving care was eaten by the servants. Later in the evening Morag loaded a tray and took it up to Isabelle's bedroom. She looked at it listlessly.

'It's kind of you but I'm really not hungry.'

'You must eat a little, my lady, especially now.' She had said nothing but the old woman had made a shrewd guess at her condition. 'I know Master Robert,' she went on gently. 'His anger never lasts long.'

'I wish that were true.'

Morag didn't know the half of it. To please her Isabelle tried to eat a little but at the first mouthful sickness rose in her throat and she pushed the tray aside. She lay on the huge bed remembering that night when they had been so happy, when the baby within her had been conceived, and wanted to weep in utter despair.

Why had Robert refused to listen to her? Why had he treated he so harshly, so unjustly? It was only gradually out of the confusion and wretchedness that she began to realise how deeply he must have been hurt. How could he believe her capable of pouring out their intimate moments to Lucien and yet . . . she sat up suddenly. How could Lucien know so much? There was something hidden there and until she found it out, until she could convince Robert that it was not she who had told him, he would never forgive her. Back and forth went her thoughts, scurrying from one thing to another trying to find reasons and failing hopelessly to understand anything except that both of them were trapped into some dark mystery.

The night passed painfully slowly. Now and again she drowsed only to wake with a start and the grim realisation of what lay in front of her. She got up early and went downstairs and out into the garden. It was cold with a chill wind whirling the leaves from the trees and whipping the last blooms from the roses while a dank white mist curled at the edge of the water. The house she had loved so much and furnished with such joy and hope for the future had become hateful to her. She was glad when Ian arrived at midday with the carriage. He was his usual laconic independent self and expressed no surprise at the change of plan. Morag said goodbye and then gave her an impulsive hug.

'Don't fret, my lady. You'll be coming back to us soon, I'm sure of it, and Master Robert with you.'

'Perhaps.'

She dropped a kiss on the old nurse's cheek. Ian handed her into the carriage and lifted in a subdued Rory, still bruised and wretched, and they drove away.

There was an ominous kind of silence about the house when Isabelle returned that evening. Everyone down to the youngest scullery maid knew that something had happened between the master and the mistress and speculated about it in hushed whispers. Robert had come back late the night before, his horse sweating and lathered, as if he had ridden hard, and had immediately shut himself up in his study. He had not even come down to dinner, only asking for something on a tray to be sent in to him with a bottle of brandy. Lady Marian had sat alone in the dining room with a worried frown and though she had knocked at his door afterwards, she had obviously received no explanation. Later that same evening Edward had been sent with a note to David Fraser's rooms in Piccadilly and had reported to the kitchen afterwards that Mr Fraser was not there but he had delivered the letter to his valet.

And now here was the young mistress returning alone and looking quite unlike herself, going straight to her room with

Rory tucked under her arm and sending word by Gwennie that she did not want anything to eat. They had plied the girl with questions but she obstinately kept her mouth shut, not that Isabelle had given her any explanation, only asked her to take Rory downstairs and give him his supper. It was all very disturbing.

When Gwennie had gone, Isabelle took off her bonnet and cloak, shivering with overstretched nerves and fatigue. As nobody expected her return, no fire had yet been lighted in her bedroom. She was standing at the window when she saw the cab draw up, saw David alight and run up the stairs. David was the obvious person to act as Robert's second if this duel should take place.

Duels were frequent enough especially among the young army officers, as often as not over some triviality, some absurd question of honour, and mostly they amounted to very little. Shots were fired, honour was satisfied, and sometimes the duellists went off to breakfast together. But Robert was no fire-eater. He had always despised such folly and she knew with a dreadful sinking of the heart that this was quite different. What had happened between him and Lucien could only be wiped away in blood and it was all her fault. She must try to stop it, but how? Even if she could make Robert understand that he was making a horrible mistake, his pride would never allow him to apologise and Lucien would still demand satisfaction.

The housemaid came to light the fire and Gwennie brought Rory back with a tray of thinly sliced chicken, bread and butter and a pot of tea. She drank the tea thirstily but still could not eat anything and wondered unhappily what David and Robert were working out between them.

'The Chevalier de St George called on me this morning,' David was saying. 'All he told me was that his principal had been grievously insulted by you and demanded that you should pay for it in the usual way. You of all people, Robert! If I hadn't had your note, I would have laughed in his face. What in God's name happened?'

375

'I found Lucien de Vosges with my wife – *in flagrante delicto* – isn't that what they call it?'

'I don't believe it,' said David. 'I would have staked my life on Isabelle's honesty. She loves you, Robert, I am sure of it.'

'I thought so too but there were other things . . .' He got up and moved away to the window, staring out unseeingly into the dark night. 'He flaunted them in my face, intimate details that only she could have told him. I'm afraid I lost my temper and hit him.'

'You should have booted him out of the house!' exclaimed David. 'Robert, are you sure about this, sure you're not making some terrible mistake?'

'I wish to God I were,' he said bleakly. Then he turned back. 'What arrangements have you made?'

'As the offended party, it is his privilege to state the terms. In three days' time on Wimbledon Common at 7.30 in the morning. It should be light enough by then.'

'Very well.'

'He made another stipulation that I refused until I had spoken with you.'

'What is it?'

'He demands the right to toss for first shot.'

'If that's what he asks, then let him have it.'

'But, Robert, it's madness. If he wins, he could disable you before you could retaliate.'

'It's the luck of the game, isn't it? I could win the toss,' said Robert calmly.

'Why are you taking it like this? It's so unlike you. I don't understand.'

'Don't you?' Robert looked at him for a moment and then walked away to behind his desk. 'I married her, David, knowing she did not love me. It was a way out of an unhappy restricted life and she was touchingly grateful. I can wait, I told myself, I refused to listen to gossip, I trusted her implicitly and during these last months since we were in Paris I believed I had won. I believed that she . . . cared for me as I care for her, but I was wrong, hopelessly wrong. She has betrayed me in the cruellest way possible, not only personally but also the work I do. I think

I could have accepted almost anything but not that. That's why I don't care very much what comes of this except that it would give me satisfaction to wipe the self satisfied smirk off the face of that damned Frenchman. Do all you have to do, David. I am relying on you.'

'It's the worst thing you've ever asked from me but I'll do it even if I have to shoot the bastard myself afterwards!'

It was dark by the time David left. Isabelle heard the front door open, heard Hawke's murmured voice and saw the shadowy figure run down the steps. Now surely Robert must come to her. He couldn't ignore her completely. She was still his wife. She had a right to know what he was going to do. She knelt by the fire still shivering, feeling she would never be warm again. An hour passed and then another but he didn't come. She felt suddenly that she couldn't endure this isolation a moment longer. She got up, pulled a shawl around her shoulders and went out and down the stairs to knock on the door of his room. There was no answer so she went in. He was in his shirt sleeves, sitting at the desk, his head in his hands.

'Is that you, Hawke?' he said wearily. 'You can go to bed. I shan't want anything more tonight.'

Then he looked up and saw her. He got slowly to his feet.

'What are you doing here, Isabelle? I thought you would have gone to bed by now.'

'Did you imagine I could sleep? I knew David was here. What is going to happen?'

'We meet in three days' time, that is all. You need not concern yourself too much. If I die, as is possible, you are well provided for.'

'How can you say that to me?' she said passionately. 'As if that is all that matters. Do you think I don't care? You are so wrong, Robert, so terribly, terribly wrong. Lucien has never been my lover, never, never!'

He looked at her for a long moment and then turned away towards the dully burning fire, kicking the sullen coal with a booted foot till it sparked and blazed.

'Why didn't you tell me about that first meeting with him

down there on the beaches? Why keep it so secret? I always knew there was something between you but I wouldn't question. I waited for you to tell me.'

'I don't know,' she said wretchedly, 'I don't know. It seemed so foolish, so childish. I grew ashamed of it.'

'Wasn't it rather because it meant so much to you, because he was all important and when you met again last year it was what you had always longed for? God knows, I received warnings enough but I trusted you absolutely and you have destroyed that trust.'

'No, no, it wasn't like that, I swear it wasn't. At first it was as if I was held in some kind of spell – I can't explain it – I had saved his life and something seemed to bind us together – I only know that in Paris when you were wounded, when I thought I might lose you, it was as if a web of illusion was swept away . . .' She paused, wanting to tell him of the child but was still fearful of how he would accept it and while she hesitated he went on with increasing bitterness.

'And everything we shared in Paris, you poured out to him, everything that was most intimate between us.'

That was what tormented him, that more than anything, was what he could not accept.

'I didn't, Robert, I swear I never said anything of what happened there. You must believe me. I have never spoken to Lucien or to anyone about that part of your life.'

'How else could he have known? Did he pluck it out of the air?' he said wearily.

'I don't know. How can I know. He could have heard it from someone else, someone in France.'

'Only one man knew what happened that night and he is dead.'

'Oh God, why should this happen to us now at this time?' Her breath caught in her throat and he turned to look at her, noting how very exhausted she was, her eyes huge and dark in the pallor of her face.

'You look worn out,' he said more gently. 'Go to bed, try to rest.' He sighed. 'Maybe in time we can work out some compromise.'

*

The next day all fashionable London was agog with it. These affairs could never be kept secret. There were those who said, 'I always knew that marriage would end in disaster,' and others who envied Lucien who had evidently got his way with that tantalising young woman. There was sympathy for Robert especially from the women who condemned her as wanton, and contempt from the clever ones who thought her a fool to be found out. But life has to go on, even though Isabelle felt as if someone had trampled brutally all over her. She had to endure Marian's reproaches. She didn't know all the details, only that her brother was going to risk his life for the sake of a young woman who put no value on his kindness, his generosity. The deceived husband is always something of a laughing stock and it enraged her.

Isabelle's pride came at last to the rescue. She held her head high. She went on as usual riding out in the morning, meeting one or two freezing looks and what was worse a sly familiarity from the more raffish members of society. She came back to her usual duties, discussing the day's meals with Cook, bathing Rory who still suffered from Lucien's cruel kick, driving to Bond Street to make one or two necessary purchases and discovering that Aunt Augusta was having the time of her life spreading poisonous gossip from teatable to teatable.

Robert was away from the house for most of the day and treated her with his usual courtesy until she wanted to scream at him. She would rather he had shouted at her, beaten her, done anything rather than become like a stranger. Meals were served and eaten either in silence or with a few casual remarks and she found herself completely unable to eat anything. She pushed the food round her plate and it went away untouched. Never had three days passed more slowly.

Robert was up and dressed and already in his study settling a few details when a tray of coffee was brought into him. He pushed it aside and was staring down at the portrait of Isabelle that had been painted in Paris when Hawke appeared in the doorway.

'Mr Fraser is here, my lord. He is waiting in the carriage.'

'Very well. I will come.'

On a sudden impulse he picked up the silver framed miniature, snapped the cover shut and thrust it between his waistcoat and his shirt. Then he took cloak, hat and gloves and went down the stairs.

Isabelle saw him from her window, all in black even to the satin neckcloth, so as to present as little target as possible, she supposed dully. There was a dreadful feeling of sickness inside her. She wanted to run after him, take hold of him, stop him from throwing away his life for nothing. The carriage rolled away and she felt she couldn't stay in the house. She could not sit waiting, waiting, she would run mad. She dragged on her riding clothes and hurried down to the stables. It was still very early but Tom was there with curry comb and brush.

'Saddle Zara for me,' she said quickly.

'But, my lady, you can't ride out, not this morning, not alone.'

'Why can't I? Do as I say and quickly please.'

At any moment Marian might appear saying it wasn't decent, it wasn't proper, she should hide herself till David brought her husband home, wounded, dying, perhaps dead . . . Tom gave her his hand into the saddle and she trotted quickly out into the mews. He stared after her as Gwennie came running from the kitchen to join him.

'I tried to stop her but she would go, God help her.'

'God help them both,' said Gwennie feelingly.

When Robert and David reached Wimbledon Common, Lucien and the Chevalier were already there. It was a grassy glade often chosen for these affairs and conveniently hidden from the carriage road by a screen of tall trees. It was a cool morning with a light touch of frost that crisped the grass and tipped with silver the cobwebs that hung from bush to bush.

Robert walked up and down while the two seconds discussed the details. Then he and Lucien were facing one another and the Chevalier produced a gold sovereign. He spun it in the air as they made their calls and then bent over it as it lay in the grass.

'Heads it is. My principal has first shot.'

So be it. Fate or chance had decided against him. While they paced out the distance Robert looked around him in the freshness of the autumn morning and with a quirk of memory suddenly thought of that day they had woken together at Sabrina House and Isabelle had flung wide the window saying how lovely it was and had run barefoot across the dew wet grass daring him to follow her and they had come back together to laugh and make love. Damn it all, he loved her still and knew that despite everything he didn't want to die.

David handed him the pistol and they took up their positions. Somewhere far above his head there came the sound of birds.

'Fire!' thundered the Chevalier and Robert felt a stunning impact on his breast that sent him staggering back. He fell to one knee but strangely he was not killed. There was no wound, no blood.

David was running towards him. Lucien had already turned away as he got unsteadily to his feet and raised the pistol.

'Stand!' shouted David to his opponent. 'Stand! It is not yet over.'

Still slightly dazed, Robert took careful aim but it requires a special kind of courage to stand and wait to be shot at. Lucien involuntarily moved and the bullet took him in the shoulder.

Robert's hand dropped to his side. David had reached him by now.

'My God, I thought you were done for. What happened?'

'I don't know, not yet. Is he . . .?'

'Winged only.'

The surgeon who had accompanied them had already gone to Lucien.

David took Robert's arm 'It's over. He'll do well enough.' He urged him towards the carriage. 'Come, let's go.'

As the carriage moved forward Robert thrust his hand inside his coat and drew out Isabelle's portrait. The bullet had gone through the silver cover, split the painting and buried itself in the heavy silver backing.

David stared down at it and then at his friend.

'Whatever pain she has caused you, one thing is sure. She has saved your life.'

'It would seem so.'

Robert passed a hand over his face. He had intended to kill and had failed. He seemed to have passed through a near certainty of death into renewed life all within the last half an hour. He found it an unnerving experience.

There were very few people riding in the Park at this early hour and certainly no ladies. A group of guardsmen went clattering by and Isabelle urged Zara forward, finding relief in a furious gallop with the wind whistling about her ears. One or two of the riders recognised her and thought it excessively improper to be riding like a madcap while her husband was fighting a murderous duel to redeem her honour. The story, greatly embellished and distorted, had gone the rounds.

Up and down she rode recklessly and as she came up to the final turn a footman exercising his master's two wolfhounds rashly unleashed them. They raced across the track like a streak of grey lightning right under Zara's aristocratic nose. A skittish creature at the best of times, she shied violently so that Isabelle lost a stirrup, tried desperately to save herself and was badly thrown. She lay for a moment all the breath knocked out of her and then realised dazedly that a little crowd had gathered around to stare and comment, the very last thing she wanted.

She scrambled to her feet pushing aside helping hands, answering questions at random, anxious only to escape.

'I'm not hurt, just bruised that's all. If someone would bring my horse . . .'

A burly guardsman had already gone after Zara and was holding the reins and grinning broadly at her.

'I'm quite all right, really I am. If you would just help me to remount.'

'With pleasure, Madam, if you are sure . . .'

The tall guardsman in his shining helmet swung her up on to Zara's back. She smiled down at him brilliantly and waved her hand as they parted to let her through.

'I don't care what they like to say about her,' remarked one elderly gentleman to another, 'but that French filly is a rare plucked 'un and Kilgour is a damned fool if he doesn't realise it!'

By the time she reached Arlington Street the pain in her back had become torture. She slipped from the saddle, saw that Tom was there to take Zara and nerved herself to walk steadily across the yard. She had no notion how she got up the stairs. Gwennie was in her bedroom tidying away discarded clothes. Isabelle clung to the door handle, her mouth so dry that the words came out in a croak.

'Is he . . .? Has my husband returned?'

'He's back, my lady, came in with Mr Fraser just a few minutes ago and not a scratch on him.'

She wanted to say 'Thank God' but somehow the words wouldn't come. The floor seemed to come up to meet her and she pitched forward into the dark.

She came round to find herself lying on the bed with Gwennie undressing her and very concerned about her condition.

'Are you sure he is not wounded?' she breathed.

'He's right as rain, my lady, and downstairs this very minute taking breakfast with Mr Fraser. Your clothes are all covered in mud and dirt, whatever happened to you, Miss Isabelle?'

'I had a tumble. It was nothing.' But her whole body felt on fire with pain and there was an agonisingly angry stab in her back.

'Shouldn't we send for the doctor?'

'Don't fret, there's no need. It's only bruising.'

But Gwennie knew of Isabelle's condition and was disturbed about her. She made her as comfortable as she could, piled up the pillows behind her and persuaded her to sip some of the hot coffee sent up from the kitchen. Then she hurried down the back stairs to find Tom. She was not going to ask permission from that Lady Marian nor from Mr Armitage. What did men know about things like this? She would send Tom for Dr Merridrew on her own responsibility.

Robert was returning from seeing David to the front door when he was surprised to see the doctor coming down the stairs.

'Is someone sick? Is it my wife?' he asked with some concern.

'Yes indeed, my lord, and I was hoping to have a word with you.'

'It's nothing serious, I hope.'

They moved into the morning room. Dr Merridrew knew all about the meeting on Wimbledon Common, was relieved to find one of the principals apparently unharmed and thought it more tactful not to mention it.

'Lady Isabelle has had a nasty fall from her horse this morning. The bruising is extensive but I hope not too serious. We must wait and see.'

'My wife was riding? This morning?'

'It would seem so.' The doctor paused. 'I am sorry to have to tell you that I fear she will have lost her hope of bearing you a child.'

Robert frowned. 'I was not aware that my wife was pregnant.'

'You didn't know? Well, in my experience young ladies are sometimes shy about these things. She was no doubt waiting for the right moment.'

'She is in no danger?'

'I pray not but I would advise you to treat her gently for a while. She is very distressed and a little feverish. No doubt she has been under considerable stress this last week. I shall call again tomorrow.'

'Yes, of course. Thank you, doctor.'

He saw him bustle away and then went quickly up the stairs and into the bedroom. Why hadn't she told him about something so important to them both? Why had she let him find out in this way? Why? There could be only one answer and the anger burned inside him.

He came to the bed and looked down at her. Isabelle was lying with her eyes closed, the long lashes dark on a face whiter than the linen sheets. The words burst out of him before he could stop them.

'Was it my child or his?'

Her eyes opened so full of dark pain that he felt a pang of shame. She didn't answer, simply turned away her head.

384

'I am sorry,' he muttered, 'I am sorry. But why didn't you tell me? Why? Why?'

'I was going to tell you ... on that day ... I had it all planned ...'

Her voice died away and he saw the slow tears, forced out of her by sheer weakness, roll down her cheeks.

She was not lying, surely to God she could not be lying, and yet if it were true, surely it altered everything. He had been wrong, utterly wrong, but the mystery, the problem still remained.

He wanted to take her in his arms, comfort her, tell her there was still time, but he could not; the doubt, the feeling of trust betrayed held him back.

She turned her head to look at him.

'Robert, did you kill him?'

'No.'

'And you are really not hurt?'

'No.'

'I don't understand.'

So much agonising and it had settled nothing. She stirred restlessly and he touched her cheek with gentle fingers.

'Don't let it worry you. Rest now. Take care of yourself.'

When he had gone, she lay and thought about it. The laudanum the doctor had administered to her was already clouding her mind. Through her own folly she had lost her dearest hope and still the question, the enigma remained, and until that was solved, they could never again be at peace with one another.

19

The Chevalier de St George was in a furious temper, a cold icy rage, which had been slowly building up in him for the past five months ever since he and Lucien had returned from their trip to Paris in the spring. Up to a couple of years ago his life had run along very pleasant lines. By luck and devious manipulation of the right people, he had escaped the guillotine and his exile in England had been considerably sweetened by discreet payments for the information he gathered and infiltrated back into France. Some of the English were fools especially in their cups and he had a way of painlessly extracting details that they never realised they were passing on. There were always those who never had enough money to satisfy their expensive tastes and convinced themselves that what they had to sell would never harm them and there were those like Scatchard, who would run with both sides if he could and never objected to dirtying his hands. All these details put together like pieces in a puzzle made an interesting whole, much appreciated in Paris. Then Lucien de Vosges erupted into his life, forced on him with the backing of that shadowy figure who had become so powerful in Fouché's secret police and ever since then everything had gone wrong.

That they were not being paid to fritter away their time in idle pleasure was made very plain to them both in Paris, and if results did not materialise before the end of the year, then the usual payments which made his days so much more enjoyable could well come to an abrupt end. And what had come of it? Complete disaster because the fool of a boy, instead of going about the business with craft and expertise, lusted after the wretched girl and provoked a scandalous duel with an enraged husband that had become the talk of London, the very thing to be avoided at all costs.

He looked at Lucien lying back on the sofa nursing his wounded shoulder and felt the righteous anger stir in him again. Damn it all, the network he had carefully set up during the last six years and which had been so successful looked like being utterly destroyed. It made his blood boil just to think about it.

'My God, didn't I do my best for you? If David Fraser had been quicker off the mark he would have known that coin was a fake. I gave you the opportunity and even then you couldn't kill him,' he said for the hundredth time.

'I know, I know. Must you go on and on about it? That shot should have done the trick,' said Lucien sullenly. 'What prevented it? He was not even wounded. Could he have been wearing a bullet-proof vest?'

'Nonsense. Armitage is no fool. He'd never risk such a slur on his honour. You can think yourself deuced lucky that it shook him a little or you'd not be here now. He has the reputation of being a deadly shot. It's about time you took a long look at yourself, my boy. All you've succeeded in doing is making yourself a laughing stock, someone not even worthy of being shot down like a dog.'

'Do you think I haven't realised that?' It was what riled Lucien unbearably. He could not rest till he had wreaked vengeance on both of them. He wanted to see them crawl. Through days and nights of fever and pain he had thought of nothing else and now suddenly he knew how he could do it. 'I've been thinking,' he said getting up and pacing up and down the room. 'I have a plan.'

'God preserve me from any more of your damfool plans!' grumbled the Chevalier. 'Our orders were to deliver the girl and boy with Armitage across the Channel and into the right hands as unobtrusively as possible and we're as far from achieving that as flying to the moon.'

'Don't you believe it.' Lucien's eyes glittered dangerously. 'Listen I have just learned something interesting. It's quite certain that Robert Armitage will be sent on a further mission very soon.'

'How the devil do you know that?'

'That little rat Scatchard still has his uses. He always has his nose to the ground. Sometimes I think he smells it out.'

'Even if it is true, how does that fact help us? He'll slip through our fingers as he has done before.'

'Not this time and not so easily. For one thing we now know a great deal about the route he usually chooses. Supposing we get Isabelle and her brother down there with him, put all three of them in the same bag at the same time?'

'You're off your head. Do you imagine a clever devil like Armitage is going to walk into your trap with his eyes wide open?'

'He has his weaknesses like other men and I'm beginning to know them. It came to me in the night, a splendid plan.'

The two heads came together, Lucien talking and the Chevalier listening. At the end he drew back, still doubtful.

'It's relying far too much on chance for my money but it could work, it just might. But one thing I will tell you here and now. This time you're on your own. I'm having nothing to do with it. It's your pigeon and you can use your own bully boys down there on the marshes, but I warn you some of them are not quite so gullible as you seem to think and I'm not risking my precious neck.'

'Have it your own way. The greater the risk, the greater the reward,' said Lucien airily.

'Reward! More likely a rope around your neck. The British hang spies, you know, they don't cut their heads off!'

October merged into November and the weather began to break. Days of rain were followed by the first fog of winter hanging like a heavy black pall over London, caused by the hundreds of coal fires burning merrily throughout the capital. There were times when Isabelle thought the fog had crept into Arlington Street. She was up now but still feeling shaky and given to private bouts of weeping which she resented but did not seem able to control. The doctor told her cheerfully it was only to be expected and in a few months when she was pregnant again, all this grief would be forgotten, but then he didn't know how impossibly remote that happy condition was. Every day she had to contend with Marian's silent reproach not only for wounding her brother's honour so intolerably but also for losing his child by her irresponsible behaviour on the morning of the duel. Sometimes she wished that Marian would scream at her. A violent quarrel might have cleared the air.

Guy, who had been away on a visit to the country house of one of his new friends, came back filled with righteous anger and most unfairly critical of his sister.

'Robert is a dashed good sort,' he said, 'he has been generous to you and to me. You ought to have more sense than to go fooling around with a wrong 'un like Lucien de Vosges.'

'I was not fooling around, as you gallantly put it,' said Isabelle indignantly, 'and not so long ago you were singing the praises of Lucien yourself.'

'Yes, well, that's different,' he said loftily. 'A married woman in your position can't be too careful. Everyone is talking about it and I don't like it above half, I can tell you, though I must say Robert does seem to be taking it very hard. It's not like him.'

But then Guy didn't know the real crux of the matter and not even to her dearly loved brother could Isabelle reveal what was causing the coolness between them.

It was David who helped her most during these wretched days. He would call in the afternoon and sit with her for an hour or so, keeping her amused with all the latest scandals, telling her how he had run down to Chatham and met Perry proudly showing off his new wife and insisting on taking him all over the *Sirius*.

He told her too how Sir Hugo Dexter had saved his pride by telling everyone who would listen how relieved he was that the flighty Venetia Brydges had seen fit to run off before marriage and not afterwards while his two daughters were clapping their hands with glee. After all who wants a stepmother younger than yourself!

It was David who told her about the portrait and the strange way in which it had saved Robert's life.

'What has he done with it?' she asked wistfully.

'He has sent it to a skilful artist to be repaired, that I do know. Why don't you ask him about it, Isabelle?'

But she shook her head. 'It must come from him first.'

'But doesn't the very fact that he took it with him on that morning prove that he still loves you,' argued David.

'I only wish that were true,' she said and sighed.

Robert and Isabelle were very polite to one another. They discussed the usual trivial details that arise in any household. He told her and Marian that Britain was now in as good a state of preparation against invasion as it ever could be, that work had already begun on the canal down on the marshes, and that one night the performance at Drury Lane Theatre had to be cancelled as all the actors were on military duty, but it seemed as if there was a barrier between them that she could not break down. The loving intimacy, the sharing of thoughts and interests and laughter had all vanished. These days she refused all invitations on the plea of ill health while Robert seemed to be always at the Foreign Office or dining at White's or riding down to Walmer to see William Pitt.

In desperation she surprised Marian one day by asking if she could accompany her on one of her visits to the Wapping Charity Centre. Marian was one of those good women who would give money and time, would dispense clothes, food, medicine and excellent advice, but who had little or no sympathy with the hapless women who crowded into the shelter, many of them the starving wives and families of men serving in the army or navy. She had no patience with the feckless ones who would buy the baby a pretty bauble instead of nourishing food and it surprised and, it must be said, somewhat irritated her to see her sister-in-law's instant success. Isabelle had learned a good deal about poverty when helping Harriet Holland amongst the poorest of the villagers and she sweetened the help she gave out with a laugh, a kiss for the baby and a question as to how they were managing and when had they last seen husband, brother or son.

'I'd like to come again if I may,' she said to Marian in the carriage when Ian drove them home, but it so happened that she never had the opportunity. Lucien's plan was slowly maturing and would all too soon trap them all in its meshes.

'You sent for me, my lord,' said Robert one morning in mid November as he was ushered into the handsome office of Henry Dundas and the door was shut carefully behind him.

'Come in, come in, my dear boy, make yourself comfortable. You are not looking too well. Not suffering one of these wretched colds that seem to have afflicted half London since that confounded fog?'

'Thank you but I'm perfectly well,' said Robert, sitting stiffly upright.

'What is it you want to see me about?'

'Oh well, yes, the fact is there is something we would like you to do for us, a mission for which you are particularly suited since you already have many valuable connections down on the Romney Marshes.'

'I have already told you, my lord, how I feel about this. I would prefer . . .'

'You'd prefer not to be involved in any more of these special assignments for us. Yes, yes, I remember what you said but this will not bring you into any danger and in the present circumstances it did occur to me that you might be glad to be away from London for a while.'

'Why should you think that?' said Robert coldly.

'My dear boy, with society still buzzing with it, I could hardly help being aware that you have been having difficulties with that pretty little wife of yours. These things happen, I'm afraid, and if you remember, I did warn you. No, don't protest, I don't want to hear anything. It's your affair. My only regret is that you didn't kill that abominable young Frenchman while you were about it.'

'I did my best,' said Robert wryly. 'What makes you say that? I don't care for the fellow, I must admit, but have you any evidence that he has been abusing the privileges he enjoys over here?'

'By acting the spy, you mean,' said Dundas drily. 'Suspicions in plenty, and of the Chevalier de St George, but not enough

391

proof to hang a cat unfortunately, but this is what I'm coming to. It is just possible we may be able to lay our hands on something useful at last. It would appear that something very odd is going on down in Kent. One of our people reported that Lucien de Vosges had been seen in the neighbourhood apparently visiting friends but I can't help feeling that the month of November with a raw gale blowing and a mist thick as a blanket is hardly the best time for pleasure trips. There must be something else. Whether he's after the plans for the canal or whether there is another reason, we can't be sure but you're the right one to ferret it out and incidentally while you're down there, you might perhaps slip across the Channel and warn those hotheads plotting a quick end for Bonaparte that over here certain members at Downing Street have been opening their mouths a little too wide. While I have no wish to see the First Consul live on into old age, his sudden death wouldn't stop the war and could well bring about an international crisis of horrendous implications. I take it you will oblige us in this matter.'

He was about to say that venturing into France at this time might be thrusting his head into the lion's cage and then knew he didn't very much care if he was being foolhardy.

He said, 'Is this an order?'

'It is between you and me but you will have our backing. You'll go.'

'If I must.'

'Good man. As soon as you can make your preparations then leave but keep in close touch before you go, the situation changes day by day.'

That evening at dinner Robert said casually, 'I shall be going away in a few days.'

Marian looked up sharply. 'Going away? Down to Kent again?'

'Partly. Certain problems have arisen down there and then I'll be moving along the coast taking a general look at our defences.'

Isabelle said nothing but afterwards when Marian had retired and they were alone for a few minutes, she stopped him as he was going out of the room.

'You're going to France again, aren't you, Robert?'

'Why should you say that?'

'I'm not quite a fool. They would never waste someone like you on a survey of the coastal defences.'

'You think too highly of my abilities.'

'Oh no, I don't and you're glad to go, aren't you, glad to leave me and everything else behind you, even though you know how dangerous it could be for you now?'

'Perhaps. It's not altogether surprising, is it?'

'Oh God, is this to go on for ever? It's as if there was a brick wall between us and I'm hopelessly battering against it.'

'I would remind you that it's a wall you built yourself.'

'If only you would believe me,' she cried desperately, 'if only you would try to understand.'

He gave her a long look. 'I think perhaps I've been understanding, as you call it, for too long already. I don't expect to be away for long.'

He went out closing the door behind him and she sank on to the sofa feeling as if she were caught in a trap with no possible means of escape. All sorts of desperate thoughts raced through her mind. Supposing she went to Lucien, demanded to know how and where he had obtained his dangerous knowledge and what was behind his relentless pursuit. It was not just her body he wanted to conquer, that was only part of it, he had some other purpose but what it was she could not fathom. But although she was sorely tempted, she realised that to go to him would undoubtedly add fuel to a fire that was beginning to die down and she shivered at the thought of Robert's anger if she were foolhardy enough to try it. Then before she could make any other move, they were all three of them caught up in Lucien's 'grand design' as the Chevalier had mockingly called it.

It began the day Robert set out for Kent. He left very early when she was still asleep and only the servants were up and about. It was barely light, a dismal November morning with a smell of fog still in the air. He took only a small valise and was too preoccupied to notice the thin man with the rat-like face who watched him from the shelter of trees on the opposite side of the street. Some hours later that same unremarkable looking man delivered a note to Hawke with a request that it should be delivered to Isabelle immediately.

The butler took the letter from him frowning, not caring for the look of the messenger, and sent it up to Isabelle's bedroom by Gwennie. She was still in her morning gown kneeling on the carpet busily grooming a strongly protesting Rory. She sat back on her heels to break the seal and open the folded sheet. She ran her eye through it and then scrambled to her feet, her face alight with surprise and joy.

'Gwennie, has Master Guy left the house yet?'

'No, Miss, he is downstairs this minute eating his breakfast and making a very poor show of it I must say. He was in very late last night.'

'Go and tell him I want to see him immediately he has finished. It's very important.'

The girl glanced at her mistress with surprise. It was a long time since she had seen her look so happy.

'Is it – is it good news, Miss Isabelle?'

'The best, Gwennie, the very best. Go on quickly in case he goes out.'

A little later when Guy knocked and came in, she had already changed out of her morning gown and was wearing a warm travelling dress of fine wool in a rich mulberry colour.

'What's the excitement, Belle?' he asked, still a little bleary-eyed from a late and somewhat too convivial night. 'Has Boney invaded or have we won the war?'

'Better than that, much better. Read that,' and she held out the letter.

It was a rough sheet of paper torn from a notebook and obviously written in haste.

'My dearest wife,' Robert had written, 'We have been at odds for far too long. I knew it when I left you this morning and it seemed to me then that it had become unbearable. As you know I am obliged to spend a few days down on the coast where we first met. Come and join me there and we will put it all behind us. I am sure Guy will be happy to escort you and if there is any trouble at Whitehall, tell him I will settle it for him. Till this evening, my love.'

Guy was staring down at the paper in his hand. The writing was Robert's right enough even if hurried, the signature was his, the seal was the family crest, and yet something about it struck a false note though he couldn't put a finger on it.

'Are you sure, Isabelle, are you quite sure that this is from Robert?'

She turned to him. 'Of course it is. Who else would write to me like that? Don't you understand how it is with him? I do. His pride would not allow him to acknowledge his mistake to my face and so he writes like this. For once, just for once, he is willing to share with me that other part of his life and it feels miraculous. I know where he always stays – at the Salutation in Rye. You will come with me, won't you? You see what he writes.'

Her happiness, her joy were so apparent, he could not spoil it for her. Surely the very fact that he was to go with her meant that no harm could possibly come of it.

'Very well, we'll go. I'll send word to Whitehall that I am sick and won't be in for a day or so and if the weather holds out we could be there by nightfall. We'll take the carriage. You make your preparations and I'll go and arrange it.'

He hurried away and she finished dressing while Gwennie put a few necessary articles in a small bag. She knew Marian was out. She was attending a lecture at the Royal Academy of Arts at Somerset House so she wrote a note and left it for her and by that time Guy was back. They would travel post from inn to inn. It was expensive but worth it. She thrust aside all thought of the weariness and bitter cold of a winter journey. Robert would be waiting for her at the end of it and that was all that mattered.

It proved a long and exhausting day. Every time they stopped to change horses, she burned with impatience, possessed with a fear that something terrible would happen, that he would believe she wasn't coming or he would be called away before she could reach him. To arrive and find him gone would be unbearable.

Tom, who had recently been promoted to act as second coachman, was driving as fast as the horses would permit but the day darkened early and a thin patchy mist had already gathered so dense in parts that he was obliged to slow up. But in spite of her impatience they made exceptionally good time and by early evening had already clattered through the tiny village of Lamberhurst. They were nearing the edge of the marshes by now and the mist thickened, spreading in places like a dank impenetrable blanket and reducing their speed to a snail's pace. Then quite suddenly Tom pulled up so sharply that they were both of them thrown forward.

'What the devil!' exclaimed Guy, climbing back on to the seat rubbing his bruised knees. He turned to his sister. 'Are you all right?'

'Yes. What is it? Why has Tom stopped suddenly like that?'

'I don't know.' Guy was trying to see through the smeared window. 'The mist seems to be pretty thick out there. I think there is some kind of a road block. Wait here inside, Isabelle, and I'll go and find out.'

He opened the door, a cloud of icy cold mist poured in and he jumped to the ground. Isabelle peered after him, seeing him appear and disappear as the fog eddied in thick clouds. She thought she could see some kind of a barrier and was almost sure there was another carriage beyond it with people moving around it. Suddenly she thought she knew what had happened. Robert would have been worried about her driving down through such a night and had come to meet her. She saw a tall figure detach himself from the group of people and move towards her. She climbed down from the carriage so filled with joy she did not stop to think.

'Robert,' she cried, 'Oh Robert, at last,' and ran towards him.

But it was not Robert's arms that closed around her. It was not Robert who looked down at her with that odd mocking smile. It was Lucien. Too late she realised her mistake.

She could see more clearly now. There were perhaps a dozen

men milling back and forth around the barrier. Tom and Guy were struggling violently in the hands of three or four rough fellows. She tried to free herself from Lucien but he only held her more tightly.

'I'm right sorry, my lady,' shouted Tom, 'but I never guessed what these ruffians be after . . .'

'Shut your mouth!' snarled one of them and struck him roughly across the face.

She saw the blood spurt from the bruised mouth and rage rose in her at the brutality.

'Where is Robert?' she said furiously, trying to fight herself free from Lucien. 'What have you done with Robert?'

'Never you mind. Your precious Robert will be here soon enough. Now, my lady, don't fight me or it will be the worse for you. Into the carriage with you.'

The barrier was thrust aside and, still struggling, she was dragged beyond it and pushed roughly into the waiting carriage. The next moment Guy was thrust in after her and the door was slammed on them.

'What does it mean?' she said helplessly. 'What do they want with us?'

'My guess is as good as yours,' gasped Guy, rubbing his bruised wrists.

'There's a dozen or more of them out there and we're pretty helpless. We'll have to play along till we find out what it is they are after. I think I know one or two of them,' he went on thoughtfully, 'they belong to a rival gang Jonty was always at odds with. It could be money they want. They know Robert has plenty. They may be demanding a heavy ransom.'

'Lucien may be using them but it is not money he wants,' she said with a fearful sinking of the heart. 'I think this means something far worse than that.'

It was only too true and Guy knew it. It was Robert they wanted and Isabelle was merely the bait that would bring him. He cursed himself for a fool in not suspecting a trap from the start. He had felt in his bones that there was something wrong about that letter. He should never have let himself be persuaded. He knew how desperately Isabelle had suffered from the rift between her and Robert but all the same he should not have let it influence him, and now what could they do? For the moment there was nothing. He put his hand on hers as the carriage jolted forward.

'We'll find a way out, I swear we will,' he whispered. 'And Robert is no fool. He'll never let himself fall into a trap like this.'

She leaned back against the soiled cushions, unable to forgive herself for her own gullibility in believing in the letter. She had longed too much to believe and in consequence had placed all three of them in unimaginable danger. The carriage smelled stale from the dirty straw on the floor and the unpleasant reek of former occupants. Behind them came their own carriage and she did not yet know that poor Tom had been left bruised and semi-conscious, trussed up in a ditch to recover as best he could and make his painful way back to London, far too late for any warning to bring help or rescue.

It was a bone-shaking journey over rough roads. They had no idea where they were being taken but there was a certain comfort in being together and in speculating over and over as to what part Lucien was playing in their abduction and what his ultimate intention could be.

At last the carriage lurched to a stop. The door was opened and rough hands reached in to pull them out. The night was so dark and the mist still so thick that for the moment they could see nothing, but Isabelle guessed that they must be near the sea. There was a taste of salt in the wind and the pebbles rolled under their feet.

'Where are we? Where are you taking us?' she demanded.

'Keep quiet, damn you!' snarled the man who had gripped her by the arm.

'Go on now. Move!' and he pushed her forward so that she stumbled and fell to her knees and was jerked up so roughly that she uttered a stifled cry.

'Leave her alone, can't you?' shouted Guy and was silenced by a thrust in the back that sent him sprawling.

'You'd best mind your manners, my young cockerel, if you want to help yourself and your sister.'

398

As Guy struggled to his feet he guessed that the man knew him and it confirmed him in his belief that Lucien was using some of the roughest elements among the smugglers to carry out his purpose.

They stumbled forward over the shingle till one of the black fishermen's huts loomed up in front of them. Inside it was pitch dark, reeking horribly of stale fish and bitterly cold. They were thrust through into a tiny back room no larger than a cupboard. Guy tried to keep his foot against the door but he was flung aside, fell to his knees and the door was slammed shut.

There was nothing in the room but a wooden bench. Isabelle had sunk down on it too utterly exhausted for the moment even to speak. Guy got painfully to his feet and began to prowl around their prison. There was a tiny unglazed window but so high and so small that it would have been totally impossible to climb through it. He examined every inch of the narrow space and then paused close to the door.

With an effort Isabelle pulled herself together. 'Guy, we've got to do something. We've got to get out of here.'

'Ssh,' he whispered and waved a hand to her to keep quiet. He was standing close to the door, his ear against one of the long cracks that ran between the rough wooden planks. 'They're talking in there. I can hear a little, not much, but it might give us a clue.'

Breathlessly she joined him at the door. The voices rose and fell. There was obviously some kind of argument going on. They could only catch a word here and there and it was not easy to make sense of it.

'Henri Rivage,' muttered Guy, 'did you hear that, Belle? Can it be he who is behind this? They're saying something about Sauvigny. Do you think that it is there they are taking us?'

'But why, why, Guy? It doesn't make sense. Sauvigny belongs to Rivage now. We learned that in Paris. We could never claim it back, never. We are no threat to him.'

'Quiet.' Guy silenced her with a gesture and drew closer to the door. 'They are talking about sailing tonight. I think it must be the captain of the ship. He says he won't go till the fog clears but Lucien is afraid of being discovered. He wants them to sail at first light. He is saying something about Robert. Oh God, if I could only hear more! Every now and then they move away and I can hear nothing. He is in a furious rage over something.'

'Robert left very early. He should be here. He could be sailing for France by now, I'm sure that is what he planned,' said Isabelle in quiet despair. 'He will know nothing of what has happened here. It could be days before anyone misses us.'

'I tell you one thing, it is obvious Lucien wanted us all together but Robert has somehow eluded him. How, Isabelle, how and where is he? That letter was a trick to get you here with him and it has failed.' He paused and then moved to the door again. 'I think they are going.' He shook the door violently but it wouldn't budge. 'Damnation, they must have bolted it.'

Outside the voices died away. There was a crunch of the shingle underfoot. Lucien and his bully boys must have gone away for the moment.

'Well, that's that. It seems we're stuck here for the time being and I'm dashed hungry,' said Guy with a valiant attempt at cheerfulness. 'I wish we had thought to bring some provisions with us.'

'Oh Guy, food is the last thing I'm thinking of,' said Isabelle.

'I had been looking forward to one of those delicious meals Mr Lambe conjures up at the Salutation and all we've got is the stink of rotten fish,' went on Guy ruefully. He put his arm around his sister's shoulders. 'Don't lose heart, old girl, we'll get out of this somehow, I swear we will.'

Huddled together for warmth, hungry and exhausted, they waited, the hours passing agonizingly slowly until suddenly with relief they heard the sound of feet coming towards the hut. There were voices and then the door was opened. They stumbled out into the icy chill of early dawn. A wind had come up in the night and had blown away most of the fog. It was barely light but they could see the shadowy figure of Lucien wrapped in a long dark cloak. There was no sign of the gang who had held them up the previous night and the two men with him were seamen by their looks, wearing heavy boots, reefer jackets

400

and stocking caps. One of them they guessed was the boat's captain.

'I'm sorry you have been obliged to pass such an uncomfortable night,' muttered Lucien. 'It will be better now.'

It was obvious that he was uneasy but he came purposefully towards Isabelle and she shrank away from him.

'Don't touch me. Where are you taking us?'

'To Sauvigny, where else? You're going home, and your brother with you. Isn't that what you've always wanted?'

There was a chilling note in his voice and here on these beaches not so far from where once had meant so much to her, she wondered how she could have ever believed herself in love with him.

Guy was desperately trying to assess the situation and the possibility of making a breakaway. He could not hope to defeat all three of them but there might be a fighting chance. If he leaped at one of them, caused confusion, it might just give Isabelle an opportunity to escape. He could see now that they were not entirely isolated. There were other huts at some little distance, boats were drawn up above the sea line. Here and there light shone like a small star. There were other people not exactly within call but she could run to one of those huts, hammer on the door, cry out for help. It was a slim chance but worth taking. The two seamen had moved away, obviously anxious to be gone.

All this had gone through his head in the space of a few seconds. He suddenly shouted, 'You're not going to get away with this, you know. I'll not allow it,' and he launched himself at Lucien with such force that, taken by surprise, the Frenchman toppled backwards with Guy on top of him.

'Run, Isabelle, run,' he gasped out. 'Run now!'

Lucien had recovered his breath and was trying to get a footing on the shifting pebbles. But Guy was fighting fit and had lately been indulging in sparring battles with the reigning champion of the ring. In a peculiar sort of way he was enjoying himself, taking out on Lucien all the frustrations of the last few months.

Isabelle hesitated, torn between anxiety for her brother and

401

the necessity of getting away. The two seamen had turned back and were making towards her. She could see the distant huts and began to run towards them, her thin kid boots slipping and stumbling on the shifting shingle. She could hear one of the men pounding after her and redoubled her pace.

A light suddenly flared in one of the huts and she ran on breathlessly until she heard the shot. It pulled her up with shock. What had happened? The pistol Guy had brought with him had been left behind in the carriage. Anxiety for her brother knifed through her. She tripped on the hidden stump of the old breakwater and fell sprawling. The man coming behind her pulled her to her feet. She tried to free herself but it was useless. He dragged her back to where Guy was lying in a huddled heap. There seemed to be blood everywhere. She fell on her knees beside him.

Lucien was staring down at him while the other man, the ship's captain, thrust the still smoking pistol back into his belt.

'We'd best hurry,' he said to Lucien. 'The tide's on the ebb and it don't wait for no one.'

'What about him?' said Lucien in a choked voice.

'Leave him. He's a dead 'un and I'm not having no dead 'un on my ship. There's too much bad luck about this business already.'

Isabelle had tried to raise Guy a little. His head lolled back helplessly against her.

'You can't leave him,' she pleaded, 'you can't. He may not be dead.'

'He's a goner all right, lady, and I've seen plenty in my time.'

He took her by the arm and pulled her up. She struggled wildly but Lucien, galvanised into action, had seized her other arm.

'No time,' he said, 'no time if we are to get away.'

'Best shift him further down the beach,' said the captain callously. 'When the tide comes up it'll put paid to him all right.'

His mate took Guy by the shoulders and began to drag him across the shingle towards the sea.

'No, no, you can't leave him like that!' she screamed and Lucien clapped a hand over her mouth stifling her cries.

She was half dragged, half carried between Lucien and the captain down to where the boat waited. She was thrust into it, the men leaping in after her. She stood staring at the bare desolate shore with a numbed despair. It was the last sight she had of her brother, a crumpled heap with the sea creeping inexorably nearer as the powerful oars carried her across the sullen water to the waiting schooner.

20

Robert came back to Arlington Street later that same evening and Marian looked up at him in surprise as he entered the drawing room.

'I thought you went down to Kent early this morning.'

'I intended to do just that but I had to call in at Whitehall and was detained there all day. I shall be leaving tomorrow.'

Marian frowned. 'But I don't understand. Isabelle has gone to meet you there.'

'Isabelle has? But why should she do that?'

'I was out this morning attending a lecture and when I came back I found she had left a note for me saying you had sent a message asking her to meet you down there at the Salutation Inn and possibly stay for a few days.'

'I never wrote such a note. It would be most unsuitable in any case. Did she show it to you?'

'No, as I've said. I wasn't there. But Gwennie knows about it. She packed a bag for her.'

'Ask her to come here, will you?'

'Yes, of course. I'll ring for Hawke.'

Robert was pacing restlessly up and down when Gwennie came in looking a little apprehensive.

'You wanted to see me, my lord?'

'Yes, Gwennie. Did your mistress receive a letter this morning?'

'Yes, sir, a letter she believed came from you. It was handed in by special messenger and Mr Hawke told me to take it up to her.' She looked bewildered, wondering what had gone wrong. What was he doing here when Miss Isabelle had gone to meet him? 'She was very happy about it,' she went on, and sent me at once for Master Guy. She wanted him to go with her.'

404

'I see. Did you read the letter, Gwennie?'

'Not then I didn't.' The girl hesitated and then went on. 'In her hurry Miss Isabelle forgot to take it with her. She left it on the dressing table . . .'

'And you read it?'

'I didn't mean to . . . I'm sorry if . . .'

'Never mind that. It's of no consequence. Have you still got it?'

'Oh yes, sir. I put it in one of her drawers.'

'Fetch it for me, will you?'

'What can all this mean?' asked Marian when the girl hurried away.

'I don't know yet.'

Then Gwennie was back holding out the note. 'I hope I didn't do wrong, sir.'

'No, no, Gwennie, you were quite right to do what you did. That will be all now.'

'Thank you, sir.'

She looked from one to the other, sensing that something was very much amiss, then she bobbed a curtsey and went out.

Robert was staring down at the hastily written note that he had to admit had a certain authenticity.

'I never wrote this,' he said slowly.

'Then who did?'

'I don't know, Marian, and that's what troubles me. This looks like some sort of trick to get Isabelle down there and I am beginning to wonder if she will ever have reached the Salutation. But why? For what purpose?'

'She couldn't have run off to that wretched Lucien de Vosges, could she?' said Marian tentatively, 'and this writing of the note simply some sort of deception?'

'No,' said Robert emphatically, 'I don't believe that, I won't believe it.'

He looked again at the letter in his hand trying to fathom the purpose behind it. 'It seems to me that someone believed I was travelling down into Kent today and they couldn't have been aware that I would be delayed because I didn't know myself. Whoever wrote this letter wanted us to be there together.'

Could it be a plot devised by de Vosges hoping to avenge

himself for the humiliation he had suffered as a result of that abortive duel? But if so, why include Guy in it? The boy had played no part in that sorry business.

'They took the second carriage and Tom was driving,' went on Marian. 'Ian told me. He was annoyed with Tom because he did not ask permission.'

'He must still be down there in Kent. There has been no time for him to return. I don't know yet what is behind this but one thing is certain, I must go after them,' went on Robert with decision. 'And as soon as possible.'

'But isn't that exactly what they want? You will be playing into their hands.'

'I can look after myself.'

'Let her go,' exclaimed Marian who still nursed a smouldering anger against her sister-in-law. 'Haven't you suffered enough on her behalf?'

'She is my wife, Marian, and no one, no one at all, is going to take her away from me, no matter who it is or whether she is willing or unwilling.'

There was a note of steel in his voice and for a moment Marian glimpsed that side of him that lay beneath the quiet manner, the side that was so seldom shown to her and had carried him through so many dangerous situations.

'But you still can't go now,' she argued. 'It's far too late and an abominable night. You must leave it till morning.'

It was true enough. Outside there was a blanketing fog and with the best will in the world he could not hope to get very far. Better to leave at first light but he fretted through the hours of waiting, lying on his bed half dressed, his mind wearily searching through one possible explanation after another. Was Marian right and was he a fool to deny it? Was Isabelle in the plot or was she the innocent victim? He had begun to realise that this was far more than a mere mischievous attempt on Lucien's part to humiliate him and Isabelle. This was part of something wider, linked with the threat that had hung over him in France during his last mission. He had felt the weight of it then and now felt it again deep within him. Dundas had warned him, hadn't he: he had outwitted them then and must outwit them again. But if Lucien had abducted Isabelle and her brother, then he and those who commanded him had a powerful threat to hold over his head and he would have to pursue his purpose with extreme caution.

The house was still wrapped in sleep when he got up, dressed warmly and inconspicuously and went down to the stables. He would take one of his best horses and ride post. He was familiar with the road and the posting houses, and prepared to ride fast. With money it was always possible to obtain good service. He was armed with a pair of pistols ready primed in the saddle holsters. His journey took him through heath and woodland where robbers or worse might lurk waiting for the unwary traveller. Ian came out as he was saddling up and wanted to go with him but he refused. He would not involve anyone else in what looked like being a dangerous and difficult enterprise.

The night wind had blown away most of the fog but once out of the city there were still pockets of dank mist and it was bitingly cold, the only advantage being that it kept traffic off the roads and he made good progress. By early afternoon he had passed through Pembury and stopped at a well known hostelry where he could be certain of picking up a good mount for the rest of his journey. He was taking a hasty glass of wine with a bite of bread and cheese in the inn yard when the London bound coach rolled in and passengers began to climb out to stretch their legs and look for welcome refreshment. One of them, a boy in a country frieze jacket and a round hat clamped down over his ears, kept staring at him.

He turned away as the ostler brought out his horse.

'All saddled and ready to go, my lord.'

'Thank you.'

He took the reins, dropped a coin in the outstretched hand and was about to swing himself into the saddle when he felt someone pluck at his cloak.

'Excuse me, sir,' said the country lad a little nervously, 'excuse me but be you Lord Kilgour?'

Robert frowned. 'Yes, I am. What do you want with me?'

The boy gave him a wide grin. 'Thought as how I'd seen you

407

afore, my lord, up at High Willows a year or so gone. I have a letter for you from his reverence.'

'A letter?'

'Aye, from Mr Holland it is. I work in his garden, see, and he give it to me and tell me to take the coach and get meself to London as quick as I could and find you and right glad I am to see you here since I en't never been to London and . . .'

'What does Mr Holland want with me?' said Robert impatiently.

The boy hunted through a deep pocket and brought out a folded and sealed sheet somewhat dog-eared and soiled.

'It's all on account of that young gentleman what used to live up there at High Willows and then went off to London a while ago. He were brought to the vicarage early this morning, in a proper bad way he were, bleedin' like a stuck pig. Miss Holland, she gave a great screech thinkin' him gone already, but then she sends me off for doctor and Mr Holland he sits down and writes this letter . . .'

During this lengthy rigmarole Robert had torn open the letter and run his eye through it.

He cut the boy short. 'You can thank heaven for the lucky chance that brought us together, lad. It'll have saved you a long trip.'

He groped in his pocket, dropped something in the boy's hand, then vaulted into the saddle and was off, leaving the lad with his mouth open and his story only half done.

Riding as fast as his horse could carry him, Robert pondered over what this further information meant. Guy must have put up a good fight and was maybe left for dead but where had they taken Isabelle? Pray God the boy was not too far gone to tell him what had happened. He was very sure that he himself could be in danger. He loosened the pistols in their holsters and kept a sharp lookout but no one intercepted him on the lonely bypath he had taken deliberately and he came up to the vicarage by late evening. It was a dark night. The mist had been blown away and it had turned to rain. He dismounted, tethered his horse to the gatepost and knocked urgently at the door.

Harriet Holland opened it, stared at him for a moment and then almost fell into his arms in relief.

'We didn't hope to see you yet.' The words came tumbling out. 'How did you manage to reach us so soon? Joe only left by the morning coach.'

'By great good fortune we met half way and he gave me your brother's letter. Could someone see to my horse?'

'Of course. Gilbert,' she called, 'take Mr Armitage's horse to the stable and then come back quickly.'

Mr Holland, looking disturbed and anxious, hurried outside and Harriet drew Robert into the parlour.

'How is Guy', he asked. 'He's not . . .?'

'He's not dead though the Lord knows he's in a very poor way. All he has kept on saying over and over was that we must find you and warn you. He seems to believe that you are in the greatest danger.' She looked at him anxiously. 'We did what we thought was right but he could only tell us very little. What is it? What has happened?'

'I'll tell you all I know later but first I must speak to him. May I go to him now?'

'You had better know how he comes to be here first. The doctor has given him a sedative and he seems to be quieter now, but I don't know, I really don't know . . .' she broke off shaking her head doubtfully. She pulled out a handkerchief and turned away her head. 'Do forgive me for being so foolish but it has been very disturbing.'

'Of course it has. I do understand, believe me. Take your time.'

'No, I'm all right now,' she went on resolutely, 'and you'll be wanting to know all we can tell you. It appears that he tried to rescue his sister from the villains who had captured them but he was fighting more than one. He must have stood very little chance of succeeding. One of them shot him, then he must have been hit on the head and lost consciousness. When he came round they had gone and he was lying on the shore with the tide already creeping up around him. It's a mercy he didn't drown. He tried to shift himself higher up the beach but the effort was too much and he fainted again. The next thing he

409

knew, one of the fishermen who live on that stretch of the coast was bending over him. All the boy could think of was my brother and he repeated the name over and over again. Mr Holland is well known among the fisher folk, the poorest of the families often come here for food and clothes when they are destitute, so he was put on the cart they use for fish and brought here. It was soon after six o'clock and I was just out of bed. He was in a shocking state. I thought at first he was dead already but we got him into bed and did what we could. Then I sent Joe for the doctor.'

'What does he say about Guy?'

'He won't commit himself. The wound is in his thigh and he would have died from loss of blood if he'd not been picked up. He has other injuries too, cracked ribs and a savage blow to the head. He had been most brutally treated. They must have believed him very close to death.'

'And abandoned him without a second thought.' Robert was shaken by a gust of anger. By God, he'd make Lucien pay for that if he could. 'It's desperately important that I speak with him,' he went on. 'Is it possible, do you think?'

'I don't know. You had better come with me.'

She led him upstairs to the bedroom where Guy was lying, his face so drawn and pale under the bandages that he might have been dead already.

'I'll leave you with him,' she whispered. 'I must see that Gilbert has looked after your horse. He has been very distressed by all this.'

She went out closing the door and Robert sat down by the bed and took the boy's hand in his.

'Can you hear me, Guy?' he said gently. 'It's Robert.'

After a moment the boy's eyes flickered open. He stared blankly for a little, then recognition came back into his face. He clutched at the hand that held his.

'Robert,' he murmured, 'thank God you've come. You must take the greatest care. It's you they want. They will be watching out for you.'

'Yes, yes,' said Robert soothingly, 'I am aware of that and of

410

how you were picked up on the shore. Can you tell me a little more about when and where it happened to you and Isabelle?'

Slowly and with long gaps in between, Guy told him how he and Isabelle had been held up on the road and then taken to the hut on the sea coast.

'Lucien was there and I recognised some of the other men. They belong to a cut-throat gang who'd murder if they were paid enough. Jonty was always at war with them.'

'Did you get any idea of what their purpose was?'

'I don't think Lucien guessed that I could hear a little of what they were arguing about through the cracks of the door,' went on Guy, trying to gather strength. 'I know that Henri Rivage is at the back of this in some way – Dr Rivage was the man who . . .'

'Who betrayed you and your father. I have guessed that. I know too that Rivage is the power behind Fouché's secret police, and that Sauvigny now belongs to him.'

'I believe that is where they will have taken Isabelle and where they would take you too if they could, but I still don't know why. What threat can Isabelle and I be to Dr Rivage now? He has everything that once would have been ours. Lucien was furiously angry that you had not come as he expected. They had been lying in wait for you all day.'

'Fortunately for me I was detained.'

'I did try to save Isabelle . . . I did try . . .' His voice died away and Robert put a hand on his comfortingly.

'I know. Those devils left you to die. It's a mercy that you were found and brought here.'

'You will go after Isabelle,' said Guy urgently. 'I know there has been some kind of rift between you but she was so happy when she believed you had sent for her to join you.'

'Don't be afraid. Isabelle is my wife and I swear I'll find a way to get her back,' said Robert grimly. 'There is still one more thing. I know that Sauvigny is in the valley of the Loire but can you give me a few more details as to where it lies?'

'I will try. It is a mile or so north of Angers. That was our nearest town.' Guy was tiring but he tried to concentrate on giving Robert a few pointers from his childhood memories. 'You

411

must take care,' he went on feverishly. 'Rivage is the devil incarnate. I was only a child when we were driven out of France but I remember how even then I feared and hated him.'

'Don't worry. I've not spent all those months in France over the last few years without learning a trick or two. What you must do is concentrate on making a good recovery. Isabelle will believe you dead and will be greatly distressed. When I see her, I want to give her the good news.'

'All I hoped was to stay alive long enough to tell you what had happened.'

'And that's what you have done and I'm grateful. Do everything that Miss Holland tells you. She is a miracle worker. She will help you to recover if anybody will.'

Guy had fallen against his pillows looking so white and spent that Robert feared for him and prayed that his youth and the care he would be given would help his recovery. He pressed his hand warmly and went down to where the Hollands were waiting for him.

'This is a wicked, evil business,' quavered Mr Holland. 'It was nothing short of a miracle that saved the boy from a terrible death. To murder the innocent in such a way – what is our world coming to?'

'Gilbert, my dear,' said his sister, putting her hand comfortingly on his arm, 'bring out the brandy. I'm sure Mr Armitage can do with it after his exhausting ride and so could you and I. Will you take supper with us, sir?'

'I'd be grateful for the brandy but I mustn't stay longer. I must find out who is responsible for the abduction of my wife and has tried to kill her brother.'

'Does it mean that you must venture into France?'

'I fear I must and there is something I would ask of both of you. This is not a local affair. I think you realise that. It has deeper implications. Say nothing of this to anyone only that Guy has been attacked by thieves and robbed on his way here. It is common enough, God knows. Can I rely on you absolutely?'

'To the last ditch,' said Harriet stoutly as she handed him the brandy, 'and that goes for both of us, doesn't it, Gilbert?'

'There is one other thing,' went on Robert a little hesitantly, not wishing to hurt their pride. 'You will be put to considerable expense in caring for Guy. You must allow me to tide you over.'

'No, no, never, not a penny!' Mr Holland put up a hand in a gesture of refusal. 'I'd be a poor minister of God if I couldn't give help to a fellow creature in distress. God willing, we will nurse him back to health. When I think of what they may be doing to that lovely innocent child Isabelle, my blood boils. Would that I could go with you. It would give me the greatest pleasure to smite down the evil doers, but alas, I am afraid it is you who will have to bear the burden.'

Robert smiled a little at Mr Holland's valiant spirit. 'You may be very sure I shall do my utmost. Pray that I succeed.'

'You may be quite certain of that. Our good wishes and our prayers will go with you all the way.'

Harriet Holland again urged him to stay at least for a little to rest and eat, but he was obsessed with the need for haste. Every hour that passed Isabelle was being taken further and further away from him. That she had gone willingly with Lucien, that she had been a party to a scheme betraying him into their hands, he could not believe and in any case all the evidence was against it. He knew that for some years now he had been a thorn in the side of French intelligence and now it would seem that to capture and destroy him would not only feed Lucien's revenge but serve his French paymasters. As he made his way through the wet dark night to the Salutation Inn he was aware of a foreboding of evil as if some corroding hatred was striking out in some way to destroy them both.

For some years now Mr Lambe had grown accustomed to his comings and goings and had been well paid for his discretion and his services. He sent up to Robert's room a quickly prepared meal with a pot of strong coffee and a measure of brandy, and was not at all surprised to see a completely different person emerge inconspicuously dressed in dark grey homespun with a tightly fitting unfashionable coat, a thick frieze cloak and a low-crowned hat, every inch the respectable, comfortably off trades-man going about his lawful business. He supplied him with a

413

fresh horse and saw him ride off in the direction of Rye Harbour. A rising wind blew around him, flapping the painted sign above his head. If his visitor was embarking on a trip to France, then he was likely to have a very rough passage.

Between Rye Harbour and Camber Castle, built by Henry VIII against another French invasion and now only a bird-haunted ruin, there lay a stretch of coast almost completely uninhabited. It was a bleak storm-driven spot, even in summer haunted by smugglers and by men who for some reason sought solitude, the only sounds the incessant pounding of the sea and the cries of innumerable seabirds.

It was midnight by the time Robert reached one of the black huts lying at some distance from the others and different only in that it was in excellent order and the fishing gear, piles of logs and other paraphernalia were neatly stacked in an adjoining shed instead of lying in an untidy muddle.

Robert tethered his horse to the iron hook in the doorpost and knocked at the door. It was opened almost immediately and he slid inside.

A lantern on the rough wooden table beside a large book barely lit the white walls, a few stools, a pallet bed in one corner with neatly folded blankets and a man who stood, dark and still, outside the circle of light.

'I guessed ye'd be here soon as I sent that last report,' he said, 'though it's quicker than I expected.'

'I want your help, Jack,' said Robert, 'now, tonight, if it's humanly possible.'

'If it's crossin' the water, you're thinkin' of, then it's a hard night ye'll have of it. Will you be wantin' food? You're welcome to the little I have.'

'Thank you but I've eaten already.'

'Sit ye down then.'

He came into the light. Lean and dark, Jack Darrow could have been any age between forty and fifty, a strange man and a secret one. He was not a native of these parts and no one knew where he had sprung from, an educated man in that he could read and write, could express himself intelligently and had a keen mind. Robert had recruited him almost accidentally some

414

years before and he had proved a useful ally, working with him off and on ever since.

He was indifferent to money and accepted the small sums given to him by a grudging government simply because they helped him to keep his rough dwelling in order and fed him when the heavy winter storms made it impossible for him to bring in the harvest of the sea. In his spare time he indulged his passion for birds and the only thing he had ever asked from Robert was a book which would give him the names and habits of the varied species that surrounded him.

He leaned across the table. 'The wind has cleared the fog but there will be a gale before morning. What part of the coast will ye be makin' for?'

'That's what we must discuss.' Robert dropped on to one of the stools and glanced at the book open at a page of coloured drawings. 'Still busy with the birds, I see.'

'Aye, it's a wonder to see how many different kinds turn up on this coast. Some of them wild and shy but others who come at my call and eat from my hand.'

Robert looked for a moment at the craggy features lit by a rare smile.

'Was it you who rescued the boy and took him to Mr Holland?'

'Aye, it was. I had heard that the gang who occasionally work along this line of the coast were unusually flush with gold, money like that is hard to come by in these times, so I kept watch for a time. Last night I was t'other side of Rye or I might have seen more. It was early this morning when I stumbled over him. He was near gone. Is he one of your men?'

'My wife's brother,' said Robert shortly, 'and thanks to you, there is a hope he may recover.'

'And your wife? Was she with him?'

'The Frenchman who has devised this ploy has taken her with him.'

'Willingly?'

'What makes you say that?'

The other man shrugged his shoulders.

It would seem that thanks to the spite of Aunt Augusta, the

scandalous story had spread even into this remote spot. He felt humiliated. There was something faintly ludicrous about the deceived husband running after his unfaithful wife.

'Willingly or not. I do not intend to be robbed of what is my own,' he said with a repressed anger that surprised the man watching him. 'In any case I wouldn't leave a dog in their hands. Now can we get down to ways and means. Is that boat of yours in good shape for a long sea trip?'

'Good enough. I make sure of that. Where were you thinkin' of?'

They bent together over the chart worn and stained with sea water on which winds and currents had been marked from Jack's own observations.

'Could we reach St Malo by tomorrow do you think?'

'That's askin' a great deal. It's a rough journey if the winds are strong and the Channel can be as contrary as a woman. Wouldn't Boulogne or Dieppe serve your purpose just as well?'

'No. It means too long a journey overland and they could be watching for me.'

'To round the bluff beyond Cherbourg could put us into serious trouble. The sea around the Channel Islands is notorious for squalls.' A calloused finger traced along the line of the coast. 'Now along here beyond Le Havre there is a small cove I know well. We could slip in there and no one any the wiser.'

Robert's eye followed the pointing finger and he thought he could make his way through Normandy skirting the larger towns and move into the Loire valley to search out Sauvigny with the few details Guy had been able to give him. What he would do when he reached there depended on circumstances but he had one possibility which he could exploit. Normandy had been a centre of protest and rebellion and there was a group in Angers still active which perhaps he could use if necessary.

'When can we leave?' he asked.

'Certainly not before first light. The tide will be on the turn about six and we could sail out with it. After that we're in the hands of wind and weather. There will be risks.'

'To hell with risks. We've done it before.'

'Not quite so far and not in November,' said Jack drily. 'But if it must be, then we'll do it. Now what we need is a good stiffener.'

He brought out a squat stone bottle of smuggled brandy and poured a measure for both of them.

Robert sipped it slowly, staring into the red embers of the fire and trying to control his impatience at the enforced delay.

'How will you return?'

Jack's deep voice broke into his thoughts and he looked up. 'I don't know yet. There are too many unanswered questions.'

'For what it is worth, there is a place further along that coast where I have a point of call. Ask for me at *Le Chat Noir* if necessity drives.'

'Thank you but I'm not willing to put you into danger from the French secret police.'

Jack shrugged his shoulders. 'What else are friends for?'

There was the faintest streak of lemon on the horizon when they went down to the shore and to the small boat tucked away in its mooring place. They were joined by Ben, a hefty solid lad in his twenties whose brain had stopped growing when he was ten years old, but who had an uncanny skill in handling boats and had often accompanied Jack on his fishing expeditions. With Robert, who had on occasions been forced to lend a hand and was not unfamiliar with the sea, they set out on their risky venture across the deceptively calm grey waters of the Channel on that bleak November morning.

The journey was too fraught with danger to leave Robert any time to do more than jump to obey orders and keep the boat heading in the right direction. Out in mid Channel they were caught by the threatened gale. Once they were blown almost completely off course and it took several hours for Jack to tack skilfully back towards the coast of France. Once the sea came washing overboard and Robert was thankful for the ancient oilskins which Ben produced from the hold reeking of oil and stale fish. It took them nearly twenty-four hours and it was still dark when at last they drew into calmer waters and followed the curving line of the shore till they could creep into the cove for which Jack had been steadily making.

It was a lonely spot without any kind of habitation. A shingle

417

beach was bordered by scrubby heathland. There was no rain but the wind was cold and Robert was now faced with a long tramp to the nearest sizeable place where he could hire or purchase a horse for the rest of his journey to Angers, a trip which could take at the very least two days and possibly longer. Jack would have pushed away the money that Robert had taken out of an inner pocket but he thrust it into his hands.

'Take it. You've earned it and more.'

'Good luck, my friend,' said Jack gruffly. 'I'm afraid you're going to need it. A couple of miles further along this coast is a village of sorts, fishermen mostly, and the dive I spoke of, *Le Chat Noir*. The woman who keeps it knows me well. She calls herself Madame Grandnez and I did her a favour once. Ask for me there and it may serve your need. I will come back how and when I can, weather permitting.'

'I'm grateful,' said Robert, 'and I won't forget.'

Jack clapped him on the shoulder and Ben gave him a huge grin and a bone-shaking grip of the hand and the two seamen watched him trudge away into the first faint light of the dawn before turning back to make the boat secure and prepare to wait till the turn of the tide would help carry them back to England.

21

The Château de Sauvigny must once have been beautiful, thought Robert, standing at the edge of a little wood and gazing at it across the ruined gardens. Even now, its scars mercifully hidden by the night, it had a dreamlike charm in the rising moonlight. The weather had changed. It was icily cold but dry with a smell of frost and the sky was clear. How strange that Henri Rivage who had destroyed his friend, had sought to ruin his children and had schemed to gain possession of his estates, had never used his undoubted wealth and power to restore it to its former glory.

'He crouches there like some monstrous spider weaving a web of violence and murder,' Jean Leroy had told him somewhat fancifully. 'The peasants who live around Sauvigny regard him with a mixture of dislike and superstitious fear chiefly, I think, because they never actually see him. He comes and goes always in a closed carriage.'

'Is Rivage there now?'

'I wouldn't be sure but I doubt it.'

It had taken Robert three days of hard riding to reach Angers but there he had been lucky. Jean Leroy, the son of an old servant of his grandmother's family, was still living in the town. As a boy he had seen his father and his elder sister brutally butchered, he had been forced into the army of the Revolution and discharged by a bullet wound that had lamed him for life. He eked out a frugal existence as assistant to an apothecary and spent his spare time plotting against Bonaparte, the hero who had turned into a tyrant. He had proved one of Robert's most trusted colleagues.

'When Rivage is there,' he went on, 'he lives in a couple of

419

rooms with a few servants but he does have guards. You must be very careful, Maurice.'

Leroy knew perfectly well who Robert really was but for the sake of caution always used his alias of Maurice Dupont.

'Has there been anything happening at the château in the last few days, Jean?'

'A coach drove up late at night the day before yesterday but whom it contained I cannot tell you, the blinds were drawn. What goes on there is kept a close secret. Neither the servants nor the guards mix with the peasants.'

'Is it possible to get close to the house?'

'There is a break in the rear wall. The villagers use it regularly, setting snares for rabbits in the woods and poaching game when Rivage is not there, and who can blame them? You'll need to use extreme caution. I understand the guards patrol regularly.'

He had obeyed Leroy's instructions scrupulously and now stood watching the house for some time. Only one window was lit, a yellow glow in the dark night, but that probably only meant that the other windows were shuttered against the cold. He edged his way carefully around the shrubberies. Grass that must once have been shaved to velvet had only been roughly scythed, roses had grown into a tangled mass that stretched out long, spiky arms to claw at him as he slid past them. Two huge stone urns flanking the shallow steps in front of the long windows were cracked and split, a headless Cupid fallen from its plinth nearly tripped him up and a naked goddess set up at the end of the terrace was pitted with bullet marks and must have been used for target practice.

As he grew closer he could see that the further wing of the château had been gutted by fire. Blackened stone had caved in. It lay open to the sky and must have happened in the first violent assault. Now creeping plants and weeds climbed over the fallen stone but the part of the house where he was standing was still in good order, though ivy clambered up the walls and hung in great swathes over the windows. He looked around him aware of a kind of brooding stillness, a silence that was almost eerie, and yet he knew that somewhere behind those shuttered windows were Lucien and Isabelle and very possibly Rivage

420

himself. What were they doing to her? An icy touch of frost made him shiver.

The lighted window was immediately above where he was standing and beckoned irresistibly. The climb presented no difficulties to a man who had scaled Scottish peaks as a boy. Half hidden by the trailing clusters of the creeper, he pulled himself up till he could lodge his booted feet securely on the carved stone moulding above the ground floor windows. Then he raised his head cautiously above the sill. Now he could see into the room. The light dazzled his eyes for a moment, then it took shape. It must have been pretty once, with satin striped wallpaper and velvet hangings. Now it was sadly faded and only sparsely furnished. Against one wall he saw the sofa and a woman lying on it, her face hidden. He saw the tangle of dark hair, the familiar mulberry coloured gown. Then Isabelle sat up suddenly and he saw the fear and loathing on her face as he had seen it once before on the child Cécile as the door opened and Lucien came into the room. He could see and yet he could hear nothing. It was like watching a play in dumb show.

Isabelle had pressed herself back against the rounded end of the day bed as Lucien came and sat beside her. He was talking earnestly and furiously almost into her face and Robert would have dearly liked to hear what he was saying. When she did not respond, he took her by the shoulders, shaking her, pulling her towards him but she turned her face away spitting out words that must have riled him to the quick because he thrust her away from him so brutally that she fell forward bruisingly on to her knees. Robert was filled with an almost irresistible desire to smash the glass, leap into the room and take her away there and then. No matter what she had said or done, no matter how much she may have betrayed his trust, he knew that he loved her still, he wanted her passionately and would never let her go. It might be weakness, it might be folly, but he could not thrust it away from him and to see her in Lucien's power was very nearly intolerable and yet to break in at this stage would be madness. There were servants, there were guards. In the space of a few seconds he could be overpowered and become as much

421

a prisoner as she was, and that would not help either of them. He was going to need cunning and resource, not a wild romantic gesture that could lead nowhere. So he hung on though his hands were cramped by the cold and his body stiffened with the strain he was putting on it.

Lucien had risen to his feet. He was lifting Isabelle up, pleading with her, but she turned to him with a swift gesture of rejection and struck him across the face. For an instant they stood glaring at one another, then he turned and strode out of the room slamming the door behind him. Isabelle stared after him for a moment before before dropping on to the sofa again, burying her face in her hands.

It could have been a lover's quarrel, it was possible, but Robert refused to allow himself even to think such a thing. He debated what he should do. Should he draw her attention, let her know that he was there? It was a heaven sent opportunity if only he could be sure of Isabelle. He was putting his safety, his very life in her hands. She had only to cry out and he would be lost and yet . . . everything was quiet again, no sound of guards or dogs, only the rustle of night creatures in the overgrown garden, only the occasional muted cry of a bird. He decided to risk it. He tapped on the window pane and waited. She raised her head but did not stir. He tapped again louder this time. She looked wildly around the room and then crossed to the window, trying to see through the misted glass. She was tugging at the stiff bolts and with a jerk opened the casement a few inches. He pulled himself up a little higher, whispering her name. For an instant she stood motionless, unbelieving, doubting her own eyes.

'Robert, she breathed, 'it can't be . . . Robert?'

Her fingers were reaching out touching his face. 'Robert, you shouldn't have come. It is you they are waiting for. Oh God,if they should see you now . . .'

'Ssh!' he said, 'listen to me. There isn't much time. Is Rivage in the château?'

'No, but he is expected soon.'

'Good.' He lifted a hand to touch hers and try to convey the urgency to her. 'I will be coming back. Tomorrow night. I have friends who will help. I have a plan. Act naturally, do what they say. I'm going to get you out of here. You must trust me.'

In her anxiety for him she was scarcely listening. 'Hurry, hurry,' she said desperately. 'They have guards. Lucien told me.'

'How often do they patrol at night?'

'About ten and again at midnight. They keep me prisoner in this room but I see them go by. They will be coming soon. They have dogs, I've heard them.'

'Did that brute hurt you?'

'A little. It doesn't matter. I was trying to make him believe that you would not come, that you were angry with me . . . I don't know . . . I thought if I told him that, then they might give up. I didn't think . . . Oh go, please go. They killed Guy, they will kill you too.'

'Guy is not dead.'

'Not dead?' she caught her breath.

'No. He told me what had happened. Did you imagine for one moment that I would leave you here in their hands? Now listen, it is important. Make sure the window opens easily. Try it tonight because this is the way we shall go. You understand?'

'Oh yes, yes,' she breathed. 'But take care, please, please take care.'

Their fingers touched, for a moment were entwined. She felt the pressure, then he had withdrawn his hand, was lowering himself down very gently. He heard her close the window above his head and latch it. He dropped on to the sodden earth amidst a tangle of leaves and ragged plants and stood for a moment listening. Somewhere inside the house a door slammed, there was a sound of voices, a laugh and then silence again. He froze for the space of several minutes but there was no tramp of feet, no baying of dogs. He began to creep along the wall hidden by the overgrown shrubbery and made his way silently towards the wood and escape. God knows he had only a few hours in which to make a plan and whatever he did must be done alone and quickly. He could not involve Jean Leroy in a plot that could well condemn him to death as well as himself.

Isabelle stood for a moment, her face pressed against the cold

423

glass, striving to see the tall shadow as it slipped away into the dark. She came back into the room dizzy with hope, still hardly able to believe, deeply thankful that Guy still lived. At least they had not succeeded in that. A burden of guilt seemed to lift away from her, and Robert had come, her heart sang at the thought even though she was filled with fear for him. He had come, he loved her still. She pressed her hands against her cheeks. Whatever happened she would have that and she hugged the knowledge to herself as a guard against whatever further humiliation and shame they inflicted on her.

'You cannot do it,' said Jean Leroy when Robert told him what he was planning. 'It is sheer madness. To snatch her away from under their very noses in this way, it is ridiculous. You will never succeed.'

'Sometimes the simplest plans work the best,' argued Robert. 'It is the devious plots that so often go wrong and now is the moment when Rivage is not there. I'm not involving you. All I would ask is that you buy me two good horses and bring them to that back entrance to the woods after ten and before midnight. You need not remain there where you could be in danger of dicovery. Simply tether them securely and then go.'

'Do you think I'm a coward to run at the first smell of danger?' said Leroy stubbornly. 'I shall stay and see you safely on your way. But there are other problems. You will need papers for Madame, your wife. We live in a police state now with petty officials who examine credentials wherever you move and you will not always be able to avoid checkpoints. There will be search parties looking out for you. Rivage has a network of spies who pass the word from one to the other.'

'I am aware of that as you know and I realise the risk is doubled with two of us, but it can be done. It must be done. Can you provide the necessary papers?'

'I'll do my best but there is so little time. Fortunately some of those jumped-up jacks in office can scarcely read even their own name.'

So they set about their preparations and Robert fretted during

424

the hours of waiting, unaware that he had not entirely escaped notice.

Roget Dufour, who served as cook for the household at the château and as usual had drunk more than he should, had come out to relieve himself. He was taking a breath of the cool night air when he glimpsed the dark shadow beneath the lighted window before it slipped away through the shrubbery and smiled to himself. He had a very healthy respect for Dr Henri Rivage but none at all for the cocky young man who lorded it about the château as if he owned it. They all knew he had an eye for the young woman whom they had been holding prisoner for the last couple of days and were inclined to laugh about it. She wasn't too willing, judging by his hangdog look when he came from her room. Maybe she had another lover, thought Roget with a tipsy giggle, and decided to keep mum about it till the right moment came to take Monsieur Lucien down a peg or two.

And while Roget hugged his little secret to himself, Isabelle was finding the long, empty hours of the night very hard to bear. Lying on the daybed, the first thrill of excitement and relief beginning to fade, she wished passionately that she had been able to escape with Robert that very night, even though she knew it would have been impossible and they would never have got beyond the park gates. Her mind went over and over the hundred dangers he might have to face so that by morning she almost wished he would not take the risk and yet didn't know how she was to get through the day till he returned with the night.

She had not been badly treated. She was brought food. A woman came to light a fire and bring a jug of fresh water and take away the slop pail, but to every question she turned a blank face. She seemed to have been living in a nightmare ever since the boat landed them on the shores of France after a rough voyage of over nine hours. Exhausted, soaked with seaspray and nauseated by the constant buffeting of the waves, she had been bundled at once into a postchaise. Travelling by day and night with only the shortest possible stops to change the horses and be brought food she couldn't eat, they had taken little more than two days to reach Sauvigny. And all that time Lucien had been strangely silent, sitting beside her, not touching her, refusing to answer her questions, simply making sure that they made all possible speed as if he were acting under some strong compulsion to reach journey's end as soon as possible.

It had been already dark when at last the carriage jolted through the gates and up the long drive and she could see very little, only that the house that in her memory had always been a place of light and beauty stood stark and desolate, a bitter wind blowing fallen leaves, dirt and debris against the shuttered windows and across the shallow steps.

Dazed and weary from lack of sleep and little food, she had not recognised at first the room to which they took her. It was only when the candles had been lit and she was left alone that she looked around her and realised with a painful stab of memory that it had once been her mother's sitting room, cosy and pretty, full of the things she loved, her music, her books, her tapestry frame, and was now bare and dirty, paper peeling from the damp wall by the windows, stripped of its graceful furniture, nothing left but the daybed with its scuffed velvet cover, a few chairs and an old rug on the floor still stained with the ink from the bottle Guy had once flung at her in a tantrum. It made her want to weep, except she would not show weakness till she knew what they wanted from her.

Last night was the first time Lucien had come to her since they had left England. He had regained all his charm, all his glamour, trying to beguile her with promises, saying that when Robert had been dealt with, he would still be there. She would be free to share with him the splendid future that had been promised him, here in the France she had always loved. She had flared out at him then, calling him liar and cheat, taunting him with his treachery, saying she would rather die than accept anything from his hands or from the Rivage who had destroyed her father and haunted her childhood.

Robert must have seen them together, she thought uneasily, even though he could hear nothing. It added to the stress of those hours that crept so leadenly by till morning came at last

426

and to stop herself thinking she began to make quiet preparations. She still had the small bag she had brought from
Arlington Street. She took a few necessities from it and tied
them into a bundle. In the evening she was at the window
moving the casement backwards and forwards on its rusty
hinges so that there should be no delay when the time should
come. The sudden opening of the door startled her. She looked
up to see Lucien standing with his back against it, his eyes fixed
on her.

'What are you doing?' he said.

'I felt stifled in this room. I needed some air.'

He came further into the room. 'Leave it and come here to
me.'

There was something wild and strange about him. He looked
as if he had just come from sleep, half dressed, his shirt open at
the throat. For a moment he seemed to become again the Lucien
she had known on the marshes, the castaway she had saved
from the sea with his charm and his impudence, and she
shivered. She half closed the window but she did not move.

He said again, 'Come here to me.'

'No.'

She would have turned her back on him but with one stride
he had seized her by the arm, swinging her to face him,
smouldering brown eyes staring down into hers. He relaxed his
grip a little.

'Take off your clothes.'

'What! No!'

She backed away from him and he came after her.

'Take off your clothes.'

'Are you out of your mind?'

She took another step back and came up against the daybed
with him almost on top of her.

'Did you hear what I said or do I have to do it for you?'

He had her wedged into the corner between the head of the
couch and the angle of the wall. There was no way out except
by fighting him and she already knew how strong he was. Very
slowly, in order to gain time, she began to unhook the neck of
her dress.

427

Impatiently he pushed aside her hands and ripped open the bodice of her dress to the waist. His eyes seemed to devour the white neck, the curve of her breast revealed by the low cut chemise, but he made no further move to touch her. She was pressed against the wall, frozen into terror, unable to stir. What was in his mind? What was he going to do? Then he stretched out his hand, gently, almost dreamily, outlining the curve of her face, her neck, her breast.

'You belong to me,' he was murmuring, 'I shall never give you up, never.' He moved closer, she felt his breath on her cheek, then suddenly there was commotion outside . . .

Lucien threw up his head. He jerked away from her. The change was so sudden, it was as if he was in the grip of some ruthless power with no will of his own.

'Who is it?' she asked. 'Is it Dr Rivage?'

'Yes, he is here,' he whispered. 'he has come back.' Then he seemed to shake himself free from some spell that gripped him. 'Better dress yourself,' he said harshly and went out slamming the door behind him.

For a moment she could not move, limp with relief. Then she crossed to the washstand and poured water into the basin. She soaked part of the towel and scrubbed at her face and neck and breast, wiping away the touch of his hand, still shaking a little as she pulled her dress together and rehooked it. Would the unexpected return of Rivage prevent Robert from coming for her? Would he be forced to change his plans? She felt sick at the thought, yet there was nothing she could do, nothing but wait and hope.

Lucien went hurtling down the stairs and collided with Roget carrying a tray to Isabelle's room. The hot soup spilled over and the bread roll fell on to the step.

'Can't you look where you're going, you clumsy oaf?' he said furiously.

'Turned you down again, has she?' muttered Roget spitefully, picking up the roll. 'It would seem your girl has another lover?'

Lucien stopped and turned back. 'What's that? What the devil do you mean by that?'

428

'I saw him late last night sliding down from her window.'

'Saw him? Who? What was he like?'

Roget shrugged his shoulders. 'How should I know? It was dark. Just a man, a villager by the look of him. I couldn't see much.'

He pushed past Lucien with his tray and left him staring after him, his mind in a whirl. So that was it. He was certain of it. Robert Armitage had come after all in one of the many disguises in which he had slipped through their fingers so often before, but not this time. He would come back, of course he would. He must warn the guards, set them to keep watch. His spirits rose. They had him now. He had been right. Lucien had succeeded after all and would have the pleasure of forcing Dr Henri Rivage to take back the scalding words of contempt which he had thrown at him when he first arrived with Isabelle.

He was so pleased with himself that he went at once to find him and tell him the good news. Rivage was in the room that had once been the heart of the old château, the room where the family had gathered, where the children had sat at their father's feet when he read to them, where Isabelle had learned to play the clavichord and sing the English ballads her mother had taught her. Now it had a forlorn look, much of its fine furniture vanished, the shutters half closed as if the present owner preferred to live in the gloom shutting off the outside world. He sat at his huge desk running through the innumerable reports that daily reached him from all over the country. The light from a shaded candle flickered over two silver mounted pistols lying close at hand.

He did not look up as Lucien burst in and poured out his story. Only when the young man had come to an end did he lay down his pen and sit back in his chair.

'Who was it who told you this?'

'Roget Dufour.'

'Dufour is a fool who drinks too much. Haven't you realised that? If he wasn't an excellent cook I'd have dismissed him months ago. By nightfall he is usually awash. If he saw a gorilla with two heads it wouldn't surprise me.'

'But you don't understand . . .'

'I understand that Robert Armitage is a clever man and very unlikely to behave in such a foolhardy manner. You know, my dear boy,' he went on with a lazy contempt, 'I've sometimes wondered if that young woman in Martinique whose name I don't even remember played me false and sent me one of her other bastards with a lying story I've been fool enough to believe.

The angry colour flooded into Lucien's face. 'You know that's not true. You know my mother did not lie.'

'Do I? Well, maybe. You go and set your guards if you want to make a fool of yourself and for God's sake dress yourself decently, not like some ruffian from the gutter.'

He picked up his pen again and Lucien stared at the father he had sought with such high hopes, who had given him money, set him to work for him, raised his expectations, but never once acknowledged him, never once showed by word or look that he regarded him as anything more than a beggar from some distant past. And yet he longed passionately to prove himself, to hear him say just once with pride, 'This is my son.' He stared at him with a mingling of despair and love and then went out of the room. He would go his own way, use his own judgment and pray that this time he was right.

Safely hidden at some distance from the crumbling wall of the château, Robert lying beside Jean Leroy could hear the patrol come tramping through the woods. There seemed to be two of them, holding dogs on leashes, and talking quietly as they came. They emerged from the trees and stood for a little where the wall was broken down, looking across the empty fields and the bridle road that wandered across them to the distant village. The night was dark and very cold. They were already impatient, little inclined to believe the cock and bull story invented by that fat fool, Roget Dufour, and acted upon by that arrogant young bastard, Lucien de Vosges. They were anxious to get back to their wine and a game of dice in the warm guardroom. They took another cursory glance around and then turned back towards the château.

Robert gave them plenty of time before he crept out of the

copse where they had been concealed. Leroy went to the horses, tethered at some distance in case some noise should disturb them and give warning that things were not quite as usual. It was a dry night but overcast, not the moonlight of the previous night for which Robert was thankful. He picked his way carefully through the trees. He had learned the art of stalking deer and other wild animals as a boy and moved very quietly. The glow from the window still shone golden in the distance. Isabelle must be waiting for him. As on the previous night everything was very still, wrapped in a hushed silence that seemed almost uncanny. He was struck with a sudden fear that it was all proving too easy. He could easily be walking into a trap. The unworthy thought flashed through his mind. Had she betrayed him, told them he was coming, delivered him into their hands? He would not believe it, he could not. If he did, then life would no longer be worth living.

He listened intently for a few minutes and then began to climb up to the window. He did not need to tap. Isabelle had been waiting and watching ever since it had grown dark. She pushed open the stiff casement and handed him the few possessions she had tied into a bundle. He dropped it to the ground and steadied himself to take hold of her as she climbed out backwards following him as he went down inch by inch, his hands always holding her firmly. Then they were standing together panting on the soggy ground, unaware of the eyes that watched them from the hidden vantage of the lower window. Let them believe themselves safe and then take them together, thought Lucien, with a sudden exultation that he had been proved right. He had already given his instructions. He watched as the two shadows melted into one another for a moment and then quietly moved around the shrubberies and began to creep towards the wood. He raised his hand and gestured to the men who crouched out of sight of anyone on the path.

Robert heard the dogs barking as soon as they entered the wood.

'Dr Rivage came back tonight,' breathed Isabelle. 'Do you think they are hunting us already?'

431

'I don't know. Maybe something has disturbed them. We must hurry. Run, Isabelle, run!'

But that was easier said than done. He had slid through the trees with practised ease but Isabelle tripped over tree roots and was caught by the long strands of low growing shrubs. He had his arm around her waist, urging her on with a horrible certainty that their pursuers were gaining on them. Alone he might have escaped them but with Isabelle he was hopelessly hampered. They still might have stood a chance if it had not been for the dogs. The men were blundering through the darkness but one of the dogs, outstripping its master, reached them just as Robert was helping Isabelle over the crumbling wall. The great brute leaped at her, bringing her down. She screamed in terror. Robert seized the dog by the collar and it turned on him snarling fiercely and by then it was too late. Half a dozen guards broke through the trees and were surrounding them.

Even if he had been able to reach the pistol hidden deep in an inner pocket, it would have been useless. Thank God, Leroy had had the good sense to remain hidden in the copse where earlier they had been concealed. He must have heard the dogs and realised that they were being followed. One of the men had a length of stout cord and tied Robert's hands behind him. For the moment there was nothing to do but submit. He couldn't fight six and win but there might be a way out. He had been in tight corners before and had got away. He smiled at Isabelle, trying to give her hope and courage, and she moved closer to him. The men were rough but not deliberately brutal. They marched their prisoners back to the château, jerking Isabelle to her feet when she stumbled and thrusting Robert away from her when he tried to remain close at her side. He knew well enough of Fouché's remorseless hunting down of spies and informers, so he had little hope for himself if he couldn't contrive an escape but perhaps Dr Rivage, now that his plan of using Isabelle as a decoy to bring him into his net had succeeded, would allow her to go free.

They entered the château by a side door leading to the servants' quarters. They were taken up a small flight of stairs along a passage and into a spacious pillared hall. Then a door was flung open and they were in that room where the long shuttered windows opened on to the terrace.

After the darkness the light dazzled him for a moment. Then his vision cleared. Lucien was standing by the huge desk piled with papers. The two pistols lying beside them caught the wavering light. Logs smouldered on the stone hearth and a man stood in front of it with his back turned to them.

'You've done well,' he said harshly to the two guards who had brought them there. 'You can leave your prisoners and go.'

The two men had remained standing just inside the door. Now they turned and went out. Lucien crossed to shut the door behind them and stayed there, his eyes upon them, a little smile playing around his mouth.

No one moved or spoke. It was as if everything waited on that figure standing by the hearth. Then he slowly turned round and the light from the candles fell full upon his face. Isabelle gave a strangled gasp and Robert began to understand.

One side of that face was perfectly normal, might almost have been called handsome, but the other was hideously scarred, the flesh horribly seamed and corrugated from the chin to the roots of the hair which had never grown fully again and lay sparse and grey across the bare scalp. The eye was half closed, the mouth twisted at one side. It was impossible to look and not be shocked and horrified but Robert knew instantly who he was, and was appalled at what he had done on that terrible night to the man he had believed dead and who still lived. He had never known his real name, had never linked him with the Henri Rivage who had become Fouché's shadow and was his own most bitter enemy. He knew too that he had been hopelessly wrong on that day at Sabrina House. Isabelle had never betrayed his love or his trust. The story Lucien had flung viciously in his face he must have learned from Rivage himself. Despite the danger that threatened them, he knew a surge of relief, almost of happiness.

'Le Hibou,' he murmured.

The scarred mouth smiled. 'So you remember, Rossignol. I've waited a long time for this moment.'

He moved to behind the desk and stood for a second looking

at them as if savouring his triumph, while Robert's eyes quietly moved around the room assessing its possibilities. It was very sparsely furnished and there was only the one door. The shutters had been closed over the windows but not bolted. It could be important to remember that.

Isabelle was staring at that ravaged face as if mesmerised, memories flooding back. She was twelve years old again on that wretched day when this man stood by smiling at her and Guy while their father was dragged away.

'Why?' she whispered, 'why have you brought me here?'

Where he stood the light of the candles was shaded. He turned his head slightly as if to hide that hideous mask.

'I'll tell you why. There was a man once, rich, handsome, a favourite courtier who liked to believe his ancestors went back to Charlemagne, bosom friend of King Louis . . .'

'My grandfather,' murmured Isabelle, her eyes fixed on him, wide and fearful.

'Your grandfather,' the deep voice was icily contemptuous. 'And in that dissolute court there was a young girl who loved him so passionately, so recklessly, that she bore him a son in loneliness, in disgrace, and died of it. The boy grew up in bitterness, hating those who called him bastard. He was sent to school, to university, never acknowledged, obliged to serve his half brother, two years younger, the heir, the favoured one, enjoying the position that should have been his. He ate the bread of humiliation and contempt. He rebelled against it and was sent to Martinique to work in the sugar refinery that gave that family so much of their wealth, and there he brooded till the moment came, that wonderful moment when France threw off her shackles and he was free to take his revenge on the man who had so carelessly fathered him. He saw him go to his death with the half brother who had robbed him of what should have been his and would have been happy to see the children he had spawned go with him, but they escaped him.'

He paused for a moment, the dark smouldering eyes watching them, before he went on, his voice changing, becoming more personal.

'I served the Revolution that had given me back my manhood

434

until the man you call husband destroyed my hopes for ever.' One hand hovered for a moment against that destroyed cheek. 'Men are ashamed to look me in the face, women turn away from me sick with disgust. He left me with nothing, only fear and hatred and the power of life and death.'

He's mad, thought Robert, the bitterness, the corroding jealousy, have destroyed his spirit and God forgive me but it was I who drove him over the edge into darkness. To plead with such a man would be useless. There must be some other way out and he had to find it. The guard who had tied his hands behind his back had failed to knot the rope as savagely as he had feared at first. As unobtrusively as he could, he tried to work his long thin hands free as he had done in similar circumstances once before.

'What are you going to do with us?'

The words burst out of Isabelle before she could stop herself.

'I wonder.' His ravaged smile sent a chill up her spine. 'We still have the guillotine, you know, for spies and informers, but that's too easy, too quick. I had in mind to stage something more dramatic, more amusing, shall we say?'

He gestured to Lucien who was still standing silent in front of the door and the young man nodded and crossed to the hearth, taking up the poker and thrusting it into the glowing heart of the fire.

Oh dear God, thought Robert, not that again. If he touches Isabelle, I'll kill him, somehow I'll kill him.

Henri Rivage had turned to him, the deep voice almost pleasant.

'Now, Maurice Dupont or Robert Armitage or Lord Kilgour or do you prefer some other of the aliases under which you masquerade, I have a few questions to ask, questions to which the First Consul, soon to be Emperor, would dearly like the answers.'

'You may ask,' said Robert, coolly playing for time, 'but I cannot promise to answer. I am not in the confidence of Britain's Minister for War.'

'Oh come, come,' and again he gave Robert that chilling smile, 'you cannot expect me to believe that. Your wife's brother, poor fool, has often enough boasted of the secrets to which you hold the key.'

Damn Guy for not keeping his mouth shut! 'Is that why you killed him?'

Isabelle made a quick movement, quelled instantly by the look Robert gave her. Let them go on believing him dead.

'That was an accident, otherwise he would have been standing here with his sister. Personally I regret it. It would have pleased me to see the last heir of that infernal race cringing before me.'

'Guy would never have done that, never!' exclaimed Isabelle furiously, but Rivage only smiled.

'No one knows what he will do till the test comes.' He turned back to Robert. One or two easy questions first. I want a clear description of those defences that are being built along the south coast, the location of each strong point, the lie of the land, the water courses, so that our invasion barges will be aware of the most advantageous places to land troops, and secondly we know there is a plot brewing to assassinate Bonaparte, a conspiracy backed by Britain and involving the last of those damnable Bourbons. I want to know the names of all those involved, no matter how slightly.'

'I am sorry but I fear you must be disappointed,' said Robert with a flippancy he was far from feeling. 'As for the first, I did not devise the plan, nor am I familiar with its details and as for the second, there have been plots against your leader ever since he assumed power, plots thought up by fools and destined for failure. How should I know those responsible for the latest foolhardy scheme?'

'Oh but you do. I am quite sure of that. Maybe this will help you to remember.'

With a sudden savage movement he struck Isabelle across the face so brutally that she staggered backwards with an involuntary cry of fear and pain.

'You bastard!' The rope bit into Robert's hands as he desperately tried to free them.

'Bastard I may be,' said Rivage drily, 'but I assure you that

436

was only the beginning. I'll ask you again and let me have some answers this time.'

Isabelle was dabbing at the blood that trickled from her mouth.

'No, Robert, no, tell him nothing. Let him do his worst.'

'Such heroics,' sneered Rivage. 'I think your husband may feel differently.' He gestured to Lucien who took the poker from the fire, the end of it glowing red in the darkened room. 'You wouldn't want to see that beauty destroyed, would you? You would not want to watch her die in agony like that other poor child? I am more merciful than you were. You've only to give me the information I want and at least you'll die together clean and unmarked.'

Lucien took a hesitant step towards them, as if reluctant to come too close and with a violent effort, the cords cutting deep, bleeding wounds in his wrist, Robert freed one of his hands. He made a dive for the pistols lying on the desk, grabbing one of them and accidentally sending the other slithering along the floor almost to Isabelle's feet. Without thinking she picked it up. Then everything happened so quickly she could never afterwards remember it clearly.

Robert fired as Rivage hurled himself at him. The bullet hit him full in the breast. He stood upright for a second, a queer look of surprise on the ravaged face, before he toppled forward across the desk sending papers and despatch boxes to the floor.

With an anguished cry of 'Father!', Lucien charged across the room, the flaming poker still in his hand. Robert dodged behind the desk, tripped over one of the boxes and fell on one knee. Lucien was almost on him. She had to stop him. She gripped the pistol in both hands and pulled the trigger. At such close range she could not miss. It hit Lucien squarely in the back. He fell forward over Rivage's body, the poker flying out of his hand and landing among the scattered papers. In a moment it could have set the place alight. Robert stumbled to his feet, picked up the poker and hurled it away from him and into the wide stone fireplace.

Isabelle shaking and appalled, the pistol still in her hand, was staring down at what she had done, unable to believe that it could have all happened so swiftly.

'Quickly,' urged Robert, 'quickly, we must go now. Those guards will have heard the shots. They will be here at any minute. There's no time to waste.'

She bent over Lucien, trembling, putting out a shaking hand to touch his cheek, sick with horror.

'Are they dead?' she whispered.

'We're not staying to find out. Come now.'

Robert was already at the shutters, easing them back, opening the long windows.

Isabelle took one last look around the shadowy room so full of ancient memories, at the two men lying together, closer than they had ever been in life, then she dropped the pistol and ran to him. He put his arm around her and they were outside, standing still for a moment to listen and then running, running for dear life towards the trees.

At the edge of the wood they paused and looked back. Light streamed out into the night from the opened windows but the walls of the château were thick and the guards, a little drunk and absorbed in their game, still seemed to have heard nothing. The fugitives did not dare to waste a second. They ran on through the wood, falling and scrambling up again, until they reached the outer wall, breathless and panting. Robert lifted Isabelle across the crumbling stone and she leaned against him, her mind still full of the horror they had left behind them.

'Where do we go now?' she whispered.

'I must contact Leroy. He will help us. It could be a long walk, Isabelle.'

She tried to smile. 'In that case we had better start now.'

'That's my brave girl.'

It was very dark, no moon or stars to light up the two figures that crept across the muddy field towards the copse where earlier they had planned to leave the horses, and the luck that had deserted them before suddenly turned in their favour. As they drew close, Robert paused for a moment.

'Listen,' he whispered.

'What is it?'

There was the sound of heavy animals stirring, a faint jingle and a shadowy figure appeared in the shelter of the trees.

'Leroy!' exclaimed Robert. 'You waited.'

'I saw what happened and kept out of it. There was nothing I could do, but I thought I would wait till dawn.'

'Good man.'

'I've seen you wriggle out of tight corners before now,' said Leroy drily. 'What happened?'

'Let's just say that we've contrived to get away but it won't be long before the guards find out what has happened.'

'Is Rivage dead?'

'I don't know. We did not stay long enough to find out, but the first necessity is for us to be as far away as possible before they sound the alarm.'

'It's long past midnight but you still have several hours of darkness and there is food in the saddlebags and a few necessities as we arranged.'

He gave a quick look at Isabelle leaning wearily against one of the trees.

'Is Madame strong enough to ride with you? I am afraid I could not procure a saddle fit for a lady.'

Isabelle braced herself. 'It doesn't matter. I have ridden astride before.'

'Don't be afraid for her, Leroy, she has the spirit of a lion,' said Robert, giving her a warm smile of encouragement.

Earlier that day they had made what preparations they could and Leroy brought out two dark enveloping cloaks of heavy wool.

'You'll need to avoid towns and villages because word will spread from one to the other and I would advise travelling by night whenever you can.'

'I realise that,' said Robert. 'I'm grateful, Leroy, immensely grateful. Take care of yourself. Find something important to take you away from here for a few weeks till the trouble has died down.'

'I will. Don't fear for me.'

'Then the sooner we go the better. Come, Isabelle.'

439

She gathered her skirts together as he lifted her into the saddle and bent down to hold out her hand to Leroy smiling down at him so that he thought, who wouldn't risk a great deal for a woman like that?

'What would we have done without you, Monsieur?'

'No doubt your husband would have thought out some stratagem, my lady,' and with a gesture quite contrary to his radical principles, he kissed the hand extended to him.

'Goodbye, my friend.'

The two men embraced, then Robert was in the saddle and they were trotting together down one of the well worn paths that would lead them into the quiet country road he intended to follow for the first few hours till dawn.

Leroy watched them disappear into the darkness. What the hell was it that drove this friend of his, this rich English Milord, to risk his life in crazy missions, when he had a wife like that? He'd never really understand the English, he thought, as he trudged away towards Angers. It would be morning before he got there and he must leave a note at the pharmacy to say he'd been called away for some days and then make himself scarce till the inevitable hue and cry was safely over.

22

Despite the biting cold, the uncomfortable saddle, the danger
and the days of hard riding that lay ahead, at least two hundred
miles between them and the sea if they avoided the main
highways, Isabelle glowed that night with a kind of wild elation.
The black cloud that had hung over her ever since the duel had
been blown away. Robert must care for her in spite of everything. Hadn't he risked his life to come for her and he must
know by now just as she did where Lucien had learned of that
fearful night which had destroyed Henri Rivage's sanity and
sent him hurtling down a path of revenge.

They were riding side by side, Robert keeping a watchful eye
when they passed through small sleeping villages or by some
lonely farmhouse. He would not stop for food or rest until they
had put as many miles as possible between them and the
château. There would be time for that later.

'It's going to be hard going,' he said warningly to Isabelle.

'I'm not afraid so long as I am with you. I would walk if
necessary.'

'Let's hope it won't come to that,' he said drily. 'These horses
have no turn of speed but Leroy has found us two strong reliable
hacks that with any luck should last out.'

To stop and change horses at the larger hostelries would
attract far too much attention. Fouché's police had a tight hold
over even these rural communities and it was possible that
Rivage still lived.

Now and again, despite her valiant spirit, a long tremor
would run through Isabelle as her mind went back to what they
had left behind them. She had once saved Lucien's life and now
she had killed him. Somehow she never doubted that he was
dead. It was an appalling thought and she shivered. She could

not forget his agonised cry of 'Father!' She saw him fall over and over again, she saw the blood. But if she had hesitated even for a second he would have flung himself upon Robert with that flaming instrument of death.

What a strange, tangled story it was. When he had first told her about his life in Martinique, did he know who she was and that the man who had sent him to England to spy and play the informer was also the Henri Rivage who had destroyed her father and had wrecked their life? Had everything he had said in those days been a lie? Somehow, despite everything that had happened since, she did not want to think so, she did not want the memory poisoned. She tried to put the unhappy thoughts behind her, tried to remember that now she was sharing that hidden part of Robert's life and with a joy that transformed the difficulties and discomforts.

Light came very late that morning with a heavily overcast sky that promised rain later. They had kept going at a good pace but the horses were blown and Robert knew they must soon find somewhere to rest them. They were travelling through a flat countryside following along beside a small river. The fields lay fallow except for the occasional root crop and here and there an apple orchard, the trees stark and black under the grey sky. Despite her strong determination to keep going, Isabelle was beginning to droop. Now and again she swayed in the saddle, half asleep, waking with a jerk when her horse stumbled, while Robert kept a sharp look-out for a possible place of refuge.

The building that caught his eye might once have been a small farmhouse but had long since fallen into a roofless ruin. The four walls that had enclosed a living room now surrounded a tangle of brambles, creeping ivy and wild briar falling in cascades through the gaping windows, but the stone shelter where perhaps the farm animals had been housed was still intact. Robert looked around him. Wide fields stretched as far as he could see. If there was a new farmhouse, then it was over the brow of a slight rise and out of sight. He dismounted and pushed open the door hanging precariously on a broken hinge. There was a musty but not unpleasant smell of apples, as if they had been stored there at some time. A bale of straw and a pile

442

of hay neatly stacked in one corner and a bin half filled with oats looked as if the farmer had used the place for storage in the summer and had abandoned it during the winter months. It had begun to rain heavily by now and Robert decided to risk it for a few hours.

Isabelle helped him to unsaddle the horses. Then he pulled the hay into a sort of nest and spread the blanket Leroy had rolled up and attached to the saddle. It was very cold but at least they would be out of the rain and wind.

'You stay here, Isabelle. I'll try and find some water for the horses.'

'I'll come with you.'

'There's no need. I'm an old campaigner. If there is any to be found then I'll find it.'

There was in fact a somewhat muddy stream linked with the small river. He filled a battered bucket, brought it to the horses, gave them a few handfuls of the mouldy oats and came to sit beside her. He began to open the saddle bags that Leroy had thoughtfully filled with meat, bread and cheese. It was not particularly appetising and they must eat sparingly, since they did not know how long it might have to last. One swallow each of brandy from his hunting flask warmed them a little, but it was still bleak and draughty and Robert wrapped their thick woollen cloaks tightly around Isabelle.

'What wouldn't I give now for some hot coffee,' she sighed.

'Me too. Poor darling, it's hard going, isn't it? But they could so easily send out messengers, the hue and cry could extend widely in a very few hours and I dare not risk staying where someone could give us away. Try to rest a little. We've a long way to go.'

They lay close together for warmth and while Robert kept alert, Isabelle drowsed, soothed by the quiet, with only the occasional stir of the horses as they munched their oats.

It must have been a couple of hours later when he was aroused from a light uneasy doze by Isabelle's stifled scream. In the dim light he could see her sitting bolt upright staring in front of her, her eyes dark with fear, her arms outstretched as if she were holding something or someone away from her.

443

'No, no, no!' she muttered, her voice rising. 'Don't touch me, don't come near me!' and she shrank back, her hands over her face, trembling violently.

Robert sat up, putting his arm around her. 'What is it? What's wrong? Were you dreaming?'

'It was horrible, horrible . . .'

'Tell me. It will help.'

'I seemed to be on the seashore and someone was coming to me out of the sea. I thought it was you. I ran to meet you but then it changed into Lucien, all covered in blood, saying "You belong to me now, I shall never give you up, never!" It was what he said to me before when he . . . when he . . .' She shuddered and turned away from him.

'When what? What did he do to you?'

'I can't tell you, not now. I was so afraid for you, so terribly afraid . . . He told me once that if you save a life, then it is yours for ever and now I have destroyed that life . . .'

'Whoever invented that saying was out of their mind,' said Robert firmly. 'Now listen to me, it was only a bad dream which is not surprising after what you've been through. I am here, very much alive and intending to remain so.'

His cheerful good sense calmed her a little. She tried to pull herself together.

'I'm being foolish, aren't I? But . . . but I've never killed anyone before. Is it always so terrible?'

'The first time it haunts you even when it is inevitable. We would be cold-blooded devils without human feeling if it didn't, but there comes a time when there is nothing else to be done and you have to face it. In any case we don't even know that Lucien is dead, or Rivage for that matter. They could still be alive and sending out a dozen guards to hunt us down. They will have no qualms about shooting to kill, believe me.'

'I'm ashamed of being so stupid. Robert, can we go? Do you think the horses are sufficiently rested?' She was still shivering a little. 'I don't like it here.'

'If you're sure you can go on. It's just past twelve. We could push on further and find somewhere better.'

As he got to his feet, the wide door swung open crazily on its broken hinge and a small boy stood in a shaft of watery sunlight. He could not have been more than six years old and stared at them with huge round eyes of surprise and alarm. Robert made a movement and he turned and bolted, screaming something as he went.

'That's settled it,' said Robert grimly. 'He's gone to fetch Papa. We must go and quickly. Help me, Isabelle.'

She scrambled to her feet. They resaddled the horses as rapidly as they could, Robert coming to help her fumbling hands. Then he led them to the door and cautiously took a look outside. There were two men coming across the fields still some way off but it looked as if they were carrying hunting rifles in their hands no doubt believing them to be vagrants or robbers. There was not a moment to be lost.

'Hurry!' he said, thankful that he had thought to pack their saddle bags after they'd eaten. He picked up the blanket, threw it across his horse, lifted Isabelle into the saddle, then they were off galloping for the road and already well away before the two men had reached the stone barn shaking their fists and shouting after them.

'That was a lucky break,' said Robert breathlessly, drawing rein at a safe distance. 'If it had not been for your nightmare, we could have been nicely caught and probably thrown into the town gaol on a charge of vagrancy or worse. Are you all right?'

'Yes, of course. Where do we go now?'

'We push on towards the north west. There is a village I know of about eight miles further on. It's a poor enough place but we could find shelter there. They'll have very few travellers at this time of the year.' He leaned across to put his hand on hers. 'Take heart. It won't always be as bad as this and at least it has stopped raining.'

For the next three days they travelled on, not able to ride as fast or as far as he would have wished since he had constantly to think of Isabelle and also of the horses. The only inns where he dared to take a lodging were for the most part filthy, disreputable places where the surly landlord could offer them little more than a thin vegetable soup with dry bread and show them up to a bug-infested room where they would sleep on hard truckle beds well wrapped in their cloaks to avoid contact with the greasy bed linen used by a dozen travellers before them.

Time and time again Isabelle had to bite back her disgust. Then Robert would make some jest and they would find relief in laughter. But although they went on together in such a close daily companionship, they were still apart in spirit. It had all happened so quickly and there had been little or no opportunity to talk, to draw closer together after the differences and the pain that had driven them apart. She was still haunted by what had happened in the first few days of her capture, still shivered remembering Lucien, his hands exploring the body that belonged to Robert even though she had been spared the worst, still blamed herself for her gullibility in being so easily taken in by that lying letter, while Robert, in between the constant worry over their safety, wondered how much she had really cared for that young bastard who had carelessly snatched at her first love, and then mercilessly destroyed it, leaving him to pick up the pieces.

One evening when they had reached the outskirts of a small town, he left Isabelle at a place called Le Mouton d'Or which boasted only one attic bedroom and went boldly into the main street, sitting at a table outside one of the better hostelries with a carafe of country wine, and listened to the gossip going on around him. The news had spread. Whether Rivage was alive or dead, and there seemed no certainty about it, there were very few who regretted it. Fouché's secret police had bitten deep into these country communities. Taxes were high, punishments severe and their sons apt to be snatched away for military duty just when they were old enough to be useful on the farm. War against Great Britain and the glorious victories in Europe were all very well but didn't fill their children's bellies. They had got rid of one king and now it looked as if they were to have an Emperor – there did not seem to be all that difference to a man living a hard life in a small town.

'They are saying the assassin was an Englishman,' said one worthy tradesman to his neighbour.

'Good luck to him and by God he's going to need it. I saw

446

the notice nailed up outside the Town Hall, a tall man, speaks good French, cunning as a fox and has a woman with him.'

'An Englishman who speaks French, that's a laugh,' said his friend with contempt. 'I've always heard those stuck-up God-damned Milords think it beneath them to speak any lingo but their own. That description could fit anyone. Could be you, mon vieux,' and he poked his companion in the belly and roared with laughter.

'I've got more sense than to go around shooting policemen,' said the other, 'much as I'd have liked to sometimes.'

If they were putting up notices already, then the guard posts would have been alerted. They would need to be extra careful. Robert returned to Isabelle thoughtfully and decided to say nothing. No need to alarm her unnecessarily. They would leave at dawn and with any luck would be at the coast in a couple of days, and it should not be too difficult to lie low there till Jack Darrow returned as he had promised. But it was then that everything began to go wrong.

In this poor place the landlord and his slatternly wife could not provide much in the way of food. They were eating their way through a tasteless vegetable stew when there was a hammering on the door downstairs, followed by the sound of voices in angry dispute. Robert quietly stepped out on to the landing and listened. Their landlord, with the French peasant's inborn distrust of the law and in particular of the police, was refusing pointblank to allow the two men standing outside to search the house.

'How do I know you're what you say you are,' he argued obstinately, 'you could be robbers, murderers. I have my wife, my children to protect. English, you say he is,' he laughed derisively, 'there's no fine English Milord upstairs in my backroom, that I promise you, naught but a beggarly fellow with his woman and she's no better than she should be by the look of her.'

Robert came back and gently closed the door.

'They're looking for us, aren't they?' whispered Isabelle. 'What are we going to do?'

447

'Get away from here – now if we can. It might be difficult to lie our way out of this one.'

Robert crossed quickly to the window. Below them was a lean-to shed where their horses had been housed. The drop was not great on to the sloping roof and from there to the ground. He looked at Isabelle.

'Can you do it if I go first?'

She peered into the darkness. It seemed a very long way to the ground. She swallowed a spasm of fear.

'If you can do it, then I can.'

'Good.'

He put their few belongings into a bundle, knotted it up and dropped it out of the window. Then he shifted the truckle bed across the floor and wedged it against the door. It would hold them up even if only for a little. Then he climbed on to the window sill, dropped to the slope of the roof, steadied himself and held up his arms to help Isabelle down. Her foot slipped and she clung to a projecting brick, trembling all over.

'Don't move,' he said. 'Stay there till I tell you. I will go first.'

He let himself drop to the ground falling heavily on to his hands and knees, then quickly scrambling up. The argument still seemed to be going on round the other side of the house.

'Now,' he whispered.

Isabelle was still clinging on for dear life. The wind blew cold and she felt dizzy. Then she closed her eyes and let herself go. Robert caught her in his arms and held her close against him for a moment.

'All right?'

'Yes,' she muttered shakily.

'Now for the horses.'

There was the clatter of booted feet on the staircase inside. The men must have won their argument. Robert led out the horses, fortunately still saddled. He had meant to come down later to feed and water them. He lifted Isabelle into the saddle and then they were away into the dark night. By the time the two policemen had forced their way in, the birds had flown and any pursuit had become impossible. They had in any case only been following up a chance remark, that two strangers had been

448

seen arriving that afternoon. They had no certainty that these were the two they sought and people run from the law for a variety of reasons. They had no intention of riding off on a wild goose chase after two doubtful fugitives.

Robert urged on their tired horses for several miles before he dared to draw rein and relax a little.

'That was too close for comfort,' he said with a deliberate cheerfulness. 'It would be a pity to fail when we are so near the end.'

'Are we?' For the first time Isabelle felt her courage, her resilience, drain away from her. She seemed to have been tired, dirty, frightened and hungry for ever. 'Supposing your friend is unable to sail his boat across the Channel?'

'If not he, then there will be others. I still have some gold and that's a powerful incentive for these poor fisher folk in winter. Don't lose heart, not now, not when you have done so splendidly.'

'Have I? But for me, you could have covered the journey in half the time. It's I who have brought all this on you,' she said despairingly. 'Why didn't I realise? Why did I let myself believe?'

He heard the shake of tears in her voice and said stoutly, 'I tell you one thing for sure. There's no other company I'd rather have with me in a tight corner and believe me I have had some in my time.'

'Is it true?'

'On my honour. Now, no looking back, no regrets. They get you nowhere. What we must be doing now is working out our next move. We're faced with an awkward problem. I know this countryside. If we stay on the bridle paths and byways as we have been doing so far, we're likely to be bogged down. It's marshy in the best of weather and now pretty near impassable especially at night. If we take the highway which is our quickest route, we stand the chance of being stopped at one or other of these damnable checkpoints and though we have papers, some of them will not stand up to close scrutiny. It's a question of the devil or the deep blue sea, and I fear it will have to be the devil and hope his wits are not at their sharpest in these rural parts.'

449

They pushed on through the night but their tired horses could not make much headway and early morning found them still several miles short of the next town which they must pass through to reach the coast. They lay up for a short rest in a little inn where the *patronne* was a buxom young woman who explained that her husband was away for a few days. She saw few strangers, was glad of the company and took pity on Isabelle, who was pale with fatigue after the sleepless night. She allowed them to feed and water the horses and invited them to share her midday meal, a good richly flavoured rabbit and vegetables. She even refused the money Robert offered her when they prepared to leave until he put the gold coin into the hand of the bouncing baby on her hip who crowed and laughed and would have put it in his mouth if his mother hadn't hastily snatched it away with blushing thanks. They went on their way, refreshed and heartened by her kindness and sympathy. But there were still hazards, and disaster hit them when they passed through the little town.

Robert had decided they would leave just before the gates were closed at nightfall on the supposition that the guards, tired and looking for supper, would be only too glad to see the last travellers on their way as quickly as possible, but for once his decision was fatal. Instead of the usual army veteran, the guard was a young brisk know-all who prided himself on his efficiency. He examined their papers minutely, told them to wait and went into the guard post. Robert had an uneasy suspicion that this time it wouldn't work. He could see the young man through the window, scrutinising the papers over again and then referring to his superior. Even if they were only detained for further questioning, it could be dangerous. He took a quick look around him. The guards did not seem to have horses available, so there was just a chance that they might be able to get away.

Under his breath he said, 'Ride on, Isabelle, ride hell for leather, stop for nothing.'

'What about you?'

'Don't worry about me. I'll follow.'

Reluctantly she kicked her tired horse into a trot and then into a canter. Robert took out the pistol he still carried in the pocket of his long coat. As the guard came out, he levelled it at him threateningly, then urged his horse forward following after Isabelle.

'Stop!' yelled the guard, taken by surprise. 'Stop, both of you!'

But as Robert had already guessed, he had to go back into the hut for his gun. He was back almost instantly, took aim and fired. Robert felt the impact in his shoulder and the sudden numbing of his right arm. Somehow he grabbed the pistol with his other hand as it dropped from his nerveless fingers and rode on till he reached Isabelle.

'What happened?' she gasped. 'I heard the shot. Are you hurt?'

'It's nothing. Ride on as fast as you can. Very soon we can draw off the road and lose ourselves in the heathland. They've no horses to follow and by the time they get hold of them, we'll be well away.'

Later when they emerged from the brushwood on to the road again, they had put several miles behind them and thankfully there was no sign of any pursuit. It was pitch dark by now and they were riding close together when Robert suddenly slumped over his horse's neck.

'What is it?' she said in alarm. 'What's wrong? Were you wounded?'

He straightened up with an effort. 'I think the damage is rather more than I thought.'

He thrust a hand inside his coat and it came out dark and sticky with blood.

'We must stop somewhere. You must let me see,' said Isabelle anxiously.

'It's only a few miles now,' he muttered, holding the reins in his left hand and thrusting the other inside his coat. 'I can last out till we reach the sea.'

'Are you sure?' She was worried. Was it just a flesh wound or something worse? 'At least we ought to try and stop the bleeding.'

He gave her a lopsided grin. 'If I dismount, I doubt if I'll be able to get up again. It's better if we keep going.'

451

They rode on with Isabelle keeping a watchful eye on him. Up to now it was Robert who had been the leader, full of resource, always knowing what to do for the best, but if he were really hurt, it was she who must shoulder the burden, must deal with this woman at *Le Chat Noir*, must find some way of bribing a sea captain to carry them to England if Jack Darrow failed to turn up, and she felt woefully inadequate.

After what seemed hours, she thought they must be nearing the coast at last. The wind had changed. It blew in their faces, cold and damp, with a salty tang in it. Some distance ahead she thought she could see a line of dark buildings with here and there a glimmer of light.

'That must be the village Jack spoke of. Now for *Le Chat Noir* and Madame Big Nose,' said Robert with an effort at gaiety.

She found it hard to laugh and it was further away than it looked. It was another hour before they emerged on to the sea road and could see clearly the scattering of small houses and one rather larger than the rest with a lantern hanging outside and the sound of voices from within that must be *Le Chat Noir*.

'Now is the moment to chance our luck,' murmured Robert. 'Jack said we had only to mention his name. Let's hope he is right.'

It was a windy desolate shore that reminded Isabelle of Dungeness, with the boats drawn up and the beaches deserted on this cold winter's night.

Robert dismounted, almost fell and saved himself by clutching at his horse's neck. With a strong effort he held himself upright. Pain, which had succeeded the numbness, combined with loss of blood, was beginning to have its effect. There was a wooden bench against the side wall of the tavern and he dropped on to it. Isabelle tethered both horses and sat beside him. In the shifting light of the lantern she could see the dark stain of blood spreading on the back of his coat.

'We must find somewhere for you to rest. We need a doctor, a surgeon,' she said urgently.

'I doubt if this place can supply either,' he said drily, struggling against a deadly faintness which threatened to overwhelm him. 'I don't think I'm going to be able to stay on my

452

feet. I'm afraid this time you will have to do the talking for both of us.'

She quailed at the thought, but Robert's very life depended on it so it had to be faced. He had leaned his head back against the stone wall and closed his eyes for a moment, looking so pale and drawn that her heart failed her. Supposing he grew worse, much worse, supposing he was to die after all he had done for her, all they had gone through together? She pushed away the chilling thought and got to her feet, shaking out her muddied skirts and tying the silk scarf over her head.

'You stay here while I go and speak to Madame. Perhaps she can give us a room or tell us where we can go for help.'

'I'm sorry,' he breathed, 'I'm sorry to let you down so badly. Of all damnable things to have happened.' He was maddened by his own weakness.

'Oh Robert, don't say that, don't ever think it, not after all you have done for me.' She sat beside him for a moment, her hand touching his cheek and he caught at her fingers with his left hand.

'Take care, my darling, take very great care.'

'I will,' she promised.

When she opened the door, the combined stench of stale fish, sour wine, sweat and the reek of close packed unwashed humanity very nearly drove her back. The small room was filled with men lounging at the rough tables, leaning up against the stained walls. A sudden silence fell as she closed the door behind her and she felt their eyes boring into her back as she walked slowly amongst them towards the far end where a woman waited for her, a tall woman tightly corseted into a black gown hung with gleaming jet, piled red hair, small black eyes in a pale face and a beak of a nose. Madame Big Nose herself. She had a nervous desire to giggle and rapidly choked it down, walking with a pride and dignity not lost on Madame who leaned across the bar staring at her.

'Women of your kind are not welcome at *Le Chat Noir*.'

'I realise that, but I look for news of Jack Darrow.'

453

The small black eyes watched her steadily. 'I never remember Jack speaking of any lady.'

'Probably not. He doesn't know me. It is my husband who is his friend.'

'And can't this husband of yours speak for himself?'

'He is outside. He is sick.'

'Sick eh? What's wrong with him? Too dead drunk to stand on his feet?'

A ripple of coarse laughter ran through the room behind her.

'No, not that.' Isabelle lowered her voice to a whisper, aware of ears that could be listening. 'He has been . . . wounded.'

'Wounded?' The response was low and cautious.

Isabelle nodded. 'We need a room where he can rest – we need a surgeon.'

'You're asking a great deal, my lady.' Raising her voice the woman said, 'So that's it. You can take yourself off, you and this man of yours. We don't want the likes of you at *Le Chat Noir*. This is a decent house.'

'We can pay,' said Isabelle uncertainly.

'Money is not everything.' Under her breath the woman said, 'Can he walk, this man of yours?'

'With difficulty.'

'Bring him to the back door. You can't be too careful these days. Wait for me there.' Aloud she said, 'You talk too much. Take that pretty face where it can buy what you're asking. There is nothing for you here.'

There was another burst of derisive laughter as Isabelle turned and retraced her steps. A big black-haired fellow stuck out his foot to trip her up. She avoided it just in time and gave him a cold stare that choked back his ready guffaw. Then she was through the door and thankfully taking deep breaths of the clean, icy air. The wind from the sea blew in so strongly that she stumbled as she rounded the corner of the building. Robert was still slumped on the seat where she had left him. In the ghostly light of the swaying lantern, his face was grey with fatigue and pain. She dropped down beside him and put her hand on his.

'She will help us but I think she is afraid that others may

454

hear and suspect there is something wrong about us. We must move round to the back of the house and she'll come to us there.'

The place was larger than it appeared. There were outbuildings, a stable where the horses could be housed and a ladder that led to a loft above it.

The pain in his shoulder had grown unbearable, every movement was agony, and loss of blood was making him feel curiously light-headed. If she did not come soon, he thought, hanging on to the doorpost and desperately summoning every ounce of strength he possessed, he felt he might ignominiously collapse. Then at last the woman was there, enveloped in a dark cloak, a hood over the bright hair. She looked long and closely into his face.

'You're the one all right. Jack told me of you last time he was here. Crazy he thinks you are and just look at you, sick to death, and begging for help from a poor widow trying to lead a quiet life and scratch a decent living.'

'I'm sorry, Madame, I would not put you into any danger. Tell us where we can go till Jack comes back.'

'Oh for God's sake,' she said tartly. 'I'd not throw out a sick dog. Jack would have something to say to me if I did, but I've got to go carefully. You of all people should know that. Now can you get yourself up that ladder? It's not luxury but it's the best I can do. It's dry and safe and I'll see you have blankets and food.'

'We're more than grateful. Do you know when Jack is likely to return?'

'Now you're asking. He's dependent on wind and weather, as you should know, and this last week there's been a gale blowing with a thousand devils in it. No boat could survive an hour.' She took a quick look around her. 'Now up you go, out of sight and out of mind.'

He looked at the ladder, was quite sure he couldn't do it and then, with Isabelle's help, managed to reach the top before collapsing on to a great mound of soft sweet-smelling hay. A few minutes later the woman followed them, her arms filled with blankets and carrying a small lantern.

'Now let's take a good look at you,' she said with brusque kindness.

She helped Isabelle strip off his coat and slowly peel away the blood soaked shirt. She stood looking down at the raw, jagged place where the bullet had torn itself in at an angle. The flesh around the wound was already swollen and had an unhealthy blotched appearance.

'Well, you've got yourself into a pretty state, I must say. When did this happen?'

'Five, six hours ago,' said Isabelle. 'The guards were trying to stop us. One of them fired after us.'

'Well, there's not much we can do just now except cleanse and bandage. He needs a surgeon.'

'Don't worry,' whispered Robert. 'I'll survive till Jack comes.'

'Not with that bullet festering away inside you. Come with me,' she said to Isabelle. 'I'll find you clean linen and a salve. It may help.'

'It's very good of you, Madame Grandnez.'

'Oh leave that,' she said impatiently. 'I was never fond of the name. Call me Grisette, everyone else does. To tell the truth, I only married Grandnez to get my hands on this place and I wasn't sorry to see him go last winter, whether he drowned or just decided to take himself off I don't know and indeed don't very much care. Does that shock you, my dear?'

'No, no,' said Isabelle quickly, 'no, of course it doesn't.'

'Come then. Let's see what can be done for this man of yours.'

And in her way she did a great deal. She supplied them with lint and linen for bandages and brought them two bowls of good meat stew with newly baked bread that smelled wonderful. Robert could eat very little but he drank thirstily the hot black coffee and afterwards Isabelle helped her to settle the horses in the stable below.

'Tell her she can sell them later,' murmured Robert. 'If she waits a little she might get a good price for them. With any luck we shan't need them again. She's a handsome piece, isn't she, in her way. I wonder what good turn Jack did her that makes her so ready to help us.'

'I don't know but it feels marvellous,' confessed Isabelle as she stretched herself beside him.

If anyone had told her that a bed on a pile of hay wrapped in coarse black blankets would seem like very heaven, she would have laughed at them, but tired to the very bone, she found it blissful. The loft was clean and fresh and though there were mice, and possibly rats, at least there were no fleas or bedbugs.

Robert lay beside her, unable to sleep because of the pain and far more worried than he cared to admit. If Jack did not come soon, and with this hellish gale blowing the chances were slim, they were faced with two grim possibilities. First, they might well be traced here or the police could be making random checks along the coast knowing that their prey would certainly try to escape by sea and secondly, he knew enough about gunshot wounds to realise that his could grow a great deal worse, setting up a fever that could render him sick and incapable of dealing with any emergency that might arise.

Isabelle woke once in the night to find him tossing and shivering in an uneasy half sleep and she grew closer, putting her arms around him, trying to give him something of her own warmth and strength.

Early in the morning she heard Grisette calling quietly and slipped down the ladder to take the jug of hot coffee.

'How is his lordship this morning?'

Startled, Isabelle said, 'Why do you say that?'

'My dear, I wasn't born yesterday. I've known men, all kinds of men, and I recognise quality when I see it. Besides Jack has hinted once or twice. He admires him, you know, and that means something if you knew Jack. Not that I'm any great believer in titles. We got rid of them once and good riddance I'd say. Now they seem to be creeping back.' It was obvious that Madame was a good republican. 'But don't get me going on my hobby horse, that's not going to help our patient, is it?'

'I am afraid he is very sick. I think there must be some infection.'

'M-m-m, well, there is a fellow who comes into *Le Chat Noir* now and again. By all accounts he was at one time a surgeon in the British Navy. They say he half killed his Captain and only

457

narrowly escaped hanging for it. He's a surly fellow but he might be persuaded to do something.'

It seemed a desperate chance, but worth trying.

'Could you speak to him?'

'He wouldn't do it for me but he just might for you. It's as he feels, but he has done something now and again. He set a broken leg for one of the fisher lads and he saved a child who fell and cracked his skull and was taken up for dead. Dr Mac, they call him, but I saw his name once on a paper he had – Torquil McFee.'

'Torquil? That's Scottish.'

'Is it? Sounds heathen to me. God knows if it is his real one. I'll point him out and then it's up to you.'

But a couple of days went by, Dr Mac did not appear and Robert grew a great deal worse, gripped by a fever, alternatively shivering and burning, hanging on to his senses by a hair's breadth so that Isabelle hardly dared to leave him until one afternoon when Grisette came to find her.

'He's turned up again. He's down on the beach walking by the sea. It's a habit of his, remembering the old days perhaps. Go and talk to him.'

Now the moment had come, Isabelle was overcome with doubts. Would he listen, would he help them and if he did, could he be trusted or would he give them away? And most important of all, was he a capable surgeon? She knew very little of the Navy. Did they demand qualifications or was he a mere botcher, a barber-surgeon? Would he do more harm than good? Then she remembered Robert that morning fighting pain and the fever that clouded his mind. Something had to be done.

It was late afternoon but not yet dark. Down on the seashore a powerful wind blew her hair into a wild tangle and flattened her skirts against her body as she struggled towards him. The stocky figure was standing by one of the boats staring out over mountainous, white-tipped waves. She approached him a little timidly.

'May I speak to you, Dr Mac?'

'Don't call me that,' he said roughly. 'I resigned my right to that title long ago.'

'Please listen to me.'

He turned to look at her then, surprised and frowning, a strong craggy face with a stubble of beard under a thatch of reddish brown hair.

'Who are you? What do you want with me?'

'You are a doctor, are you not?'

The eyes surprisingly bright and clear in the ravaged face, scanned her from top to toe.

'I was once.'

'Doctors are like priests. They never lose their skills.'

That took him by surprise. 'Are you a Catholic?'

'I was brought up as one.'

'I too believed once, till I found that like all religions it was no more than milk-sop for babies. Who is it who needs me?'

'My husband.'

'What's wrong with this man of yours?'

Now was the moment. She must take a chance. 'He was shot three days ago. I think there is serious infection.'

'A bullet wound, eh? It's a long time since I did anything like that. I doubt if my hand is steady enough.'

'But you have instruments, you have the knowledge,' she said quickly.

'Maybe.'

'If you won't help, he could die.'

'Who is he, this wounded man of yours?' His eyes narrowed. 'An English spy on the run?'

'What makes you say that?'

'Never mind. Just give me one good reason why I should lift a finger to help an Englishman.'

'He is not English. He is a Scot, like you.'

He stared at her and then laughed, a harsh bitter sound. 'So you found that out, did you? Grisette, I suppose.'

He was still for a moment, his mind turning back to those long years at sea, peaceful some of them, with little to do but care for the ills of a ship's crew and spend hours with his books, terrible when the battle raged overhead and down in the bowels of the ship he probed for bullets, and amputated arms and legs, bound up hideous wounds, sometimes unbelievably saved a life and more often than not, able to do no more than prolong the agony when a quick death would have been more merciful – the blood, the stench, the reek of rum poured down the victims' throats to deaden the pain, and yet a life he had loved, took pride in . . . how agonisingly he had missed it. Abruptly he made up his mind.

'Very well, I'll come. Where is he, this husband of yours?'

'In the loft behind *Le Chat Noir.*'

'Hiding eh? Grisette, I suppose. She's a good soul.'

'Yes.'

'I'll come as soon as it is dark. Tell her to have plenty of boiling water. I may need it, and more light, as much as she can provide. I promise nothing but I'll do what I can.'

'Thank you, thank you a thousand times.'

'Don't thank me yet. I'm no miracle worker and nobody knows better than I how quickly a man can die.'

He turned and walked away from her across the beach towards the houses at the far end. Had she done right? She prayed she had. In a queer way he had given her confidence.

He came as he had promised, as soon as darkness fell. Grisette had provided another lantern and there were extra candles, with a bowl and a large iron kettle of boiling water. Robert lay propped up on the contrived bed and looked at him with fever-clouded eyes. He had little trust in this uncouth stranger but he knew something had to be done. He hated his weakness, loathed to be so utterly dependent on Isabelle.

'My wife tells me that you are a Scot,' he said in English.

'Aye, I am that. If you want to know my father is Minister to the Kirk in Ullapool.'

'Is he indeed? And mine is Francis Armitage of Glenmuir.'

The doctor's eyes widened in surprise. Isabelle had never hinted at who they really were.

'And why the devil is the son of a belted earl skulking in this God forsaken place?'

'Maybe I should be asking you the same question.'

'That's my business.'

'As this is mine. Shall we get on with it?'

460

'Aye, that's what I am here for.'

He put down his case of instruments. There had been days during the last five years when, driven by hunger and despair, he had been tempted to sell them but they had been hard won after long years of study and semi-starvation at Edinburgh and he still clung to them as a sort of sheet anchor. One day, surely one day he would regain what he had lost in that one moment of sad folly.

With Isabelle's help he removed the bandages. He frowned at the swollen and discoloured flesh around the wound, noted how Robert flinched at the lightest touch, but said nothing, simply taking off his coat and rolling up the frayed cuffs of his shirt. Scrupulously he scrubbed his hands in the bowl provided and opened the case, the knives, the lancets, large and small, saws, all gleaming evilly in the shadowy light.

'Now,' he said turning to Isabelle, 'are you going to assist me or shall I call Grisette?'

'She is busy with *Le Chat Noir*. I can do it.'

'No fainting at the sight of a little blood, I hope. I don't want two patients on my hands.'

'I've never done so yet.'

He gave her a long look. She had a steady nerve, this slip of a girl. He wondered if the blue-blooded aristocrat lying there knew how damned lucky he was.

'This is going to hurt like the devil,' he said brusquely. 'Do you want to numb yourself with brandy?'

'Do you take me for a child? For God's sake, get on with it!'

'As your lordship commands.'

There was a slight antagonism between them. To the surgeon Robert represented the class who had broken his career, sent him into the outer darkness because he had rebelled against one of them, the Captain whose sole notion of discipline was to flog and flog and flog again. He couldn't now remember the number of maimed and broken bodies he had tried to mend, often uselessly, till the day he could stand it no longer and seized the lash from the Bos'n's hand, slashing it across the hated sneering face.

461

Memories best forgotten. He put them behind him and turned to the task in hand.

Isabelle thought she would remember the next few minutes as long as she lived – the loft with its high raftered ceiling, the dim glow of the lanterns, the candle flames shaking in the draughts that eddied through the many cracks, Robert's face greenish white glistening with sweat, the dark stocky figure bent over him with the gleaming knife, the grunt as he plunged it in and took the towel from her to wipe away the pus, the long probe as he bent closer searching for the bullet with delicacy and expertise. She saw Robert suddenly go limp, the hand that gripped the edge of the palliasse relax, and looked at the surgeon in alarm.

'Don't worry. He's fainted, that's all, not surprising. It helps me to work more quickly.'

It was only a few minutes but it seemed like hours before he raised his head and slowly straightened up.

'I have it. Here it is, the little joker that's been causing all the trouble. It had flattened itself against the bone. See.' He held it out for her to look, the tiny bullet with a fragment of cloth still adhering to it.

For a moment she thought she would faint in sheer relief, but there was still too much to be done. She brought the bowl of water, handing him the swabs of linen which Grisette had provided and watched him cleanse and bandage with speed and precision. Afterwards, with a surprising strength, he lifted his patient into a more comfortable position and examined him carefully, heart, chest, pulse.

Robert's eyes flickered open.

'Is it done?' he breathed.

'Aye, it is done. You'll live to fight another day, my lord.'

There was still that faintly mocking note in his voice. Grisette had provided them with an old linen shirt that had belonged to her husband. He put it over Robert's head with surprising gentleness.

'Isabelle . . . will pay you . . . whatever you ask,' muttered Robert, still lost in a world of pain.

'Keep your gold for those who need it,' said the doctor, with a sudden fierce anger.

'I'm sorry . . . I thought . . .'

'Never mind.'

He frowned as he finished cleaning his instruments and replacing them carefully in their case. Then he moved to Isabelle, drawing her towards the door.

'Will he recover?' she whispered in trembling anxiety.

'I don't see why not. He has the will and the courage and that counts for a good deal, but he's going to be in a good deal of pain and there is little I can do for that except administer these few drops of laudanum, all I have left from my medicine chest.' He grinned lopsidedly. 'I have kept it to use myself when the nights become intolerable, but he needs it more than I do. Use it sparingly, it's all I have. I'll come again tomorrow.'

He brushed aside her fervent thanks and climbed down the ladder. She watched him disappear before she closed the door. She had sensed the integrity beneath the rough and ready manner and felt comforted. Then she turned back to Robert.

23

Robert began to improve more quickly than even the doctor had anticipated, but he did counsel extreme caution.

'The fever has abated but there could still be infection,' he said warningly. 'These are not ideal conditions for a sick man. Go slowly if you don't want to undo all the care your wife lavishes on you.'

Robert knew the advice was sound but he was impatient of the weakness that kept him chained to the loft and desperately anxious to get Isabelle away from France as soon as possible. He was very conscious of the fact that for the first time in his life he had put personal matters before public ones. Dundas had entrusted him with a mission that he had abandoned deliberately to go in search of his wife. There was little doubt that he had killed Henri Rivage, Fouché's most trusted colleague, which could have serious political implications if he were arrested and charged in his own name. He could not, must not allow that to happen. Very little news filtered through to this isolated community but how long before someone picked up the scent and came looking for them? It seemed a long time since they had shot their way out of the Château de Sauvigny but it was actually not much more than a fortnight and the search would certainly not yet have been given up.

The weather had not improved. In fact the gales that whipped the Channel into a frenzy had increased in strength. No fisherman would dare to take out a boat in such conditions, not even the experienced Jack Darrow would attempt anything so foolhardy, as Robert knew only too well. There would seem little point in escaping Fouché's widespread net only to drown in mid Channel.

So he lay and fretted and one afternoon when Isabelle was

not there, he fought his way on to his feet, managed to take a few unsteady steps and then fell heavily, wrenching his wounded shoulder so that she came back to find him lying face downwards on the bed, the bandages stained with fresh blood.

Dr Mac was not unduly perturbed. 'Sometimes a flow of blood can be beneficial. It carries away any latent infection. I don't think he has done himself too much harm.'

During these days drawn close together in their care for Robert, Isabelle had grown to like and trust Torquil McFee. Sometimes when she could escape out of the loft for a little she would walk on the seashore, finding exhilaration in fighting the wind and there she would run into him on one of his lonely walks, and found to her surprise that when he forgot his shy gruff manner, he could be an entertaining companion.

One afternoon she came in from one of these excursions, her cheeks scarlet, her eyes bright, her hair damp with sea spray, laughing as she took off her wet cloak and shook it out.

'Where have you been?' asked Robert.

'Walking on the beach. I like it there. The wind is stronger than ever but I enjoy fighting against it. I could hardly keep on my feet. If Dr Mac had not been there, I would probably have been blown away.'

'You seem to enjoy the company of our dour Scot,' said Robert with a slight edge to his voice.

'Yes, I do. He can be an interesting man.' She was trying to comb the sticky tangles out of her hair. 'I don't think he talks to many people here. Do you know,' she went on, turning to face him, 'that the girl he was to marry turned him down after the court martial? How could she have been so cruelly disloyal?'

'Very easily, I imagine. Most young women look for a home, children, protection, and he must have seemed a very poor bargain after that happened. How do you know? Has he been pouring out his heart to you?'

'No, of course not. He only hinted. I guessed the rest.'

'And naturally you lavished all your sympathy on him. Lucky devil!'

She gave him a quick look, then put down the comb and went to kneel beside him.

465

'Robert, are you jealous?'

'Yes, I am, furiously jealous because you can walk and talk with him and I'm tied to this abominable place, with every day the danger of being captured coming closer and closer.'

'But there's nothing we can do about that, is there?' she said reasonably. 'We have to wait and make the best of it and while we do . . .'

'You enjoy yourself with Dr Mac.'

'I won't walk with him ever again if you don't wish it.'

'Oh for God's sake, Isabelle, when have I ever forbidden you to do anything?'

'No, you have left me free always and that binds me to you all the more closely.'

'Does it?'

'You know it does.' Suddenly she had to know, she had to be certain. She put out a hand and turned his face towards her. 'You do trust me, don't you? You're not still thinking of Lucien?'

'That's in the past, forgotten.'

'Sure?'

'Absolutely sure.'

He sat up suddenly, seizing her hand and pulling her towards him so that she fell against his chest.

'Robert, do mind your shoulder!'

'Damn my shoulder! If you knew how I long to wipe him out of your mind, out of your heart.'

'You did that long ago.'

'Sometimes I'm not so sure.'

Then he was kissing her, ignoring the pain, kissing her almost savagely till he felt her tremble, felt her hand tangling in his hair pulling him closer to her. For a moment his senses whirled till pain shot fiercely through him, forcing him to relax his grip and Isabelle was looking at him, breathless, laughing a little.

'I'm not at all certain we should be doing this.'

'Maybe not.' He lay back against the pillow, smiling at her flushed face, a wave of new confidence surging through him despite his throbbing back. 'Does our Scottish friend kiss you out there in the teeth of the wind?'

'No, certainly not.' She was indignant. 'He wouldn't dare.'

'I don't know so much. If he's half the man I think he is, he is probably in love with you already.'

'Rubbish!' she said flatly, sitting back on her heels. 'But I have been thinking, Robert. Couldn't we do something for him?'

'Here we go again,' he said drily. 'What do you want me to do? I've no influence with the Navy, I'm afraid. He's not like Rory, you know, my love. There is no man more proud or more stubbornly independent than a Highlander. If I were to offer to set him up in practice, he would throw it back in my face. He despises me in any case. He's a strong radical at heart.'

'Perhaps he might,' she said thoughtfully.

'I'm quite sure of it.'

'I wonder. I've just had another idea. You know how Marian is always talking about how splendid it would be if she had a resident doctor at her East End Clinic. I think he'd like that. One of the reasons why he joined the Navy was because he thought the surgery and medicine throughout the ships was not always as good as it ought to be.'

'A one-man crusade, is that it?'

'Don't laugh, Robert. It meant a great deal to him.'

'I'm sure it did.'

'And you could make it seem as if he were doing us a favour instead of the other way round,' she went on eagerly.

He smiled and touched her cheek. 'Clever girl. It's certainly an idea if we ever get out of this wretched place.'

When the doctor came that evening for his usual examination he frowned down at Robert.

'What the devil have you been up to? There is considerable inflammation. Trying to use your arm, I suppose. I warned you to be careful. The bullet chipped the bone. That takes longer to heal than a flesh wound.'

'I'm sorry,' said Robert, 'but time is growing short. We've got to get away from here and somehow or other I must be on my feet when the chance comes.'

'That may be sooner than you think,' remarked Dr Mac perching himself on an upturned barrel that served as a stool. 'I smell a change in the weather. I noticed tonight that the wind

467

has lessened considerably and it's turning colder. There could be frost.'

'Then the sooner we move out of here the better.'

'Not quite.' The doctor looked from Robert to Isabelle and then said earnestly, 'Listen to me, both of you. I've been keeping my ear to the ground. Up to now, though there has been a deal of talk about you, the folk here have not yet realised who they are sheltering in their midst. The latest rumour is that Grisette is taking care of an old flame of hers from the past – oh yes, she had a past, you know, before she settled for respectability – and if you'll forgive me for saying so, my lord, you scarcely fit the part, a little too young for one thing. Should they realise that they are hiding an English spy with more than likely a price on his head by now, it might be quite another story if someone comes along asking awkward questions.'

'Is there someone?' asked Isabelle quickly.

'I'm not sure. Before I came here tonight, a man was knocking at the door of *Le Chat Noir* asking for a bed for the night with an air of consequence I did not care for. Grisette sent him off with a flea in his ear but he could come back. It may mean nothing but take great care, my lord. Exercise yourself up here if you wish, walk about, try out your strength, but be careful not to stick your nose outside. You too, my lady,' he went on to Isabelle. 'Tomorrow if I may, I'll borrow one of your horses and take a ride along the coast road. I could take a look at where Jack usually lands his boat and at the same time I may hear and see something that will give us a clue as to how the land lies.'

'That's uncommonly good of you,' said Robert.

'Well, we're on the same side, aren't we?' he said drily. 'I'd not like to see you both marched off to a French gaol. I've seen the inside of some of 'em.'

'I told you he was a good man,' said Isabelle when he had gone. 'Do you really believe that they could have traced us here?'

'It wouldn't surprise me,' said Robert thoughtfully, 'and I wouldn't like to put the good people here into serious trouble on our account.'

468

The doctor came early the next morning, reported that all seemed as usual, saddled the better of their two horses and trotted along the sea road towards the small cove where Jack Darrant had landed Robert on that morning which seemed like years ago and was not yet a month.

The day passed very quietly. Now the wind had dropped and the tumultuous sea quietened, some of the men were examining their boats, shaking out fishing tackle and scanning the weather prospects with experienced eyes.

The stranger did not return and Isabelle, venturing down to the back door, had a consultation with Grisette. She came back to report that there was a copse of trees some short way inland and a disused hut where animals had been kept.

'If this man comes again asking questions,' went on Isabelle, 'she will try to keep him occupied so as to give us time to slip away and lie hidden there till she lets us know it is safe to come back.'

'If I can walk as far,' said Robert gloomily. 'Of all the maddening things to happen. I never felt more useless.'

Most of that day he spent on his feet, resolutely refusing any help from Isabelle, trying to regain strength and balance, with his right arm in a sling to save any sudden wrench on his damaged shoulder, till at last he collapsed from sheer exhaustion. Then he drew out the pistol, carefully cleaning and reloading it and finding a place for it within easy reach.

'It's lucky I can shoot with my left hand pretty near as well as my right,' he said.

'Surely you won't need to use it.'

'It's just as well to be prepared.'

Dr Mac did not return that night but they had not expected him to do so since he might well have prospected inland before turning back. They woke to a cold dry morning with a light frost on the bare branches. One or two boats had ventured out to sea very early and they began to make a few preparations, putting their scanty possessions together and hiding them, pulling up the ladder when not in use to make the place look uninhabited to prying eyes.

All day they were tense and watchful, but by early evening

469

everything seemed quiet and Isabelle went down to the kitchen to collect their supper.

Grisette had it ready for her on a tray. She had reached the door when a man burst into the room, not in uniform but with all the authority and aggressiveness that marked Fouché's select force of secret police.

'Stop!' he bellowed. 'Where do you think you are going with that?'

She was so startled that she couldn't think of a ready answer and Grisette replied for her.

'What right have you to come pushing your way into my private quarters and bullying my servants? If you want to know, she's carrying that food to an old tramp I've been feeding for the last few days. I have my charities same as everyone else. Anything wrong with that?'

'And where is this so-called tramp of yours? Housed in your stable?'

'No, he's not as it happens. Too verminous for my clean place. He's lying in a stone byre out in the field. Do you want to go and look for yourself and collect a few fleas while you are about it?'

'A likely tale, I must say! I've been talking to some of the people here and a more stubborn set of numbskulls I've yet to meet, but I can put two and two together quicker than most men and come up with the right answer. You've got this English spy holed up here somewhere, so don't try to put me off with stupid lies. A murderous Englishman and his doxy, and I swear I'll lay hands on him before the day is done.'

'Oh and how do you think you're going to accomplish that when he's not here,' said Grisette sarcastically, wondering how much was bluster and how much he had guessed.

Isabelle had quietly put down her tray and seizing her chance made a dash out into the yard, but the policeman was too quick for her. He grabbed her by the arm, swinging her back roughly against the outside wall.

'Perhaps you'll tell me what I want to know, my pretty. You don't come from these parts that I'll swear.'

'No, she doesn't and what's that to do with you?' improvised

Grisette quickly. 'She's my niece, my sister's daughter here on a visit and she's a decent girl so you keep your hands off her, you great bully.'

'Your niece eh? That's a laugh.' He had drawn out a long, narrow knife gleaming wickedly in the light of the lantern already lighted above the back door. 'One more word from you, Madame, and I'll slice you up, both of you.'

He was a big man and he had them cornered against the angle of the outer wall. Grisette made a quick move to escape and the knife cut a long thin streak down her bare arm from which beads of blood instantly sprang.

Isabelle drew a startled breath and he turned back to her.

'That shocked you, did it? Well, that's a mere taster, there's plenty more to come if you won't co-operate. Come now, where is he? Where is he hiding eh? Skulking somewhere like some cursed coward, I'll be bound. Tell me and then it will be over for you and for the rest of the folk in this god-damned place.'

'I don't know what you're talking about,' said Isabelle bravely. 'I've never heard of any Englishman, nor seen any stranger, nor has my auntie. Someone must have given you the wrong information.'

'Oh no, he hasn't. You tell me or I'll line up these dumb villagers and pick them off one by one beginning with your auntie here. How would you like that, eh? Now where is he? Where?'

'I don't know. How can I tell you what I don't know?'

He moved a step nearer.

'I could carve a fancy pattern on that pretty face of yours.'

The knife touched her cheek, drawing a spot of blood, and then moved to her throat. She felt the prick and dug her nails into her hands to stop herself from crying out. He was so near she could see the sweat on his face and knew he was enjoying her terror, prolonging it deliberately.

'Speak, damn you, speak!' he said thickly, and again the knife pricked the soft flesh and there was a trickle of blood.

The sound of the shot so startled her that she fell back a step. There was a look of shock on the face so close to her, then the knife fell from his fingers, he spun round and collapsed on to the flagstones of the yard.

For a moment neither of them could move, then Grisette fell on her knees beside him.

'Oh my God, he is . . .'

She looked up and met Isabelle's eyes, the same thought in both their minds.

Two or three men, hearing the shot, had pushed into the kitchen from the front room of *Le Chat Noir*, others had come into the yard. They stood staring down at the man lying on the wet flagstones.

Isabelle was frozen into fear. Why had Robert done it? Why? Why? He had put himself into the most terrible danger.

There was an uneasy moment of silence, no one moved. Then the door of the loft opened and Robert came unsteadily down the ladder. In the old shirt Grisette had given him, with stained breeches, his arm in its ragged sling, his hair falling untidily across his forehead, no one could have looked less like the wealthy English Milord who was also a spy. With a little dry sob, Isabelle ran to him. He put his left arm around her and drew her close against him.

He looked across at Grisette.

'Is he . . .?'

She got slowly to her feet. 'He's dead all right.'

His eyes went round the ring of faces watching him.

'It was the only way I could stop him. He would have done what he threatened, you know. I've seen it before. Men, and women too, shot down one by one till they got what they wanted. I could not let that happen here. But they will come back in search of him. They will demand a price.'

Isabelle held her breath. He was putting himself in their hands. He was taking a chance.

There was another long pause, then one of the men took a step forward and she recognised him, a big fellow with a mop of black hair and a sweeping moustache, one of those who had laughed at her on the day she first came to *Le Chat Noir*.

'Reckon as how you've done us a favour, M'sieur,' he said laconically, 'never did care for the flics, set of interfering

472

busybodies, ready to poke their noses into what doesn't concern them, asking questions, taxing us out of existence.'

Suddenly it was as if in this tight, isolated community they had their own rules, their own set of morals. They had sheltered two fugitives and were not prepared to give them up to men they distrusted and feared.

Their leader summoned one of his comrades with a flick of his fingers.

'Jacques Martel, you can help me take this carrion down to the boats. Out beyond the reef there's good fishing now the sea is quiet. A couple of weights will send him to the bottom and help to fatten 'em. If those others come asking questions we'll know nothing, we'll have seen nothing, agreed?' A murmur ran from one to the other and a burly man came out from their midst to join him. 'More than one man has been lost on these coasts in stormy weather so why not he? But as for you, M'sieur,' he went on turning to Robert, 'better not wait till they come. Take your woman and go before the night is out, eh?'

'You have my thanks,' said Robert, 'my most sincere and heartfelt thanks.'

'Chut! What are thanks? She's the one you should thank, Grisette here, the heart of a lion and the cunning of a vixen, isn't that so, m'dear?' and he put an arm around her shoulders.

'You keep your hands off me, Jean Marius!' she said tartly. 'And don't just stand there, the rest of you. Get this filth out of my back yard and scrub it clean with a pail of water.'

The body was carried away, someone washed off the blood with a broom and she came to where Robert still leaned wearily against the wall of the stable.

'You had me on a knife edge for a few minutes,' she said, 'but thank God it worked. They're a rough lot but they mean well. Jean Marius is right however. If they come back, you must not be here.'

'I realise that.'

'You have a few hours yet. His comrades will not come looking for our dead friend yet awhile and by that time he'll be fathoms deep in the sea and no doubt Dr Mac will be back. Get up there again and I'll bring you some food.'

'I don't think I could eat a thing,' sighed Isabelle.

'Yes, you can. Always take care to eat when you can if times are hard. That's something every soldier will tell you,' she said sternly.

So they climbed up to the loft room again which in its bare comfortless way had become almost like home and Grisette brought them meat and bread with cheese and apples.

'It's cold, I'm afraid, but the best I can do this evening.' She put a bottle of wine between them. 'It's a good one I keep for my friends. You are a brave man, Monsieur Robert. It could have gone horribly wrong.'

'I was aware of that.'

'But it didn't, so all is well. Drink up and be happy.'

Impulsively Isabelle threw her arms around her and hugged her.

'We're so grateful for all you've done.'

'Oh well, shall I tell you something? I enjoy a bit of excitement now and again, reminds me of the old days even if I have settled for a quiet life. I'll be on the watch. Now the storm is passed, I'm pretty sure Jack will be here and if not – well, Jean Marius will do a lot for me and he's a good seaman. So eat your supper and don't fret too much.'

Robert looked after her as she clambered down the ladder and they pulled it up again.

'I bet you anything you like she's an old campaigner,' he said, 'and at some time in her life has followed the colours.'

'You had me terrified too,' confessed Isabelle. 'I'm still shaking when I think of it.'

'Did you imagine I'd allow that dirty-minded bully to carve you up?'

'Not only me but the others too.'

'Yes, the others too. There comes a time when you must act even if it means imprisonment, even if it means death.'

'I know,' she said softly.

'But now we've got a reprieve, though God knows for how long, so we'd best make the most of it.'

He leaned across to kiss her and unexpectedly it was like setting a candle flame to dry tinder, the danger, the relief, the

474

mounting tension of the last few weeks ever since that night of revelation at the château carried them into a frenzy of desire and passion that took them both by surprise. It was as if suddenly they could not wait, could not get close enough together. Robert forgot pain, forgot the stiffness of his shoulder. They fumbled with clothes while their mouths clung together.

'A one-armed man is at a disadvantage. You'll have to help me,' he murmured and she was unbuttoning his shirt while his hand sought and found her breast. The urgency drove them on swiftly, almost savagely, until at last they were locked together in a welter of discarded clothes and blankets, all the pain and wretchedness, the doubt and misery, swept away into a triumphant moment of joy until at last they lay exhausted but blissful. His finger touched the streak of dried blood on her cheek and he kissed it gently.

'I'd kill ten men rather than allow your face to be scarred, my darling.'

'It's not that important.'

'It is to me.'

She looked around them, laughing at the confusion.

'Not exactly a love nest, is it? I wonder what our friends would say if they could see us now?'

'Envy us our happiness.

Better a dish of herbs where love is
Than a stalled ox and hatred therewith'

'Proverbs, can't remember the verse. It was dinned into my ears by a Calvinistic tutor when I was about six, till Grandmother discovered what was happening and sent him packing. I always used to wonder why a stalled ox should be so wickedly luxurious when Grandmother's herbs smelled so sweet.'

Isabelle giggled as she sat up and began to pour the wine into the cups. They solemnly toasted one another, then Grisette, then the villagers, until she said, 'Robert, if I don't eat something I shall be drunk.' So they set to on the meat and bread and cheese and felt unutterably and quite ridiculously happy.

After all that, the arrival of Dr Mac and Jack Darrow later

that same evening was almost an anticlimax. There was still such an air of hilarity about them that the doctor glanced suspiciously at the half empty bottle and Robert laughed.

'Grisette made us a present of it but we've not drunk it all. We've left some for you. By God, it's good to see you, Jack.' He went on holding out his left hand in greeting. 'There have been times when we almost gave up. Your Madame Grandnez has proved a jewel of a woman. We'd have been lost without her. Fill up the cups, Isabelle, we'll drink another toast to her.'

So she poured out the rest of the wine and looked curiously at the lean dark man whom Robert called friend and who smiled but said little.

'You seem in very good spirits,' said the doctor, putting down his cup and looking from one to the other. 'Has something happened? Have they called off the search?'

'Very far from it,' said Robert grimly. 'We've had a visitor and a damned unpleasant one. Isabelle can tell you more about him than I can.'

Laughter forgotten, they told the grim story between them while the other two listened in silence.

'You took a most fearful risk,' said the doctor with a certain reluctant admiration. 'Didn't you realise how easily it could have gone wrong?'

'Oh I realised it all right,' admitted Robert. 'I was nervous as a cat in case my ability to shoot straight with my left hand wasn't as good as I thought it was, but sometimes you are left with no choice. If the people here had demanded that I must give myself up to save them from Fouché's vengeance – and he's capable of burning the whole place down – all I would have asked from them was Isabelle's freedom. Luckily for me they decided otherwise, and that's enough about that. Now tell us what fortunate chance has brought you two together.'

It seemed that the doctor had prospected along the coast road, gone inland asking one or two cautious questions, and then went on to the cove where Jack Darrow usually brought in his boat. He spent most of the night there and met up with him in the early morning. They had returned together leaving Ben

476

with the boat and taking a devious route so as to avoid arousing suspicion.

'I can tell you one thing for sure,' he went on to Robert. 'From all I have heard, your life is forfeit. They would do everything in their power to get you behind bars so there is no time to be lost.'

'It seems to me,' said Jack Darrow, speaking for the first time with his quiet air of competence, 'that the sooner we get you and your lady on board and away from these shores the better. There is only one problem. The sea is quiet enough now particularly inshore, but there is a considerable swell out in mid channel and it could grow stronger. I don't know whether Ben and I can crew the boat alone if a heavy gale should come up.'

'We have little choice,' said Robert frowning. 'To stay till I get my strength back and run the risk of being clapped up in a French prison or leave now and stand a chance of drowning in the Channel. It must be your decision, Jack, it's your life too, yours and Ben's, but I would point out that I'm not entirely helpless. My left arm is still good enough and at a pinch I daresay I could use the right.'

There was a moment of silence, then the doctor said gruffly, 'You could do yourself very serious damage if you did. I have had experience of sailing and I've certainly still got my health and strength. I could lend a hand under instruction.'

'You mean you would come with us?' exclaimed Isabelle.

'There is nothing to keep me here and I can starve just as well in London as on the shores of France,' he said drily.

'Oh but . . .' began Isabelle and was instantly silenced by Robert's quick gesture, fully aware that to hint at any reward for his generosity would offend his pride and independence intolerably.

'If you're as good a sailor as you are a surgeon,' went on Robert with his easy charm, 'I know Jack will be eternally grateful to you, as we all will.'

'That's settled then. Hadn't we better start making preparations immediately? From what I've heard and from what has happened here today I don't imagine they will lose much time in coming in search of you or indeed of all of us,' said the doctor getting to his feet.

There was little enough to be packed up but there were farewells to be made. Grisette hugged Isabelle, and greatly daring, kissed Robert on both cheeks. He gave her most of the money he had left which she was very reluctant to accept.

'I didn't do it for this,' she protested, 'but for Jack and for the two of you.'

'I know but use it how you wish. The people here are poor enough, God knows, and the winter could bring problems.'

Jack kissed her cheek and Isabelle couldn't help noticing how she clung to him for a moment and wondered if at some time these two most unlikely people had once been lovers.

Then they must go, Robert and Isabelle riding the two horses and carrying such baggage as they had, with the doctor and Jack trudging beside them. At the last moment Grisette came out with a package of food and handed it up to Isabelle.

'What about the horses?' said Robert, impatiently pushing aside the doctor's helping hand and hoisting himself into the saddle. 'They are yours now, you know.'

'Leave them tethered there among the trees. It's a quiet spot and as soon as Jean Marius comes back with his boat, I'll send him along to fetch them. He has been wanting to buy a horse all this past year but the money has been hard to come by. Now he can keep one of them as a gift from the Englishman.'

She laughed and waved, watching the incongruous little cavalcade setting out bravely into the dark night.

They reached the cove shortly after five o'clock. It was still dark with only a faint lightening of the sky over the sea and Isabelle caught her first glimpse of the boat that was to carry them to safety looming up out of the shadows.

'It's so much bigger than I imagined,' she exclaimed.

Robert smiled at her. 'What did you expect? A rowing boat?'

'I don't know quite what I thought, something like that, I suppose,' she confessed.

'Don't ever say that to Jack. The *Seagull* is his pride and joy.'

'Did you provide it?' she asked curiously.

'Not exactly. The Foreign Office had a hand in it too.'

Ben had used a piece of sail canvas to rig himself up a rough shelter within a copse of scrubby trees and had started a little fire, partly to keep himself warm, partly to boil a pannikin of water for breakfast. He leaped to his feet grinning broadly with relief and pleasure as the little party came into view.

Robert slid from his horse, horribly stiff and aching in every limb. It annoyed him to find he was not nearly as fit as he had hoped. The days of sickness had taken a heavy toll but he took care to hide his weakness from the others.

Jack was scanning the sea with an experienced eye. 'A good hour or so before the tide turns. We'll wait and warm ourselves at the fire.'

'Good idea,' said the doctor. 'We'd better eat too. We have a long cold trip before us.'

'We have the food that Grisette gave us,' said Isabelle.

'I'm afraid I have no coffee or tea,' apologised Jack, 'but I do have chocolate. Build up the fire, Ben, and fill the pan with water.'

'Aye, Master, aye, I'll do that.'

The big lad, who had been standing shyly gazing at Isabelle as if she were a being from some other planet, hurriedly knelt down again and picked up the pail of water.

'I'll help you, shall I?' she said, giving him a dazzling smile and going to kneel beside him.

'Thank 'ee, Miss, my lady,' he stammered turning bright scarlet. 'I were just goin' to make it for myself.'

They gathered around the little fire. They had no milk or sugar but the hot bitter chocolate was comforting and Grisette's bread and tasty sausage went down well. The fear of discovery was still there tensing their nerves but they tried to ignore it, laughing, joking, urging Dr Mac to tell of some of his adventurous voyages though Jack could not be persuaded to join in, saying nothing in his life had been worthy of record. These two with their lifelong love of the sea and ships had already drawn close together.

When the light began to strengthen, it was time to go. Isabelle had saved two apples for the horses. She gave them one each and kissed the soft noses. They had proved good friends during so many hard days of riding. Then she followed the others to the edge of the sea.

The tide was beginning to ebb. She hesitated, looking at the stretch of water she must splash through to reach the *Seagull*. At any other time Robert wouldn't have hesitated. He would have picked her up with ease and carried her through. Now infuriatingly he could do nothing, was forced to stand by while Dr Mac came to her side, saying cheerfully, 'With your permission, my lady,' swinging her up in his arms, striding through the water with her. It was absurd to feel so irritated by it, but he did and angrily pushed Ben away when the boy came to him shyly offering his assistance.

The *Seagull* was rough and ready, it boasted no luxuries, but it was spotlessly clean and had certain comforts. There was a tiny hold where there were blankets and cushions and Jack with the doctor's backing urged Isabelle to take shelter there out of the wind and Robert with her. He refused absolutely to do any such thing and obstinately remained on deck doing what he could lefthandedly, leaving the other three to manage the intricacies of sailing.

For the first few hours everything went well with them and they made fair headway, despite a contrary wind that was not strong enough to blow them off course but slowed them up and needed constant skilful manoeuvring to keep the head turned towards the south east.

The short winter's day was already drawing in when the gale that Jack had dreaded caught up with them. The first gust came so suddenly and with such force that it nearly overset them. Water flooded across the deck almost sweeping Isabelle off her feet. She skidded on the wet planking and cannoned into Robert who held her tightly braced against the rail. Then miraculously the *Seagull* righted itself and she was able to laugh a little shakily.

For the next few hours it was a desperate struggle to survive. Robert begged her to go below into the tiny cabin, but she would not. It was too claustrophobic. She had an inner fear of the *Seagull* foundering when she would be trapped, fighting for air, unable to break out.

It was maddening that it should have happened now when they were comparatively near home. Jack was all for making for a safe harbour no matter where it was but that was easier said than done. He had never known such a contrary wind. It seemed to come from all directions and there had to be a constant wrestling with the sails. When he tried to turn inshore it came blasting across the south downs blowing them back into mid channel, with the harbour he was hoping to reach receding further and further away.

In the midst of this turmoil there was one moment of quiet, one moment of sudden calm, when they stopped to look at one another, laughing at themselves, windblown and wet with seaspray, exhausted but triumphant, then it had vanished. With an ear-splitting shriek like some evil banshee there came the wind again, taking even Jack by surprise, temporarily whipping the tiller from his hands. An enormous wave poured across the deck, caught Isabelle unprepared and took her back with it, slipping and sliding into the swirling white-tipped water.

For a split second they stared unable to believe, then the doctor said agonisingly, 'Christ, I can't swim!', but Robert, regardless of his aching shoulder, tore off the heavy oilskin he had put round his shoulders, kicked off his boots and went in after her.

The icy cold of the water hit him hard. It took his breath for a moment but he could see her as she came up through the waves, choking and terrified, and he swam towards her driven by a force stronger than pain, stronger than disability.

He caught hold of her. 'Don't struggle,' he gasped breathlessly, 'let yourself go. I've got hold of you.'

Through her fear she heard his voice. It gave her strength and she did as she was told.

Jack had swung the tiller, trying to steer the *Seagull* towards them, peering into the darkness only lit by the faint light from the lantern swaying crazily above his head. The force of the water plunged Robert back towards the boat. Willing hands leaned over catching hold of her dress, dragging her over the

481

side. Then the boat heaved again in the wind and the surge of the sea carried Robert away. He tried desperately to reach out, to hold on to the rope thrown to him, but his strength was ebbing, pain and cold were taking a grip on him, his hand slipped and he was being carried further and further out of their reach, and all Jack's desperate manoeuvring could not bring the *Seagull* any closer to him. The boat rocking in the wind was like a live creature in their hands. They could not control it. Jack peered into the darkness with a chill at his heart. By now Robert could have been swept into any direction. To find him in that stretch of wild sea seemed hopeless and yet they went on searching. He and Ben called out again and again until they were hoarse but there was no answering cry.

Isabelle, half-drowned and semi-conscious, didn't realise at first what was happening. Dr Mac had carried her down into the cabin, stripped off her sodden clothes and wrapped her in blankets.

Her first conscious thought was of Robert. She sat up looking wildly around the tiny cabin.

'Where is he? Where is Robert?'

'Don't worry,' he said soothingly. 'Jack and Ben will find him.'

'Find him? What do you mean? He brought me back to the boat. I remember that. What have you done with him?' She was beating at his breast in a kind of frenzy. 'You have let him drown.'

He caught her hands and held them in his. 'No, Isabelle, no.'

'Then where is he? I must go and find him. He can't die. I won't let him die.'

But swaddled in blankets she could not move and he pressed her gently back against the cushions.

'Believe me there's nothing you can do. Stay here. I will go. They will have picked him up by now, I'm sure they will.'

He went out and up on to the deck. Immediately the wind caught him and threw him forward on to his knees. He struggled up again. One look at their faces told him how hopeless it was.

'We're still searching,' said Jack.

'My God, what are we going to tell her?'

'That there is still hope.'

482

But there wasn't. They knew that, so did he and so did Isabelle when he went down to her again.

One look at his face and she turned away from him, her eyes full of an anguish that tore at his heart.

Robert's first reaction when he realised that the sea was carrying him further and further away from the *Seagull* was anger, a furious anger that after all they had been through and when safety lay only a few hours away, blind chance should have done this to them. It was that grim feeling of rage and the desire to fight it that kept him afloat for a while, battling with the deadly chill, the pain, the weakness. He turned over on his back and let himself float for a time to ease the deadly ache of his shoulder, his senses blurring a little, carrying him back to his boyhood when he and David had swum together in the icy Scottish lochs with nothing to fear and everything to hope for . . . Something bumped into him, a log, a ship's timber, he wasn't sure what it was but he held on to it with his left hand and it gave him a few moments of respite . . . He knew he was tiring, wondered vaguely if he could strike out for the shore and guessed he would never reach it. How absurd it was to die just when everything had straightened itself out, when he and Isabelle had reached a new depth of understanding . . . Some kind of a current was carrying him along more quickly now but the cold was too intense, he had begun to realise he couldn't hold on much longer when he saw the light, bobbing and dancing in front of him . . . Was it the *Seagull*? He let go the wood and swam towards the light. The effort took all his remaining strength. He thought he could hear someone shouting . . . was it in French? Couldn't be. He was escaping from France, wasn't he? In any case he had no breath to answer. He made one last enormous effort, then could do no more. A weight of exhaustion seemed to drag him down, down . . . The sea closed over his head and he sank into a soft thick darkness.

'Isabelle, my dear,' said Harriet Holland, knocking at the door and then coming into the bedroom, 'that gentleman is here again, that Dr McFee. He is asking to see you very particularly.'

Isabelle looked up quickly from the chair by the window. 'Has he come with fresh news?'

'He did not say so.'

The hopeful gleam faded from her face.

'No, of course not. How could he? It's six days now. It's foolish to go on hoping, isn't it? It's time I faced up to the truth, forced myself to believe that he has gone from me for ever.'

'Oh my dear, if you knew how deeply I feel for you.'

'I do know. You have been so good to me, both of you. Will you tell him I'll be down in a few minutes?'

'I will and I'll make you both some coffee.'

'Thank you.'

Harriet hurried downstairs, an ache at her heart.

'If only she would break down, if only she would weep, it would be so much better for her,' she said to her brother in the kitchen. 'I don't seem able to reach her. She just sits there as if some spring was broken inside, as if she did not want to go on living.' She put the kettle on to the hob and began to measure coffee beans into the grinder. 'She can't go on like that, Gilbert.'

'You must give her time, my dear. She is still in shock.'

'She will not even let me write to her brother or to her sister-in-law. They must be suffering great anxiety. When Lady Marian came here that day asking questions, to which of course we could give no answers, she told me that the Earl himself had come down from Scotland.'

'She will go on to them in her own good time,' said her brother, patting his sister on the shoulder. 'We know so very little, Harriet, it is not for us to interfere.'

Upstairs in the pretty bedroom with its flowered linen curtains and the patchwork quilt worked by Miss Holland herself, Isabelle was thinking the same thing. She must take up her life, shoulder her responsibilities, however hard it was going to be. She must not delay any longer. She would have to go back to London tomorrow.

She got up and glanced listlessly in the mirror. Harriet had loaned her a dress in dark grey wool with a little lace at neck and cuffs. The last six days seemed to have passed in a kind of blur of numbed despair ever since that night when, exhausted

484

and deeply grieving, they had limped into Rye Harbour at last. She knew that Jack and Dr Mac had been wonderful. They had taken her to the tiny hut. Jack had built up a huge fire while the doctor massaged her frozen body back to life, wrapping her in warm blankets, pouring brandy and hot coffee down her throat, taking her as soon as it was feasible to the Vicarage, where Gilbert and Harriet Holland had willingly taken her to their heart. It seemed strange to her that she had suffered so little physically, it was the terrible knowledge that it was she who had brought Robert to his death that tormented her, that shut her into a despair from which she could not escape.

She went slowly down the stairs and into the front parlour where Dr McFee waited for her. He got up as she came in and she went to him stretching out her hand.

'Miss Holland said you wanted to see me.'

'Yes.' He took her hand and held it for a moment looking into her face with a professional eye. 'I have come every day to ask her how you were. I feared that you might have suffered from the cold, from the exposure.'

'I am perfectly well, no ill effects at all, thanks to you and Jack.' She withdrew her hand gently and moved to the small table. 'I see there is some coffee. May I pour it for you?'

'Thank you.' He took the cup and sat down again.

They were being desperately formal with one another, unable to speak of what was closest to both of them.

'Will you try a griddle cake? Miss Holland is famous for them. Robert used to say . . .' Then she faltered, turned away her head unable to go on.

He wanted to put his arms around her, try to comfort her but knew he dare not.

'Thank you, nothing to eat. I must go soon. I really came to say goodbye. I can't trespass on Jack's hospitality any longer. I must go to London, look for some kind of employment, but I could not leave before, I had to wait just in case . . .'

'In case there might have been some good news, but there is nothing. I don't know how, but I must learn to accept that.' Her voice trembled and then steadied. 'Will you come and see me in London? There was something – something Robert and I

485

spoke of together – something that might be of assistance to you.'

'I would not wish to trouble you in any way,' he said stiffly.

'It would be no trouble, rather it could be of assistance to us – it concerns his sister. Will you come? Please do.'

'Of course, if you wish it.'

'It is Glenmuir House in Arlington Street, just off Piccadilly.'

'I will remember.'

He did not stay long and when he had gone and Harriet came in to collect the tray, Isabelle got up with a new determination.

'I've made up my mind. I must go back to Arlington Street tomorrow.'

'Perhaps that is best. How will you go? Shall I send Joe to book a place on the London coach?'

'Yes, I'd prefer that.' She made a little helpless gesture. 'I have no money. I shall have to borrow from you till I reach home.'

'You mustn't let that worry you.'

She had moved to the window. 'What kind of a day is it? I would like to walk down to the sea.'

'Oh my dear, is that wise? It's not raining but it is bitterly cold and you should not walk there alone.'

'Why not? I always did in the old days.'

'Well, if you do go, you must take my warm cloak and put on my new boots.'

'Oh Harriet,' she exclaimed with a little laugh that was half a sob. 'What would I have done without you?'

She gave her a little impulsive hug and went to get ready.

Half an hour later she set off. The air was icy as Harriet had warned her but the sky was clear and she walked quickly down the familiar bridle road. Every bough and twig was lightly tipped with frost but there was very little wind. That vicious gale having done its evil work had blown itself out. She went past the Ship and Anchor and on to the lighthouse. Beyond stretched the empty beach where she had found Lucien, where Robert had come on that day and seen her bathing half naked in the sea that had torn him away from her. It was hard to remember that it was December, and Christmas only a couple of weeks away. There seemed an immeasurable gap between now and the morning she and Guy had set out so joyously, a gap of time that was out of time during which she had grown so much older and wiser.

She walked on and then sat for a while with her back against one of the smaller boats pulled up high on the beach out of harm's way. The sea that could be so cruel was deceptively calm, grey and still, lapping gently at the water's edge. Perhaps if she walked out into it, walked and walked, then she would die too. It might be a way out. She did not know how she was to break the news to Marian, how she could meet the bitter reproach in her eyes. Then there was the Earl, that formidable figure, who was only now learning to accept Robert's kitchen-maid bride and now must be told that she had drowned his only son. She would have liked to run away and hide herself somewhere, but that would be the act of a coward. She shivered, feeling the bitter cold beginning to creep up her back. She pulled Harriet's thick cloak more closely around her and got to her feet.

The beach had been empty that morning, too bleak even for the children who usually played around the lighthouse. Now there was one man coming from the direction of the Ship and Anchor, a fisherman by the look of him, a thick padded coat, heavy boots and peaked seaman's cap that had a foreign look about it. One of the smugglers must have brought it back with him, she thought idly, and then she stopped, staring. He had quickened his pace, had taken off the cap, was waving it above his head, the thick brown hair grown too long was blowing in the breeze . . . she drew a quick breath . . . it wasn't . . . it couldn't be . . . it must be a dream, a hallucination conjured up out of her thoughts and her misery . . . then she was running, they were both running, struggling across the loose shingle, till she collapsed in his arms.

'Robert!'

She was gasping, stammering, crying, all at once, hanging on to him as if she would never let him go, tears pouring down her face.

'Well, this is a fine welcome, I must say, weeping all over me as if I haven't had enough of salt water,' but he was holding her tightly against him. They stood locked together for a moment, not wanting to move till the first exultation, the first relief and joy had eased a little.

'But where have you come from? Out of the sea? Has the wind relented and blown you back to me?' she asked when she could speak coherently, still gripping his arm as if she thought he might vanish at any moment.

'Nothing so romantic, I'm afraid. I have come from the Ship and Anchor.'

'But how, why, when?'

'It's a long story.'

'I want to hear it, all of it. Why didn't you come to us? We've been in such agony over you.'

'It was past midnight by the time I arrived there. I was coming to the Vicarage this morning in search of you when Mary Hope said she believed she had seen you walking past the inn so I came after you.'

She was looking at him more closely now. He was very pale with bruising shadows under his eyes and she saw that he still kept his right hand tucked into his coat.

'Tell me what happened.'

'I ought to see the Hollands as soon as possible.'

'Tell me as we go.'

'I was picked up by a French lugger if you please, one of those plying their illegal trade between here and France. They turned me upside down, shook the sea water out of me and poured contraband brandy down my throat till I passed out. It was twenty-four hours later before I had any idea of what had happened to me. By that time they were safely moored in a harbour somewhere near Boulogne. I was lying in the cabin wrapped in blankets. They must have stripped me down, kept me warm, and undoubtedly saved my life.'

'Did they know who you were?'

'No, thank God. What identity papers were in my pocket were in the name of Maurice Dupont. I was feeling pretty groggy by then but I had enough wits left to concoct a tale of quarrelling with my own particular gang, being shot up and heaved overboard. They swallowed that since it is the kind of thing that sometimes happens. They were even sympathetic but, mother naked, and with as much strength as a sick cat, I couldn't do much about anything. My clothes had vanished including what money I had left, but they were kind enough in their way, found me these rather odd garments and brought me food at intervals. The one thing they were not prepared to do was to make a special trip back to these shores for my sake. I could be there still if some emergency hadn't arisen and they decided to make a quick trip while the sea was in a good mood, and so here I am.'

'It's so incredible, I still can't take it in,' she breathed.

'Do you know who was the first person I met when I stepped ashore last night and they were arguing over some contract or other? Jonty, of all people! And he knew me even in this disguise. For one horrible moment I thought he was going to give me away, but though he frowned and grunted and looked daggers at me, he kept his mouth shut otherwise I would have been shipped back to France or held up for ransom and I tremble to think what the Foreign Office would have had to say about that!'

'What are you going to tell them at Whitehall, Robert?'

'Very little I hope. It depends on what has filtered through.'

'Will you have to tell them about me . . . and Lucien?'

'Not if I can help it. To all intents and purposes, my love, you and I have been indulging in a secret holiday for the past six weeks.'

She giggled, far too happy to worry very much about anything.

'Marian will never believe that, nor will your Father.'

'Oh Lord, is Papa in on this?'

'I am told Marian sent to him and he has come down from Glenmuir.'

'Oh well, just another problem to be faced.'

'I was intending to book a seat on the London coach tomorrow. Shall I ask Joe to reserve two places?'

'To hell with that! I'll go along to the Salutation. Mr Lambe will arrange all that for us. We'll take a postchaise. The sooner I get out of these clothes the better. Have you noticed? There is a very ancient fishy smell somewhere. Do you think the Vicarage could run to a bath?'

Epilogue

NEW YEAR'S EVE
1803

'I don't believe a word of it,' said David. 'You arrive in a hired postchaise, you looking like death, and Isabelle as if a puff of wind would blow her away, not an item of baggage between you, and ask us to believe that you've just returned from a six weeks' holiday. Come on, Robert, it's just not good enough. Don't you think you ought to tell us what really happened?'

They were in his study the very next day after the carriage brought them back to Arlington Street. The first moments of joy and relief, the house buzzing with excitement, the dogs' frenzied welcome, the servants all agog with curiosity, were all over. The time had now come for explanations which for various reasons Robert was very unwilling to give.

'I'm sorry but that's really all there was to it.'

'Poppycock!' exclaimed the Earl, heaving himself out of the armchair and straddling the rug in front of the fire. 'It's very far from being all. That tale may serve to fob off your London acquaintances but it won't do for me. I'm your father, remember? I want the truth. Damn it, I deserve it after having been dragged all the way from Glenmuir to find Marian in floods of tears, the house in an uproar, the women servants going off into the vapours at the slightest thing and that confounded little dog of Isabelle's howling night and day, and after all that, in you walk, the pair of you, calm as you please, with some balderdash about enjoying a second honeymoon.' He snorted angrily. 'I wasn't born yesterday, you know.'

'Believe me, Father, there's very little else to it.'

'And do you expect me to swallow that? It's no use looking daggers at David. He shuts up like an oyster at the first question. Now you listen to me, my boy. I may live out of the world but I'm not deaf or blind or in my dotage. I still hear a good deal of

493

what goes on. What about that unpleasant business with your wife, eh? And that duel of yours. Why the devil didn't you finish the fellow off when you had the chance? You used to be a crack shot. It's pretty obvious to me that your kitchen maid bride after playing fast and loose with you all the summer, ran off with that wretched frog, leaving you with no alternative but to chase after them. That's about the truth of it, isn't it?'

'No, it damned well isn't!' said Robert, 'you've got it all wrong.'

'Have I? Then perhaps we might have the truth for once. Damn it, don't you think I have a right to know?'

'Oh hell!' Robert exchanged a hunted look with David and wondered how little he could say that would satisfy his father. Tell the whole story and more than likely he would go boasting of his son's exploits as if he were some hero of romance. The very last thing he wanted.

'Come on, boy,' said the Earl impatiently. 'Must we wait all day?'

'Oh very well,' he said reluctantly. 'If you must know, some of the work I've been engaged in during the last few years has made me enemies in France. I believed I had escaped them, had preserved my incognito, but it seems I was wrong. Lucien de Vosges was simply their instrument. They sought to get at me through my wife. Briefly Isabelle was tricked into going down to Kent believing she was to join me. She was attacked and abducted. Guy who was with her, tried to save his sister but was left for dead. Mercifully he was picked up and able to tell me what had happened and where she was being taken, so I went after her.'

'And you brought her back.'

'Yes.'

'I hope this time you gave that unpleasant young man what he richly deserved. Did you kill him?'

'No. It so happened that Isabelle did.'

'What!' exclaimed David. 'Are you telling us that . . .'

'She shot him in the nick of time otherwise I would not be here with you now.'

'Well, I'm damned!' said his father. 'Good for her. You know, I always thought that young woman had pluck.'

'Did you?' said Robert ironically. 'You could have fooled me.'

'It must have been the very devil getting away from them, wasn't it?' went on David.

'It certainly had its problems.'

'Which you don't intend to tell us.'

'No, not until I have made my report. I must see Dundas as soon as it can be arranged.'

'Well,' said the Earl, 'all I can say is, let it be a lesson to you. Give up this work of yours. They've done their best to kill you, next time they could succeed and then what is to happen to Glenmuir? It is going to be yours, Robert, isn't it time you took an interest in it? I'm not going to live for ever, you know. I want my son . . . and my grandson.'

Robert looked up quickly. 'What is all this? You're not sick, are you?'

'No, no, no,' said his father testily. 'I'm as well as ever I was but life's damned uncertain. You of all people should realise that. And that reminds me, I saw that doctor fellow hovering about the house this morning. Was it you he came to see or your wife?'

'I met with an accident. I have had trouble with my shoulder.'

'I thought perhaps Isabelle might have found herself in a certain condition.'

Robert laughed. 'Father, you are incorrigible. Isabelle is not pregnant so far as I know.'

'Pity.'

Robert was spared any further questions by Hawke knocking and coming into the room.

'I am sorry to interrupt, my lord,' he said respectfully, 'but Lady Isabelle would like to know if the gentlemen would care to join her and Lady Marian for a light luncheon.'

'Excellent idea,' exclaimed Robert seizing upon it with relief. 'Tell her we will be with her immediately, all three of us.'

To his surprise Robert was given something of a hero's welcome when a few days later he reported to Henry Dundas. His rather

495

stiff confession that he had neglected his instructions in order to follow his own personal affairs was brushed aside as of no consequence.

'My dear Robert,' said the statesman, 'it is the mark of an intelligent man to know precisely the right moment to abandon the rigid lines laid down for him and act on his own initiative, and it is that very quality that I have always admired in you.'

'You're very kind, my lord,' he said drily. 'I gather the news has filtered through to you.'

'Indeed it has. They tried to hush it up but that colleague of yours in Angers contrived to send it through one of our agents. No names, of course, but we knew who was responsible. My congratulations. You have rid us of one of our most troublesome enemies in that field. A number of loyalists, and I daresay not a few Frenchmen, will be breathing a sigh of relief that Dr Henri Rivage is no longer pursuing his evil career. There is something else too that should please you. The Chevalier de St George has been given his marching orders. Not enough proof to hang him unfortunately but we've put a stop to his little games and I'm told he is decidedly sick at losing his comfortable pension from Bonaparte's jackal. Lady Vernon has been warned to close down her little gaming house though I don't doubt that resourceful lady will come up with some new scheme sooner or later. Well, that is my news, now what of yours? The trouble with your arm is a temporary disability, I take it.'

'Oh surely. The sling I'm wearing is on doctor's orders. I have been using it too much for his liking.'

'Good, good, because I have something very particular to discuss with you.'

'No,' said Robert, 'no, my lord, not this time. My mind is made up. No more missions into France.'

'Who said anything about France? Come now, my dear boy, take a few months off, get fit, go out and enjoy yourself. I'm pretty sure that what I'm going to suggest will appeal to you. You can have time to think about it, even discuss it with your wife.'

'My wife?' said Robert frowning.

'Certainly. This time you can take her with you. Indeed it would be to our advantage and to yours if you did.'

'I am afraid I don't understand.'

'You will, you will, but a glass of claret first. I have a case of a really excellent vintage and daren't ask my wine merchant where he procured it. I'd value your opinion. We'll share a bottle and you can tell me how you contrived to escape Fouché's clutches, and I'll give you the details of what we have in mind for you.'

When Robert returned home that afternoon he came into the drawing room to find Isabelle on the floor poring over a large map with Dr McFee kneeling beside her, and noticed with wry amusement that his eyes were fixed on Isabelle's flushed, excited face rather than on what she was pointing out to him. He wondered if he would ever be able to accustom himself to the plain fact that other men desired his wife. He was not the only one to be caught in her spell.

'May I ask what all this is about?' he enquired.

Isabelle sat back on her heels and the doctor sprang to his feet looking slightly embarrassed.

'Lady Isabelle asked me to call when she returned to London, my lord, and she has just told me the splendid news. I can't tell you how happy I am to see you looking so well after such an appalling experience.'

'Thank you. I still shudder occasionally when I remember it.'

'Does that wound of yours still trouble you?'

'Scarcely at all. The sling is a mere precautionary measure advised by my doctor who, I may say, expressed strong approval of your surgery.'

'I only did my best.'

'In the circumstances a great deal more than your best.' Isabelle had scrambled to her feet and was rolling up the map. He glanced from one to the other. 'What is it you two have been planning this afternoon?'

'I was showing the doctor where Marian's clinic is in Wapping. He is not familiar with London and I thought he might be interested.'

497

'I see. Actually it is my sister's pet scheme. Perhaps Isabelle has already told you that for some time Marian has been talking of establishing a medical unit there. Perhaps you would like to meet her if you have not already decided on what you intend to do.'

'Oh no, not yet, there has scarcely been time.' He hesitated. 'But I would not wish to be asking any favour – your sister may have made other plans.'

'My dear fellow, there is no question of that, I assure you. You would be doing Marian a favour and I strongly advise you not to make any rash decisions till you have seen the place. The centre is housed in an old ramshackle warehouse and your patients are likely to be the very dregs of humanity.'

'I would still be interested.'

'In that case why not come and dine with us and discuss it with her.'

'I – I don't know,' he gave a hunted look around the richly furnished room, 'I'm not sure if I . . .'

'Just ourselves, quite informally,' went on Robert smoothly, 'I don't feel up to facing company yet and neither does Isabelle. Leave your address with Hawke and we'll send word.'

'Thank you. I shall look forward to it. Now I must go. I shouldn't stay and tire you. It has been a great pleasure to see you both again.'

He bowed to Isabelle and to Robert and somehow got himself to the door where the butler appeared to show him out.

'Oh Lord,' said Robert dropping on the sofa as the door closed behind him, 'I nearly put my foot into it, didn't I? The poor devil probably only has the clothes he stands up in.'

'You got out of it beautifully, the perfect diplomat,' said Isabelle coming to sit beside him and slipping her arm through his. 'Are you very tired?'

'No, not at all, but I have had a long session with Dundas and have drunk too many glasses of his excellent claret.'

'He is not persuading you to undertake some further mission, is he?' she asked in some anxiety.

'Would you mind very much if he did?'

'Oh Robert, you won't agree to anything, will you? I still

haven't recovered from the agony of believing you drowned. I couldn't, I simply couldn't go through all that again.'

'You won't need to.'

But despite his firm decision he had been greatly intrigued by the proposal made to him that afternoon. It was new, exciting and appealed to that restless desire to be of use, to do something worthwhile, which he could never entirely subdue, and today for the first time the pain and sickness and fatigue had begun to leave him at last. He felt the surge of renewed health.

'Robert, are you listening to me?'

'Yes, of course I am,' he said guiltily, 'you were telling me something about a wonderful idea.'

'It came to me while I was dressing this morning. Why don't we have a New Year's Eve party down at Sabrina House?'

'Isn't that a little rash at this time of the year?'

'Not if I go down and spend a couple of days with Morag arranging it all. We could take some of the servants, Hawke and Gwennie of course. Not a big party, just those nearest and dearest to us.'

'If you're sure it won't be too much for you.'

'Oh no, I should love it.'

'In that case we'll do it.'

She has grown up, he thought, she wants to spread her wings, play the hostess in her own house.

'You're looking particularly lovely this afternoon,' he went on, 'do you know that? No wonder our friend Torquil was gazing at you as if he could eat you.'

'Oh what nonsense.'

'Just as I'm doing now.' He slipped his arm out of the sling and pulled her close against him.

'Oh Robert, you shouldn't, not here!' she gasped as soon as she could recover breath. 'Marian could come in at any moment or one of the servants.'

'Upstairs then,' he said cheerfully, getting up and pulling her to her feet. 'It must be nearly time to change for dinner.'

When all the guests were gathered in the drawing room of Sabrina House on the last day of that momentous year, Isabelle looked around her with satisfaction. They were all there just as she had planned.

There was Marian of course, rather against her will, with Guy and David, the Earl in his usual place on the hearthrug dominating the company as he loved to do, Venetia with Perry, who had just returned with despatches from Toulon and had been allowed two days' leave before being given fresh orders and battling his way through the winter seas to the Mediterranean, the Reverend Holland whose curate was taking his Watch Night Service and his sister resplendent in a new gown of lavender wool trimmed with bands of purple velvet, which was Isabelle's gift, and last Dr McFee still a little on the defensive but wearing a new black coat which was only half paid for.

They were just about to go in to dinner when there was an unexpected disturbance outside.

Hawke opened the door looking a little perturbed and announced, 'Sir Joshua has called, my lord.'

For a moment everyone was paralysed with surprise, then Robert stepped forward with outstretched hand.

'This is an unexpected pleasure, Sir Joshua,' he began courteously and was almost immediately forestalled by Venetia who had turned white, then scarlet, and ran across the room to throw herself into her father's arms.

'I have no wish to intrude upon you and your guests,' he was saying, one arm still around his daughter, 'but I happened to be in the neighbourhood and it seemed only right to call and convey my good wishes to you.'

Venetia was still holding on to him as if she could not bear to let him go and Isabelle came to kiss his cheek.

'How kind of you, Uncle, to think of us at this time,' she said and thought it more tactful not to enquire after Aunt Augusta. 'You will stay and dine with us, won't you?'

He had left soon after they had eaten with the polite excuse that he must return to his wife who was not well, but his visit had delighted Venetia and put a finishing touch on a most successful day, Isabelle thought happily, when the celebrations were over, the guests had retired to bed and she and Robert were left alone at last. They had welcomed in the New Year with hot mulled wine, with chestnuts exploding on long iron shovels thrust into the glowing fire, with a great bowl of plums in brandy which had been set alight, all of them shrieking with laughter as they tried to snatch at the fiery fruit.

Now long after midnight she was still flitting around the room, putting it to rights while Robert lazed at ease beside the dying fire.

'Leave all that to the servants,' he said, 'and come here to me. I have something to tell you.'

'What is it?'

He caught at her hand and pulled her to sit beside him. 'You have the gift of making everyone feel happy,' he said, 'do you know that?'

'I just gave them plenty to eat and drink.'

'You did a great deal more than that.'

He was leaning back, smiling at her, and she frowned.

'You're looking very sly and secretive all of a sudden. Has something happened?'

'Yes, in a way. How would you like to go to Russia?'

'Russia!' She sat up. If he'd said fly to the moon she could not have been more surprised. 'Russia! But Robert, you promised faithfully . . .'

'Not for some months yet,' he went on, 'and they tell me St Petersburg is a beautiful city and Tsar Alexander is young and very handsome.'

'But why, Robert, why? What would you be doing there?'

'It would seem that the King has gone off his head again and very soon now Pitt will almost certainly be recalled to power. There will be a new war strategy. Britain needs European allies but the Russians are still shilly-shallying between Bonaparte and us. I would be attached to the Embassy as an observer probing into the attitude of the Tsar and his ministers, meeting them socially, talking to them informally, finding out the reactions of the whole country and then reporting back.'

'But you don't speak Russian,' she said doubtfully.

'The language of the court and the government is French, with a little German, so that is easy and I have time to pick up a little useful Russian between now and then. And you, my darling, are to come with me. You will organise delightful parties and all the infatuated Russians will pour out their souls to you.'

'Don't laugh at me, Robert, this is far too serious. Do you mean we would be working together?'

'That's the idea. You don't need to decide now. We won't be leaving for a few months.'

'And if I should say no, you would still go?'

'I'm afraid so.'

'Then that settles it. I don't need to think about it. I've decided now. I shall go with you.'

'Good. That's what I hoped you would say.'

Later when they were lying close together in that huge bed, she thought how far she had come in the five months since they had last slept there and a thrill ran through her that at last she would be sharing that other life of Robert's.

Presently she said dreamily, 'If our son was born there, does it mean that he would be Russian?'

'Not if he were born in the Embassy. It is British territory.' Then suddenly he sat up. 'Isabelle, does this mean . . .? What are you telling me?'

'Well, I'm not absolutely sure yet, but I think so.'

'Oh my God, it doesn't seem possible.'

'Remember that night in Grisette's stable after you killed Fouché's policeman?'

That crazy night when they had come together like two demented, starved lovers. He suddenly gave a shout of laughter.

'Father was right after all.'

'What do you mean? What has your father to do with it?'

'Nothing, nothing at all. Oh my love, what can I say?'

'If I am pregnant, you won't go without me, will you?'

'Never. We're partners in this and in the future.'

She had longed for him to say that and now he had. It proved his trust, his love, and made all the pain and stress of the past weeks worthwhile. Once she had believed all she wanted was to live in peace with him beside her but she knew now that could never be, not while the war lasted, not while he believed himself of use. She would live with danger and uncertainty but it didn't matter, nothing mattered beside his love and his need of her.

His arm tightened around her and she sighed happily. The wind from the sea had blown him back to her and that was enough.

A Selected List of Fiction Available from Mandarin

☐	7493 0003 5	**Mirage**	James Follett	£3.99
☐	7493 0134 1	**To Kill a Mockingbird**	Harper Lee	£2.99
☐	7493 0076 0	**The Crystal Contract**	Julian Rathbone	£3.99
☐	7493 0145 7	**Talking Oscars**	Simon Williams	£3.50
☐	7493 0118 X	**The Wire**	Nik Gowing	£3.99
☐	7493 0121 X	**Under Cover of Daylight**	James Hall	£3.50
☐	7493 0020 5	**Pratt of the Argus**	David Nobbs	£3.99
☐	7493 0097 3	**Second from Last in the Sack Race**	David Nobbs	£3.50